Siren Enslaved

Other Books By Lexi Blake

ROMANTIC SUSPENSE

Masters and Mercenaries
The Dom Who Loved Me
The Men With The Golden Cuffs
A Dom is Forever
On Her Master's Secret Service
Sanctum: A Masters and Mercenaries Novella
Love and Let Die
Unconditional: A Masters and Mercenaries Novella
Dungeon Royale
Dungeon Games: A Masters and Mercenaries Novella
A View to a Thrill
Cherished: A Masters and Mercenaries Novella
You Only Love Twice
Luscious: Masters and Mercenaries~Topped
Adored: A Masters and Mercenaries Novella
Master No
Just One Taste: Masters and Mercenaries~Topped 2
From Sanctum with Love
Devoted: A Masters and Mercenaries Novella
Dominance Never Dies
Submission is Not Enough
Master Bits and Mercenary Bites~The Secret Recipes of Topped
Perfectly Paired: Masters and Mercenaries~Topped 3
For His Eyes Only
Arranged: A Masters and Mercenaries Novella
Love Another Day
At Your Service: Masters and Mercenaries~Topped 4
Master Bits and Mercenary Bites~Girls Night
Nobody Does It Better
Close Cover
Protected: A Masters and Mercenaries Novella
Enchanted: A Masters and Mercenaries Novella
Charmed: A Masters and Mercenaries Novella
Taggart Family Values
Treasured: A Masters and Mercenaries Novella
Delighted: A Masters and Mercenaries Novella
Tempted: A Masters and Mercenaries Novella

LEXI BLAKE WRITING AS SOPHIE OAK

Texas Sirens
Small Town Siren
Siren in the City
Siren Enslaved
Siren Beloved
Siren in Waiting
Siren in Bloom
Siren Unleashed
Siren Reborn
The Accidental Siren
The Reluctant Siren

Nights in Bliss, Colorado
Three to Ride
Two to Love
One to Keep
Lost in Bliss
Found in Bliss
Pure Bliss
Chasing Bliss
Once Upon a Time in Bliss
Back in Bliss
Sirens in Bliss
Happily Ever After in Bliss
Far from Bliss
Unexpected Bliss
Wild Bliss

A Faery Story
Bound
Beast
Beauty

Standalone
Away From Me
Snowed In

Siren Enslaved

Texas Sirens Book 3

Lexi Blake
writing as
Sophie Oak

Siren Enslaved
Texas Sirens Book 3

Published by DLZ Entertainment LLC

Copyright 2018 DLZ Entertainment LLC
Edited by Chloe Vale
ISBN: 978-1-937608-81-1

Sign up for Lexi Blake's newsletter
and be entered to win a $25 gift certificate
to the bookseller of your choice.

Join us for news, fun, and exclusive content
including free short stories.

There's a new contest every month!

Go to www.LexiBlake.net to subscribe.

Dedication

2011

To the Wednesday night chatters. A better group of righteous perverts doesn't exist. I've grown to appreciate your support and friendship more than you can know.

As always, thanks to my family and friends. And to Kim G and Shayla Black for all the help with nursing me through my "Julian" period.

2018

I'd forgotten how hard this book was for me. Julian was the most closed off character I'd written up to this point in time. But Dani and Finn were truly halves of me. When I wrote this book, I was coming to grips with the fact that my vision of success wasn't the reality. As many small press and erotic writers found, we weren't always welcome at the table. We walked into many writers' groups and RWA chapters with enthusiasm and real book sales, only to be told we weren't good enough. It didn't merely happen to me. It was the beginning of the indie and erotic revolution and change is painful. I realize now that this particular book was my reaction to that painful rejection. Fast-forward seven years and the world is a different place. And not. While we're readily accepted by our romance sisters, the greater publishing world still looks down on us. And yet I am reminded that we have stories that mean something to you—our readers. We have a voice and a unique perspective. So this book is dedicated to all my sisters (and some brothers) who fight every day to have our voices heard, to bring you these stories that are close to our hearts, to show you that you are not alone.

This book is for the writers.

This book is for the fighters.

This book is for you.

Chapter One

Julian Lodge gingerly flicked the four-foot single tail whip and was pleased at the slender line of pink that appeared across Sally's back. The entire dungeon was silent as was right given the gravity of the ceremony. He quickly laid three more across the skin of his longtime slave's back and thighs. She never once moved or showed that she even felt the lash. Sally was practically perfect. She never disobeyed or questioned him. She took every punishment he handed out with grace. She was his match, a lovely masochist to match his control freak with a slight streak of sadism. He had been her Master for over two years, the longest he'd ever kept a slave. She'd been his only slave since the incident with Jeremy Walker years before. She'd lived with him, served him, honored him with submission.

He was letting her go.

"Rise, slave." Julian heard the words come out of his mouth. He pushed them forward, saying all the proper things to keep this ritual moving along. He believed in ritual and routine, was devoted to both, but now he wanted it all over with so he could go back to his penthouse apartment and…he wasn't sure what came after this.

All around him, he heard the whispers. The Club was like any other social group. There was always gossip, much of it about him.

Sally rose gracefully to her feet. She turned and looked luminous as her eyes met the man beside him. Julian's heart clenched. She'd never once looked so happy at anything he'd done, but she glowed for Stephen Mann.

The high-powered attorney looked just as happy as he took the whip from Julian's hand. Julian walked to his former sub and took the collar from her throat.

"Be happy, pet," he said, meaning every word. He genuinely liked Sally. She'd been a good sub. It wasn't her fault he wasn't capable of true commitment. During their years together, he'd never thought of making them exclusive. Their relationship had been comfortable and convenient. He'd known he needed to find her a permanent Dom for the last year. He'd kept up his obligations to her, but his heart wasn't in it.

Permanent. The word played through his brain like a mystery he had yet to solve.

Nothing in his life seemed permanent.

Sally bowed her blonde head. "Thank you for everything, Sir."

She wouldn't call him Master, not ever again. An odd sensation made Julian's eyes feel strange. His face felt hot. His vision started to cloud. Was he… Oh, hell, no. He ruthlessly tamped down the sentimental feeling that started to overtake him. He wasn't going to cry. He wasn't going to think about the fact that he was forty-one years old and had absolutely nothing to look forward to. He had a life most people would kill to live. He was a billionaire, an ultra-powerful financier, and he owned the hottest BDSM club in the south. Unless one considered Sanctum, his security team's club, but it was only hot because they couldn't afford an air conditioner.

He had absolutely nothing to feel sad about.

Sally knelt at her new Master's feet, her head bowed in perfect submission. Stephen Mann's hand cupped her head, and he offered his thanks as well. Julian moved to the side of the stage as Mann took over. It was only moments before Sally wore a new collar and the couple was accepting congratulations from the members of The Club.

He had a few moments before the crowd broke up. He needed to see if the penthouse was ready for the party that was about to start.

If he could have avoided it, he would have. He felt the odd need to completely pull into himself. But this party was his final obligation to Sally and he intended to honor it.

He stepped up to the private elevator that in twenty minutes would bring everyone to his penthouse where he would fête the happy new couple.

A large man in a dark suit stepped in with him. Ah, his security detail for the evening. He was roughly six foot five and built like a linebacker. And quiet. So not one of the Taggarts or that annoying Miles fellow. He had to admit he liked the broody ones.

"Mr. Lodge," the man said. He was almost sure the name was Scottish.

McDonald? Nope. This was the other partner. McKay. "Mr. McKay."

The ex-FBI agent. Yes, he was definitely the broody one.

"It's Alex," he said, his voice low. He stared up at the place where the elevator marked each floor. "Tonight I'm your main contact. Adam is monitoring the building's CCTV and Sean is backing us up. Everyone in the building right now has been vetted. The doors are locked so it's smooth sailing from here."

"Have we had any issues?" There was always something going on, someone angry with him for a decision made. It was precisely why he had a security firm on call.

"We've been quiet for days," McKay explained.

He'd made a good call investing in McKay-Taggart Security Services. "Thank you. Are the caterers prepared?"

"Yes, unless you ask Sean, and then they need to redo their dumplings," McKay said with a shake of his head. "You'll have to forgive him. He's a foodie. I have no idea where he got it from because we grew up on Spam, if you know what I mean."

He didn't. He'd never experienced a day of material wanting, though that didn't mean he'd never wanted.

He rather wanted now. The problem was he wasn't sure what he wanted.

"Are you married, Alex?"

The man beside him stiffened, and Julian regretted the question. He was about to take it back when Alex replied. "I'm divorced but I wish I wasn't."

And that was all he needed to know. Why was he even asking the question? He wasn't chatty. He didn't need to know about people's lives. "What did you get out of being married? That you didn't get from being single? Please feel free to not answer if I'm intruding. It's been an odd night. I find myself disconcerted and when I am I tend to ask questions I probably shouldn't."

Alex McKay's lips turned up slightly, a rueful smile. "I'm surprised to see you so human."

"Oh, I assure you, I'm the very definition of human." He made more mistakes than most. He was simply excellent at covering them up.

The door opened and McKay held it for him. "I was a better human being when I was married to Eve. I don't know if she made me that way or if loving her made me strive to be better, but the result was the same. I felt more. I was more."

"And you divorced why?"

McKay's face flushed, but he stood tall. "I made some terrible mistakes and she couldn't forgive me. Love isn't invincible, it turns out. It's actually quite fragile if you forget to work on it. I suppose love and marriage is like everything else. It is what you put in it. I forgot and mine died. Is that what happened with you and Sally?"

He brushed that line of inquiry off. "Not at all. Sally was a close companion, but that word never came up. I never once thought it. I will miss her though. My apologies for intruding on something private."

Alex stepped out behind him. "If you could give her up, it wasn't love."

Really? Not that they weren't in accord, but there was one point he needed to make. "I agree, but I wonder about you. You divorced your wife."

"She divorced me, and I haven't given up. I might never. She's smart. We worked together at the FBI and I put my job before her. It was the biggest mistake of my life."

He'd studied up on the group. He could only be talking about Eve St. James, the psychologist. "Ah, the blonde. She's quite beautiful."

"She's everything." There was such longing in the man's voice. "She's the smartest woman I've ever met, the most loving. She was my sub and I let her down. I should have cared more about her than my job. Fuck. I should have listened to her. That's where I made my real mistake."

He'd never once longed for any one specific person, never wanted anyone in that way. Well, maybe once. Maybe once he'd thought about taking on a long-term project. He was sure the man in front of him would balk at the idea of him calling a relationship a long-term project. "Well, I hope you get what you're looking for."

McKay nodded his way. "I hope you figure out what you're looking for."

Julian stared out at his penthouse. Everything was immaculate. His life was perfect. So why was it also empty?

"So do I."

Two hours later, Julian wondered when his hosting duties could end. He hadn't been able to stop thinking about what the security guy had said, hadn't been able to forget the hollow look in the man's eyes. He walked out onto his balcony, the sounds of the party fading. The lights of Dallas twinkled around him, but he didn't really see them.

"It's a good thing you did."

He turned to look at Leo Meyer as the younger man walked out onto the balcony, two beers in his hand. The thirty-two-year-old former Navy SEAL was his Dom in residence. He pressed a longneck into Julian's hand. "It was time."

He'd been looking forward to some alone time. "I'm glad you think so."

Leo took a sip of his own beer as he looked out over the city. He stood next to Julian, a smile on his face. "Come on, man. I know beer isn't your speed, but you gotta drink a little. It's tradition."

"Tradition?"

Chuckling, Leo turned to face him. He'd changed out of his leathers into more comfortable jeans and a T-shirt. Julian despaired of him ever becoming fashionable. Rather like another of his protégés. "You broke up with a girl, man. It's perfectly traditional to drown your sorrows in cheap beer."

Julian seriously doubted that the beer in his hand was cheap.

He'd had the entire affair catered in, and it had cost him a small fortune. Still, if it was tradition, he didn't see why not. He took a sip of the cold brew. It wasn't half bad. "Should I drown my sorrows even when I willingly gave the sub away?"

Leo's mouth turned down. "It was the best thing for her, boss."

It had been necessary. Though he knew he would miss Sally, he found himself no longer capable of giving her what she needed. He refused to fail her, so he found her someone else. "Sally deserves to be happy."

There was a long pause. The cool air prickled along Julian's skin, reminding him he hadn't bothered with a jacket. He didn't even think about getting one now. At least the cold meant he felt something. He hadn't in a long time, not until earlier this evening.

"Don't you deserve to be happy, too?"

"I am happy." It was an automatic response, though he knew it was something of a lie. He wasn't sure what happiness was. His armor came up around him, and Julian felt his face go cold. He turned to Leo. "I have everything I could possibly need. Who wouldn't be happy?"

Leo sighed and tipped back his beer. "And I spoke too soon. Well, when you're ready to talk, I'll be around." He shoved off the railing and turned to go.

"And what would I talk about?"

Leo's hand was on the door. "The fact that you're frozen. When you're ready, we'll talk about the fact that you aren't moving forward with your life."

That was the absolute last thing he wanted to talk about. "You're fired. The next time I hire a Dom in residence, I'll make sure he doesn't have a degree in psychology."

"You do that, boss," Leo said with a smile that let him know he didn't take his threat seriously. "One of these days I'm going to put that degree to good use. For now, I'm enjoying spanking pretty subs. I just psychoanalyze you in my spare time."

"Well, stop, please, or I might make good on my threat." He didn't want to be psychoanalyzed. He was certain he wouldn't be happy with what he would find.

"I doubt it. You like me, Julian. You'll do amazing things for the people who get past that shell around you. You can actually be quite tolerant when your heart is engaged. That's what those people in there don't understand. You have a heart. You simply prefer not to use it."

The door closed behind Leo, and Julian stared out at the night, the words echoing in his brain. Perhaps Leo didn't know him as well as he thought. Julian had no idea how to use his heart, or perhaps he would have been able to keep the people he loved close to him. There hadn't been many, but every one of them had left for greener pastures. Not a single one had truly known him.

Hell, he didn't know himself. Perhaps the time had come to be alone for a while. For the first time in years, he didn't have a slave and he didn't particularly want one.

He thought about the lovely blonde. Eve. What had her husband done? He'd put his job before her. Julian rather thought the man's true crime was allowing her to leave in the first place. She was smart and competent and submissive. With the right Master she could find heights she'd never thought possible.

That was what he wanted. He wanted to be necessary. To want and give as much as he received, and yet he hadn't found the right submissive.

Not slave. He was fooling himself about the slaves. He needed more than a slave could give him.

He thought about a phone call he'd taken earlier that day. Jackson Barnes had called. He called at least once a week, reaching out. Each time Jack called, Julian asked what was wrong, and Jack simply responded that he was calling to "shoot the shit." It was confusing. Why would Jack call if he had nothing important to say? Julian would never have used the phrase himself, and yet he found he looked forward to the weekly calls more and more. He and Jack talked about their lives, and Jack often spoke of the wife he shared with Sam Fleetwood. Abigail was pregnant again and due any day now. Jack and Sam were younger than he was. He'd trained them, helped them along, and they had found their happiness elsewhere. They had a family.

Julian wasn't sure that was what he wanted. He simply wanted to want something.

I was a better human being when I was married to Eve. I don't know if she made me that way or if loving her made me strive to be better, but the result was the same. I felt more. I was more.

That was what McKay had said. What would it feel like to be more?

He breathed in the night air. He needed to think about it. Yes, some time alone would do him good.

* * * *

Finn Taylor needed to be alone. He needed to get some fucking air in his lungs, and he couldn't do it surrounded by all these yokels. He pushed out of the Willow Fork Community Center's double doors and into the chilly night.

Dani was getting married. She was really going to marry that idiot redneck and have his redneck babies. Damn it. How was he supposed to handle that?

He nodded at a group walking into the party. He didn't recognize the family, but that was probably a good thing. Willow Fork, Texas, hadn't been a great place for him to grow up. It was hard being gay anywhere, but small-town Texas was pretty much hell on the adolescent homosexual. He'd been beaten up, cussed out, told he was going to hell by just about everyone, and who could forget the time the football team thought it would be hilarious to tie him to the flagpole with the word queer written in lipstick on his forehead?

Yeah, he fucking loved to come home.

Only one thing could have coaxed him from his gorgeous condo in Dallas. Danielle Bay's thirtieth birthday. When he'd gotten the invitation a month ago, he'd thought long and hard about the fact that it was way past time to confess to Dani. Her sister was out of college. She'd done her duty. It was time to come out of the closet and tell Dani that he was bisexual. It was time to admit that he was in love with her and wanted her to move to Dallas to be with him.

All of those plans had been crushed when freaking Jimbo Smart—there was a misnomer—had announced, beer in hand, that he and Danielle would be married this summer. His Dani was going to marry a man who Finn was pretty damn sure was the product of his mother's union with a goat. It was the only thing that explained

Jimbo's facial hair. Finn took in a deep breath of chilled air. Motherfucking son of a bitch.

"Do you need help, son?"

That voice. Finn had to take another deep breath. Jack Barnes got to him. Something about the man's voice went straight to his cock. He turned to look at the richest man in Willow Fork. He was married to Dani's boss, Abigail Barnes. Of course, if what Dani said was true, Abby Barnes was also married to Jack's business partner, Sam Fleetwood.

Finn would really like tickets to that show.

"I was just getting some air, sir." The *sir* came naturally. The man in the snowy white dress shirt and slacks commanded respect.

Jack Barnes's lips curled in a secretive smile. God, he was hot. "Me, too. My wife loves this shit, but I am one antisocial son of a bitch. How do you know Dani?"

The dark-haired man sounded so sure. "How do you know I'm not a friend of Jimbo's?"

A sharp laugh cut through the cool night air. "You don't look like a man Jimbo Smart would befriend. Sorry, but you're far too educated and urbane for the Smart clan." Dark green eyes assessed Finn, and he found himself curiously awaiting Jack Barnes's judgment. "You're white collar. Maybe an accountant—no, a lawyer. You're a lawyer. My brother is a lawyer, so I know the type."

He was good at guessing professions. Not as good at remembering faces. Finn wasn't surprised. Sometimes he faded into the background. "Yeah, I'm a lawyer. I know your brother. We work together. I actually met you at a party the partners threw a couple of months back."

Jack snapped his fingers and grinned. "That's where I remember you from. I knew you looked familiar. You're Lucas's friend. You're also friends with Dani, and you're not at all happy that she's getting married."

Finn felt himself flush. Barnes had pegged him perfectly. He'd also summed up Finn's problem neatly. Finn was about to make junior partner in his law firm, a veritable wunderkind to make partner at his age. None of his professional success mattered since he'd done it all, accomplished it all, in order to build a life for him and Dani.

21

Now he was fucked. "He doesn't deserve her."

"But you think you do."

Finn forced himself to laugh. Now that he knew what was going to happen, he damn sure wasn't going to announce to the world that he'd played the fool again. "Of course not. I don't guess you've gotten the lowdown on me. I'm Finn Taylor, Willow Fork's most famous queer."

"Well, I am horribly offended by your lifestyle, Finn." Jack Barnes's slow drawl dripped with amused sarcasm.

"What's got you offended, Jack?"

Finn turned to find Sam Fleetwood walking up. He was wearing jeans and a western shirt that did nothing to hide his magnificent body. Sam Fleetwood was a Greek god.

"It seems Finn here is of a homosexual bent, and he's a bit miffed by it." Barnes grinned at his partner.

"Nah." Sam shook his blond head. "He's at least bi. He was staring at Melissa Paul's chest." Sam turned to him. "You should stay away from that. Seriously, man, she's trouble."

He'd only taken a little glance. He knew a hot mess when he saw one. "I don't care about Melissa Paul."

"You should keep it that way. Now, I need to borrow Jack. We have a small situation." Sam's voice was perfectly even, but Barnes went shock white. There was no mistaking it, even in the moonlight.

"Abby? I knew we shouldn't have come out. Damn it, Sam. You two need to mind me. I swear if something goes wrong, I'll have the both of you over my knee."

If Sam Fleetwood was worried, it didn't show. "Yeah, that should be an interesting night. Look, discipline is going to have to wait a couple of weeks. Abby's water broke."

Jack Barnes had no answer for that. He simply took off running. One minute he was there, and the next his boots were stirring up dust as he sprinted for the doors.

Sam's chest moved with the force of his laughter. "Sorry, man. You have to forgive him. He is the coolest customer in the world until me or Abby gets sick. It's a baby. This is perfectly normal, but he's got to freak out. It's why we didn't mention it until now. She's been having contractions all day. Well, he makes up for it by being a beast in the sack." Sam slapped his back jovially. "You should get your girl, man. She's not married yet. Don't wait or it'll be too late."

"Sam, we're leaving now!" Jack Barnes's voice boomed across the parking lot.

"Gotta go have a baby. This one's number two. Got my fingers crossed for a boy. Otherwise, we'll be hopelessly outnumbered." Sam practically glowed as he turned and jogged for the big truck, whose engine was gunning furiously. Gravel flew when the black truck sped out of the parking lot.

That truck was speeding toward a future. Finn was stuck hopelessly in the past. His stomach twisted. What was he supposed to do? His first instinct was to march his ass back into that party room and beg Dani to reconsider. He could kiss her and tell her he'd always wanted her. He could explain to her that he'd lied all these years. Yeah, that would go gangbusters.

"There you are!"

Heart skipping a beat, Finn turned, and Danielle Bay walked toward him, a light sparkling in her blue eyes. Her honey blonde hair was pulled back in a loose bun, and the dress she wore showed off her round, glorious breasts. How many times had she complained about those tits when all he wanted to do was get them in his mouth?

"Well, my engagement party is off to a spectacular start. My boss went into labor. My future mother-in-law is mopping up what she calls the wages of sin. Apparently she doesn't truck with the ménage lifestyle. She won't say that to Jack Barnes's face, though. That man scares the crap out of everyone. I love it." She wound her arm around his waist, cuddling temptingly close to him.

"He seems pretty intimidating." He'd been a junior in high school by the time Jack Barnes and Sam Fleetwood had bought their spread. Thirteen years later, they ruled Willow Fork, despite the fact that most of the narrow-minded town considered them sinners. They were sinners with an atrocious amount of money, so the sin was tolerated. Finn knew his wouldn't be.

"He's an interesting guy." Dani ran her free hand across his cheek. It was an affectionate gesture. She couldn't know what it did to him. "Abby is an amazing woman. I can't tell you how great it is to work for her. She's opened a free clinic here in Willow Fork. She's making a difference."

"That's great," he managed to say. He forced his hand to curl around her hip in a perfectly nice "we've been friends since high school but never managed to have sex because one of us is gay" kind of way. "I'm glad you found a good job."

He was happy that she wasn't working at the Buys A Lot anymore.

"I have a good job, and now I'm getting married."

Finn heard the hitch in her breath. "Are you sure about this? The last time we talked you didn't even mention that you were dating Jim." He left off the *bo* part. It was simply too surreal to think that his lovely, sweet Dani, who read Jane Austen and watched foreign films with him, could possibly be marrying someone named Jimbo.

He felt her sigh against him. "I didn't talk about him because I know how you feel about anyone from this town. Look, Finn, I love you. You're my best friend in the world, but I have a life here."

"You could have a life in Dallas, too." He hated the slight whine in his voice. Damn it, why couldn't he be forceful?

"Not anymore. I don't have a degree. My only work experience is in minimum wage retail. There's no way I can get a decent job in the city. I was damn lucky Abby Barnes hired me as her clinic manager. This is as good as it gets in Willow Fork. I'm not smart like you."

"That's not true."

There were tears in her wide eyes as she looked up at him. "Please say you're happy for me. I couldn't stand it if you were disappointed. I've missed you so much, Finn."

The pleading in her voice was more than he could take. He hugged her close. "If this is what you want, then I'm happy for you."

Her head sagged into the crook of his neck. "I'm glad because you're my maid of honor. Don't tell me no. I had to fight Jimbo's whole family to make this happen. They don't think it's proper to have a male bridesmaid."

Every muscle in his body went tense at the thought. He was sure that conversation had been worse than Dani was saying. They wouldn't want a gay to tarnish their special day. Fuck. He couldn't hurt her this way. He loved her. He had to be strong.

"Of course, I'll be beside you." He would stand there, wanting her, loving her.

Her smile was as brilliant as the sun. "I'm so happy. I couldn't do this without you, Finn."

She started talking a mile a minute about everything from her dress to the wedding cake she wanted to order. Finn nodded and tried to figure out how to face the future without her.

Chapter Two

Six Months Later

Julian turned his Audi R8 Spyder down what appeared to be Main Street. The June air was warm on his skin, but he still felt the strange restlessness that had been plaguing him for the last few years. Being alone had only seemed to make it worse. His recent string of bad luck incidents had convinced him that he needed a more radical change. First his car had been vandalized. Then there had been a fire in his building. He'd had a nosy reporter on his case about the possibility of an underground sex club in the Dallas area.

Of course, there was an underground sex club. He ran it, but he certainly didn't want publicity. The car had been a mere nuisance. He simply bought another one, and the fire was apparently an accident. Still, it all added up to serious stress, so Julian was doing something he hadn't done in years.

He was taking a vacation.

He glanced around the small town. It looked like something out of a Norman Rockwell painting. It was three o'clock on a Saturday afternoon, and Julian seriously expected to be assaulted by visions of boys and their faithful dogs, perhaps playing stickball and trading baseball cards. Willow Fork, Texas, was a sleepy town.

His car purred as he moved down the street. He had the top down. It was a stunning day outside, but he was rapidly discovering that, with no one to share it with, the days seemed to blend together. Each was as empty as the next. Julian stopped at a stoplight. He drummed his fingers along the steering wheel. It wasn't that he missed any one person in particular, but rather that he didn't like to be alone. Perhaps he'd spent too much of his childhood in that state that now he simply couldn't stand the silence. He'd been on edge for six months, but he wasn't sure how to get off. The last thing he wanted was another pretty-faced sub in his bed who didn't challenge him at all.

But he was tempted. It had become a bit of a game at The Club to see which sub could find his or her way into the Master's bed. It wasn't that he didn't want sex. He was horny as hell. He simply wasn't interested in anyone in particular, and sex for sex's sake had gotten boring.

He blamed Jackson. His former protégé had found something magical. He was living happily with his two subs, Samuel and Abigail. He'd started a family. He had a life beyond work. Julian couldn't get Jackson's words out of his head. A few years back, Jackson had given him a bit of advice. He'd warned Julian not to let his rules run his life. He'd warned him that rules might keep him from something wonderful. So far, Julian hadn't found anything wonderful. He'd only found sexual frustration and loneliness.

He hit the gas and drove past some sort of church. He intended to use this week to reconnect with old friends. When he got back to Dallas, he would get on with his life. He would spend this vacation deciding on whom to take as his new subs. He would stop putting it off and select based on logic. He would pick one man and one woman, and then begin training them to suit his needs. He was done waiting for some mysterious thing to happen to him.

The light in front of him turned red. It looked like he was going to hit every single one. He thought about the stack of files he had in his luggage. He was sure Jackson would be horrified by the way he intended to choose his new lovers. He had a system. He would weigh the pros and cons of each, input the numbers into a spreadsheet, and presto, he would have two lovely bodies in his bed. The one time he'd followed his heart and offered a permanent contract to a sub, the man had declined and run off...with Jackson Barnes. He wished Samuel Fleetwood well, but he had learned his lesson. He wasn't a man who would have something as elusive as love.

His cell phone trilled. Julian looked down and saw a picture of his longtime personal assistant. Candice was almost sixty. Her stern face was a comfort to him. Nothing got by her. Julian moved his thumb across the slide bar to answer the call. "This is Lodge."

"Mr. Lodge, that reporter called again." The normally unflappable Candice sounded distinctly flapped.

"Have security block her number." The nosy *Morning News* reporter would undoubtedly try again. If she gave him too much trouble, he would simply change his number. It would cause a headache, but it would be worth it if it got rid of her. The last thing Julian needed was an exposé run on his underground activities. There was a reason he kept a low profile.

"You don't understand. She called your private line, Mr. Lodge."

The light turned green, but Julian didn't care. He sat there, his foot firmly on the brake as her words settled in. He jealously guarded his private line. It wasn't a number he gave out to his business associates or people from The Club. Only close friends and his submissives had that line. "Did you ask her how she got that number?"

"Yes, sir. She said she has an inside source." Candice's voice softened. "Mr. Lodge, I don't think it's anything you should worry about. She's asking questions. That's all. It's not the first time this has happened. There are always rumors. I merely wanted you to know before I called the boys in."

He took a deep breath. The "boys" in this case was how Candice referred to his security team. McKay-Taggart was actually made up of a bunch of ex-Special Forces soldiers and an extremely competent former FBI agent who happened to be female. But Candice hadn't worked with Eve St. James. She did, however, dote on the men when they came in. He rather thought his secretary found them both attractive and amusing. What they were was highly reliable.

The light changed back to red. He was lucky there was no one on the road. "Are you sure? Perhaps I should come home and coordinate with Taggart."

Maybe it was for the best. He wasn't sure what he was doing out here anyway.

"No, no, you promised me you would take a vacation." Now she was stern and unmoving.

Julian felt his lips tug up into a small smile. When she talked to him like that, he could almost see her the way she was thirty years before. Candice Holloway had been the tenth nanny his uncle had hired. He'd run through nine in the years after his parents died in a car accident. He'd intended to run her off as well. She'd flatly refused to be dismissed. She'd told him she wasn't going anywhere, no matter how hard he tried to push her away. Candice promised that she would never leave him, and she never had. When he no longer needed a nanny, he'd convinced her he needed an assistant. Along the way he'd managed to convince her to let him pay for her children's college education and set up a retirement plan for her. He believed in gratitude. "It isn't much of a vacation spot."

"That will be good for you, sir." She sounded more relaxed now. "A little peace and quiet is exactly what the doctor ordered."

Something caught Julian's attention in the rearview mirror. On the hill behind him it looked like a wedding party was breaking up. He would need to move soon. He didn't like to talk and drive. He believed in concentration. "The doctor didn't order anything. You did. I'm almost to the ranch if my GPS is to be believed. Do call Taggart and have him attempt to figure out how that woman got my phone number. Is there anything else I should know?"

Julian watched as a ball of white appeared on the sidewalk several blocks down from him.

"Lucas Cameron was in the dungeon last night."

Nothing odd there. Jackson Barnes's younger brother had become a regular at The Club ever since he finished law school and began working at a prestigious firm in Dallas. It hadn't hurt the young man's chances that he came with a small, but lucrative client list made up of Barnes-Fleetwood and Julian himself. Julian sighed as he realized why Candice would mention it. "He brought Lexi with him?"

"Yes, sir. I thought you would like to know. They performed a scene and left. Ms. Moore was reportedly very upset."

Julian's hands tightened on the steering wheel. Lexi Moore was rapidly becoming a problem. He wasn't sure what he was going to do about those two. He'd thought about calling her mother, but Lexi was twenty-three. Though she didn't have a membership at The Club,

Lucas did, and he acted as her Dom. Unless he was willing to seriously argue with Lucas, he had to allow it to continue. He'd offered to talk to Lucas. Lucas had declined. That boy was wading into dangerous waters. Lexi Moore was on an emotional ledge after breaking up with her fiancée, and she and Lucas seemed to think they could solve her problems with public spankings. Julian sighed and felt tired at the thought of trying to deal with it. If he revoked Lucas's membership, he and Lexi would more than likely find another, perhaps more dangerous club. Julian didn't like the thought of that. At least this way, he and Leo could keep an eye on the situation.

"Thank you for telling me, Candice. Please call me if the situations, either of them, worsen. I'll see you in a week. Until then, I will enjoy my vacation. You needn't worry. It appears absolutely nothing interesting ever happens in this town."

He hung up the phone as he looked in the rearview mirror again. He felt his eyes widen. It appeared as though a large marshmallow was barreling down Main Street. The frothy confection had a blonde head sticking out of it. Julian stared in the rearview, unable to look away. A man raced after the white puff ball. He wore a tuxedo and screamed something that sounded like "Annie" at the top of his lungs. A large crowd was pouring out of the church. Very interesting. He wondered if the marshmallow intended to run all the way to Mexico to get out of her wedding. Julian didn't blame her. He probably would do the same thing if he had been foolish enough to agree to something like a wedding.

He had to admit that the puff ball had stamina. Though he couldn't see her legs through the sea of taffeta surrounding them, he knew they had to be pumping overtime. As she came into sharp view, Julian could see that her mascara was running in dark rivers down her face. Her ridiculously long train trailed behind her. The man, who seemed to be the groom, tried to chase down his frothy prize. He would probably make it. All he had to do was get within twenty feet of the fleeing bride and he could put a foot down on the satin trail behind her. If he had any sense at all, he would have a length of rope on him. Julian always had a length of rope. The groom could tie up the fleeing bride and drag her back to the church. If he was really serious about this whole marriage thing, he would spank her first to start the marriage on the right foot.

Julian sighed. It wasn't his concern. Still, he enjoyed a good train wreck as much as the next person.

The marshmallow steamrolled down the sidewalk. Her arms pumped, her legs strained. Her eyes widened and locked on...him. Before Julian could think to gun the engine, he was assaulted by a sea of satin and lace.

"Drive!" The woman practically screamed the words as she threw herself into the front seat.

Julian struggled to find his way through the cloud he found himself caught in. Why hadn't he thought to keep the top on? Oh, yes, because it was a beautiful day and he hadn't expected a stranger would jump in and attempt the high-jack him. "Excuse me?"

"I said drive." The words were strong, but the tone was shaky.

"Yes, I speak English. I wasn't asking what you said. I was rather shocked that you had said it. Were you raised in a barn?" He shoved down the mountain of fabric that covered his face. He looked at the woman now in the seat beside him.

"Please drive," she beseeched him. Her tearstained face went straight to his gut. "I am begging you to please drive and quickly." She hiccupped through her tears and managed one last word. "Sir."

Julian practically growled. She'd said the one thing that he couldn't ignore. She'd called him Sir in that oh so sweet way that let him know she would be soft and submissive if he played her properly. She would submit and lie beneath him with no demands of her own except to please him. Perversely, it made him damned determined to meet her needs. She'd done the one thing guaranteed to manipulate him each and every time.

He thought about it. Waiting would do the trick. The tuxedoed groom was close. Another few steps and he would haul this sugary piece of trouble right out of his convertible. Then Julian could drive on to Jack's ranch and spend the next week catching up with friends. He wouldn't get involved. He wouldn't get in trouble.

"Please, Sir. I am begging you." Her breath hitched and blue eyes pleaded with him.

The groom closed in as Julian gunned the engine.

Trouble, it seemed, just followed him.

* * * *

The man beside her finally gunned the engine and took off down Main Street. Dani took a deep breath and tried to get her hands to stop shaking.

What the hell had she done? She'd panicked and fled, leaving 122 wedding guests sitting in the pews at the First Methodist Church of Willow Fork. Only they hadn't been in pews at the end. She'd looked back long enough to see the wave of people coming out of the large doors to gawk at the idiot running out of her own wedding.

She tried to shove down the ridiculous amount of satin and lace currently assaulting her. God, she couldn't breathe. She glanced out the rearview mirror of her handy getaway vehicle. Finn had stopped running. He stood at the stoplight, his face contorted in concern. She turned to look back at him.

"Dani!"

She shook her head as best she could with Jimbo Smart's great-grandmother's monstrosity of a veil. It had been bedazzled within an inch of its sad little life. Of course, the whole damn dress was that way. She had rhinestones everywhere. She weighed an extra fifty pounds. Finn was running a hand through his dark hair and pulling out his cell. She knew who he was calling, but she couldn't answer. Her phone, along with her purse and everything else she had brought, was in the bride's room at the church.

She'd run out on her wedding. She'd run out on her whole freaking future.

What had she done? What the hell had she done? Her chest ached.

"Breathe."

Dani turned to look at the man driving the car. She hadn't thought that through, either. She'd known that Finn was going to catch her, and she couldn't face him. She was with a complete stranger. Her hands shook, and her breath hitched again.

"Calm down and breathe. Focus on one thing and one thing only. Let the world narrow to a single point."

It wasn't a suggestion. The man next to her commanded. His

deep voice ran over her like warm, rich chocolate. She took a long, steadying breath, filling her lungs with humid air. She gripped the door but found herself doing exactly as he ordered. She settled her eyes on the air conditioner vent. Four little lines. That was all that mattered. She stared at them.

"Excellent. Now concentrate on slowing your breathing. Flex your hands. Remind yourself that you are in control of your body. It does not control you. Say the words for me. Hear them for yourself. *I am in control.*"

"I am in control." The words felt foreign. She hadn't been in control for a long time, most of her life. Most of her life had been about outside forces controlling her.

Her concentration slipped. Panic threatened again. She panted. What was she going to do?

The car came to an abrupt stop. Dani looked around. They were on the edge of town, just off the highway. Was he going to leave her here?

The man beside her turned in his seat, and Dani got her first good look at him. Holy crap, she'd gotten in the car of some damn movie star. He had to be. He was absolutely perfect. She felt her jaw drop. He had dark brown hair that was pulled in a low ponytail at the back of his neck. His silvery eyes dominated a face made of strong bones and sharp angles. From what she could see, his body was long and lean. His shoulders were encased in an expensive-looking dress shirt, though he wore no tie, leaving a *V* of smooth, tanned skin exposed.

He looked a bit like an angel, but one who had fallen from grace long ago.

He took her hand, sliding it between both of his. Her hand, so cold a moment before, was surrounded by warmth now, and that warmth started creeping up her skin.

"Focus on me, Annie."

She thought about correcting him, but the panic was a tidal wave threatening to drown her again. It had been like this for six months. The panic attacks were getting worse. She'd nearly passed out the night before. Finn had held her and asked her over and over if she was sure she wanted to do this. Damn it. Finn was part of her problem.

She'd started down that aisle, and he'd been beautiful standing there. Her groom. Finally she was where she belonged, walking down the aisle toward her love, Finn. Only Finn wasn't there for her. He never had been, not that way. Jimbo was the one standing there, and he'd been wrestling with his bow tie.

In that instant she'd seen her whole life play out like some tragic movie. She would have a few kids. He would drink a lot and go out with his buddies while she took care of the kids. He would do as he liked and she would do her duty. She would waste her life on him. She would spend all the good years either taking care of kids or nursing him because he would drink and party his life away.

She would still be alone, even with a ring on her finger.

She'd turned and ran, and now she was in a car with a gorgeous god of a man who might be a serial killer. The way her luck went, he probably was. She would end up chopped up and buried all across East Texas.

And it still might be better than the life she would have had with Jimbo.

"Oh, you are such trouble." He sighed, those gray eyes rolling, and then he pulled her close. "Luckily, I know how to handle you." He let go of her hand and twisted in his seat. One hand captured her face, cupping her cheek, and the other went to her waist. He pulled her in, a mountain of tulle between them. "The key is giving you something to focus on."

She was focused all right. But if his plan was to get her heart rate under control, he was going about it all wrong. She could feel it pound, though not in panic anymore. It was something else, anticipation. Was he going to kiss her? He leaned in. She could see the dark beard beginning to come in all along his jaw. She could smell the mint on his breath and feel the heat of his body. She was completely paralyzed as he pressed his mouth against hers. He moved his soft lips along her mouth gently, as though simply exploring. Dani felt her shoulders relax. This was so nice. This was in another league from Jimbo's sloppy, halfhearted attempts at kissing before he gave up and simply stuck his penis in. This was meltingly sweet. Dani gasped a bit, and her mouth opened.

He took immediate advantage, his strong tongue invading. Dani heard herself groan and let her whole body go soft in his hands. As his tongue danced around hers, she realized she'd never been kissed, not once in her life. She'd been pecked and assaulted by men who didn't know what they were doing, but this, oh, this was a kiss. This was an overwhelming request for her every sense to come alive for him. His hands didn't move, but she wanted them on her skin. She wanted to be under him. She wanted this to never, ever end. She didn't know his name. He didn't really know hers. It didn't matter because for the first time in her life, she wanted, really wanted, to spread her legs and let someone in.

Not even Finn affected her the way this stranger did. He'd never wanted her physically, but this man was kissing her five minutes after they'd met. She felt her nipples get hard, begging for his lips to find their way there.

He raised his head in a smooth motion. Dani stared at him. Her skin felt flushed and alive.

"Now, are you more in control, Annie?"

Nope. Not a bit. But he was. As far as Dani could tell, he was completely unaffected by the kiss that had blown her mind and had her body begging for more. She swallowed and nodded her head, turning back in her seat. "Yes. I am feeling much better. Thank you."

"So polite," he murmured. His hand found the stick shift again. "I don't suppose there's anywhere I can take you, Annie?"

"It's Dani. Danielle." Her mind raced, but the panic was gone. She needed to think straight. Lust was not an option. "Just drop me off at the diner. It's called Christa's Café. It's a couple of blocks over."

It was where the bus stopped. Although she didn't actually have any money for a bus. Maybe she could call from there and her sister could bring her the purse and bag she'd left at the church. She couldn't face Finn. She might never be able to face Finn again.

"Hungry, are you?"

"No."

"Then why should you go there?"

It was none of his business, and yet she answered immediately. And then felt bad because she was being rude. "It's where the bus stops."

Not that she knew where she would go. The bus could take her to

San Antonio or Austin one way. The other way went to Dallas and up to Oklahoma City.

Would she really run that far?

"Ah, you intend to flee for good, then. Well, you'll have to buy two tickets because I doubt that, um, dress you're wearing will fit in one. Buy the whole row, little one." He put the car in first gear and the sports car purred down the road. He turned onto the highway, away from town.

She watched as the street he needed to turn down was left behind. "Hey, the diner is back that way."

He nodded. "Yes, you mentioned that."

The car kept on its path.

"You're not taking me to the diner, are you?" She found herself settling into the seat, relaxing. Any more time in this car with him meant another moment before she had to face the fact that she no longer had a home to go to, or a future. She knew she was being an idiot. She could hear her sister bitching at her. *She didn't think about anything. She wasn't careful about selecting her friends. She didn't fit. She was an embarrassment.* Now that she thought about it, maybe she wouldn't call Val at all.

It was easy to push aside her sister's constant complaints as he drove. She looked up at the wide Texas sky and something eased inside her. She found herself actually smiling. "Where are we going?"

It didn't matter. Somehow, someway, she knew she would be safe with him. After a lifetime of doing everything that was asked of her and getting next to nothing in return, she felt like she didn't know what her next day would be like. It was exciting.

His head turned, and he arched an elegant eyebrow as he looked at her. The left side of his face tugged up slightly, and the sweetest dimple formed in his cheek. "We're going on vacation. You should be glad I packed light since I seem to have found a bit of extra baggage along the way. My name is Julian Lodge, though I suspect by the end of the night, you'll call me Sir."

"Yes, Sir."

Dani had no idea why, but it seemed to fit him.

She sat back and let Julian Lodge take the reins.

Chapter Three

Julian turned the Audi down the long gravel drive that led to the Barnes-Fleetwood ranch. A warm sense of satisfaction poured over his system. Jackson Barnes was a man he admired. Jackson had done well. He'd come from less than nothing and truly built a life for himself. The house in the distance was lovely. He could see a large main house and a guesthouse. From Jackson's descriptions he knew there was also housing for something Jackson had called the "hands." It was his first visit to the ranch, and he suspected his former protégé would teach him all about ranching. Despite having been born and raised in Texas, Julian had never been close to a cow that wasn't sitting on his dinner plate and cooked to medium rare.

"You know Jack Barnes?" Danielle sat up straight in her seat now, her eyes on the house in front of them.

It had taken roughly ten minutes to get from that tiny town she was fleeing to the ranch. He'd been amused at how quickly she'd relaxed and allowed her eyes to drift closed. She trusted quickly. It could be a dangerous thing if she met the wrong person. He had the feeling the woman beside him was a true submissive. She'd probably been taken advantage of all her life for that reason. She needed a strong, dominant partner. It was a good bet she wouldn't find one here.

"He's a friend," Julian replied simply.

She didn't need to know that Jackson Barnes used to be the Dom in residence at the sex club Julian owned and operated. The Club was his own personal haven. It was for experienced Dominants and their submissives. This soft little thing was obviously submissive, but she would never see the inside of a BDSM club. It simply wasn't her world. Despite her attempt at freedom, Julian knew she would end up right back in that church marrying the yokel next door.

People didn't change.

He studied the curve of her porcelain cheek. She wasn't a delicate girl. She was all curves and breasts. And the ridiculous gown she was wearing still overpowered her. If he had been dressing her, he would have kept it simple. He would have put her in a simple tailored gown that showed off her perfect skin and what looked to be an hourglass figure. Julian was surprised at how aroused he'd been while kissing the woman beside him. She'd gotten to him, and he wasn't sure how. Somewhere between making the decision to calm her down and that moment when she sighed and went languid in his arms, she'd flicked a switch on. Julian wasn't sure he wanted it switched off again. His cock certainly didn't. He was still hard.

"Are you staying here, or just saying hello?" Danielle asked.

He had an almost irresistible urge to reach out and place his hand on her hair. He wanted to smooth it down and calm the panic he could see was clearly rising in her. He forced his hand to stay on the steering wheel. "I told you I was on vacation. I'm spending the week here with my friends."

He had to admit it felt good to want someone. He would enjoy peeling back her layers and getting to the woman underneath. A smart idea? Perhaps not. Danielle seemed to be trouble. The tight feeling in his groin told him he might not mind a bit of trouble. He would have to ponder it. He never made snap decisions. Getting involved with the woman next to him carried certain risks he would have to carefully contemplate. He would sit down after dinner and give the decision the consideration it deserved. She obviously needed kindness. He had to decide if he could give that to her.

She was staring at her hands. It seemed to Julian that she was trying to make a decision. Perhaps she needed a bit of space. "When you're ready, come inside and find me. If you choose to stay, I'll have Jackson make up a room for you. If you choose to go, I'll arrange transportation. Is there anything you need right now?"

She shook her head and didn't look at him, instead staring at her hands as they twisted in her lap. He thought briefly about kissing her again. It had worked the first time. He discarded the idea as dangerous. He set the parking brake as the door to the ranch house opened.

Jackson was suddenly in the doorway, a wide smile on his face and something odd attached to his chest. It moved, then appeared to yawn.

"Julian! Damn, man, it's good to see you." Jackson Barnes's voice carried over the huge front lawn. He was a tall, broad man with dark hair. It wasn't covered with a cowboy hat this afternoon. Julian had rarely seen Jackson without a Stetson on his head in years.

Julian slipped out of the car and had his hand out as he crossed the yard. "I thought I would never get here. This is a beautiful place you have."

"That's all Abby's work. She's whipped this place into shape. She has your room all fixed up." Jackson's face split in a wide grin as he shook hands with Julian.

Julian studied the contraption Jackson was wearing. It looked like someone had tied a large scarf around his neck and back and formed a pouch. It was not what he had expected his tough cowboy friend to wear. The small child on his chest opened its eyes. Emerald green orbs studied him carefully. A tuft of dark hair sat on top of the baby's head.

Julian stared at the small human. "Well, there is no question who fathered this child." He was the spitting image of his father. He yawned like a tiny lion.

Jackson flushed slightly. His big hand came out to cover the baby's belly, holding him close. "They tricked me. Abby wanted one more baby. I agreed. What I didn't agree to was Sam getting a vasectomy while I was away on business. Let me tell you, that was a whipping he won't forget."

"Why on earth would Samuel do that?" The very thought made his blood boil. If one of his subs had done that, he would have dismissed him immediately. Any decision like that should have been cleared through the sub's Dom. But of course, Jackson couldn't dismiss Sam. They had a family together. This was why marriage could never work for him. "If Abigail wanted another child, why should Sam cut out half of her chances?"

"They wanted this baby to be mine."

The black-haired baby smiled. His sleepy green eyes were barely open. He was a cute thing. "I thought the three of you decided you wouldn't do a paternity test on Olivia unless it became medically necessary."

Jackson's hand gently smoothed the baby boy's hair down. "Yeah, well, sometimes you don't need a paternity test. Look at Josh here."

"But Olivia looks like Abigail. You can't know which one of you fathered her."

There was a tremendous crash as the front door slammed open, and a small ball of energy ran out of the house at breakneck speed. Julian had a brief glimpse of a red-haired girl in overalls and sneakers.

"Look, Daddy!" the girl screamed at the top of her lungs. "I'm running. I'm running, Daddy!" She motored across the yard and then began sprinting in circles, giggling madly. Her small face was turned up to the sun. "Watch me, Daddy."

Jackson watched the girl with the softest look in his eyes. "We're watching you, baby girl. Josh and me wouldn't want to watch anything else." He kept his eyes on the three-year-old. "She has Sam's smile. She might look like Abby, but everything else is pure Sam." Jack turned, and his whole face was lit up. "She is hell on wheels. Keeping her alive is a full-time occupation. She's already climbed the bookshelves. She's brilliant at escaping any crib or playpen we put her in, and she loves to try to ride the dogs. She's only three. I can't wait to see what she tries next."

It sounded perfectly atrocious to Julian. A child couldn't be reasoned with. A child wouldn't understand what he was willing to give and what he needed to withhold. A child simply needed everything. There was no contract one signed with a child. There was no out clause. Being a parent was messy. Like being a husband was messy. But being a Dom, that was neat and clean, with firmly placed boundaries.

He stared at the tiny girl. She was petite with a mass of wild red hair. She grinned as she ran, her joy completely infectious. Like Sam. Sam had a child. Six-month-old Josh was more awake now. He watched his sister with a lazy smile on his face. The baby looked almost indulgently affectionate, just like his father. What did Jack feel when he looked into the face of his son? A strange sentimentality stole across Julian. His own father had died when Julian was a child. Had his father had the same odd look of wonder on his face when he looked down at Julian as Jackson had on his?

Olivia Barnes-Fleetwood continued her crazy play. Jackson's eyebrows crept up, and he suddenly was focused on the car in the drive. "Is there something you would like to announce, Julian? Has this vacation turned into a honeymoon? It looks like your bride is getting away."

Sure enough, Danielle was making her way slowly down the drive. She walked lopsidedly, as though one of her heels had broken. Where did she think she was going? It was apparent to him that she had no one to rely on and nowhere to go. He checked the sudden urge to chase after her. If she wanted to go, he should allow her to do so. He'd never once forced a girlfriend to stay with him. Girlfriend? He hadn't had one of those in so long, he almost didn't remember the last one's face. He didn't have girlfriends or boyfriends. He had submissives. And he had never forced one to stay when they wanted to leave.

Although he couldn't allow her to simply stumble down the road in that hideous dress. She would get into trouble.

"She says her name is Danielle." Julian was well aware that his former protégé was studying him carefully. He'd trained Jackson himself, and one of the things he had been good at was reading body language. Julian worked to keep his face as placid as possible.

Jack obviously had lost that particular talent. His eyes went wide, and his mouth dropped open. "Danielle Bay? You married Abby's clinic manager? I thought she was supposed to marry that mechanic Jimbo today. Sam and Abby went to the wedding."

"Not my bride, but she is very insistent on running away. Oh, look, your daughter is much better at catching her than her poor groom."

Jackson threw his head back and laughed as Olivia parked herself on Danielle's train. She sat right down on the extra-long satin extension.

"Daddy, I'm getting a ride!"

Danielle stopped and pulled at her train. When she couldn't dislodge the child, she pleaded for a moment. Julian waited to see if she would shove the child off. She simply sat down next to the little girl in the middle of the driveway. It was mere seconds before she began to sob into her hands.

"Damn, things must have gone awfully wrong for that girl." Jackson started to walk across the lawn.

Little Olivia stood, walking across the white train. She placed her hand on the strange woman's head and started to speak. Whatever the girl said made Danielle open her arms and draw the child in. She clung to her small body and wept.

Julian sighed and couldn't stand another moment of indecision. He gave in to his instinct. He reached the crying bride long before Jack could. In the end, he simply kneeled and wrapped his arms around both woman and child. As Dani's hands found his shoulders he realized how much trouble he was in.

He really shouldn't have stopped at that light.

* * * *

The air conditioner hummed to life, blowing cold air into the hallway of the church. Valerie Bay was grateful for the chill. The heat outside was nothing compared to the flames when she thought about what had happened. That cool breeze hitting the back of her neck was the only thing she was grateful for today.

"Well, I never. I swear this town is going straight to the d-e-v-i-l." Audrey Miller always spelled out the devil's name because to actually say it was to invite him in.

Her friend Miranda Knight shook her head in agreement.

Idiots. Valerie was surrounded by them. She was in a church full of them, but she couldn't run away. Her stupid bitch sister had already pulled the vanishing act for the day. She needed a drink, but she wasn't going to find that in the First Methodist Church of Willow Fork.

Audrey Miller shook her finger Valerie's way. She was dressed in her very best ankle-length cotton skirt and button-up shirt. It was, of course, buttoned all the way to the top, as though she was worried anyone would want to catch a glimpse of those old boobs. Her thin lips pressed together. "Your poor mother would simply die, if the good Lord hadn't already called her home."

While Val couldn't stand the old woman, she was on the church's social board. Audrey Miller had power in Willow Fork. Val forced herself to nod. "You're right. It's the only thing to explain my sister's actions, Mrs. Miller. The d-e-v-i-l must have gotten to Dani."

Something had gotten to her, that was for sure. Danielle had started walking down the aisle, looking like a fat cow in white satin, then her face had gone as white as her dress, and she turned and ran. Jimbo had looked surprised, but that queer of hers had been the one to take off after her. Finn had made an even bigger scene than Dani. He'd screeched her name all up and down Main Street until Dani had hopped into someone's car and it had driven off. God only knew where she was now. If she had any sense at all, she would get herself murdered and spare them all the shame of having to see her again.

"And she must have been planning it." Hillary Glass's voice grated on Val's last nerve. The terror with a walker wrinkled her nose in obvious distaste. "She had a car waiting for her and everything."

Val checked her instinct to flee. The elderly were circling like judgmental sharks sensing blood. Val moved back from Hillary Glass. Many a toe had suffered damage from the old biddy's walker, and Val was pretty sure they weren't all accidents. "I don't think she planned it. Dani has impulse control issues."

She had to turn this around, find a way to illicit sympathy for herself or all might be lost. All her hard work gone because Dani was chicken shit.

"Poor Jimbo's momma is crying in the bathroom." Miranda Knight had strangely bright blonde hair for a woman her age. It formed an old-style beehive and might weigh more than the woman herself. She was cadaverously thin. "Leah says she should have known the lord was trying to send her a message by allowing the engagement party to be ruined by That Woman deciding to have her child right there in the community center. It was scandalous."

Val nodded, eager to pile on Abigail Barnes. They never said her name out loud, either. She was simply That Woman. They claimed Abby Barnes had killed Ruby Echols. Any woman who could take on that nasty old witch and come out on top was a woman Val didn't want to cross. Not that she would mention that to this group. Hating Abby Barnes was practically a religion to these women. "I tried to convince Dani she shouldn't invite That Woman, but she never listens to me."

And she damn well should. She'd been left to pick up Dani's mess. At least she had some sense. She'd moved everyone into the reception hall where the gossip had started to flow thicker than molasses in winter. The older people were all discussing Satan, and by Satan, they meant Jack Barnes. The rancher and his wife and whatever the hell Sam Fleetwood was were the subject of most of the gossip around town. Oh, no one in their right mind would be anything but polite to the trio. They were far too scared of Barnes, and then there were the rumors about what Sam could do to a person who insulted Abby.

When Dani had gone to work for Abby Barnes, everyone had said it was only a matter of time before she got pulled into whatever crazy sex things went on at that ranch. Val had tried to talk Dani out of it, but she was adamant about working in the clinic. Now look what had happened. That fat cow had walked out on the only man who ever gave her a second glance.

"You poor thing." Audrey Miller patted her shoulder. "You've had to put up with so much."

Val felt herself flush as shame flooded her body. She prayed no one noticed. She hated to be the object of their pity.

"First your father up and runs away," Audrey continued.

"If that was her father. You can't ever be sure with that type." Hillary said it to Miranda, but Val didn't miss the jibe. There was nothing to do but take it.

"Then your mother dies, and you have to depend on Danielle. We all know she doesn't make the best choices when it comes to friends."

Just like clockwork, the doors opened and Finn Taylor walked through looking like a zombie. His face was slack, and he sort of stumbled through, not paying any attention to the people around him. He disappeared behind the door to the bridal room.

"It's wrong." Hillary shook her head as she stared at the door Finn Taylor had closed.

Val mumbled something about getting a glass of water and fled. She avoided the reception hall, needing a moment. She turned down a quiet hall that led to the Sunday school rooms.

Val glanced at herself in the reflective glass of the trophy case. The Methodists regularly trounced the Presbyterians in softball and had the trophies to prove it. Damn, she looked good. She had picked out the bridesmaid dresses herself. The pink brought out her delicate skin, and the sheath emphasized her slender figure. She could still fit into her old cheerleader uniform. Not many people could say that. Certainly not Dani, though Dani had already been portly in high school.

Damn her. Val had worked her ass off to make sure this was a great social event. She'd intended to use this as a stepping stone. She wasn't going to be one of those trashy Bay girls anymore. The Smart family might not be the cream of the crop, but they were a definite move in the right direction. They owned their own land and attended the right church. They didn't live in a rundown old house and scrape for every penny the way the Bays had for decades.

She was grateful to her sister for sticking around after their mom died. Dani had put her through college. Of course that had been the sensible thing to do. She was the one with potential. She was the one who made good choices. By the time she was in junior high, Val had already eclipsed her older sister in every way that mattered. Dani might have been a straight A student, but that wasn't what counted, not really. What counted was how well you fit in. Val had ruled the school with an iron fist. She'd been the Queen Bee.

She was going to be that again. Marrying her sister off had been the first step. Then all she had to do was get Dani to sell Val her half of the land they'd inherited. How the hell was she going to do that if Dani didn't leave? She was on a timetable. Sooner or later the mayor was going to announce the development of that land, and then Dani would get half of the six figures their pitiful piece of Willow Fork was going to go for. The only reason John Hartley hadn't announced the development yet was the fact that Val would cut him off. She couldn't keep him on her sexual string forever.

"You got any idea where Dani went?"

Val spun around. Jimbo Smart stood behind her in his tuxedo jacket and black denims. She hadn't been able to convince him to wear the trousers. Jimbo might be all right in the sack, but he was a dumbass everywhere else. It briefly ran through Val's mind that maybe her sister had found out she was screwing Jimbo. She decided the only way to deal with the situation was to power through. "None whatsoever. You want to tell me what you did?"

That was the way to do it. Put the blame on everyone but herself. It worked almost every time. Sure enough, the dumbass mechanic reddened.

"I didn't do nothing, Val. Hell, I ain't even talked to her in a couple of days except at the rehearsal dinner. I did exactly what you told me to and laid low." His boots moved restlessly across the floor. He kept his voice quiet. "I let Momma handle her. I have no damn idea why she did that. She seemed fine last night. She spent all her time with Finn, but she seemed happy."

Finn. Damn him. Finn was the cause of all this chaos, Val knew it. Dani had been fine with her fate right up to the minute Finn drove into town and got out of his fancy car. It was pathetic. Val wasn't stupid. She knew her sister was in love with a man who would never return it, not the way a woman needed to be loved. Jimbo would have given Dani kids and a house to keep and some sort of place in the community, besides her current place of pathetic doormat old maid. Now Dani was going to be the crazy, pathetic doormat old maid. And Val was her sister, painted with the same damn brush.

"Obviously she wasn't happy or she would still be here getting ready to toast her new marriage."

Jimbo shrugged out of his tuxedo coat. "Maybe it's for the best. She's a nice enough girl and all, but she's pretty damn cold in the sack." He winked at Val. "Not like you, sweet thing."

She rolled her eyes. "Not here. Will you try to look like a sad groom?"

He leaned against the faded paneling beside the trophy case. "I'm not really. Look, Val, my momma told me I had to get married. Dani was sweet, but she sucks in bed. I don't get it. She's got a rocking body. Anyway, she doesn't want to get married. Fine. I'll find someone else. You're available, right?"

Val's stomach twisted in revulsion. As much as she enjoyed Jimbo, she was never going to be the wife of a mechanic. Now, the wife of a politician, that she might be able to handle. But John Hartley was never going to leave his middle-aged wife for a retail clerk. She had to bring in some cash of her own. And that meant getting rid of her sister. One way or another.

Val turned on her stilettos, not bothering to answer the redneck who couldn't even get someone like Dani to marry him. It had all gone to hell. She strode into the reception hall, determined to figure out a way out of the mess her sister had left her with.

Chapter Four

Dani sat on the sofa and looked between the two men who were carefully studying her. She decided she'd been more comfortable with her boss's husband when he had a baby attached to his chest. He'd seemed far less dangerous with a toothless infant dangling in front of him. Now Josh and Olivia had been put down for naps, and she was the object of both men's attention. She tried hard not to feel like an insect they had carefully pinned and made ready for dissection. Jack Barnes and Julian Lodge seemed perfectly comfortable with the silence that hung heavy in the air.

"Thanks for the clothes." She had to say something. She smoothed down the cotton T-shirt Jack had found for her. The jeans were slightly too big, but a belt had taken care of that. She glanced at the clock, wondering if there was any way she could get out of here before her boss came home. Abby Barnes was away this afternoon attending a wedding. *Her* wedding. But where was she going to go? A part of her wished she was still in that car with Julian, just driving. She hadn't had to face reality while she was in that car. Well, she had to face it now. She wasn't some dreamy-eyed teen. She had to take her medicine. She would have loved a day or two to sort things out, but she wasn't going to get it. "If I could use a phone, I'll get out of your hair."

"Who do you intend to call, little one?"

Dani sat up straighter. God, couldn't the man ask a simple question without the words going straight to her crotch? And why did he have to call her little one? She obviously wasn't little. Val was the slender one. Maybe he wasn't as nice as she thought he was. He wouldn't be the first person to make fun of her. She crossed her legs and gathered her last shred of dignity. She should never have gotten in the car with him. She shouldn't have run in the first place but getting into a stranger's car was ludicrous. If she couldn't handle Jimbo Smart, she had no idea how she was supposed to hold her own with Julian Lodge. Perhaps it was time to grow a backbone. "That is none of your business, Mr. Lodge."

One elegant eyebrow arched, and the room seemed to get cold.

"Sir." So much for a backbone.

Jack Barnes laughed sharply. "Well, that was inevitable."

Julian slid a glance Jack's way. "Any possibility there's someone I can pass her off to?"

Jack shook his head, crossing his booted foot casually over his knee. He made the leather chair he sat on seem like a throne. "Here? Not a chance. And it's worse than you think. If she ran out on her wedding, those old biddies in town will make life hell on her. They can't take her job, but they can make sure she's isolated. Do you know what that will do to a woman like Dani?"

"If this is what being a part of the community has done for her, then perhaps she should try isolation," Julian murmured. "Any chance you need a fourth?"

Emerald green eyes rolled. "Yeah, I'll get right on that. Let's just say I would like to keep all of my man parts in their current position. If you don't want her, call Leo. Hell, look at her. If you walk her into The Club, you'll have to beat the Doms off her."

Dani had no idea what they were talking about. She didn't know a Leo or a man named Dom. Anger started to build in her gut. She was used to people talking about her behind her back, but at least they didn't do it while she was sitting right in front of them. There was such a thing as common courtesy.

A slow smile spread across Jack Barnes's face. "You don't like that idea, do you, Julian?"

"I didn't say that." He sounded like he was gritting his teeth.

"You didn't have to." There was a wealth of satisfaction in Jack's tone. "Fine. I'll call Leo myself. He's been looking for a permanent sub for a while now. It will be my pleasure to get him down here. Maybe once he takes a look at her, he can forget about Abby. I swear I'm going to kick his ass one of these days."

Julian's jaw tightened, the words grinding from his mouth. "Don't you call him. She's my problem, and I'll take care of her."

The words hit her like an out-of-control train, slamming into her, making her sick with shame. Problem? She was starting to process his words, though they didn't all make sense. Julian Lodge thought she was a burden and was trying to foist her off on someone else. She wasn't a burden. She never had been. She'd always been the one to take the load off someone else. She was the one who never complained and never argued. Until she'd run out of that church, she'd never caused a single scandal, with the exception of being friends with Finn. Dani had given up her whole future to take care of a sick mother and put her sister through school. She did not deserve their scorn. She stood, sick to death of people who didn't value her.

"Don't talk about me like I'm not here. If you won't let me use your phone, then I'll just walk, but I won't stand here while you two jerks make fun of me. I don't know about this guy." She gestured to Julian, whose face had gone stony cold. "But I thought better of you, Mr. Barnes. I didn't think you were the type to kick a person when she was down. I guess I was wrong. Please tell Abby that I won't be in to the clinic any more. I'll find something else."

God, she'd quit her job. She loved her job. It was the one bright spot in her dreary life. Why had she done that? But there was no backing down now. She turned to leave. She would mail Abby her clothes later. Right now, it was a long walk back to town.

"Danielle!"

Julian's sharp bark caused her to stop in her tracks. She turned almost unwillingly.

"That was a good start, but you didn't understand," he said, patience molding his every word. "We weren't making fun of you. We were rather making fun of me. But I'm proud of how you stood up for yourself. Now please sit back down and we'll talk about what to do next."

So he could make fun of her again? "You city types are all alike. Of course, I thought Mr. Barnes was better. I'm so disappointed in you. I guess you're more like what those people in town say than I thought."

Barnes's brow rose. "And what do they say, Danielle?"

When that man wanted to freeze a person out she felt the cold. "It doesn't matter. Good-bye."

"Danielle!" He hadn't moved from the couch, but she felt the will pouring off his body. "You will come back in this room, and you will stop behaving like a brat."

She felt her eyes widen. No one had ever called her that. "Brat? You're the one acting like a bully, Sir. I mean Mr. Lodge."

She had to stop calling him that.

He moved gracefully off the couch, stalking to her. He towered over her, six foot two inches of pure intimidation. He invaded her space, and her heart started to thud in an unfamiliar rhythm. "You were right the first time, Danielle. Now I was willing to give you a pass because I believe it took courage for you to stand up the first time. I admire courage. But I explained that we weren't attempting to hurt you. Can you tell me exactly how I've bullied you today? I didn't force you into my car. You jumped in and refused to get out. I didn't leave you on the side of the road. I brought you to the safest place I know. My friend gave you clothes. Please explain to me how we bullied you?"

Put like that, she wanted to crawl away and hide. But they'd said things. "You were talking about me like I wasn't here."

"I assure you I was well aware of your presence every second we've been here," he said. "And like I said, Jackson was joking about me, not you. He's a gentleman."

Tears pricked her eyes. Had she been wrong?

Julian stared at her. "You will apologize to Jackson, and then we're going to have a private talk."

The front door opened suddenly.

"Damn, Jack, you missed a hell of a show. Dani finally got a lick of sense and motored herself right out of that church. It was the best show this town has seen in a long time."

Sam Fleetwood strode into the living room with a broad smile on his handsome face.

The wife he shared with Jack followed behind, though she was frowning. "We need to find her, Jack. She's in trouble."

Jack simply pointed.

Abby sighed. "Thank God. You scared us, Dani. Not that I don't absolutely support your decision to not marry that man, but you shouldn't have run away. You got into some stranger's car. Anything could have happened to you. I've been so worried."

Abby's eyes moved between Dani and Julian, who, despite the addition of two new audience members, hadn't once moved those cold eyes off her. Dani wanted to run, but she'd done enough of that for one day.

"Jack, what's going on?" Abby put a hand on Jack's arm, concern plain on her face. She started to walk toward Dani, but Jack held her back.

Sam threw his head back and laughed. "Can't you tell, baby? Damn, Dani, of all the cars in the world you could have hopped into, you got into Julian Lodge's. That man is a sub magnet. I've always said it."

Julian growled a bit. "Your sarcasm is duly noted, Samuel. Now, may I have a moment alone with Danielle?"

"Are you sure about this?" Jack was holding Abby's hand. He sent Sam a look that had the blond man getting serious all of a sudden. "If you aren't, then I'll take care of her. I can get her a job in another town and see that she's all right."

"Why does she need a new job?" Abby asked, her voice rising.

That scenario didn't seem to satisfy Julian. "She doesn't need a new job. She needs a new life. If you simply move her somewhere new, she'll get in trouble again because she is untrained."

"I'm not a dog, you jerk!" Her fists were clenched at her sides. Humiliation washed through her.

He turned quickly. "I didn't say you were, Danielle. And, as I have been nothing but polite with you, I expect a modicum of courtesy. I understand that you have been through a lot today. I understand that you require some tenderness. None of that gives you the right to belittle me and our hosts."

Tears were threatening again. She disliked him greatly in that moment. He made her feel like a child. "Then I wouldn't want to force you to be around a brat. Like I said, I'll get out of your hair."

He ignored her. "I'll deal with her, Jackson, and if you question my rights again, we shall have trouble."

Jack's mouth thinned, but he nodded.

"Jack, what's going on?" Abby asked. She attempted to pull away.

"No. This is between Julian and Dani. Abigail, go to our bedroom now."

"But Jack."

Jack Barnes stared down at his wife, his face colder than Dani could ever remember it being. "I said now. Do you want to test me?"

"No, she doesn't." Sam slipped his hand into Abby's. "Come on, baby. Let's go check on the kids. Julian isn't going to hurt your friend, and you know it. You also know exactly what she is and what she needs. We've talked about it before. It's why you practically cheered when she ran away. Now she might figure a few things out. Don't take that from her."

Abby nodded, and with one last look Dani's way, she walked out with Sam, leaving Dani alone with Jack and Julian.

Dani shuffled nervously, wondering exactly what Sam had meant and what she was supposed to figure out. Julian's eyes were still on her.

"Do you have something to say, Danielle?"

"I want to leave. I want to go home." She wanted to get away from him. The very fact that she felt a desperate need to apologize and do anything it took to get his approval made her want to flee in terror.

His jaw tightened, but then he took a step back. The iron will on his face turned to a mask of smooth indifference. "Of course. Do you have someone to call, or would you like me to drive you? If you feel uncomfortable with me, I am sure I can find someone else to take you wherever you would like to go."

She didn't like the way he looked through her as though she was something he'd already dismissed from his life. He was giving her what she wanted. He was being polite, nonthreatening, and utterly distant. She hated it. She had spent so much of her life feeling invisible, the thought of this man looking through her made her eyes water. She nodded, unable to speak.

His hand came out and slid over hers. The touch of his skin sent tingles across her whole body. "Don't cry, Danielle. I promise I'll make sure you get home. Jackson?"

He nodded, but she could sense his disappointment. "I can have one of the hands take her home. She knows Ricky and Tom. She should feel comfortable with them."

Panic threatened again. Home? She'd moved all of her clothes and things into Jimbo's house. She could go home to the house she grew up in, but Val was there. The thought of listening to her baby sister rage about how she'd screwed everything up was more than she could handle. And Finn could find her there. She couldn't stand the thought of seeing pity on his face. She also couldn't stand the thought of never seeing the man in front of her again. It was stupid. She'd just left her groom at the altar. She wasn't in Julian Lodge's league. She should have Ricky or Tom take her to the church, and she could figure out what to do from there. Her hand curled into Julian's large one, and she shook her head. "Please let me stay the night."

His mouth turned down. "That is up to Jackson."

Jack watched the scene with his arms crossed over his solid chest. "I don't think that's what she's asking."

"Then she needs to have the courage to ask me for what she wants." His foot tapped against the hardwood floor.

Dani swallowed as she looked up at Julian. His perfect face was staring down at her patiently. He was going to make her ask. "May I please stay the night?"

He stilled his foot and focused that intense attention on her. "You have to be clear, Danielle. Are you asking for a room for the night, or are you asking to spend the night in my bed?"

Damn him. Why did he have to put it like that? It was so blatant. And she wasn't thinking that way. Well, she was, but she wouldn't go through with it. She was insanely attracted to him. Any woman with eyes would want him. But she knew she wasn't a sexual person. As much as she wanted him, she would only be disappointed in the end. "You're safe from me, Mr. Lodge. I promise not to attack you. I'm not…interested in that kind of thing."

That was a lie. She was beyond interested. She simply wasn't any good at it. She lacked something. While she heard other women boast about their sex lives, Dani didn't get it. She'd had three lovers her entire life and not one of them had managed to get her to that magical place other women talked about. After Jimbo failed, she had to wonder if the problem didn't lie with her.

He snorted regally. His lips turned down in an expression of complete disbelief. "Really? You have no interest in sexual intercourse?"

"None. Consider yourself safe."

"You have no interest in a man, a dominant man, bending you to his will? No interest in pleasing him? Let me tell you how it would go, little one. You would do it on your knees, on your back, however he wanted you. You would kneel before him and trust him to give you the discipline you require to come to orgasm. And you would come, Danielle. This man would make sure of it. You would come many times. He would train you to accept pleasure and that edge of pain that enhances it. He would train you to pleasure him, and in giving him pleasure, pleasing that part of you that needs to give. You would be tied up, tied down, forced to accept a crop's sting across your flesh. He would bind your arms and legs and whip your backside when you displease him. You would learn to love the lash because it takes you someplace special, someplace where only a person like you can go. After, you would be worshipped, with his hands, his lips, his tongue, his cock. There is no piece of you this man wouldn't claim. He would invade your pussy, your mouth, your tight little ass. You would belong to him, and in exchange, he would protect you, cherish you for the gift you have given him. He would see to your comfort, your peace of mind. You have absolutely no interest in such a relationship?"

Her mouth had gone dry a long time ago. She forced herself to swallow. His words had gone straight to her pussy, and she shifted, feeling an odd softness at the juncture of her thighs. She should definitely run now, and she knew she wouldn't. She'd spent twelve years giving to others. She'd given up her dreams for her sister. She'd been the doormat of Willow Fork. Today was about what she wanted.

It wouldn't last. She wasn't foolish enough to believe that Julian Lodge would sweep into her two-stoplight town and carry her away. But, if he could make her feel something for a day or two, that would be worth it. The heartache would come, and strangely she welcomed that, too. It would mean that something had happened to her, something she chose.

"I would like to spend the night with you."

A slow smile spread across his face, making her heart clench at the thought that she had put it there. "Excellent. I would enjoy that as well."

"I thought you were on vacation." Jack was shaking his head.

"Yes, and now I am taking a vacation from my celibacy."

"Celibacy?" A distinct note of incredulity seeped into Jack's tone.

"Later, Jackson. For now, Danielle and I need to work out her punishment."

She forced herself to breathe. "Punishment?"

"Yes, you were rude to me and our hosts."

She liked the way he said "our" far too much. She was getting in too deep and couldn't seem to stop. There was one thing she was sure of. He hadn't been teasing her. He seemed to really want to be with her sexually. She wasn't sure why, but she wasn't going to get stubborn now. And the truth was, she had been rude. "I am sorry, Sir."

"I do not require your apology. I require your submission. Twenty swats over my knee, right now. And then you may apologize to our host."

Dani felt herself flush. Julian walked to the sofa, sat down, and patted his knee. She turned to Jack, who simply nodded as though giving his assent to the proceedings. Julian wanted her to lie across his lap and allow him to spank her? A vision of the way she would look spread out across his lap assailed her. She would be helpless. He would be utterly in control.

"It's up to you, Dani. If you're scared, then you can talk to Abby and figure out what you want." Jack sounded imminently sensible.

"You do this to Abby, don't you?" She'd known that her boss's marriage was odd, to say the least. From the lunches she'd had with

Abby, she'd started to see that she was very freethinking in her sexual beliefs. It didn't put Dani off. It made her think that Abby Barnes was a woman to admire. Abby loved and was loved and didn't apologize for it.

Jack's lips quirked up. "Yes, I do. But I understand that it might be intimidating to a newbie. If you're scared, know that I won't toss you aside. You're my wife's friend. I will take care of you."

That was the easy way out. That was the way "careful Dani" would go. This Dani wanted to know what it felt like to be with Julian. This Dani wasn't backing down. She walked to Julian. She started to lean over him. His hand came up, stopping her.

"Pull the pants down."

She hesitated. Julian simply waited. His face was open and showed no signs of intimidation. He was waiting to see if she complied. Why did he leave it up to her? She cast a glance at Jack, but he didn't seem to be leaving.

"She should have a safe word," Jack murmured Julian's way as he watched them.

"Fine," Julian assented. "Danielle, select a safe word. This is a word you say if you wish for everything to stop. If you say this word, I will stop what I am doing and we'll talk. It should be a word that you wouldn't normally say during intercourse, so try to avoid yes, no, god, and please, please, please."

She laughed at his unwavering confidence. It lifted her spirits and made him even more attractive.

"How about hippopotamus?" She hoped that word wouldn't float through either of their heads when they had sex.

"Excellent." He patted his knees again.

No more procrastination. She was either in or out. She really wanted to be in. She could lie to everyone else, but her pussy wasn't lying. It was throbbing in a completely foreign way at the thought of Julian's hand striking her ass. She undid her belt. Her fingers went to the fly of her borrowed jeans. She wished they were alone, but it was obvious this was a test of sorts and she meant to pass it. She shoved the jeans down past her hips and quickly lowered herself over Julian's lap, hoping Jack Barnes didn't get a view of her cootchie.

Julian's hand smoothed across the flesh of her ass. She felt him start at her waist and trail all along her skin down to her thighs. Every nerve stood at attention, as though waiting for his further consideration.

"You are lovely, Danielle. I can't wait to see you naked."

That deep, dark voice was completely serious in its intent. He wasn't teasing her. He honestly wanted to see her naked. He wanted to see her without her bra or panties. He wanted to see her breasts and her pussy. No one had ever simply said he would like to see her. She wiggled her ass, unable to remain still.

She felt his cock get hard against the side of her torso. "Yes, that's what I want."

She squealed as his hand struck the fleshy part of her ass. If he was holding back, she couldn't tell. It stung harshly. Her eyes watered; her breath hitched.

"I need you to count, Danielle. I wouldn't want to lose track."

Bastard. "One."

Immediately she felt the second blow. She hissed as her other cheek went up in flames.

Tears threatened at swats three and four. On five she gritted her teeth and decided she hated him.

"You're doing well for a novice." His soothing tone slid across her.

Six and seven made her whimper, but she made another decision. She wasn't going to let the pain win. She would show them all she wasn't so fragile and delicate.

Eight and nine weren't so bad.

"Ten." She wasn't about to disappoint him now. She could handle this. The fire that started on her cheeks had warmed to a deep heat that sank into her flesh. It felt almost pleasurable. He struck again, and her eyes watered. "Eleven."

His hand struck again, merciless in its intent. She felt her head sag. She gave over. She'd made the decision not to give in to the pain, and now that pain was turning into something else. She allowed her whole body to relax. Her knees softened, and she felt boneless against him. Her hands found his ankles, seeking something solid. She called out each number.

"Nineteen." Her voice was the only thing with a lick of will now.

Her ass was on fire, and damned if that didn't feel interesting.

His final blow landed along the crease of her ass. She simply sighed and waited for the pain to turn to something more. She let the rest of the world go and concentrated on what she felt. This was a special place. Nothing existed here except her feelings.

"Little one, I need a count." Julian's amused voice pulled her out of her warm, safe place.

She stiffened. "Twenty."

Strong arms pulled her up. Gray eyes looked into hers. "I am so proud of you. You did very well." He kissed her soundly. "Now pull up your pants and apologize so we can go and have dinner. Tonight I will thank you properly for your good behavior."

She managed to force her way up to standing and quickly rearranged her jeans. Blushing furiously, she turned to Jack Barnes. "I am sorry, Mr. Barnes."

Jack was flushed. He nodded shortly. "Apology accepted." His eyes shifted to Julian. "Dinner should be served in thirty minutes. I might be late, you bastard."

He practically ran from the room.

Julian was grinning broadly. He sat back, not bothering to hide the enormous erection he was sporting. "Sit down beside me. I believe our host will be a while. We can sit and cuddle."

She sank down next to Julian Lodge. His arm came around her shoulder, and she leaned into his heat. She let her head rest against his chest and felt safer than she had all day. She fell asleep to the steady beat of his heart.

* * * *

Finn sat in the bridal room with his head in his hands. The air conditioner came on, filling the room with cold air that didn't penetrate his body. He couldn't seem to make himself care about what was going on around him.

He didn't even know where she was or who she was with. A slow anger started to build, pushing through the sadness. She'd run. She'd jumped into a stranger's car and fled as he called out for her. That idiot fiancé of hers had stood back, but Finn had sprinted, trying to catch her. He could understand her leaving Jimbo behind, but he couldn't fathom why she would leave him.

She'd never left him. Not even when they were kids. Not even when she'd found out how different he was. She'd been the first one he'd come out to, when he was so confused he wasn't sure what he was. She'd stood by him when everyone else turned against him. Why had she run today?

With a bitter feeling in the pit of his stomach, he gathered her things. No one else would do it. They were all too busy gossiping and eating pie. It was what these people did. They had started whispering the second it became apparent the wedding wasn't going to go as planned. The buzzards had started to circle. Those old ladies who moaned about their hips had moved pretty damn quick to get a good view of Dani's escape. He'd had to make his way around them to follow her. By the time he'd gotten back to the church, they were all sniping about how they'd always known she wouldn't come to anything. After all, she was thirty and only had a job because That Woman took pity on her.

He hated them. Not all of them, of course. It wasn't like he'd never found a moment's kindness here. There were teachers who had encouraged him. The town librarian had always given him a place to hide when the bullies got to be too much. Christa's Café had been a haven, too.

But through it all, Dani had been his anchor.

When they had graduated from high school, he'd been the one who had left her behind.

Finn shoved her sneakers into the small travel bag they had prepared the night before. She and Jimbo hadn't planned much of a honeymoon. They were supposed to spend the weekend at a casino in Shreveport. He'd shuddered when she'd told him. A couple of nights in some smoke-filled casino wasn't his idea of a romantic trip. If he'd married Dani, he would have taken her to Europe. He would have let her plan the trip of her dreams. Italy, France, England. He would have taken her to all the places they'd dreamed of visiting when they were kids. It should have been him.

This was his fault.

"It's your fault, you know."

Finn turned at the sound of Val's voice. Dani's sister was seven years younger but had ages of conniving bitch experience on her. "Thanks for your input, Val. Feel free to go back and gossip to your heart's content. I'll deal with Dani's things."

It would give him something to do. He couldn't imagine that he would get a wink of sleep until he figured out where she was.

He sighed as he found her cell phone. There went one shot at reaching her.

"They're starting to clean up in there," Val said with a sniff.

No wonder she'd come looking for him. Val had always managed to get out of any kind of work. Finn couldn't stand the sight of her. She was almost sickly thin. Though both she and her sister were natural blondes, Val had bleached out the honey color to a full platinum. Both women had green eyes, but somehow Val's were harder, colder. Finn didn't like Val, never had. Even as a small child, she'd been deceitful and cruel. She'd taken everything Dani had to give and, as far as Finn could see, gave nothing at all back.

"I'll take Dani's stuff with me. She'll call me when she's ready to talk." Finn wasn't about to leave it up to Val. Val would sell Dani's things if she thought she could make a buck.

Her eyes went wide, and she bit into her bottom lip. Finn immediately went on high alert.

"Please tell her to call me. I'm so worried about her." Her voice hitched as though she was about to cry.

This was the time when the man was supposed to get all soft and willing to listen to her bullshit. Finn was not that man. "What do you want?"

She always wanted something.

Her arms crossed defensively over her chest. "She's my sister. Can't I be worried about her?"

If she had a heart, maybe. Val had gotten rid of her heart long ago in an attempt to get back to her birth weight. "No. You have an angle. I want to know what it is."

She dropped the innocent act. Her lip snarled briefly. "You're an asshole, Finn. I don't care what you think. I need to talk to my sister. If you find her before I do, tell her to call me. We need to figure out what we're going to do with the house. She was supposed to sell me her half of the house, and I mean to keep her to that promise. I'm an adult. I can't have a damn roommate forever."

He would have said Val couldn't shock him. He'd been wrong. "That's the house she raised you in. She gave up her whole future to keep that house so you had a place to live. She didn't go to college because the state would have put you into foster care. She worked two jobs most of the time. Do you have any idea how hard that was for her?"

Val shrugged and flicked her nails. "I'm offering her a good deal. She can find someplace else. She's lived there all her life. You would think she'd be sick of it by now. I'm doing her a favor."

He huffed and zipped the bag closed. He didn't want to spend any more time in Val's presence than he had to. "Some favor. I bet you'll try to cheat her somehow. I will take a look at any paperwork you want Dani to sign."

She paled a bit, but her voice was filled with malice. "Why don't you take her back to the city with you? Don't you need a hag or something?"

"Fuck you, Val."

"Only a real man could do that." She rolled those cold eyes. "That's why you're perfect for Dani. She wouldn't know a real man if one tried to marry her. Oh, yeah, she fucked that up, too. She has pissed off a bunch of the women in this town. Trust me, she'll be damned grateful I'm willing to buy her out. She is not going to want to live in this town after her stunt."

Val turned on her stilettos and slunk off.

A slow heat started to spread through Finn's body as Val's words sank in. Dani had stayed for Val. After Val finished college, Dani had stayed because she didn't know anything else. What if she had to leave? What if the town became completely unbearable? She would need a friend. She would need him.

Once he had her on his home turf, he would show her that they could make a relationship work. She would be surprised at first, but she would come around.

He slung the bag over his shoulder. He would make it work.

He simply had to figure out where she was.

Chapter Five

Julian looked at Danielle across the living room. She sat next to Abby with Olivia in her lap. She'd barely touched her steak, salad, and mashed potatoes, or the excellent chocolate mousse the Barnes's housekeeper had prepared for dinner. Though she played with the little girl and managed to hold a conversation with Abby, he could practically feel her anxiety from across the room. He smiled, trying to encourage her to calm down. It had been a while since she'd made the decision to spend the evening with him and she was obviously second-guessing herself. He wanted that. He wanted her to second- and third-guess herself. She should wrestle with the decision. It was a huge step to take in what already seemed to be a big day of change for Danielle Bay.

He'd sat down with Jackson directly after dinner and questioned him about Danielle. It was as he'd suspected. She was very submissive and completely untrained. She'd spent her entire life attempting to please the people around her. Most of them had taken full advantage of her nature. She'd given up her hopes and dreams to care for a mother dying of a brain tumor. When her mother was gone, she'd raised her sister, who Jackson had referred to as a waste of flesh. If she hadn't fled from her wedding, she would have been taken advantage of by her husband, and her life would have continued on the same sad path.

A warm feeling suffused his skin. This might be exactly what he'd been waiting for. The subs at The Club were mostly professionals, men and women who knew exactly what they wanted. Training those submissives merely meant teaching them how he preferred things and then allowing them to find their places in the community.

Danielle was different. Danielle wanted but had no idea how to have. There was a well of untapped potential in her that merely needed the right person to encourage her that strength didn't have to mean arrogance, that her voice was something she could listen to.

He could teach her and potentially find a permanent Dom for the gorgeous thing. The thought of keeping her for himself nibbled at the edge of his consciousness. He disregarded the idea. He wasn't cut out for long-term, but he knew many men who were. He would do what he'd always done. He would train her, enjoy her, and match her up to the perfect Dom.

"Baby hog." Samuel held out his arms to Jackson.

Jackson rocked back in his easy chair, Josh against his chest. He glanced up at Samuel. "How about a please?"

Samuel's lips turned up. "I thought I already pleased you enough for one night, Jack."

Jackson's face lit up as he shook his head. "I'll give you that one." He kissed the top of Josh's head and allowed Samuel to pull the baby into his arms. The little guy lit up at the sight of his other father, and Samuel carried the baby to the couch. He sank down beside Abby and cooed at the child.

Jackson sat up. "He's going to kill me one of these days."

And yet the content look on his face told Julian it wouldn't be a bad way to go. He studied his former protégé for a moment. Jackson's lips turned up.

"Are you ready to ask me about it?" Jackson made the question seem almost like a foregone conclusion.

"Ask you what?" He wasn't aware he had any burning questions.

"Aren't you going to ask me how settling down feels? You're not exactly a young man anymore. Haven't you thought about settling down?"

He was mildly affronted at the thought. "I'm only five years older than you. I'm not exactly an old man."

Jackson held his hands up in apology. "Of course not, and don't raise your voice. You're almost the same age as Abby, and I do not want to have that conversation with her. All I'm saying is you're in the prime of your life, and it's time to think about the future."

His gaze stole to Danielle, who quickly averted her eyes. She was so shy. He would have to rid her of that condition, at least around him. His immediate future looked quite bright. Danielle was beautiful and completely untrained. She would prove to be an amazingly rewarding challenge, he just knew it. "I'm happy with my life the way it is. Not all of us get a white picket fence. Not all of us want one."

But the words rang hollow, even to his own ears. He kept his face perfectly even, but Jackson's words sent a strange restless feeling through his gut. He'd hoped that enforced celibacy would cause him to work through the odd longing he'd had in the last couple of years, but it had only seemed to sharpen the hunger. He'd finally decided to take up his old life again. He would take two subs, carefully chosen from a plethora of eligible candidates, and continue as he had before. He would ignore the unsettled feeling he got when around his "settled" friends. His future would be orderly.

Then Danielle had jumped into his car.

Chaos suddenly didn't seem like such a bad thing.

"You need to be careful with her." Jackson leaned forward, his voice low.

"I am always careful."

His hands tightened on his knees, and Jackson's eyes studied him carefully as though deciding how to continue. "I wasn't talking about physically. She isn't some submissive who knows the score. The subs you've taken up until now know that eventually you'll pass them off to someone else. They know that you will give them what they need as a submissive, but not much else."

Julian felt his eyebrows draw together. What was that supposed to mean? "If you are accusing me of something, I would rather you stated it plainly."

"You are so touchy about this. That's what I mean. You look at Dani and you see a submissive in need of training. I know that you'll give her everything she needs as a sub, but she needs other things. She

65

needs you to see her as a woman, too."

The whole conversation was making him uncomfortable. "Of course I see her as a woman."

Jackson sighed, disappointment plain on his face. "I'm talking about something beyond tits and a heart-shaped ass. She needs more than an affectionate Dom. That woman needs a lover. She needs someone who won't dismiss her because she acts out, and she will act out. It's inevitable in a real relationship. People get mad at each other. People in love really get mad at each other."

Julian looked at the woman in question. She was lovely and obviously in need, but he couldn't see himself ever getting mad at her. Disappointed, yes, but he rarely got angry. Anger meant a loss of control, and he would never do that. Though he wanted Danielle, he wasn't willing to upset his oldest friend over her. He felt his jaw tighten. "If it bothers you, then by all means, make different arrangements for her. I wouldn't want to offend you in your own home."

Jackson sat back, and he had the terrible feeling that he'd done exactly what he'd sworn he didn't want to do. "I wasn't telling you to leave her alone. Forget I said anything. I had Benita move your things to the guesthouse. We converted the upstairs of the guesthouse to a playroom last year after Abby's mom got remarried. You should be perfectly comfortable there. There's a stash of new toys in the closet."

Julian sat back, unsure of what to do. This was why he didn't have many friends. He didn't know how to act around them. It had been easier when Jackson was his employee. And yet, he found himself unable to cut the tie. "I didn't mean to be difficult. I just don't understand. Why don't you tell me plainly what you think I should do?"

Jackson's face relaxed. "You really don't understand, do you? Here's what I want you to do, I want you to keep an open mind. I want you to go into this relationship with Dani with no thought to when it's going to end."

That should be perfectly clear. "Well, it will end when she no longer needs me."

"And what if she always needs you?"

Julian had absolutely no answer for that.

* * * *

Dani felt her hands tremble as Julian opened the door to the guesthouse. She stared at the broad plane of his back, encased in an expensive-looking dress shirt. She longed to run her hands across those shoulders, to feel the muscles beneath his tanned skin, but she held back.

What was she doing?

He turned as the door swung open, gallantly inviting her to go first. She hesitated. If she walked in that house with him, she was agreeing to have sex. She doubted it would be regular, normal sex after that speech he'd given her. It would be super kinky, monkey sex. Was she ready for that?

His hand touched her hair, smoothing it back. "It's all right, little one. You don't have to do this. I won't throw you out because you don't want to have sex with me. You can spend the night in the main house, and we'll figure out what would be best for you in the morning."

How did he do that? One minute he scared the crap out of her, and the next she wanted to melt against him. A sudden vision of Finn crossed her mind. Finn was the only man she'd ever really loved. She remembered the one time she'd kissed him. He'd been so embarrassed he'd walked away from her. When he'd come back, he'd acted like nothing had happened.

It had been the only time she'd tried to be aggressive. It had been a miserable failure, and she wasn't good at it in the first place. It felt wrong. Unnatural. Yet, when Jimbo was aggressive, she'd wanted to get it over with. Kneeling over Julian Lodge's lap this afternoon had been the most sensual experience of her life. She was scared, but she wanted to see where this path led.

"I know what I want."

His finger traced the line of her jaw. "Brave sub. Did Abigail explain what you needed to know? We can talk for a while if you want."

She swallowed. Abby had explained a lot. She'd fully explained what a safe word was and why Dani needed one. Abby had explained about the playroom/dungeon and some of the things Julian would probably want. It had been a bit awkward in the beginning, but Abby had been patient. By the time Sam had joined them, she'd put Dani at ease. She'd also assured Dani that Julian would honor her safe word. Abby wasn't Julian's biggest fan, but she claimed he was good to his…subs. He was the Dom, and she was the submissive. "I think I understand."

"Very good." He gestured for her to enter.

Dani glanced around the nicely decorated space. The Barnes-Fleetwood guesthouse was way nicer than the house Dani had grown up in. She found herself in a living area. It didn't look anything like a dungeon. There was a comfy-looking sofa and love seat. She could see there was a kitchen and a small dining area. Off to the side were the stairs that led to what Jack had called the playroom. She was interested in seeing what was in that playroom. Abby had gone over some of the things in there, but she wanted to see them with her own eyes.

"Should I go upstairs?" She wasn't quite sure what to do.

"I think we should begin down here." He didn't seem at all uncomfortable. He walked straight to the couch and lowered himself onto it. He'd unbuttoned the top three buttons of his shirt, and Dani couldn't help but look at the smooth skin he'd uncovered. He looked like a man who didn't mind hitting the gym—a lot. He patted his lap. "Sit with me."

It wasn't a suggestion. His voice had gone deeper than normal. She sank onto his lap. One arm anchored her at the waist while the other found her neck and drew her head down onto his shoulder. She could smell his masculine scent. Sandalwood. She breathed it in.

"See, this is nice."

She felt his low rumble all along her skin. He nuzzled her neck, causing her to shiver, but not from the cold. This was very nice indeed. His hands moved soothingly across her curves. He did everything with a seductive deliberation that had her hormones simmering.

"Let's set our ground rules for the evening."

"Rules?" She thought he would just take her. She was surprised he hadn't already. She could feel the thick line of his erection against the cheeks of her ass, yet he seemed content to cuddle against her.

"Oh, yes, there will be rules. I think we'll take it easy tonight. I'll ease you into high protocol. For tonight, you may speak without express permission. I want you to be able to ask questions if you're afraid." His hand trailed along her leg. "Do you understand what a Dom is?"

"Apparently someone who doesn't want me to speak."

His hand came down on her ass in a short, sharp arc. "No sarcasm allowed. I don't take well to Sams."

His slap hadn't really hurt, but it left a lingering warmth. She squirmed a bit. "Sam?"

"Smart-ass masochist. Samuel Fleetwood was aptly named. It fits him to a *T*, but this is lingo we use for a submissive who talks back."

She shook her head. She knew what a masochist was. It wasn't a good thing to be. "I'm not a masochist."

His hand fondled her breast. "Yes, you are. Maybe only a bit, or you wouldn't be here. You liked your spanking. Don't try to lie to me. Lying to me means punishment. Rule number one. Rule number two is stop thinking like a tourist. I can see the way your brain is working. With me, there is no right or wrong. There is only what feels good and what doesn't work. That's what we'll discover. The only way we can do that is if you're honest with me and with yourself. Now, answer me honestly. Did you enjoy your spanking?"

"Yes." It actually felt good to not lie. It felt good to admit it. She'd spent so long denying herself that there was a sort of freedom in admitting she was a bit of a freak.

His hand tightened on her nipple. It was through her shirt and bra, but she felt the warning in it. "What do you call me?"

That pinch on her nipple sent a flare of heat that fired into her pussy. "Sir."

He lessened the pressure but kept his hand on her breast. "Excellent, Danielle. For now, I am Sir. If we choose to move on, perhaps sign a contract for the duration of your training, you will call me Master, but for the time being, Sir will do. Now, take off your clothes and let me inspect you."

She immediately pulled back. The thought of standing in front of him naked made her stomach roll. She wasn't exactly a hard-bodied girl. She was short and curvy and could stand to lose ten, maybe fifteen pounds. Certainly not the fifty Val thought she needed to lose, but she could lose some. Her boobs were too big. They sagged a little. She had cellulite on her ass.

"Is there a problem, Danielle?" His calm voice held an edge of impatience.

She swallowed. "I thought we would turn off the lights maybe."

"No, we won't turn off the lights. Nor will I rip your clothes off your body. You will make the choice every submissive makes every time her Dom gives a command. You choose to obey and continue the session, or end the session with your safe word."

She chewed on her bottom lip, indecision banging through her head. "It would make it a lot easier if you would do the rip-my-clothes-off thing."

He chuckled, his chest moving against hers. "I'm sure it would. If you have any rape fantasies you would like to explore, I would be more than willing to play with you, but that is for later. For now, you will either obey me or use your safe word."

She scrambled off his lap. Several scenarios played in her head. He could take one look at her without her clothes and run screaming from the room. He could laugh and tell her it was all a joke. Or, he could really, really want her.

How the hell would she know if she never took the chance? It suddenly struck her that she'd had it easy all these years. Yes, she'd had to give up what seemed like a promising future to help out at home. That was awful, but what about the last couple of years? What about after Val got through school? She'd gotten used to not trying. She'd gotten used to being able to blame her crappy life on circumstances. She'd gotten used to thinking that staying in this town and marrying someone she didn't love was simply something that had happened to her. But it wasn't. It was a choice she'd made. And so was this.

Her hands went to the bottom of her shirt. If he laughed, that was on him. She couldn't live her life making choices based on the worst-case scenarios, not if she ever wanted anything good to happen to her. She pulled the shirt over her head and tossed it aside. Without stopping, she undid the clasp on her bra and let it fall to the floor. Her nipples puckered. Her breasts felt heavy on her chest. When she looked up, Julian had a faint smile on his lips. His normally chilly eyes suddenly seemed warm.

"I think you're beautiful, Danielle. I also admire your courage. It took a lot for you to do that. Your breasts are lovely. Now, I'd like to see the rest of you. Take off your jeans and turn around slowly. Then I want you to sit down on the love seat and spread your legs."

Really? That was all he wanted? Dani took a deep breath. She wasn't backing out now. She unbuckled her belt and shoved the jeans over her hips, painfully aware of how clumsy the act of undressing could be. She wasn't moving gracefully. She was more robotic than anything else, but she managed it. She was forever grateful for the shower she'd been able to take. At least she was clean, and her legs were shaved. Because she had been about to go on her honeymoon, she'd decided to go a little crazy and shave her pussy. What would Julian think of that?

The air was cool on her skin. There was no way she could hide the fact that her nipples were standing at attention. She felt awkward as she placed herself on the leather sofa. With a long breath, she let her legs fall open.

Julian sighed. His hand came out in an elegant sweep that told Dani she wasn't open enough.

She let her feet find the coffee table in front of her, spreading her legs wide. Julian nodded and then went silent as he looked at her. He studied her carefully, as though she was a piece of fine art he was interested in collecting. As his stare moved from her breasts to the *V* of her legs, Dani felt her skin flush.

"Touch yourself, Danielle."

Her hands were on her knees. "Where?"

Even as she asked the question, she figured out the answer for herself. She moved her right hand over the smooth flesh of her pussy. It felt different, softer than before, without the harshness of pubic hair. She decided immediately that even if this didn't work, she would keep up the landscaping. She slipped a finger across her clit and between the lips of her pussy. She was already so wet.

"That's right. Enjoy it. It should feel good. I'm going to do the same. Don't stop fingering yourself, but don't come or we shall have some punishment."

She felt a sudden rush of cream coat her fingers as he shrugged off his shirt. He stood up, revealing a broad, well-muscled chest and abs that Dani thought only happened on sports stars. She stared at the indentions at his hips. Her finger swirled around and around in her pussy, imagining it was Julian touching her there. What would it feel like? Would he be rough with her? Or smooth as silk?

His hands unbuttoned his slacks and slipped them off. She had a brief glimpse of cream-colored boxers before she felt her mouth drop open.

He calmly folded his clothes, but Dani was watching his cock. She'd never thought of a penis as being a beautiful thing, but she'd never really had a chance to look at one before. Julian's cock was thick with a purplish head. She could almost feel her hand stroking him. She wondered if she could get her hand around that glorious monster. He was hard as a rock, but the skin would be so soft.

He strode forward and placed himself between her spread legs. If he was bothered by the fact that he was completely naked, he didn't show it. He stared down at her pussy. "Give me your hand."

Dani lifted her hand to his. He grasped her wrist and brought her fingers to his lips. He sucked her cream-coated fingers into his mouth. Dani shivered at the sensation of his tongue swirling around and around her fingers. His gray eyes were dark with desire as he knelt down in front of her spread legs.

"You taste delicious, little one."

She closed her eyes briefly, imagining his mouth on her pussy.

"Come here and taste yourself." His hand cupped the back of her neck and pulled her forward. He pressed his lips against hers the same way he had earlier in the day. She softened instinctively beneath him, opening her mouth, letting him in. He controlled the kiss. His tongue moved into her mouth with silky grace. She tasted her own tangy essence. One hand tangled in her hair, holding her still for his kiss. The other wandered across her flesh. She felt a painful longing deep in her cunt. She wanted him to take her, to shove that hard part of him into the softest piece of her. She wanted to be beneath him.

He slanted over and over her mouth. His hand cupped her breast, pinching at her nipples before slipping lower. Dani moaned against his mouth. When his fingers were almost at her clit, she shifted to make him move faster. Some shimmering experience was right there, and she couldn't wait for it.

Julian pulled away abruptly, leaving her awkward and unsatisfied.

"No." He stood quickly. "You are not in control of this. I did not give you permission to come."

He stepped away and went back to the couch. Dani felt tears well in her eyes. What had happened? One minute she was close to her first honest-to-god man-given orgasm, and the next she was sitting alone and naked.

"Should I get dressed?" The quicker she got out of there, the better.

"If you like. Just say your safe word, and we'll be done."

He sounded so cold. It was like there hadn't been a bit of heat between them. The connection she'd felt between them had been severed, and now she wondered if there had really been one in the first place. His cock was still standing straight up, but there was no passion on his face. He was obviously an experienced lover. He could more than likely give her the orgasm of a lifetime, but was that what she needed?

She forced herself to smile even as she felt tears roll down her cheeks. She knew it probably summed up her existence quite neatly— smile through it all because she wouldn't want to make anyone uncomfortable. "Hippopotamus. I'm sorry I couldn't...I didn't understand. I still don't. I appreciate you helping me out, though."

She pushed herself off the couch. It was leather, so she winced as she peeled herself up. So awkward. That summed up her life, too. It was time to get her clothes and call Finn and figure out what to do. He would be mad, but he would stick by her. Dani reached for her panties.

Julian had gotten up when she did. He stood there unmoving, his face still. His pants were on top of hers. She picked them up and held them out to him.

"Do you want these?"

"No." He sounded as though he couldn't believe his answer.

"No? Do you want me to get you something else?" It seemed odd to leave him standing there naked. Beautiful and remote. There was still some part of her desperate to reach him.

He stared at her, his eyes stony. "Did I frighten you? I didn't mean to."

She shook her head, well aware that she still wasn't wearing much. "No, it wasn't that. I just changed my mind. I'm not cut out for this."

"But you are. You are very submissive."

She pulled the shirt over her head, his every word making her more certain of her decision. "See, you keep calling me that. Maybe I am submissive. Maybe I'm a sub, as you say, but I'm Dani, too. You talk about contracts, and I don't know what you mean. You talk about training me. I want to know what your childhood was like. I want to know what TV shows you watch and what makes you laugh. I'm completely fascinated by you, and you want to train me. I might be submissive, but I know when I'm wanted, and I'm merely convenient for you. I wanted this to be different. I've been convenient all my life. I want to be special. I won't ever be that to you, Mr. Lodge." She pulled her jeans on and shoved the bra into her pocket with shaky hands. She would probably regret this for the rest of her life. "I'll go back to the main house and call a friend to come get me. Thanks again."

She made it to the front door when he pulled her back by the elbow.

"I don't watch television beyond the news and the occasional financial report and baseball. I like baseball. I don't talk about that with the guys because I don't have some group of guys. I have subs, and for the last six months I haven't even had those. I don't laugh a lot. And I haven't had sex in more than twenty years that wasn't fully detailed and covered by a contract between myself and the person or people I was having sex with. Yes, I said people, as in more than one. I've had sex with men and women, sometimes at the same time. I don't know how to not be in control. I have to be in control."

His voice was as calm and disciplined as an anchor reporting the nightly news. There was nothing about his face or manner that told Danielle he was feeling anything at all, but somehow she knew he was. She felt his hand tighten on her wrist as though he was afraid if he let go, she would flee. Her heart softened. He didn't not care. He was afraid to. She might not be his dream woman, but he did need something from her. She brought her free hand up to cup his cheek. She thought she might be imagining it, but she felt him move into her hand, as though savoring the contact.

"All right, Sir."

He shook his head. "The session is over. You said your safe word."

Always in control. She let her hand slide from his face. She couldn't help herself. She went up on her tiptoes and kissed his cheek. He was absolutely the most beautiful man she'd ever seen, and he'd been kind to her. She wished the night had ended differently. "All right. Good night, then."

"Don't go." There was a hoarseness in his voice as he hauled her against his chest.

She tipped her head up to look at him. He was still remote, but now, pressed against him, she could feel the heat of his body, the fine shudder that went through him as his hands wrapped around her waist. He pulled the T-shirt back over her head, and his mouth was on hers. This was different than before. He plundered her mouth. His tongue moved against hers; his hands tightened on her waist. She was pulled close to his body, his cock nudging her belly insistently. He tipped her head back, his hold just short of painful. One hand tugged at her hair, and the other found its way to the cheeks of her ass. She was pushed and pulled into the position Julian wanted her in, but she didn't fight, didn't even think about it this time.

He needed this. He needed to be in control, and he needed her.

When he started to pull at the waist of her jeans, she wiggled her hips, helping him shove them to the ground. There was no thought to folding the clothes. He tossed each and every piece he pulled off her body to the ground. Dani groaned as he left her mouth and kissed his way down her neck.

"Spread your legs." He growled a little as he issued the order.

She opened herself to him. His hand immediately trailed over her stomach and teased at her pussy.

"Are you getting wet, Danielle?"

"Yes. I've never been so wet in my life."

And yet she wasn't embarrassed by it. The hungry look in his eyes as he knelt down in front of her made her feel hot and wild. Unlike the awkward moments before, she wasn't the only one desperate for this. She wasn't alone. She spread her legs and squirmed when Julian's big fingers slid across her clit. His hand came out and slapped her ass.

"No moving. This body is mine for the night. Mine."

The possessive way he said "mine" caused a fresh coat of arousal to gush from her body. She heard Julian groan his approval but held herself still. His fingers played in her pussy while his tongue delved into her navel. He kissed a path down until his mouth was right over her pussy. She could feel the heat of his breath. She moaned as he shoved a single finger up inside her.

"Tight. You're going to be so fucking tight."

Yes, she was going to be tight because that cock of his was a monster, and damn if she wasn't ready to ride it. Her hands became fists at her sides as Julian's dark head leaned over, and she felt the first strong glide of his tongue against her clit. He worked her clit over and over, sliding across it with firm pressure, eating her pussy as if she was a delicious treat he couldn't get enough of. He licked all the way down to where his finger curled up inside her, coaxing and pumping into her.

"All right, come for me, Danielle. Come all over my mouth."

There was no denying his deep, commanding voice, and she couldn't resist his mouth. He fucked her with his fingers, and his teeth bit down slightly on her clit, sending shock waves of pleasure shooting across her body. Dani screamed, her hands winding into Julian's thick hair. The orgasm spread across her body, a wildfire she didn't want to put out. It was so far beyond anything she'd ever felt. The pleasure coursed through her, hot at first, and then a languid laziness stole through her bones as sweet in its way as the orgasm itself. Her hands came out of her lover's hair, and she thought about trying to get to the couch. Her heart was racing, her breath pounding out, her mind drugged with the experience. She giggled because she couldn't get her legs to move. Julian stood, and she leaned into his chest, needing his strength to continue standing.

"That was amazing, Julian."

"The other men, they didn't make you come." It wasn't a question that came out of his mouth. It was a gloriously arrogant certainty.

She shook her head. The thought to lie about her experience didn't occur to her. She wanted to give credit where credit was due. "Not even close."

"Remember that." He swept her up into his arms like she weighed next to nothing.

Dani let her hand drift around his neck. His thick, dark hair had come out of its queue and shifted around his shoulders as he began up the stairs.

"Where are we going?" She didn't really care. He could take her up to the "dungeon," and she wouldn't mind. She would let him tie her up and spank her with the implement of his choice, and she wouldn't complain. He'd taken her someplace she hadn't even known existed.

She got a brief glimpse of a huge space filled with the oddest things. There was an X on the opposite wall and what looked like a doctor's office in the corner. She was only able to glance around what Jack called his playroom before Julian walked through a door, and she found herself being tossed onto a huge bed. He walked to the nightstand and turned on the light. He opened the drawer and pulled out a condom.

"On your back, spread your legs." He slid the condom over his cock, covering it.

She scrambled to obey. She twisted her body, but Julian was already on her. His hands wound around her ankles, pulling her across the bed. She slid over the comforter, the silky material soft against her back. She let her muscles go lax beneath his hands. He quickly settled himself between her legs, and she felt the head of his cock prod at her pussy's entrance. He slid in and inched back. She groaned at the sensation. He wasn't thrusting yet, but he felt so big inside her.

"Wrap your legs around my waist." He pushed his dick in another inch before pulling out.

Dani complied, wrapping her legs around his middle, hooking her ankles together. She braced her arms on his shoulders as he worked his cock inside her. So full. She felt so full as he finally pressed himself in. He groaned and ground himself into her body. She tilted her hips up, the sensation bordering on pain, but filled with pleasure. He held himself still for a moment, leaning over to capture her lips with his own. Her pussy throbbed around his huge cock, softening, accommodating him. His tongue danced against hers, rubbing, dominating. His hips moved, thrusting shallowly, giving her time to adjust.

Dani let her hands run down the length of his strong back, reveling in the feel of the muscles under her fingers. She moved her greedy hands all the way down to his muscled ass.

Julian hissed as she sank her nails into his skin. "That's right, little one. I don't mind a bite of pain, either. Just know I might pay you back later."

"Bring it on, Julian." She said it with a smile. She could handle him. Now that she knew he needed her, she could handle whatever he threw at her. If he tied her to that cross in the playroom and whipped her, she would let the pain sink into her skin. She would take anything he gave her if it meant she got to that place where they melded together again. She felt so close to him, closer than she ever had to another human being.

His lips quirked up. "I will. I fucking will."

He pulled his hips back and slammed home. His pelvis ground against her clit as his dick hit some crazy spot deep inside her. Her bold statement seemed to break something in him. He went wild on top of her. He pounded into her pussy. A low moan drifted from her throat as she met his velocity. She slammed her hips up, that magical place so close she could feel it rushing toward her. She clamped down on the huge cock invading her. He went deep, fusing them together, and she came in a rush of electric pleasure, the heat sparking through her, stronger than before. She opened her mouth and let the groan flow out of her. She fought to keep the orgasm coming, slamming her hips up, grinding against him.

Julian twisted his hips, sending her headlong into another screaming orgasm. This time he joined her. His gorgeous face contorted, and he stiffened above her, his whole body rigid as he held himself close. He pumped into her, his butt muscles tight under her hands. Finally he came down, slumping against her. She held him close and smiled at the connection she felt. His breath was warm on her body. His heart pounded against hers. She let her hands drift back up to his hair, loving the intimate connection between them.

"Don't think I'm done."

She smiled at his arrogant words. She wasn't done with him either.

Chapter Six

Finn pushed through the door to Christa's Café with a heavy heart. He hadn't slept the night before, and he felt the lack in every weary muscle. He'd stared at the ceiling of his crappy motel room and wondered where the hell Dani was spending the night. A hundred scenarios had played through his brain, most of them ending in something terrible. It was all his fucking fault since he'd been the idiot who let her go. He should have seen that she was terrified. He probably had, but he'd been terrified, too. He'd been thinking about himself. He'd been thinking about the fact that he was going to lose her. He hadn't thought about what Dani was going through at all.

He looked around the café. It was half-empty this early on a Sunday morning. He forced himself to walk up to the counter. He wasn't leaving this town until he found her. He'd made the decision last night that he was hiring a private investigator the first chance he got.

He'd gotten a good look at the car she'd jumped into. There couldn't possibly be too many Audi R8s in the state of Texas. It was a two-hundred-thousand-dollar car. Whoever owned it was probably from a big city. Given Willow Fork's placement in Northeast Texas, he would bet the man was from Dallas. He had the first two letters of a license plate. He would figure it out in the end. He had a ton of resources. Though he was a corporate lawyer, he'd done a bit of time in the prosecutor's office. He still had connections there, and those lawyers knew cops. When he knew who she'd run away with, he would track the asshole down and find his girl.

If Audi guy had taken advantage of her, then he would figure out a way to ruin him.

"What can I get you?" The woman behind the counter had dark hair and a professional smile. He'd seen that smile every single time he came home. Christa Wade had always been kind to him, so he always gave her his business.

"Coffee, please. I don't need sugar or cream." He couldn't stand the thought of eating at this point. His stomach churned at the smell of food. He could barely stand the thought of coffee, but if he didn't have a cup, he'd be a zombie by noon.

He needed to be able to focus if he was going to find Dani.

"That all?" She looked up from her notepad for the first time. A wide smile covered her face. "Hey, Finn. How are you doing? You okay?" Her voice took on a distinctly sympathetic tone. She reached out and covered his hand with hers.

This was why he'd really come in here. He knew he'd find a friendly ear to bend. "I'm fine, Christa, but I'm worried about Dani. I can't quite believe she did something so impulsive. It's not like her."

Christa's eyes lit up. "Well, I was thrilled. Let me tell you, when I saw her take off, there was a part of me that wanted to tackle Jimbo to make sure he didn't catch her. Of course, turned out I didn't need to. What a jerk. He was hitting on high school girls at the reception. Dani was right to get the hell out of there. Even if Jimbo wasn't a cheating SOB, Dani should have run because his momma is one crazy bit...well, you know what I mean. She would have made Dani miserable."

He sat back against the barstool. Yes, this was what he needed. He needed someone who understood. "I know. She was making a huge mistake, but I can't see how running off with some stranger is going to help it."

She should have told him. He would have carried her out, put her in his car, and been on the way to Dallas before anyone knew what was happening. He would have given her everything. He would have made sure she was safe and had a home.

Christa patted his hand. "I know it seems crazy, but it's for the best. Don't worry. She's in excellent hands. Abby will make sure she's fine."

He stilled, his whole being suddenly focused on what Christa had said. "What do you mean? Abby Barnes knows where Dani is?"

Christa nodded. "Oh, yes. Don't worry a bit. I talked to Abby early this morning. Dani spent the night at the ranch. Jack will handle everything. He kind of lives to handle stuff like this. Abby said she was upset, but she'd calmed down by dinnertime and was going to spend a couple of days out there. It'll do her good. She can play with the kids, and Jack will scare the shit out of Jimbo and any of his relatives if they go after her."

Finn only heard part of what Christa said. "She's at Jack Barnes's ranch? How did she get out there?"

Christa put two hands on the counter. She leaned in and looked around. It was obvious to Finn that gossip was on her mind. This was another reason to come to the café. Christa was the worst gossip in town. Information flowed through the café as freely as the coffee. "That guy whose car she jumped into was one of Jack's oldest friends. He's from Dallas, some real rich guy. Name's Julian Lodge. He took her out to the ranch. He was on his way out there for a visit, it seems."

He breathed a deep sigh of relief. Dani was out at the Barnes-Fleetwood ranch. At least he knew she was alive. "That's good news. She left me a voice mail that told me nothing."

The voice mail had asked him for forgiveness, and she'd promised to call him later. Apparently later hadn't meant last night, but he felt enormously better knowing that she'd spent the night sitting up with her boss. They'd likely had a glass of wine and Abby would have talked to her about how to handle the next few days. She would have probably cried herself to sleep, but at least she was safe.

Christa waved a hand. "Don't worry. She's fine. Abby says she's well on her way to recovery, if you know what I mean."

He didn't, and he didn't like the saucy wink Christa gave him. Exactly what kind of recovery were they talking about? "Who's this Julian person?"

Christa turned and poured him a cup of coffee. She slid the mug in front of him. "Abby said he's intimidating. He has a ton of money and owns a club or something. I don't know. There are certain things me and the BFF don't get into. I love Abby and support her every decision, but she's closemouthed when it comes to her sex life. Trust me when I say it's frustrating. When you have two amazingly hot guys, you should share. Right? Wait. I didn't mean it exactly like that. I'm happily married, but I would totally listen to crazy stories."

"She's met this Julian?" Finn couldn't care less how much Abby Barnes shared with her best friend. He wanted to know about the guy who had spirited his girl away.

"She said she's known him for a couple of years, but Jack has known him for more than two decades. He used to work for him or something." Christa's eyebrows rose. "Apparently he and Dani are getting along really well."

His spine straightened. "What is that supposed to mean?"

Someone from a booth near the window waved his hand. Christa nodded toward her customer. "I'll have to get back to you, Finn, but don't worry about Dani. She's in good hands. There's no way Jack or Abby or Sam lets anything bad happen to her." She winked his way. "Be back in a bit. Think about breakfast, okay?"

She walked off to take the other customer's order, and Finn pulled out his cell. If this Julian person was a friend of Jack Barnes's, then maybe one of his coworkers knew who he was. Finn worked for one of the most prestigious law firms in Dallas. They knew all the power players. He dialed the person most likely to know this Julian guy. As luck would have it, Finn knew the lawyer who handled the Barnes-Fleetwood account. He was more than Jack Barnes's lawyer. He was Jack's brother.

"Hello?" Lucas Cameron sounded like he was half awake. He was a couple of years younger than Finn, but they had bonded almost immediately. They had a lot in common. Lucas had spent some time in Willow Fork, and they were both bisexual. Lucas was a gorgeous man, but Finn had known from the minute he met Lucas that they were destined to be friends and nothing more.

Besides, both he and Lucas had fucked-up love lives. Both of them seemed to want women they couldn't have.

"Hey, Lucas, it's Finn."

"Good for you, Finn," Lucas growled into the phone. Finn could hear a soft voice in the background. "Go back to sleep, Lexi. It's nothing to worry about. What do you want, Finn? I thought you were on vacation. This better be an emergency."

He got straight to the point. This was an emergency for him. "I need to know everything you can find out about a man named Julian Lodge."

"Julian?" Lucas suddenly sounded wide awake. "What's going on with Julian? That's my account. He hasn't called me. What's happening?"

"Nothing in his business. I need to know for personal reasons. He's seeing someone I know."

There was a snort from the other end of the line. "Seeing? Julian doesn't see people. Julian screws people six ways to Sunday, but only after a careful vetting process. You should see some of the shit he has me dig up on his potential subs. Wait. I thought you were going back to Willow Fork. The only person you like in Willow Fork is Dani." There was a brief pause. "Are you telling me that Julian is fucking Danielle Bay?"

"You put him on speakerphone now, Lucas."

Damn it. He should have remembered that Lexi had spent time here. Lexi Moore was Abby's daughter and involved with Lucas in some weird way no one could quite figure out. Lucas was madly in love with her, and she often spent the night with him, but Lucas insisted they were casual. Lexi had a friendly relationship with Dani. Damn, now he had to deal with Lexi. Lexi was sometimes a pain in the ass. She ran an art gallery and could be a bit bossy.

"Finn, what's going on with Dani and Julian?" Lexi sounded fully awake and in charge now.

He sighed. "I don't know. I only know that the wedding was a bust. Dani walked into the church in her wedding gown, turned, and ran away."

"Yes."

He could practically see the fist pump Lexi was undoubtedly giving. Lexi had declined to come to the wedding, giving some excuse about a big gallery show, but he knew the truth. After Lexi's own wedding had been canceled at the last minute, she couldn't handle talking about anything vaguely marriage related.

He continued, not willing to listen to Lexi's inevitable lecture on how futile love was. "She ran down the street and hopped into some guy's convertible."

"Audi?" Lucas asked.

"Yeah. The next thing I know, she's gone, and I heard Christa say that she's at Lexi's mom's house recovering nicely. What the hell is that supposed to mean?"

"I think it means that my mom is taking care of her. Dani is a sweetheart. She thought about it and rightly panicked. Stop worrying. Mom and Sam will get her laughing, and Jack will make sure that asshole she was going to marry doesn't hurt her." Lexi yawned. Finn could hear her covering her mouth. "And Julian will be perfectly polite. He always is."

Lucas spoke up. "Sweetheart, did you think about the fact that Dani is incredibly submissive?"

Lexi got quiet.

"Will someone tell me what's going on? And who the hell is Julian Lodge?" He was moving past frustrated.

"Julian Lodge is my biggest client," Lucas replied.

"I thought that was the Masters' account." Lucas was already a legend at the firm. He'd walked in the door with a billionaire as a client. The Masters' account covered the Masters' Fund, a superrich group of investors.

"Julian Lodge runs the Masters' Fund."

Finn nearly dropped his coffee mug. Dani had jumped into a car with a billionaire? What were the chances of that? Deep breath. Maybe that wasn't so bad. What would a billionaire want with his Dani? Dani was sweet and beautiful. He thought she was the most beautiful woman in the world, but she didn't have a Hollywood glamour. She was a small-town girl. Now that he thought about it, she'd been lucky. She'd managed to find someone who could take her to the one place where she would be perfectly safe. Yeah, this was a good thing.

He relaxed. Everything was going to be okay.

He'd sit in the café and have breakfast. When the stores opened, he'd find the nicest bouquet he could and then go out to the Barnes-Fleetwood ranch and talk to Dani. By this evening, he'd have her on the road to Dallas. He'd have to remember to send Julian Lodge a nice thank you card. Though he would absolutely have a long talk with Dani about how dangerous that stunt had been.

"Finn, are you okay?"

He laughed at Lucas's nervous question. "Of course. I just wanted to know she was safe. It sounds like she's in good hands."

Lexi's husky laugh poured into his ear. "Damn, I'll say she's in good hands. I kind of wish I was in her place."

"Alexis!"

He held the phone away from his head as Lucas had a few choice words for his...well, whatever Lexi was to him.

"Sorry, babe." If Lexi was at all intimidated by Lucas's stern words, it didn't show in her tone. "I know it's a little perverse, but that man is sexy as hell. Oh, he scares the crap out of me, but I don't know a sub alive who wouldn't do almost anything to kneel at his feet. If he's decided to train Dani, then all I can say is good for Dani."

A cold chill went through Finn's system. Train? Kneel at his feet? That could only mean one thing.

"Are you talking about that BDSM crap you're always going on about?" Why Lucas wanted to spank Lexi, Finn had no idea. But the thought of Dani—sweet, eager–to-please Dani—in the clutches of a leather-clad sadist had him reaching for his keys.

Lucas sighed. "It isn't crap, Finn. If you would come with us, you would see. The club Lexi and I go to is Julian's. He's an expert. There's nothing to worry about."

But he wasn't listening. He threw down some cash to pay for his coffee and ran to his car. Like it or not, the Barnes-Fleetwood family would be waking up early this morning.

* * * *

Dani woke to the sound of something thumping. The pounding was rhythmic and pulled her from the sweetest dream. She sat straight up in the enormous bed and looked around for Julian. He wasn't in the room with her. The door to the bedroom was open. She stretched and felt the most delicious soreness permeating her every muscle.

Wow. The night before came rushing back, and all she could think was "wow."

Julian Lodge was absolutely the most insatiable, perverse, decadent man she'd ever had the enormous pleasure of meeting. Now she understood why women chased after a man. If other men had half the skill and wild imagination that Julian had, she might have to chase down a few.

Except that she couldn't imagine doing anything like that with another man.

An image of Finn with her and Julian flitted across her brain.

It worked for Abigail Barnes. Why couldn't it work for her?

She let the thought go. She wouldn't be able to keep Julian for long, much less convince Finn to give a girl a whirl. It was a fantasy, and that was exactly where it would stay. She'd made the decision last night somewhere between orgasms eight and nine that she would hang out at the ranch while Julian was on vacation. It would do them both good. He said he'd been celibate for a while. She couldn't imagine why, but he seemed really happy to end it. If it was okay with Julian, she would enjoy this week with him. After that, she would have to decide what to do, but whatever the future was, it wouldn't involve Julian. He would go back to Dallas and whatever job he had there. She would pick up the pieces and figure out what to do with the next fifty years of her life.

Not going there. She shoved the covers back, walked to the closet, and hoped that she could find a robe or something. It appeared Julian's clothes had been neatly hung. There were elegant dress shirts and slacks. Not a single pair of jeans. That was a real shame, because his ass would look good in a pair of Levi's.

"Where is she, you perverted motherfucker?"

She turned to look out the open bedroom door. Was that Finn? She quickly pulled a dress shirt off the hanger and shrugged into it like a robe. The clothes she'd worn last night were downstairs, strewn across the living room. The shirt would have to do. The good news was Julian was a big man and the shirt came down almost to her knees.

She rushed out of the bedroom. Someone was talking—Julian,

probably—but he was speaking quietly. Finn was not.

"You better show me where you put Dani right now, or I swear I'll make you wish you had."

"I wouldn't threaten me, whoever you are, although I suspect you're Danielle's ex-fiancé. Might I speak for her? She has no intention of marrying you. She made herself plain yesterday." Julian's voice was low and had almost no emotion to it.

She ran through the playroom toward the stairs. Though she hadn't known Julian for long, she'd already figured out that he was at his most dangerous when he was perfectly, completely calm.

"I'm here." She had no idea why her best friend had decided to go commando on Julian's ass, but he would lose that battle. Julian was one amazing specimen. While Finn was incredibly fit, she figured Julian would fight dirty. It was best to stop the fight altogether, especially since there wasn't a thing to fight over. She raced down the steps.

Finn wasn't alone. It looked like the entire clan was invading her and Julian's love nest. Jack Barnes was dressed in denims and a T-shirt. Sam Fleetwood hadn't bothered with a shirt. Abby had wrapped a robe around herself and had a hand on Jack's arm.

"Thank god." Finn let out a deep breath and started toward her.

Dani tripped on the last step and started flying. One minute she was going to break her neck, and the next she was wrapped in Julian's arms. He was wearing a pair of slacks and nothing else. His chest was male model perfect.

"Slow down, little one." His gray eyes seemed warmer this morning. His hands tightened around her briefly, and then a wall slammed between them. "Your fiancé is here."

"I'm not her fiancé. Now let her go." Finn started to reach for Julian, but Sam stopped him.

"I wouldn't do that. Look, man, I know you're pissed, but you don't want to fuck with him." Sam pulled Finn back.

Julian set her on her feet and immediately let go. She felt the loss of the intimacy. This was not the way she'd seen the morning going. She'd expected that she and Julian would spend some time in bed and then plan out their day. He didn't look like a man desperate to spend time with her now. All of her self-doubts came creeping back like the fog that came off the lake, pretty at first, and then she couldn't see anything but mist. She turned from Julian to look at Finn.

"What are you doing here?" She'd left a message on his voice mail telling him she was okay. How had he even found out where she was?

He pulled away from Sam and walked straight to her, catching her hands in his. "I came for you, of course. Dani, you don't know what you've gotten yourself into. You have no idea who that man is."

A bitter smile passed across Julian's face. "And I suppose you do, whoever you are."

"His name is Finn Taylor. He works with my brother, and he grew up here." Jack didn't look impressed. He watched Finn like he was waiting for an excuse to do something really nasty. What the hell had Finn done to put that black look on Jack Barnes's face?

"Ah, so he works at a law firm in Dallas. The law firm where you and I are the biggest clients. That is interesting." There was a silky threat in Julian's voice.

Finn didn't seem to care. "Fine, get me fired. I'm still not leaving Dani here. I'm not going to let you beat the hell out of her and call yourself her Master. You're a sick fuck. Jack's own brother is the one who told me."

"Somehow, I think Lucas would have used different words," Jack said slowly. He smiled and moved forward. Abby had dropped her hand, a sure sign that Jack had been let off the leash and things were going to get bad fast.

She needed to get the situation under control and quickly. "Will you calm down, Finn? I don't know what Lucas told you, but Julian has been nothing but nice to me. He got me away from the wedding and helped me find a place to stay. I'm grateful to him."

"Yeah, I bet I can guess exactly how he wants you to show your gratitude." Finn turned back to Julian. "You better be glad you slept on the couch."

Dani swung her head around to the couch. Sure enough, there was a pillow and blankets. He had left her sometime after she'd fallen asleep. He'd come down here instead of staying in bed with her. "You didn't want to sleep with me?"

"Our relationship isn't about sleep, dear." Julian enunciated the word sleep.

It had the intended effect on Finn. His face twisted and got really red. "You don't have a relationship with her. You don't even know her."

Julian's lips rode up in an arrogant version of a smile. "I obviously know her better than you. Only in a biblical sense, of course."

"Stop." She got in the middle of them, putting a hand on both chests. "I have no idea what's happening here, but I want it to stop."

Julian's dark head came forward in a courtly gesture. "Of course. I am so sorry to have caused you distress. Please feel free to leave with your friend."

The whole place went perfectly quiet and she could feel every eye on her. It was like the night before hadn't happened. He was being brutally polite. If he wanted her to leave, he should say it. "What is that supposed to mean?"

Abby stepped forward, sympathy on her face. "Why don't we head back inside, Jack, Sam?"

Sam glanced from Julian and Dani back to Abby. "Why would we do that? The show's out here, baby. If it weren't so early in the morning, I would say let's make some popcorn."

"Don't think about snacks until after Julian decides if he's going to kill Finn." Jack took a step back, obviously more comfortable now.

Finn ignored their audience. "Dani, baby, I don't care what happened with him. Let me take you away from here, and we can talk. Please, you don't know who you're dealing with. Lucas told me about him. He's into all kinds of things."

"And that's important to you, why? Finn, you're my best friend. I am asking you to walk away. I'm fine. I'm more than fine. I know what I'm doing. Please go back to Dallas, and I'll talk to you on Monday." She needed to figure out what the hell was wrong with Julian. He'd completely shut down.

"He won't go back to Dallas, Danielle." Julian's eyes slid between her and her best friend, finally stopping on Finn, who paled slightly under his stare. "He won't go anywhere without you."

She sighed, frustration in her every breath. Did she need to do this in front of her boss? "Finn, I'm an adult. I made the decision to spend the night with Julian. I know exactly what he's into."

"Did you know he sleeps with men?" Finn made it sound like an accusation.

"Well, let the lightning strike, buddy. So do you. He's bisexual. Why on earth do you care?" Dani stared at Finn, waiting to see when the horns would grow out of his head. For the life of her, she didn't understand what this drama was about. Before she'd gone to sleep, she'd thought about inviting Finn out for lunch and to meet Julian. She'd envisioned them fighting over who got to sleep with him. In her wildest dreams she'd never thought it would go like this.

"He's upset because he wants you."

She softened slightly at Julian's tone. She got why Julian was mistaken. Finn was doing an awfully good impression of a jealous male. "No, you don't understand. We're just friends. We've been friends since we were kids."

The silence that fell over the room made Dani's stomach turn. She watched Finn and saw the blood slowly drain from his face.

Sam leaned over to his wife. "Does Dani not know that Finn's bi, too?"

"No, he's not." She said the words, hoping she could make them true. If they weren't true, then that part of her world that had always been the best piece was utterly false. She'd always known that she and Finn were meant for each other. It had been one twist of fate that kept them apart. But if Finn wasn't gay, then he'd chosen not to be with her.

"Dani, I can explain." Finn's words fell flat and heavy between them.

She turned to Julian, hoping for something, anything from him. He looked slightly amused, but nothing more. There were no open arms for her to run to, no encouraging look. He was remote, untouchable. Despite the intimacy shared between them the night before, there was nothing between them now. Like there was nothing between her and Finn.

She was making a fool of herself. Again. Like she'd done all these years with Finn.

"I can explain." Finn tried again, and this time he took a step toward her.

She moved back. "Don't. I don't want an explanation. I want a yes or no answer. Have you ever slept with a woman?"

Finn swallowed, the movement visible. He started to say something, but finally nodded, turning his eyes from her.

"How many?" Now that the wound was opened, she couldn't seem to stop picking at it to find out how deep it went.

"Damn, Dani, I don't know. They didn't mean anything."

But they meant something to her. They meant the world to her. Tears blurred her vision as she turned, picked up her clothes, and started to walk into the small bathroom. She passed the couch. Julian wouldn't have been terribly comfortable on it. He was too tall to stretch out. His knees would have been bent. Still, he'd chosen discomfort over sleeping beside her. She paused briefly at the bathroom door, but no one tried to stop her. She walked in, locked the door, and got dressed.

When she was done, she sat down on the toilet seat and put her head in hands. Her time with Julian was done long before she thought it would be. And her time with Finn…that was over, too.

Chapter Seven

Julian watched the SUV drive down the long path that led to the highway. Danielle was running again.

This time she was running from him.

And that Finn person. Though she wouldn't get far since he was in the vehicle with her. That fact rankled far more than it should.

"I can't believe you didn't try to convince her to stay." Abigail's hazel eyes were laser beams trying to cut him in half.

He rather wished they hadn't been here to witness the scene that had played out. "Why would I do that?"

He knew why he should have done that. He should have done that because he'd enjoyed her. He should have asked her to stay because he'd hated that moment when the light in her eyes had died. The impulse to gather her close and hold her to his heart had been almost impossible to ignore. He didn't ask her to stay because a part of him didn't want to ask. A big part of him wanted to force her to his side, and that meant something to him. That meant she belonged to him.

"Abby, why don't you and Sam go get some breakfast?" Jackson asked.

Abigail sighed and then did something that completely surprised him. She walked up and put her arms around him. "It'll be okay. I know why you did it. I just wished you hadn't.'"

Before he could figure out what to do, she stepped away. She gave him what he could only take as an encouraging smile and walked back into the main house.

Samuel was grinning, his gorgeously cut chest on full display. There was a tattoo on his right bicep, the same logo they used on their brand. "Damn, now she's going to try her hand at matchmaking. Good luck to you, Julian."

He felt his jaw tighten as Abigail and Samuel walked back toward the house. He kept his eyes completely off the SUV that he was sure would be making the turn to the highway soon.

It was all for the best.

He ignored the sick feeling in the pit of his stomach that screamed at him to get in his fucking car and go after her. It was the same voice that had him curling around her and drifting off to sleep the night before. He'd caught himself seconds before he made the mistake. He did not sleep with his slaves. He didn't sleep with anyone. But then Danielle wasn't a slave. There was no contract between them and no real talk of one. He shouldn't have had sex with her in the first place.

The night before, he'd forced himself to roll out of bed and walk away from her. He'd grabbed a pillow and blanket and slept very little. The way she felt, the moans she made, the soft submission she'd given to him completely naturally had kept him awake most of the night. She'd been perfect, and for the first time in a long time, he'd lost himself in the sex.

It wasn't what he'd intended at all. He'd intended to warm her up and then take her to the playroom. He had planned on introducing her to the pleasures of Dominance and submission. It was supposed to be a teaching session. He was the Master, and she the slave. He was in control.

He'd meant to have sex. He'd had no plans to make love.

He didn't lie to himself. It was a self-defeating exercise. He'd made love to Danielle. He'd taken her without a contract, without any thought put into it. He'd simply felt. He'd felt her heat and softness, her willingness to please him. She'd flowered under his dominance, and he hadn't been able to hold himself back.

It was a relief to see her go. Danielle Bay could be very disruptive.

"I'll handle Abby. She means well. She wants everyone to be as happy as she is." Jackson strode to the love seat where Julian's shirt from the previous night lay folded. He picked it up and tossed it back Julian's way. "Come on. The livestock don't give a damn that you have woman troubles."

He shrugged into his shirt and slipped into his shoes, hurrying to keep up with Jack. "I do not have woman troubles."

His woman troubles had conveniently driven off, leaving him alone, and that was how he liked it. Danielle had the good sense to know when to leave, and he'd shown remarkable restraint in allowing her to go. He buttoned his shirt as he wondered exactly where Danielle was going. Home? He was given to understand that she had already moved her things to her fiancé's home. How would she handle getting her belongings back? He didn't like the thought of her with nothing to her name. Would that mouthy prick who'd come for her this morning take care of her?

He had to check himself. Finn Taylor had narrowly avoided being knocked on his ass and shown his place in the world. The minute Finn had started spouting bile his way, he'd had the most ferocious urge to take the little shit by the back of his neck, shove him to the ground, and not allow him to get back up until he'd acknowledged who his Master was. Something about the younger man had brought about a ferocious sexual reaction in him. It had proven to him beyond a shadow of a doubt that Danielle wasn't for him. He'd known the second a vision of himself between the two of them flashed across his brain that he would let Danielle go.

He really needed to take new subs. It was starting to affect him in undesirable ways.

Jackson strode across the lawn. The early morning air was warm, and the sky above was seemingly endless. Julian stopped and stared at the perfect blue sky. It was quiet and calm after this morning's roiling emotion.

"Nice, huh?" Jackson had a tranquil expression on his face as he stood and looked up at the big sky. "You don't get this in the city. You don't get to feel like you're the only person in the whole world.

This is what I love. This is why I get up early, you know. I get up before Abby and Sam and the kids, and I get a whole hour when everything is quiet." He frowned suddenly. "Which is why I nearly took that little shit's head off this morning. He interrupted my alone time. Do you know how hard it is to get alone time with two babies in the house?"

He turned on his boot heels and made a beeline for a large structure Julian was a bit worried was an actual working barn. When the smell hit him, he was certain. Definitely a barn.

There were several stalls. Each looked to be carefully maintained and contained a prime piece of horseflesh. It was surprisingly quiet and peaceful in the barn. There was only the sound of the horses breathing and Jackson speaking soothingly. Jackson was running his hand over the muzzle of a large brown horse.

"This must be Ranger." He'd heard all about Jackson's favorite horse. It was a magnificent animal.

Jackson tossed him a bright orange carrot. "Make friends, Julian. Ranger here is like everyone else. He has to be courted. Offer it to him on the palm of your hand with your fingers flat or he might decide your fingers are tasty, too."

Yes, the horse was obviously like all creatures, willing to take far more than he wanted to give. Still, if he was careful, Julian knew he could control this as he did everything in his life. He held the carrot out, and the horse nickered gratefully before biting down.

"Let's take a ride, my friend. You've been on horseback before, right?"

Julian shook his head. "Despite the fact that I'm a native Texan, I've rarely been in the country. They don't allow horses in my condo."

Jackson threw back his head and laughed. He walked over to another stall and started prepping a second horse, this one black and powerful-looking. "Oh, I am going to have so much fun this week. By the end of it, Sam and I will have you riding like a pro. We'll make a cowboy out of you, yet."

He wasn't sure he wanted to be a cowboy but figured he would handle it like he'd handled everything. He would figure out the tasks Jackson gave him and master them with intelligence and discipline.

Discipline was the key to everything.

He hadn't been able to properly discipline Danielle. He'd only spanked her one time, but she'd responded beautifully. The flesh of her ass had pinkened and gotten warm to the touch. Her breath had started out in gasps and fits and then become softer and more languid. Truly submissive. By the time he was done, she was relaxed and dreamy. If he'd ordered her to her knees to suck his cock, she would have done so. She wouldn't have thought about the fact that they weren't alone. She simply would have followed instructions because pleasing him was part of what gave her pleasure. He could have molded her to be exactly the type of companion he'd always wanted.

He leaned against the stall as Ranger continued to chew. He could have molded Danielle, but why? He'd molded Sally into exactly what he wanted and kept her for years past that first contract, and still, he'd felt compelled to give her away. He'd been comfortable with Sally, but the restlessness had taken over. Maybe he did lie to himself. Maybe what he wanted and what he needed were two different things.

"See, I can hear you thinking from here." Jackson eased a blanket over the black horse's back.

"Well, I will try to think more quietly then."

"Don't. I'm deeply enjoying your confusion."

Julian turned to face his oldest friend. He thought briefly about dismissing the subject but decided to try that friendly discussion thing Leo said he lacked. "Well, I am not. And I'm not really confused. I'm simply surprised that I allowed myself to be pulled into Danielle's problems."

Deep green eyes assessed him. "Oh, you're confused. Dani knocked you flat on your ass the same way Abby knocked me on mine."

He was not going there. "This is nothing like what happened between you and Abigail. I don't even understand what happened between you and Abigail."

Jackson cinched the saddle into place and moved to get Ranger ready, too. "If you don't understand it, how can you say it's not the same?"

"I have no intentions of marrying Danielle. I'm not serious about her." But it had felt serious the night before. He could admit that to himself. Making love to Danielle had been like sitting in front of a warm fire on a cold night. He'd huddled too close and gotten a bit singed.

Jackson worked with skill and had the horse saddled quickly. He had his hands on the reins as he opened the stall door. "I wasn't serious about Abby. It was a fun fling. It was never supposed to go beyond a night or two. And then one day I woke up and there was a ring on my finger, and I had to deal with it."

He said it with a perfectly straight face. Julian had to give it to his protégé. He had learned a thing or two. "That's complete bullshit, Jackson."

The smile that crossed Jackson's face was one of pure joy. "Damn straight. I knew I was going to marry that woman pretty quick. I'm smarter than you. I was just trying to put you at ease."

Jackson handed him the reins to the black horse and showed him how to lead the animal. The big black horse was a fascinating study of power and beauty. He found himself looking forward to the morning's lessons. It had been a long time since he'd tackled something new. Perhaps physical exercise would get his mind off Danielle.

Jackson stopped both horses outside the barn. He was very serious as he looked Julian over. "I've known you all of my adult life. I know there's only five years between us, but you've been a father figure to me for a long time."

"I prefer to think of myself as a slightly older brother." Julian was warmed by Jackson's words. He'd always thought of the younger man as his spiritual son. He'd seen something in the rough young man that called to him. Though Jackson had been broke and spent most of his childhood living off the charity of others, Julian understood him. He understood his need to be in control. He'd been the one to teach Jackson to control and refine the impulse. And Jackson had taught him that it was okay to give a damn about someone. Jackson might owe him, but Julian owed Jackson as well.

"My point is, I know you pretty damn well. I saw the way you looked at her. I haven't seen you look at a woman like that. I've only seen you look like that once in the entire time I've known you. You were crazy about him."

An unfamiliar sense of embarrassment flooded Julian's system.

He had been unaware that Jackson knew how he'd felt about Samuel all those years ago. It was over, of course. It had never really started. Samuel hadn't been interested. Samuel loved Jackson and now Abby. There had been no place for him. "I wasn't in love with him."

"I wouldn't blame you. He's intensely lovable. He's a lot like Dani. So eager to please and so sweet that the world kind of lights up when they smile. She's a good match for you. She'll keep you on your toes, and she won't settle. She'll force you to love her, really love her, if you want to keep her. Can't you see that's what you need?"

"It sounds perfectly atrocious, Jackson." Julian was done. There was a reason he didn't chat about his feelings. "I'll leave the whole marriage and love thing in your hands. I prefer to relax. I only have a week. Are you going to teach me to ride or not?"

Jackson sighed. "I'd teach you more if you would let me, but let's start with this." His nose wrinkled up. "Wow. We're going to have to get you some boots. Cow pats can be hell on dress shoes."

Julian looked down. Sure enough, his thousand-dollar shoes were firmly planted in a cow's refuse. He scraped his shoe against the grass and wished he'd stayed in bed.

* * * *

Dani held herself as far away as she could from Finn. She pressed up against the passenger door of the SUV. If Willow Fork had taxis, she would have called one, but the idea of standing there with everyone feeling sorry for her had made her agree to allow Finn to take her home. And she couldn't stand another second of Julian looking anywhere but where she was.

"Are you sure you want me to take you back there?" It was the first time Finn had spoken since they'd gotten into the car.

Of course she didn't want to go back to the dilapidated two-bedroom house she shared with her sister. Val was going to be insufferable, but she didn't have anywhere else to go. She'd thought about a motel, but they cost money. She had two hundred dollars in her bank account. Everything else had been spent on her wreck of a wedding.

When the bills started to roll in she would be happy she'd had that two hundred bucks. She seriously doubted Jimbo's family would come through with their half now.

Finn's voice was ragged as he spoke. "I could take you back to my motel room, or we could drive to Dallas. My condo has two bedrooms."

She snorted. "Yes, obviously I would need a separate bed. You wouldn't want to sleep with me. Hell, even the guys I have sex with don't want to sleep with me."

She could still see the leather couch that had been more enticing to Julian than the comfy bed. At least tonight he could sleep on a mattress since she wouldn't be there.

She watched as Finn's hands tightened on the wheel. "I only suggested the second bedroom because you're pissed at me right now. If you want to share a room with me, I'm ready."

"Sure, Finn, like I'm going to believe anything you say at this point." Bitterness welled up, threatening to choke her.

Finn turned down the road that led to her childhood home. She knew every bump and crack in this road. It was as familiar as the back of her hand, but it brought her no comfort. Going home this time felt like utter defeat.

"That's not fair, Dani. I love you."

It seemed cruel now for him to say those words to her. "I thought you did. We don't lie to the people we love. I would have been hurt, but I'd have gotten over it. That's what friends do. Friends tell each other the truth, even when it hurts. I want to know one thing. I want to know why you lied to me."

He paused as though trying to decide how to put it. "I was scared I would lose you."

"Bullshit. You knew how I felt about you. I told you so many times it was practically engraved on my forehead. I told you how much I loved you and that I wished you were straight. Every single time I got my heart broken, I went running to you and said the same thing. If only you weren't gay... So you're telling me that never once in all those times did it occur to you to say, 'Hey, guess what, I like boobs'?"

"It's more complicated than that."

She shook her head. "No, it's not. It's simple. You didn't even have to talk. You could have reached out and grabbed one."

"Damn it, Dani, stop. Just fucking stop. This is serious."

"Oh, I am serious. Don't think I'm not. What did you expect me to do? Did you expect me to turn to you with grateful tears in my eyes and say thank you? Well, I can do that for you. Thanks. Thanks for lying to me. Thanks for making a complete fool out of me. Did you sleep with girls in high school?"

"No." The answer came quickly, almost tripping out of his mouth. "I didn't sleep with anyone in high school. I lost my virginity to a guy named Greg halfway through my freshman year of college. I swear I didn't sleep with anyone in this town."

At least she hadn't had some bitchy girl laughing behind her back. Of course, she should have known that. If Finn had slept with someone in Willow Fork, everyone would have known it. "When was the first time you slept with a woman?"

His eyes were suddenly back on the road, his face a bright red. "About twenty minutes after I slept with Greg. His girlfriend was very open-minded."

She huffed. Well, no wonder he had no interest in her. He was too busy having kinky sex. He probably thought she was some dried-up prude. She hadn't felt that way last night. Something wicked picked at her, making her feel mean. "Julian's pretty open-minded himself."

His eyes were right back on her, burning with something righteous. "Julian's a prick who took advantage of you."

"At least someone did," she grumbled.

"Do you have any idea what he's into? You need to talk to Lucas. He knows this guy."

"I don't care what Lucas thinks. The only opinion that matters here is mine, and I liked him."

He'd been difficult and remote, and when he'd made love to her, she'd felt like the only person in the whole world. He'd been just as focused on her during sex as he was distant this morning. It had been an incredible experience. Of course, Finn had probably had a lot of those. Finn had ménage sex. The thought of Finn on his knees in front of Julian made her heart flip. She would watch and get hot while Finn got Julian hard enough to fuck her.

Damn. One night with Julian Lodge and she was a lustful pervert.

But what was perverted about it? What she and Julian had done hadn't hurt anybody. Why should it matter that she had fantasies that were slightly outside the mainstream? She'd spent her entire life being a good girl and what had it gotten her? She was forgotten in the community until someone needed something. Finn had found other girls to sleep with. Her sister treated her like crap. The one crazy thing she'd ever done in her whole life had netted her a night in bed with a veritable sex god.

Maybe being good was for the birds.

"I don't like the look on your face."

"Too bad."

She was about to let loose, to tell her lying best friend that she didn't give a damn, and he could go to hell. The smoke rising from her house made her stop. She felt her mouth drop open as he turned, and she could see a plume of gray smoke rising from her front yard. "What the hell?"

"Is that your house on fire?" He hit the gas, charging forward.

Up ahead, she could see that the house was fine. The yard was not. The yard was littered with piles of trash, and it was, or had been, on fire. The small Willow Fork volunteer fire truck was out front, and they had put out the fire. They were rolling up the hose as Finn stopped the car.

Val stood in the front yard talking to a man in uniform. His name was Andy McKenna, deputy and resident all-around asshole. She squinted. A piece of bright pink fabric stuck out among the char. Dani's heart sank. She knew what that was, or rather had been. It was a big pink elephant Finn had won for her at the county fair when they were sixteen. She'd moved it to Jimbo's along with everything else she owned in the world. Now it was gone.

"What the hell happened?" Finn's question came out as a shocked gasp.

She slammed out of Finn's SUV and made a beeline for Val, who had a judgmental frown on her lovely face as she listened to Andy. Dani heard Finn's door slam and felt him behind her. Despite her anger with him, she was damn glad she wasn't alone.

"Well, look who decided to crawl home." Val's frown got

deeper, putting creases on her face.

Andy turned toward Dani, a glare in his cold, dark eyes and a smirk on his face. "Looks like you pissed someone off, Miss Bay." He emphasized the Miss. "Take a look around and tell me if you recognize any of this stuff. Your sister was sleeping, and when she woke up, all this crap was in her yard, and it was on fire. She seems to think it has something to do with you."

"Shit," Finn hissed as he surveyed the damage. He kicked at a pile of books. A half-burned copy of Keats' poems disintegrated before her eyes. She saw his face go red, but this time it was all about anger. He turned to Andy McKenna. "Are you going to call that fucking redneck in for questioning?"

McKenna stared through Finn, not bothering to take off his mirrored sunglasses. "I have no idea who you're talking about, son. And I would appreciate you watching your fucking language around an officer of the law."

She had the most insane urge to clock the son of a bitch. He was a year Finn's junior. The "son" was pure insult. Anger rushed through her system. She wouldn't get a lick of justice out of this man, but she felt compelled to push anyway. "He's talking about my ex-fiancé. He obviously dumped my belongings here and then torched them. There has to be something illegal about that. If nothing else, isn't there a burn ban?"

McKenna's lips quirked up. "Now, Miss, if I were going to write a ticket for ignoring the burn ban, I would have to write it to the homeowner. That would be you, correct?"

"Obviously she didn't destroy everything she owns." Finn's jaw was clenched in impotent anger. His fists pumped at his sides.

Tears burned in the backs of her eyes. She looked over at her sister, the woman she'd put her life on hold to raise, to put through school. She was shaking her head and rolling her eyes.

"After yesterday, who knows what Danielle would do?" Val proclaimed. She stood there in the jeans and flouncy top Dani had bought for her birthday and shook her head, looking at her sister like she was a pest to be dealt with.

Everything she owned. The truth raced through Dani's system like a wildfire. All her clothes, her books, the chair her mother used to rock her in, all gone. Even her car was at Jimbo's shop. She had nothing but her purse and the clothes she'd gone to the church in yesterday. Finn had picked those things up. It was the only reason she had a damn thing in the world. Her hands started to shake. Finn's arms came around her.

"It's all right, baby. I'll take care of you." His breath was warm against her neck.

She suddenly wanted to call Julian. She wanted to call him because he would come and take care of the problem. He would step in and shield her, and she wouldn't have to worry about anything. If Finn tried to deal with this, he would get in trouble. He might get hurt. No one would hurt Julian.

He hadn't given her his number.

She stepped out of Finn's arms and turned to face Deputy McKenna. There was no one she could rely on but herself. Finn was standing by her because he felt bad. They were friends and nothing more. She couldn't put him in the line of fire. "I would like to file a report."

"You don't have any witnesses." The deputy frowned at her and crossed his arms, showing his obvious disinterest in the process. "Val here was asleep, and there are no close neighbors. I already called Jimbo, and his mother is willing to say that he dropped these belongings of yours off late last night since you made it real clear you weren't moving into the house he bought for you. I doubt this crap burned all night. This shit is so cheap it probably went up in no time at all. What did you do? Set it on fire and then drive around the block?"

No help was forthcoming from the Willow Fork Sheriff's Department. It didn't surprise her. Andy was Jimbo's drinking buddy. There was no way he took her side over his. The thought that Andy would do his job with no bias was completely laughable. "So you aren't going to do anything at all?"

He shrugged as the volunteer fire department finished packing their equipment. "Unless you have an alibi, I would back off, Dani. Everyone knows you aren't acting much like yourself lately. A lot of folks around this town are thinking you're out to get as much attention as possible."

Val stepped forward, getting between Dani and the deputy. "Back off, Dani. You can't prove you didn't do this. You don't want to get into more trouble than you already are. Everyone is looking at us like we're the trashiest family in Willow Fork, and that's saying something."

"What is wrong with you people? There's no way she did this herself. That's ridiculous. She was out at Jack Barnes's ranch," Finn countered.

Andy laughed, a sharp, short bark. "Yeah, I wonder what she was doing out there."

"A man who's way better looking than you." Dani ignored her sister's gasp of shock and turned on her heels to walk into the house. No one would help her. She might be able to force them to make a report, but unless she had irrefutable evidence, these good old boys would protect their own. Jimbo would get away with his revenge.

She walked up the rickety steps and started to slam the door, but Val was there following her.

"What do you think you're doing?" Val's claw clamped down on her elbow, whirling Dani around to look at her.

"I'm tired. I'm going to bed for a while." Her old bed was still here. Val hadn't gotten rid of it yet. She would curl up and try to forget that any of this ever happened. Maybe she would wake up and find out it was all a dream and Finn was still gay and her world was still crappy, but familiar.

"This is my house." Val got between Dani and the hall that led to the bedrooms. She looked model perfect for a woman who'd recently gotten up. Dani had to wonder if she'd taken a flat iron to her hair before she called the fire department.

"It's still half mine. Where do you expect me to go?"

"I don't know. Anywhere but here. Look, I'm not trying to be a bitch, but there's nothing left for you here. You should go somewhere else. No one is going to accept you in Willow Fork. Go to Dallas with Finn and let me buy your half of the house. You're gonna need the money. It's what we agreed on in the first place." Val's flip-flop tapped on the linoleum.

A heavy weariness permeated Dani's body. She hadn't slept much the night before, and the emotional roller coaster of this morning was taking its toll. She was sore, tired, and wanted nothing more than to cry herself to sleep after a nice long shower. "We decided that when I was moving. I can't move now."

"Of course you can. It'll be easy. You don't even have stuff to pack. You can move to Dallas with Finn. You talked about how much you wanted to do that before Mom died."

Finn stood in the doorway. Her heart skipped a beat. He was so gorgeous. His shoulders were broad and his body fit, but his face was what always caught her. She'd had so many fantasies about that face cuddling close to hers, those sensual lips saying "I love you" as he worked over her.

He'd never wanted her. He was one more in a long line of men who didn't want her for who she was. She needed time to figure out how to move forward.

"I can't move to Dallas. I might cramp Finn's sex life." She saw Finn pale but turned away. He wasn't hers to comfort anymore. She turned and walked down the short hall. After she slammed the door, she sank to the bed. Though exhausted, it took her the longest time to fall asleep.

Chapter Eight

The bartender opened a small cabinet and pulled out a bottle of Scotch. Julian sighed at the thought of something civilized. He might be at a place called The Barn, but it looked like the Scotch, at least, was a connection to his privileged world.

The bartender set two glasses in front of them and poured out a finger apiece. Julian frowned and slightly shook his head. The fellow was obviously well trained as the line of pure amber liquor went up in his glass.

Beside him, Jackson chuckled lightly. "You should probably leave the bottle, Kevin. My friend had his first full day of ranch work. Never been on a horse before."

Kevin smiled and nodded in a deferential fashion that made Julian believe he was a man who was usually tipped well. "Absolutely, Mr. Barnes. Cigars, sir?"

Jackson shook his head shortly and turned, his eyes flashing around the bar. Samuel slid onto the stool beside him, a smirk on his ridiculously perfect face.

"Abby's in the bathroom with Christa. Your cigar habit is still a secret." Samuel slapped his Dom on the back affectionately and nodded as he was passed a beer.

Julian stared at the two. There was so much about the way their relationship worked that he didn't understand. For years he simply let it slide, but now he found he wanted to know why Jackson did the things he did. "And you keep this a secret why?"

Jackson took a quick swallow of his Scotch. "I keep it a secret because I married a nurse. She takes particular exception to smoking. It's why I rarely do it."

"Then simply tell her to accept it." That was the way it worked. Jackson was the Dom and Abigail the submissive. That's what a sub did. She submitted to the will of her dominant partner.

Jackson and Samuel both broke into fits of laughter, further confusing Julian. His muscles ached. He probably had bruises in places where he didn't want bruises. He now understood why they called it punching cows since he'd given serious consideration to doing exactly that. Cattle, it turned out, were not very smart creatures. They did not mind and couldn't care less where they defecated which, at least twice that day, had been on him. He was sick of cows, sick of horses. He was sick to death of feeling like he was the only one who didn't get the joke. To top off his perfectly horrible day, he'd gotten word from Candice that several threatening letters had made their way into his personal box, and the reporter had called again.

He'd spent an hour on the phone with Ian Taggart, and that had done nothing to change his state of mind.

And he missed Danielle. He'd spent the whole day wondering if Finn was taking care of her. This was his vacation. No wonder he'd never taken one.

"Sorry, Julian," Jackson said, coughing a little. "There are some things on which our wife is utterly unmovable. My healthy lungs are one of them."

"Yes, I'd forgotten how vanilla you've gotten," he replied, well aware that there was a nasty tinge to his voice. "Abigail took your balls as surely as Samuel paid someone to take his."

"Hey! My balls still work perfectly," Samuel stated. "The boys still jingle. They just don't jangle anymore, if you know what I mean."

He didn't. He was pretty sure he didn't understand anything. Scotch. He understood Scotch. He took a sip. The smoky flavor was a pleasant sensation as it burned slightly down his throat. "I would have dismissed you had you done that as my slave."

"No, you wouldn't." Samuel leaned forward and grabbed the

bottle. He refilled Jackson's glass and did the same for Julian. "You would have done exactly what Jack did. You would have tanned my ass red."

A smile curled Jackson's lips up, making him softer, younger looking. "Well, I spanked you until you actually used your safe word."

"Damn straight I did," Samuel replied. "Only time I've ever used my safe word. He was pissed at me."

Jackson turned to his partner, his voice deepening. "I wasn't pissed that you had done it. I was pissed that you hadn't told me. I hadn't approved of the doctor. I hadn't checked out the procedure. If you ever do anything like it again, you won't come for a month. You'll take care of me, but there will be nothing for you."

"Oh, are we talking about Sam's balls again?" Abigail frowned as she slid onto the stool next to Samuel. "Are we ever going to stop talking about this?"

"You, too. You won't come either. Never again."

Abigail looked around both of her husbands and gave Julian a saucy wink. "He spanked the hell out Sam, but ten minutes later he was holding a bag of frozen peas to Sam's swollen balls. Did you know they can swell up after surgery?"

Both of her husbands shuddered, but he couldn't miss the way Jackson's hand slid over Samuel's neck, or how Abigail's hand found Jackson's, connecting the three of them. For a moment, Julian was sure in their minds they were the only three people in the universe. Their easy intimacy staggered him. The look in their eyes made him avert his own.

Perhaps this had been a terrible mistake. He wasn't cut out for intimacy. He sipped his Scotch as they talked, nodding when it seemed appropriate, but his mind was far away. Sitting with Jackson, Samuel, and Abigail made him feel like he was twelve again, watching families eat together, fathers playing with sons, mothers clucking over their babies' welfare. He remembered vividly watching from the back of his limo as parents walked their children into school. Even on the first day, every year he'd been alone. Until Candice had come, even his nannies simply told the driver where to take him and where to pick him up. Poor little rich boy.

Yes, perhaps it was time to go home.

"Come on, baby, let's dance." Samuel took her hand and led her away, leaving Julian alone with Jackson.

"I know what you're about to say."

"Ah, so you're a mind reader now, Jackson."

"Nope, I just know you. You're about to tell me that this was all a mistake and thanks for the invite, but you should get back to Dallas in the morning."

He clutched the crystal glass in his hand like it was a lifeline. That had been precisely what he'd planned to say. He'd trained Jackson far too well. "I don't believe I'm cut out to be a cowboy. I make a much better billionaire playboy."

Jackson snorted and pushed back the brim of his hat, giving Julian a better look at the surprise on his face. "You haven't been a playboy a day in your life. You're the opposite. You demand commitment from your lovers before you'll even bother to touch them." His eyes narrowed. "Is that what's bothering you? You're upset because you slept with Dani without a contract?"

It did bother him. It went against his own rules. "That contract is there to protect both of us. You know that."

"I know that you think the contract can protect you, but it also builds a wall around you. I'm encouraging you to stay for the week. If you don't want to work the herd, I can handle that, but give Dani a call. Hang out with us. Spend time with Dani. You don't have to promise her anything. She's a big girl who has a better head on her shoulders than even she knows. See where it goes. No contract. No promises. No end date."

It sounded strange and oddly intriguing. "You're asking me to play Dani's boyfriend."

"No, I'm asking you to be Dani's friend who she might happen to sleep with. You did sleep with her, right?" Jackson asked.

"There was very little sleeping involved."

"Did she not enjoy submitting?"

Julian felt his dick go hard at the thought. "She submitted beautifully. I could have tied her down, and she wouldn't have questioned it."

Jackson's eyes narrowed inquisitively. "I'm surprised you didn't.

Did you use the playroom at all?"

He hadn't even thought about it. Once he'd gotten Danielle on the bed, he'd been too busy fucking her. He'd fucked that pussy over and over again. He'd fucked her from behind, slamming his cock inside as his hands molded the gorgeous, voluptuous curves of her hips and her ass. He'd propped her ankles on his shoulders and enjoyed the super tight entry he got that way. At one point he'd picked her up and put her in the shower. He'd soaped her hair and suckled her breasts. She'd been perfect.

"We didn't need the playroom." He took a much longer sip of the Scotch and tried to shake off the images of Danielle waiting for his command. "Besides, she made her decision today."

"And you know damn well she would have stayed if you'd given her any indication that you wanted it."

"Perhaps she and this Finn person are meant to be."

Jackson groaned. "God, I hope not. Damn. That would be like Abby and Sam without me, only worse. At least Abby can take charge when the occasion calls for it. Those two are true subs. I'm not surprised he hadn't slept with her. He isn't aggressive enough. I bet the women he has slept with took charge, or he was ordered to sleep with them by his Dom."

"He didn't sound like he'd had a Dom."

Jackson sat back. "I didn't say he knew he'd had one, but any relationship that worked for Finn had to have a dominant partner there. He's one of Lucas's friends. Lucas likes the hell out of him, but he thinks Finn's fooling himself. He's been trying to get Finn to go to The Club with him."

Julian toyed with his glass. He thought about how angry Finn had been. "He didn't seem submissive to me."

Except something inside him sparked off the younger man.

"Lucas is sure, and I've seen the way his eyes slide down when I stare at him," Jackson was saying. "He knows instinctively who could master him."

Yes, he could believe that. Finn had a certain air about him. If Finn was a sub, then it had taken a lot of love and no small amount of bravery to stand up to him. He admired bravery. "If he is, then he'll need to change. Or Danielle will. Otherwise the entire world will walk all over them."

He didn't mention that they would always be missing a piece of themselves that went beyond sexuality. They might be happy, but they would never be complete.

"Or they could find a Dom," Jackson said. "That's why Lucas has been trying to get him to The Club. I know he was planning on asking you to match up Finn. He'd even mentioned that he thought you and Finn would get along. Lucas said you were taking applications."

He felt his lips curl slightly at the admonishment in Jackson's voice. His protégé had never understood the screening process. Of course, now that Julian thought about it, Samuel would never have made it through his screening process, and he was the only person he'd ever offered a permanent contract to. Danielle wouldn't have made it, either. The thought of finding Danielle another Dom caused a knot to form in his stomach.

"I thought it was time," Julian said.

"Maybe it's time to try something else. Give Dani a call tomorrow. See how she's doing. Look, tell me honestly you're not worried about her and I'll back off."

There was something about the way Jackson said it that warmed Julian. Jackson truly gave a damn about him. It wasn't that Jackson needed him. He'd passed that long ago, and yet he continued to come back. He'd known Jackson Barnes for almost twenty years. He'd been Jackson's mentor, his patron, and at one point his partner in crime, but now it really hit him that Jackson was his friend.

That revelation made it much easier to be honest. "I am worried about her."

A slow smile spread across Jackson's face as he poured another finger of the fine Scotch. "Then call her. I have her number right here in my cell. If that ex of hers is causing trouble, then we can take care of it. And if Finn comes with her, well, maybe you can see if you can help him, too."

He slid the phone across the bar, but at that moment, the door flew open, and Julian realized he wouldn't need to call to find out how Danielle was doing.

She was already here.

* * * *

The door practically slammed back into his face. Finn had to quickly put a hand out in order to keep his nose in the right place. Dani was pissed, but he wasn't backing down. If she felt the desperate need to dance, then he was going to dance with her. Well, he would watch from someplace safe. She definitely wouldn't let him dance with her.

Hell, she wouldn't let him get near her. She'd slammed the damn door in his face more times than he could count today. And when she'd finally smiled sweetly at him and asked if he could retrieve a CD from his car because she really needed to hear a song, she'd locked the door and not let him back in. He'd sat on the porch texting her until she'd finally walked out wearing a ridiculously short denim skirt, cowboy boots, and a shirt that had to be two sizes too small. When he'd opened his mouth to mention the fact that she'd put on some Barbie doll clothes instead of real actual human clothes, the look on her face had had his mouth closing. She'd announced she was going to The Barn, the only honky-tonk for miles, and that he could drive her or she would walk.

She had not said a word in the car. Now she marched across the smoky, loud bar like a woman on a mission.

Finn felt his whole body sag. He'd fucked up and had no idea how to fix it. He only had a few days before he had to get back to work, and somehow, he had to convince Dani to come with him. He was pretty sure if he didn't break through to her soon, he never would.

"Excuse me," a familiar, though unwelcome, voice said.

Finn sighed when Val started to walk past him. "What the hell are you doing here?"

Her skirt was even shorter than Dani's, though she had sticks pointing out of it instead of real legs. Dani's denim skirt hugged her luscious ass, and he would swear if she bent over, those sweet cheeks were going to pop out. Val's skirt was flat against her body.

"It's a free country, isn't it? I told some of my friends I would be here." Her cold eyes slid around the room like a predator seeking prey. When they narrowed, it seemed to Finn that she'd found it. "Wow, who the hell is that? Damn, that man is fine."

He looked around Val, who tottered on what had to be five inches of stiletto. He caught a glimpse of a dark-haired man sitting at the bar. Even from here, he could see the man was dressed in an expensive shirt and slacks. Then he turned as though looking for someone, and Finn got a look at his face.

Damn it. Julian Lodge. Why did he have to be here?

Finn felt his face flush and averted his eyes before Julian could catch him gawking. This was the reason he'd stayed away from Dani all these years. A man like Julian walked in and Finn couldn't help but want him. He didn't want to admit it, but maybe Lucas was right. Lucas went on and on about how submission was in Finn's nature and how attracted he would be to strong Dominants. Julian Lodge was proof of that.

This morning, it had taken every bit of courage he had to face the man. When Julian had opened the door, the first thing Finn wanted to do was stare and maybe drool a little. He'd stood there in the doorway wearing nothing but a pair of black slacks, his elegant face a mask of irritation. He'd taken one look at Julian's muscular chest and his perfectly defined abs and wanted to ask if Julian would take him, too.

Dani would have loved that.

"Oh, now that is one gorgeous man. And he looks rich, too." Val was practically licking her chops.

"He's a billionaire."

Val turned, her mouth dropping open, eyes wide. "You're kidding me."

"Nope." A kernel of evil joy lit in his breast. "He's my firm's richest client. He's also the man Dani ran away with. That was his car she hopped into." And his bed. Damn, but Finn wished he'd been there.

Val was spewing some serious venom about how lucky Dani had always been, which was pure bullshit, but he was thinking. Dani was attracted to Julian, no question about it. He'd talked in length to Lucas as he'd sat on Dani's porch, and he'd found out a bit about the infamous club owner. Julian Lodge liked it both ways. Lucas had explained that Julian liked to keep a male and female slave. Slave. He wasn't sure he liked the sound, but that was the word Lucas had used.

Finn had to wonder how far he would go to stay close to the

woman he loved.

He might not be the most aggressive man in the world, but he would be damned if he didn't do everything to get what he wanted.

"Oh, wow, he's coming this way." Val patted her hair and pulled down on the neckline of her shirt. "Introduce me."

He gasped, the breath shocking into his system. Julian was walking his way, and there was no question who he was coming for. There was an almost gritty look to the man's face that had his whole body vibrating with anticipation.

"Finn," Julian said, not an ounce of friendly greeting in his voice. It was a challenge.

"Sir." Finn did what came naturally. He allowed his eyes to slide away. He gave the man in front of him the greeting Lucas warned him he required. If this afternoon had taught him anything, it was that if he wanted Dani, he was going to have to go through Julian. When he'd come up with the plan during the long, lonely hours of waiting for Dani, he'd realized he wasn't going to be sacrificing much. Getting into Julian's bed alongside Dani would be a pleasure. And a way to make damn sure he was there to clean up the mess Julian was sure to leave behind.

Julian leaned back as though regarding him seriously. "A different approach? Well, this one is bound to work better than attempting to decapitate me."

Val elbowed him.

"Oh, uhm, this is Val. Val, this is Julian Lodge," he managed to mumble. His eyes darted between Julian's muscular chest and the dance floor where Dani seemed to be trying to grind some redneck asshole to dust. "Julian, this is Valerie Bay, Dani's sister."

He was completely satisfied with the disinterest Julian showed in Val. His eyes held no heat as he glanced over her and dismissed her entirely. His focus immediately came back to Finn, and there was nothing bland about the look Julian gave him.

"You allowed Danielle to leave the house dressed like that?"

The forbidding tone in Julian's voice had him standing up straight. "She didn't give me a choice."

Julian's arms crossed, his eyes flaring. "Your choice should have been to pick her up and tie her down if she chose to disobey you."

"What the hell is he talking about?" Val asked, hand on her hip. "Why does he care what Dani wears? I mean, she looks like a stuffed sausage, but that's her damn choice. The girl never did have a lick of fashion sense."

Now Julian was interested. "You're Danielle's sister?"

She shrugged but inched closer. She thrust her chest out, and her voice took on a breathy, little-girl quality. "She's my older sister. Much older, if you know what I mean."

"I don't. I didn't ask Danielle for her birthday, much less yours, before I went to bed with her." Julian turned back to him. "Does Danielle live with…this? She's around this all the time?"

It took everything he had not to laugh. "Yeah."

"She needs to move."

"Yes, Sir." He believed that more than anything. She needed to leave Willow Fork. If Julian Lodge could get her to pack her bags, Finn was good with him.

"You slept with my sister?" Val's shrieking could be clearly heard over the loud country-western music.

Julian's gray eyes became positively arctic as he turned his attention to Val. Finn watched as she lost her seductive posture and shrank back.

"Go away." The words were deep but there was nothing sexy about them.

Val took a sharp breath. Her well-shaped brows came together in a *V*. "Well, I never."

"I couldn't care less what you have or haven't done. Leave my presence." Julian's eyes found Dani on the dance floor. His mouth turned down sharply. "I don't like what she's wearing. She's showing too much skin. Her breasts are going to fall out of that shirt. Damn it, is she wearing a bra? She better be wearing a bra."

Val huffed and stomped off, her body vibrating with a rage that gave Finn a deep satisfaction.

"I tried to get her to change, but she ignored me."

The world seemed to flow around Julian as though he had his own plane of existence and the rest of reality moved to make way for him. People walked all around him, moving through the small area, but hugging the walls as though in deference to his space. Finn himself was jostled and shoved, but Julian remained unmoving, untouched.

"And you expect to take care of her in this manner?" Julian asked. "By allowing her to dress as a hooker and ignore your reasonable requests?"

He wasn't sure what Julian expected him to do. "She's not a child. She's an adult. I can't just tell her what to do."

Julian shook his head, all that dark brown hair waving like handfuls of silk. "Can't you see that is exactly what she wants from you? She is not behaving as an adult should. She is acting out. I'm not questioning her intelligence. I'm not saying she's immature. I'm pointing out that most of us act out when we want attention. Even the most rational human will push the boundaries to test the people around us. Danielle was given a harsh blow today. She's going to push you away in an attempt to see if you will go. She will shove and fight and scratch at your soul to see if she can get you to leave her because she would rather hurt now than later. Are you going to allow her to do that?"

Finn felt Julian's words like a physical blow to his body. "No. I won't leave."

An almost soft expression came over Julian's gorgeous features. His hand came out, cupping Finn's left shoulder. "It's all right. I can teach you how to take care of her. You might not like how I do it, though. Are you willing to learn?"

His head was nodding before he could get the words out. "Yes, Sir."

"Good. Let's start now." Julian turned and began to walk toward the dance floor.

Finn hurried to follow.

Chapter Nine

Dani tried to let the music guide her, but mostly she wondered what she was attempting to accomplish. Her hips swayed to the country-western beat, and her partner led her around the floor, his eyes almost never leaving her chest. She kept her eyes firmly fixed on the cowboy's hat. It was way safer than doing what she wanted, which was to look around to see if Finn was watching.

"Hey, Dani, you might want to go easy on the bump and grind there."

She turned, startled at the familiar voice. Sam Fleetwood had his hands all over his wife. Abby grinned at her and nodded.

"Yeah, sweetie, you really should behave. Julian's here. I don't think he's going to like you dancing like that with someone else. Sam and I know what we're talking about," Abby managed to shout over the loud music.

The cowboy, who Dani seemed to recall was named Brett or Brad or something, tried to whirl her away, but Sam followed easily.

"You gotta understand, there are rules to be followed, and the first one is don't play around with other dudes. I think Julian is going to be inflexible on that one." Sam two-stepped with a light smile on his face.

Dani searched the bar frantically. Julian was here? What the hell was Julian doing here? But, yes, there he was. She couldn't mistake those broad shoulders or the lush, dark hair pulled back in a sexy ponytail. She remembered what it looked like when it fell around his neck and past his shoulders. When he'd leaned over her, his hair had fallen around her face, making an intimate world where there had only been the two of them.

"If you don't watch it, Julian's going to tan your hide," Abby said with a cheerful smile. "That's the good part. The bad part is when he doesn't let you have any fun, if you know what I mean. I wouldn't push him that far. You've done what you set out to do. You absolutely have his attention."

She stopped in the middle of the dance floor to the obvious chagrin of Brad whatever-his-name-was. The cowboy frowned and threw his hands up before stalking off in search of a less distracted partner. Dani allowed Sam and Abby to move her off the dance floor to the far end of the bar.

"I don't understand. He doesn't care about me." She wasn't sure why he was here, but he wasn't here for her. He'd made that clear this morning. Craning her neck, she tried to see through the sea of dancing couples. Julian looked like he was talking to Finn and a woman. Her heart ached as she realized who was standing so close to Julian, batting her heavily mascaraed eyes up at him. Her sister. Val was trying to sink her perfectly manicured claws into Julian.

"Don't worry about that," Sam said, passing Dani a longneck. "Julian likes boobs on his females. If he's in the mood for some manloving, he'll find a guy. That sister of yours doesn't stand a chance."

Sure enough, Val turned from the two men, her chest heaving with obvious anger. She shot Dani a cold stare before marching to the bar where she met up with Cecelia Smith, her cool, blonde BFF. Cece was a terrible gossip. The tall, willowy twenty-four-year-old was already whispering behind her hand to her equally skinny blonde cohorts. The former cheerleading squad of Willow Fork High School might no longer wear tiny red skirts, but they stuck together, and they loved to cause trouble.

"See. I know what Julian's into," Sam said with that easy confidence of his.

A secret smile played on Abby's face. "I wouldn't mention that to Jack if I were you."

"Mention what?" Jack slid an arm around his wife's shoulders.

"Not a damn thing." Sam winked at Dani. "I was explaining to Dani here that perhaps she should have thought about actually wearing the other half of her skirt to this particular establishment."

"Yes, that might have been smart. I do believe Julian took exception to Danielle's wardrobe choices this evening." The words were a lazy threat coming out of Jack's mouth.

She was righteously confused. Finn was upset. She understood that, but Julian had dismissed her as though he couldn't have cared less whether she stayed or went. Why should he care that she was wearing a skirt she'd bought as a part of a Halloween costume? It was one of the only things she'd left behind when she'd moved her things to Jimbo's house. "My skirt has nothing to do with Julian Lodge. And from what I understand, he shouldn't care either way. I talked to Lexi a couple of hours ago and she told me all about his club. People run around there naked."

When Lexi had explained exactly what kind of club Julian ran, Dani had been shocked, amused, and very, very interested. It wasn't like she didn't know places like The Club existed. She wasn't that naïve, but she'd never met someone who went to one. Except she had. Abby went to Julian's club with her husbands. Lexi went there with Lucas. Lexi said it was one of the only places in the world where she felt truly comfortable.

If it worked for Lexi and Abby, why couldn't it work for her?

"There are rules at The Club," Jack stated implacably. His shoulders squared, and he seemed to get even taller. Dani noticed Abby and Sam both looked up to him, their eyes soft.

"There are laws everywhere," Dani countered.

Jack shook his head. "I'm not talking about laws. I'm talking about rules. Julian's club has rules, and the people there know they damn sure better follow the rules or they're in for some serious trouble. There are no real rules here, and no one to enforce them even if there were. It's not fair, but it's a fact of life that you'll get treated differently because you're wearing that...I wouldn't even call it a skirt. It looks like a denim Band-Aid you wrapped around your ass.

And you should be wearing a damn bra, Danielle."

She had always wondered what it would be like to have an overprotective father. Jack Barnes was doing a fine impression of one. There was a big part of her that wanted to apologize and slink home to change. But she wasn't letting that part of her win tonight. Tonight she was in charge.

"I'm sorry you don't like it, Mr. Barnes, but it isn't any of your business." The man Dani had come to see walked into the room from the back porch where they played horseshoes and smoked. Yes, this was why she'd come. Not to catch anyone's attention. Dani felt her eyes narrow and her fists clench. Jimbo Smart was laughing and drinking like he hadn't put a torch to everything she owned. "Now, if you'll excuse me, I have to go make a few things clear to my ex."

She heard someone shout at her, but she moved through the crowd quickly before one of her friends could catch her and stop her from making a mistake she really wanted to make. The Barn was ridiculously crowded for a Sunday night. Shouldn't these people be at church? Dani moved past the pastor of First Presbyterian, who was dancing with his wife and looked like he was having a great time. Dani seriously doubted Pastor Robert Cornelious of the First Methodist Church had ever two-stepped to "Save a Horse Ride a Cowboy." Maybe she should change churches. After all, she was going to need forgiveness for what she was about to do.

One of Jimbo's friends elbowed him, and the bastard looked up. His jaw dropped open as she approached.

"Damn, girl, you look good!" He whistled and gave his friend a return elbowing. He leaned over, but Dani could hear what he said. "I hit that."

Joe, who worked at Jimbo's shop, shook his head. "Yeah, we all know. That's probably why she bolted. You gotta hide that tiny dick or you're never gonna get a woman to marry you."

Jimbo doubled over laughing. The bastard was drunk off his ass. When he came up for air, there was a pleading look in his eyes. "Come on, babe, defend my honor. It isn't the biggest thing in the world, but it's got stamina."

No, it didn't, but she wasn't getting drawn into an argument over the size of his dick, which, compared to Julian's, was tiny.

"Come on, babe, you gotta admit you owe me. The least you can do is take out an ad or something proclaiming that you didn't leave me over the size of my dick—or you could say you did because it was too big for you to handle. Yeah, that's what you should do." Jimbo's face was red from beer and laughter, and she couldn't handle one more second of it.

She picked up the nearest napkin holder and fastballed it right at Jimbo. It took the cowboy hat right off his head.

"Damn, girl, what was that for?" Jimbo held his head in his hand while Joe laughed his ass off.

He was going to play dumb? She wasn't about to let him get away with it. "That was for what you did to me. How could you? That was everything I owned. You could have burned down my house. Did you even think about that?"

Jimbo's eyes got big and wide. "What the hell are you talking about? Are you pissed that I left your stuff in the yard? I tried to call, but you didn't answer. You didn't answer the door, either. I thought you would want your stuff back. Besides, Momma already set me up with this girl from Alba, and she probably won't fuck me if my house is full of some other girl's shit. It didn't rain or nothing. I don't see what the big deal is."

"Danielle!"

Julian's voice carried across the room, the crowd, the loud music. He shouted, and Dani turned immediately. She saw Jack shaking his head with an "I told you so" air about him. The dancing stopped, and everyone moved out of Julian's way as he stalked the distance between them.

"Holy shit, Dani, what kind of trouble are you in?" Jimbo asked, still rubbing his head.

The kind that got her spanked. Julian looked like a righteously pissed-off bull must look right before he gored the cowboy who'd tried to ride him. She took a step back, coming into contact with Jimbo's front. She was surprised that his hands came up to her shoulders.

"Maybe you should get behind me," he said, his voice uncertain.

"I wouldn't do that if I were you, Dani," Finn said, walking up and taking his place beside Julian.

When had they started working together? Well, she wasn't about to hide behind Jimbo. She forced her spine to straighten. "This isn't your business, Julian. And it isn't your business either, Finn."

That single eyebrow arched up. "What did you call me?"

"Julian, Sir." Damn it, she had to stop that.

"I didn't call you anything. Nope. Nothing at all, sir." Jimbo took a step back, leaving her alone.

"See that it stays that way," Julian said. "Danielle, are you attempting to start a bar fight?"

She pointed Jimbo's way. "I am attempting to show this asshole that he can't torch everything I own and get away with it."

"What?" Jimbo shouted the question. When Dani looked back there was unmistakable confusion on his face. "I didn't torch nothing, Dani. Why the hell would I do that?"

She turned to fully face him. "When I got home this morning, the fire department was putting out the fire in my front yard where you had burned everything I owned because of how pissed off you were that I left you."

"No, babe, that's not true. Damn, how did I miss that story? Everything was fine when I left. Look, I'll be real honest with you. I like you, but I ain't in love with you. I was actually kind of relieved. Although, the way you look tonight, if you want to, you know, have some righteously nasty breakup sex, I am all over that."

"You asshole," Finn shouted as he surged from behind Julian. His fist was back and quickly connected with Jimbo's face.

Curses started flying as Finn let go. He had Jimbo on the floor before Dani could scream. Jimbo's friend got in on the action, double-teaming Finn. She heard Finn groan as Joe's fist connected with his gut. Jimbo managed to get a good kick in. Dani couldn't stand by. As angry as she was with Finn, she still loved him. She tugged at Joe's shirt, trying to pull him back. All around her the crowd moved in. Bar fights were a regular form of entertainment at The Barn.

"Stop!"

Dani felt an arm go around her middle, lifting her away from the fight.

Jack and Sam were in the middle of the fight, pulling people off one another. Jack held the back of Finn's shirt even as his fists continued trying to pummel an opponent who wasn't close enough to hit. Finn's face was bloody, his nose bruised.

"Don't even think about it," Julian whispered harshly. His arm tightened around her. "Finn, I believe you've made your point clear. Jackson, is there a place where I can take these two? I need to clean Finn up and make both of them very clear on the way their evening is going to go."

Her heart started to race, and it wasn't from the adrenaline of the fight. Julian was using that deep, almost hypnotic voice on her. She opened her mouth to protest. She shouldn't go anywhere with him. He would only break her heart again.

Before she could even get the first word out of her mouth, Julian's hands tightened around her. "I would watch my words, Danielle. I won't hesitate to start your punishment here and now. You know I have no problem with showing you off."

"Punishment?"

"Yes, and Finn is due some as well."

Finn's head turned. "Me? What did I do?"

"Acted like an ass," she said under her breath.

A sharp smack hit her bottom. "Your running commentary is not required, little one. Speak up again and I'll have that skirt up and your panties down while I redden that ass of yours." Dani could hear him sigh. "You are wearing panties under that thing, correct?"

"Of course, though it's really more of a thong," she admitted.

"That will do." Julian let her go and walked to Finn. He lifted Finn's chin, seeming to inspect him. After a moment he nodded before turning back to Jack. "Should I take them home?"

The big cowboy shook his head as he handed Julian a key. "Nah, I have a place upstairs for just such an occasion. Take the back stairs, and it's the first door on the left. There's a shower and some clean clothes and other items should you need them."

"Excellent." He turned to the stairs. Despite the fight and all the chaos around them, Julian seemed perfectly in control. Finn was a bloody mess. She knew she had to look atrocious, but Julian was neat and pin perfect. What would it take to mess him up?

He paused at the bottom of the stairs. "Danielle, Finn, come along."

He turned and walked as though it was a certain thing that they would follow.

He hadn't gotten more than two steps up before Finn was reaching for her hand, pulling her along.

* * * *

Val watched as her sister—her pathetic, can't-keep-a-man sister—walked up the stairs after the gorgeous billionaire. What the hell was going on? Her mind raced. Maybe this Lodge guy was feeling sorry for Dani. Maybe he viewed her as a charity case.

That had to be it. Except he hadn't looked at her like she was a charity case. He'd stared at Dani like he wanted her. She'd managed to get close enough to hear a bit of what he said to her. He'd been upset at the way she was dressed and talked about punishment. Dani had closed her mouth fast at that. What the hell had Dani gotten into?

Val watched the three of them disappear up the stairs. Jealousy curled in her stomach. *That bitch*. Had she known what she was doing when she fled her wedding? This billionaire guy seemed to be a friend of Jack Barnes. Maybe Dani had known exactly what she was doing.

Val felt her hands fist at her sides. She thought about what had happened this morning. She'd called that two-timing asshole John Hartley and asked him to find a way to get her sister out of the picture. He'd been utterly unwilling to help her. In fact, he'd told her that if she couldn't get the house in her name in the next couple of days, he was going to announce the coming deal. It turned out fall elections were more important to mayors than mistresses. Val was going to get the shaft—again.

"You want to explain what the fuck that was about?"

Jimbo hauled her around, a nasty gleam in his eyes.

This was so not what she needed. She saw Cece start to point their way. Cece would have a rumor going in no time at all. Val pulled Jimbo toward a darker, more private part of the bar. There was only one man sitting at a table in here. He nursed a beer and didn't seem to pay particular attention to anyone.

"Will you keep your voice down?" Val shoved him into a corner.

Jimbo's eyes gleamed with suspicion in the low light. "No, I won't. You want to explain to me why Dani thinks I torched her shit? I was damn careful with all that crap. I even made sure that stupid-ass elephant she loved couldn't possibly hit the ground and get wet. So how did it all manage to burn? I'm betting it was you, Val. What the hell have you got against your sister?"

Everything. Everywhere Val went, she was always Danielle Bay's little sister. Even when she ruled the school, all any teacher could talk about was how smart Dani was, how kind. No matter how gorgeous and thin Val managed to make herself, there was someone who thought Dani was better than her.

"You can't prove anything." Val would never let this redneck hick get the best of her. She loved what he did for her in bed, but she would be damned if he pushed her around. "Besides, what the hell do you care? She left you at the altar, or has half a dozen beers made you conveniently forget that fact?"

"She came to her senses is all." His calm infuriated Val. "Dani was always too good for me, and we both know it. She's a nice lady."

Nice? She'd left her fiancé and gone to bed with a practical stranger. "She's fucking that guy, you know."

"Yeah, I kind of got that feeling when he stared a damn hole through me." He chuckled as he glanced over to where Dani had disappeared up the stairs. "If I'm right, she might finally get around to getting into Finn's pants, too."

"Finn's gay, dummy."

He waved that off. "Nah, Finn's just real flexible, if you know what I mean. My sister went to the same college as Finn. He got around with a lot of people. Girls, boys, maybe the occasional goat, but I always knew he had a thing for Dani."

Why wouldn't this asshole get mad? "That guy she went upstairs with is loaded. She left you for money."

"I doubt that," he replied with a sigh. "Dani's not like that at all. But hell, if that guy's loaded, then good for Dani…and Finn. I get the feeling that dude is open-minded like Jack Barnes. I gotta wonder why all the crazy threesomes around here are dude fests. I need to start a new trend. Two girls and one guy, namely me. That's more sensible."

"You're an idiot."

"Probably. I was sure as hell a dumbass for sleeping with you. Here's the deal, Val. I won't open my mouth about this because I think it would hurt Dani, but you back off. Maybe she'll leave for Dallas with the rich dude and Finn, and then you can have that pitiful excuse for a house all to yourself." He pushed past her and walked back to his friends.

Val felt tears threaten. How had her sister won again? After all the times she'd slept with that asshole, he still defended Dani.

"You look like you could use a drink."

Val turned. She'd forgotten about the guy at the table. He had a trucker hat pulled low over his face, but he seemed young to Val, maybe mid-twenties. He was clean shaven and thin, almost to the point of being gaunt. Still, he had a certain prettiness about him.

"I don't think I'm good company tonight." She wasn't in the mood for a hookup, not when her sister was busy screwing more money than Val could ever imagine.

"Oh, but you might find out we have a lot in common."

Val rolled her eyes. As pickup lines went, it was pretty pathetic. She was just about to put the imbecile in his place when he spoke again.

"Like you want to hurt your sister, and I am intensely interested in hurting Julian Lodge."

Much better pickup line. Val took a seat at the table. "I'm listening."

"I thought you might." He pushed his hat back, showing off big, dark eyes. "By the way, my name is Jeremy."

Jeremy started to talk. Val leaned in, not wanting to miss a single word.

Chapter Ten

Dani looked around the room and wondered exactly what Jack Barnes used it for. It was a small bedroom with a bed, closet, one dresser, and a door that led to a bathroom. She felt Finn beside her, his hand trying to tangle with hers. Their fingers brushed, but after her initial shock, she'd been unwilling to allow him the intimacy. She'd dropped his hand as they headed up the stairs, and his disappointment had been tangible. He stood beside her watching Julian as he opened drawers.

"Ah, yes. I knew Jackson wouldn't let me down." Julian pulled out a small wooden paddle. He turned to her. "You can dispense with the skirt, Danielle. The rest of your clothes, as well. Bend over with your elbows on the bed and your ass in the air."

Dani took a step back.

"Hey, you're not going to use that on her." Finn's words came out somewhere between a statement and a wary question.

One arrogant brow rose over Julian's eyes. "I am going to use it on both of you. Danielle, I am punishing you for your attempts at making me jealous. I won't be manipulated in that fashion."

"I didn't…" she sputtered, her eyes still on that paddle in Julian's hand. "How could I know you would be here?"

"Can you tell me in all honesty that you didn't think about me when you chose to dress in this fashion? Why did you dress so out of character? Or do you intend to tell me this is your regular dress?"

"I thought it looked nice." She didn't. It looked trashy, but she'd talked to Lexi and found out that Julian's women tended to wear no clothes at all.

His expression didn't change. "All right. We began with five swats. We're up to ten now. Would you like to lie to me again?"

Tears pricked at the corners of her eyes. She knew what she wanted. She wanted Julian. Hell, she was alone in a very intimate room with the only two men she'd ever really felt anything for. And she was so scared she couldn't see straight. She couldn't stand the thought of being another in a long line of submissive females for Julian.

Of course, Lexi also said he never slept with a sub without a contract in place. It seemed a foreign idea to her, but it was the way Julian worked. Except with her...

"Danielle, you have a safe word," Julian prompted.

And so did he, she realized suddenly. That contract was his safety net. That contract was a safe way for Julian to keep his lovers at arm's length. Lexi had been more than willing to spill everything she knew about this man. He had rules, so many rules. He never took a sub without a contract. He never had sex that didn't involve some form of BDSM. He generally kept both a male and a female, yet the subs were not involved with each other, only him.

Why was Finn here?

The night before, Julian had made love to her. Sure it had been rough, but it had also been very...vanilla. That was the term Lexi had used. He'd broken his rules for her. Now he'd brought Finn in here. Julian had to know how she felt about Finn.

This was what Sam and Abby had been talking about. This was why they'd been so nonchalant. Julian had made a decision to include Finn. To please her.

"Dani, let's go. We don't have to do this." Finn's hands tangled with hers, and this time she allowed it.

"Hush, or you'll get in trouble with Sir. He likes to be called Sir." She gave Finn a reassuring smile because she wasn't going anywhere.

The warmth that came over Julian's normally chilly gray eyes gave Dani the boost she needed. She squeezed Finn's hand and started to work the skirt over her hips. It wasn't easy.

"Finn, I believe Danielle needs assistance. Is it glued to your body?" The paddle tapped against the palm of his hand.

"Kind of feels like it right now." What had she been thinking?

Finn's hands were suddenly at her waist, warm and strong. They skimmed under the band of her skirt and made contact with skin. Her every nerve came to life like a live wire sparking.

"Hold still." His voice was right in her ear.

He was behind her, and she could feel…oh, boy, she could feel that. "You have an erection."

There was a warm chuckle in her ear. "Yup. Get those a lot around you. Kind of reaching epic proportions tonight." He pushed the skirt off her hips and down her thighs.

"You want me." It was a revelation. She'd heard the words before, but the proof was currently attempting to hump her hip.

"Finn, help her out of her clothes before you prematurely ejaculate all over her." Julian sounded amused at the prospect.

"I wasn't…fine." Finn's hands ran under her shirt, pushing it up and over her arms.

"I would prefer a *Sir* when you speak to me, Finn," Julian stated. He set the paddle on the bed. A single finger came up, and he twirled it as though asking her to turn for his inspection.

Dani slowly turned around, wearing nothing but boots and her black thong and matching bra. It was embarrassing until she caught the look on Finn's face. His jaw was slightly open, and his eyes were glazed and right on her boobs. He *wanted* her. Julian had a bit more decorum, but there was no mistaking the erection tenting his slacks.

"Finn, I am waiting."

"Yes, Sir. Should I take off the rest of her clothes?" Finn seemed to have trouble concentrating.

"Yes, that would be a good way to start." Julian continued as Finn began unhooking her bra. "Let me explain the way this works, my little subs. I am the Master. You will obey me. You always have the choice of saying your safe word and walking away. If you choose not to, you will do as I say and there will be no argument. I top you both, but Finn tops you as well, Danielle. Do you understand?"

Sort of. Between Lexi and the Internet, she'd done a whole lot of research this afternoon. It meant she had two Masters. The thought sent a shiver of arousal through her.

Julian stood and moved to her. His hands went to her breasts, flicking at her ridiculously hard nipples. "I can see by your tight nipples that you do. Now Finn and I have been talking. He has a safe word, and I believe he understands the boundaries. I'm in charge, but he has the right to discipline you if you step out of line. I intend to play out a scene with the two of you tonight. This scene will more than likely involve Finn and I having sexual contact. Will that bother you?"

Julian's hand slid into her thong. He chuckled as his fingers easily moved through her ripe and wet pussy. Dani shuddered, her hands coming up to brace herself.

A ridiculously sexy smile crossed his handsome face. "Finn, I believe our small-town girl has exotic tastes. If the state of her pussy is any indication, she has no problem with this scene of ours."

"Y'all planned this?" The thought of the two men talking about how to pleasure her, how to be together, warmed her in a way that wasn't all sexual.

Julian leaned over and his lips brushed her forehead, an oddly sweet gesture. "Oh, yes, though our careful planning was interrupted by your attempt to decapitate your ex-fiancé. If this doesn't go as well as it should, it will be your fault."

"You should add another couple of swats for that." Finn sounded hoarse.

"Perhaps I shall. And to yours as well, Finn. Now go clean yourself up. If you don't hurry, you'll miss Danielle's punishment."

The bathroom door slammed before she could turn to watch Finn go.

"Why are you doing this?" She had to know.

Julian shrugged, and for the first time this evening, seemed less than all-powerful. "Perhaps I'm simply magnanimous. I see that the two of you want each other quite badly, but it can't work if you're both too afraid to try. Finn has spent years longing for you. I suspect it has been the same with you. Neither of you understand your own needs. Off with the boots and that strip of fabric covering my property."

He was talking about her pussy. She knew she should protest, but her hands didn't seem to have a problem with it. They moved as though of their own accord, shoving the soaked thong off her hips. She stood in front of him fully naked.

"Excellent. We'll begin your formal training. When I ask you to present yourself to me, you will find the nearest flat surface and place your hands palms down on it, lifting your ass high in the air. Do it now, Danielle."

On trembling limbs, she walked to the dresser and did as he asked. She felt unbelievably vulnerable as she moved into the position. Then she felt a big warm hand run the length of her spine, and she let herself sigh at the contact.

"Spread your legs further apart. I require access to you."

She took a long, calming breath then did as he asked. "Is that better?"

"No talking. I'll let you know what I want from you." His hands cupped the cheeks of her ass. "I'm going to push you tonight. I'm going to challenge your boundaries. This is as much for Finn's sake as it is for yours."

Oh, she wanted to talk. She wanted to ask a hundred questions, but she bit her lip and stared forward. She watched in the mirror as he inspected her. His hands ran all over her skin, and his eyes missed nothing.

"Very good, Danielle. I know you're curious, but you followed the rules, so I'll share a bit with you. Finn believes, mistakenly to my mind, that you will never be able to accept what he needs in a relationship."

She heard Julian opening a drawer in the nightstand. She heard the sound of a package being opened but didn't turn around. He came back into view carrying something pink and a tube of lubricant. Dani had to force herself to breathe. She had an awful suspicion about what he intended to do with that pink piece of plastic.

The grin on his face was slightly sadistic. "Never had a plug up this sweet ass before, have you? I thought not. Well, you should get used to it." He set the plug on the small of her back. He poured lube down the crack of her ass, parting her cheeks. "You'll soon discover I have a certain sick obsession with assholes. I like to fuck them. This should stretch you a bit, to accommodate me."

She felt a weird pressure as Julian began to press the plug against her anus. She couldn't help but whimper as he ruthlessly pushed the plug against her asshole.

"Yes, I love that sound, Danielle."

She looked up at the mirror. Julian's eyes were heavily lidded, his mouth slightly open. The picture of decadence. The door to the bathroom opened and Finn walked out. He stopped at the scene before him.

"Holy shit."

"She's taking the plug quite nicely, Finn," Julian commented. "Press out against the pressure, dear."

She didn't want to. It felt foreign and painful. Yet she found herself flattening her back and allowing Julian to slide the offending material deep inside her body.

"Very nice." Julian pulled her cheeks even further apart, as though showing off his work. "Perhaps tomorrow we can move her up to a larger plug. In a few days, she should be able to handle a cock."

Larger plug? Dani felt her whole body flush. They were looking at her asshole. It was…really getting her hot. What the hell was wrong with her?

"But for now, we should get to the punishment portion of the evening," Julian announced. "Do you need a gag, little one?"

Her head came up to lock eyes with Julian in the mirror. A gag? How bad was this going to get? "I don't know."

"I would rather not use one. I enjoy your whimpers but screaming could bring unwanted attention. We should save the extremely heavy scenes for places where no one notices a sub crying out."

Dani couldn't help it. She laughed. He said it so seriously, as though it was perfectly normal to find a place where no one could hear her scream. "I bet I can make them notice. I can scream loud, Sir."

A wide smile broke out over his normally closed-off face. It made him seem younger. It brought Dani great joy that she was the one who put it there.

"I look forward to it. But for tonight, please indulge me. Little whimpers and mewling cries will get your Master hard and ready to fuck. If you manage a pretty tear or two, oh, I can't tell you what that will do to my cock, love."

Finn's mouth came open. "You're a sadistic bastard."

Julian shrugged. "I thought that was obvious. Do I need to wear a button? Or one of those *Hello, My Name is…* badges?"

She frowned and turned her head back. Was Finn ready to bolt? Her arousal dimmed as she felt the weight of Finn's stare on her backside. Maybe this was a bad idea. What Julian made seem normal and almost loving was counter to everything she'd been taught. Nice girls didn't accept anal plugs and call their lovers Sir.

Julian walked straight up to Finn and sank his fingers into Finn's thick, dark hair. He pushed Finn to his knees, a completely feral expression on his face. "Do you have any idea what you did to her? You prissy fuck. She was perfectly happy until you set your ridiculous morality on her. There is no right or wrong in this room. There is only what works. You think she can't handle your sexuality? You're the one who has a problem with it, Finn. Tell me something. Why is your cock hard? I see it straining against the fly of your jeans. Is it hard because you want to spank her sweet ass?"

She watched as Finn swallowed once and then again. He didn't fight Julian's hold. He was on his knees with Julian above him. They made a gorgeous picture.

"No. That's not it, Sir."

"Then what is making you hard, Finn? I suspect it's not the idea of disciplining Danielle. I suspect you want to be disciplined yourself."

Finn's head nodded, though there was almost shame in the gesture.

Julian let Finn's head fall forward. He sighed. "You're not ready. Go. I won't have you infecting Danielle with your ideals. She's more open and accepting of her nature than you are. You're the problem here, not Danielle." He turned to her. "Who is not in the position I left her in."

Dani turned quickly and got back into position. The plug filled her ass and jangled against her nerves every time she moved.

"I don't want to go," Finn stated, his voice sounding small.

"I...want this. I just...it's hard. I want so many things that place me on the outside. I'm always on the fucking outside."

Julian sighed. "You are only on the outside because you're trying to fit into your idea of the normal world. The world is what you make it, Finn. There are as many worlds as there are people. This is your world. You are the only one who can force yourself out of it. Now, Danielle and I would like to play. If you can properly submit, you are welcome to stay. I suggest you take your clothes off and join Danielle. I can get all of the discipline out of the way, and we can move on to the portion of the night where we take care of each other in more pleasurable ways."

Dani waited, breath held in, as Finn slowly stood. He stared at her. She could see the longing in his eyes. He slanted a glance at Julian as well. That was pure lust. She couldn't miss that. Finn seemed to reach some decision, and his hands quickly tackled the fly of his jeans. She watched as they hit the floor. No underwear for Finn, just a big hard cock. Holy cow. He was gorgeous. Finn was naked, and there was no hiding how beautiful he was. Broad shoulders led to a tapered waist and washboard abs. He was chiseled to perfection.

"Stop." Julian issued the order, and Finn stopped on command.

As he had with her, Julian carefully inspected Finn. He ran his hands along Finn's skin, no expression on his face. He traced a line from Finn's chin all the way down, through the valley of his chest, past his navel, all the way down to his cock. Julian took that hard cock in his hand, stroking, pumping. Finn's eyes closed, but not before she saw the pleasure there.

"You'll do nicely, Finn. You're beautiful, too. Now, take your place beside Danielle. Ass in the air."

There was no hesitation this time. Finn jumped to do Julian's bidding. He was beside her in a heartbeat. His hand brushed against hers. Their eyes met.

"I love you, Dani."

He whispered the words. Dani let their pinky fingers tangle together.

"I have a plug up my ass," she whispered with a grin. It was so much better because she was exploring this world with him, with her best friend, her love. They would explore what Julian had to offer.

"What's he gonna shove up yours?"

The tense look on Finn's face disappeared, and a wide grin took its place. "I have a feeling it's going to be bigger than your plug."

"No talking. I normally don't do this, but the two of you look sweet together. Finn, I don't have another plug handy, though I doubt you need one. Is your ass used to taking a pounding?"

Finn flushed, but she winked at him, trying to let him know that she accepted all of him, his past, his present, god she wanted a future. "Yes, Sir. I'm more than ready for you, Sir."

"Excellent. Twenty swats apiece. No talking unless I give you express permission, is that understood? No count is required this evening."

She nodded at the man in the mirror. He'd taken his shirt off and stood behind them in nothing but his slacks. His long, dark hair had come out of its queue and fell around his shoulders. He pulled back the paddle.

Thwack. The sound rang through the small room. Dani hissed at the pain that spread across her ass. The plug lit up every nerve in her rectum, making her eyes water with a weird sort of jagged pleasure. There was no mistaking the bite of pain, but she felt her muscles clench around the plug, desperate to keep it in.

Finn's fingers wound around hers as Julian continued the torture. He smacked her ass over and over. The wide paddle was different than his hand. He struck hard and fast. Unlike her previous spanking, he concentrated on her ass. There was no moving, merely the quick strike of hard paddle against soft flesh.

It hurt. There was no doubt about that. She cried. Tears flowed down her face, but all the while her pussy was throbbing and her heart seemed to open up as though a pressure valve had been turned and she was releasing all the bad stuff that had happened. Her breasts dangled, jiggling with each and every swat. By the time Julian brought the paddle down for the last time, a nice floaty feeling had started to take the place of the hot pain.

His hand caressed the cheeks of her ass, and a single finger found its way to her weeping pussy.

"Yes, that's what we both want. Do you have any idea how much this pleases me? You're ripe and ready for me, but it has to wait.

Kneel down on the bed and watch Finn's punishment. Don't lose that plug, Danielle. I'll find something bigger if you do."

She moved gingerly to follow his directions. Her ass was still on fire, and now her pussy ached. She wanted to beg Julian to take her, but she was curious. She wanted to watch them together. She knelt on the bed, careful to clench her ass cheeks together.

"Do you understand why I'm punishing you, Finn?"

"Sort of," Finn replied. "I shouldn't have started that fight. Dani could have gotten hurt."

"You could have gotten hurt, too. It is my responsibility to keep you both safe. That is part of the reason. The other part is that it's my responsibility to give you what you need. I believe you need this."

Julian's hand reared back, and the paddle struck Finn's muscled ass with vicious force. She gasped as Finn groaned, and his head fell forward. Julian struck again and again. This couldn't be what he'd done to her. Her ass was still sore, but Finn's was bright red. She could see tears dripping from his eyes, and his bottom lip was ground between his teeth. His guttural groans filled the room as Julian beat his ass over and over again. When it was finally over, Finn slumped forward. He would have hit the floor had Julian not caught him, his big arms going around Finn's middle.

Dani held her breath.

Finn's eyes opened, and a slightly loopy grin crossed his face.

"Did you come, sub?" Julian's gaze was fast on Finn's cock.

"No, Sir, but it was a close thing."

"That was good, Finn. For a beginner. Lie down, face-first. I'll treat you to some aftercare."

Finn stretched out beside her and sighed. "I think I'm going to like aftercare, Dani."

Dani stroked his head. She thought she would like it, too.

* * * *

Julian fumbled through the drawers in the bathroom before checking himself. He was behaving quite out of sorts. He caught a glimpse of himself in the mirror. His hair was wild around his face, and there was a slightly desperate look in his eyes he didn't recognize.

Wrong. He did recognize it. It had simply been far too long since he'd seen that expression on his own face. Want. He wanted. Quite desperately. It had been so long since he really wanted sex. Sex was a pleasure, for sure, but it was a transitory thing. It was a bodily function. One did not long deep down for a bodily function.

He breathed deeply and forced himself to focus on the matter at hand. His subs had taken their discipline with grace, and the Master owed them his tender care. He calmly opened the drawers and found what he needed. A small tube of salve lay there along with other first aid items. Of course, Jackson would stock this place thoughtfully. As naughty as Samuel could be, Jackson would need to be ready to discipline him at all times. He rather thought Finn would be that way as well, though his Danielle was far more obedient than Abigail. He was surprised to discover he trusted Danielle. He'd seen the way her whole soul had sagged under the weight of Finn's ridiculous shame. She was an accepting woman, tolerant beyond what most people understood, and yet the very thing that made her so attractive to Julian also made her vulnerable to shame. She needed to please those around her. She needed to fit in. It was his job to take that need and focus it. She would be trained to please her Master, herself, and those she truly loved. Everyone else would be secondary. Danielle's first loyalty would be to him and Finn.

Fuck. When had he started to think that way? An odd sense of irritation gnawed at him. He didn't have a contract with them. He'd practically promised Jackson he wouldn't push for a contract for at least a week. They hadn't gone through any of his processes. McKay-Taggart hadn't run a background check on them. His physician hadn't checked them out. He hadn't sent either one to Leo to be cleared on a psychological level. He always did that now—after Jeremy.

That was a thought to hold on to. Jeremy was the perfect poster boy for why he shouldn't walk back into that room. He should call Jackson and have him finish the aftercare. He should pack his things, head home, and begin proper procedures to find proper slaves. Two. One male and one female. That was the problem. After the incident with Jeremy, he'd kept Sally alone for far longer than he should have.

That was why Finn had gotten to him. He needed a man. Danielle was special. She was a natural submissive with a sweet disposition who still managed to have a backbone. It was a perfect combination of the traits he found attractive. Seeing the way they looked at each other, he knew that in order to keep Danielle, he would have to take Finn on as well.

Or did he? He could take her from her friend. She was far too curious. Finn had hurt her. All it would take was a few well-placed words, some kindly logic, and Julian could drive off with Danielle. She would follow him because he was the first Dominant man to truly show an interest in her. The key would be to keep them away from each other. If he allowed Finn no sexual contact with Danielle, they couldn't bond further.

He really was a sadistic son of a bitch.

"Sir."

Julian started at the sound of Danielle's voice. She stood there with a sheet wrapped around her lush form. Her lips were made for kissing, and for taking a man's cock in between them. Her bright blue eyes were large and trusting as she looked up at him. His cock tightened. *Walk away.*

"You were gone for a while. I was worried."

She really was. He could see it in her face. She cared about him. She was on the precipice of falling in love with him. He felt a little sick at the thought that there was no contract between them. He had no real rights to her or Finn. There were no boundaries. There was nothing to tell them how to act or to inform them exactly how much he was willing to give. There was nothing to stop them from walking out…

Julian felt his heart clench. He couldn't breathe. He shoved the salve at Danielle and pushed past her. "Rub that on Finn's abrasions. He'll probably need some form of analgesic. Jackson should have some. I'll send him up in a moment. He'll take care of you both."

He needed to get dressed. He needed to leave before the damn walls closed in on him.

"Julian?" Finn sat up from his reclining position. His handsome face was open with worry and confusion. He winced as his ass hit the bedding. He was on his feet quickly. "Is something wrong?"

They were both looking at him with that wide-eyed innocence that kicked him in the gut every single time.

"Did I do something wrong?" Finn's voice suddenly sounded very small to Julian's ears.

"No, sweetie. It wasn't you." Danielle was at Finn's side. She clung to the sheet wrapped around her breasts, but her free hand smoothed over his shoulders. "It's fine. Julian changed his mind. That's all. It'll be okay."

"I'm sorry, Dani." Finn was talking to only her now. They turned in toward each other. Though he couldn't see it, Julian could almost feel a wall being closed around them. Like they were the only people in the world.

"Like I said, I'll send Jackson up. He knows what to do." Jackson would see them like this. Jackson would be the one to care for them. Though he knew Jackson would never take advantage of them, a savage part of Julian rebelled at the idea of him coming in here at all. "Get dressed before he comes up."

Danielle shook her head, her shoulders squaring. "Don't send him. I'll take care of Finn, and he can take care of me. That's the way it's always been, always will be."

Well, he'd sent Danielle right back into Finn's arms. She was already directing him to lie down. Julian picked up his shirt. It was wrinkled. He hadn't had one of them take care of his clothes the way he normally would. He stood there for a moment, watching them. Dani tried to get Finn into the proper position, but she was obviously struggling with her own tender ass and the plug. Would Finn be able to get the plug out? Would he have to call Jackson? He couldn't stand the thought of Jackson's hands on Danielle. It made him...very angry.

"We'll be fine, Julian." Danielle sounded distant. All that softness and warmth seemed to be reserved for Finn now. When she turned to him, there was a dullness to her eyes, as though she was looking right through him. He'd been utterly dismissed.

As he'd dismissed her.

If he walked out, he wouldn't be allowed back in. He could fool himself into thinking that he could have access to these two whenever he liked it. He was the Dom. They were the subs. They were supposed to accept what he wanted to give. Unfortunately, the exchange only worked if the subs trusted the Dom. The subs had to love the Dom, even a little. If he walked out, Danielle would place him in a long line of people who took advantage of her nature.

"Move out of the way, Danielle. You need it, too. Lie down beside him." Julian allowed the shirt to drop once more. He would have to train them to see to his clothes, but now was not the time. Now he had to repair the damage his waffling had caused.

"I don't think…" Danielle began.

"That's right, Dani, don't think." Finn's head came up, and Julian was surprised at the grin on his face. He gave Julian a beatific look and patted the place beside him. "Lie down with me and let the Dom take care of us. This is supposed to be our time. At least, that's the way it was explained to me."

Julian felt something calm come over him as he realized Finn was accepting him. That odd irritation that could only be described as jealousy drifted away. He walked to Danielle and cupped her cheek. She stared up warily.

"One spanking and Finn is an expert. Danielle, I did not give you leave to cover your body. When we're alone, you're to be naked for me." He pulled at the simple knot she had fashioned, and the sheet hit the floor.

She looked up at him. "You were going to leave us."

"And now I'm not."

Dani frowned but was smart enough not to attempt to cover herself again. "You can't just…"

"Dani, come on, baby. Give the man some time. He's here now. Can't we just enjoy it?" Finn practically pleaded with her.

Julian decided to take a different tactic. If he was staying, it would be on his terms. He thrust a hand into Danielle's thick blonde hair and hauled her up against his body. The minute he made contact, she softened against him. "Danielle, you will do as I tell you or take your place for further punishment."

A stubborn expression took up residence on her face. "So I don't get an explanation of what happened?"

"Not tonight." He wasn't going to have a long, drawn-out discussion about this. He had zero intentions of exposing himself. He was opening himself as much as he could right now. "Do as I say or use your safe word."

"Can't you see how unfair that is?" She wasn't giving in.

"I never said it was fair." That restless feeling was back. What exactly did she want from him?

"How do I know you won't take what you want from us and walk out?"

He finally felt her arms go around his waist. This, he could handle. "Because I won't, little one. I promise I will stay with you for the rest of my vacation. You and Finn and I can explore this thing between us, and at the end of the week, we can decide if we wish to continue."

He forced her head back and took great pleasure in looking at her face. She was so soft and open. Even the way she questioned him pleased him on some level. She was willing to fight for herself. He just had to make her understand she didn't need to fight him. Julian let his instincts lead him. He closed his mouth over hers and dominated. He ravaged her, forcing his tongue deep inside. She gasped and then allowed him his way. Her mouth flowered open for him. Her nipples hardened against his chest.

When Julian came up for air, he turned to Finn. Finn was on his knees watching, his eyes moving from Danielle to Julian and back again like a kid who couldn't decide which treat he wanted to eat first.

"Aftercare can wait for a bit, can't it, Finn?" He was ready to play. Perhaps Danielle wasn't the only one who would have her boundaries expanded this evening.

Chapter Eleven

Finn watched Julian's hands move on Dani's lush body and felt his cock harden to the point of pain. *Aftercare? Who the fuck needed aftercare?* He needed something else.

"No, Sir. The aftercare can wait." The voice that came out of his throat sounded almost foreign. It was husky and filled with longing. It was the voice of a man who wasn't ashamed that he wanted both the people in front of him. He loved Dani. He loved her so much, but he wanted Julian.

What was wrong with that as long as Dani was fine?

Since that moment when Julian had forced him to his knees, Finn had thought of nothing but how much damn time he'd wasted. He'd always placed the blame on Dani's tender feelings, but Dani was the strongest woman he knew. Julian was right. Dani wasn't the problem. He was.

"Finn, I believe this pretty sub and I could use your attentions. I'm feeling magnanimous tonight, and a bit curious. I think I would like to watch you fuck our Danielle. Would you like that, little one?"

Dani looked up at Julian, a brilliant smile on her face. Her previous worry seemed to have been washed away with the Master's kiss. She nodded before turning to Finn. "I've always wanted that."

Julian leaned down, and when he kissed her this time, there was no mistaking his tenderness. "On your knees, then. You and Finn take care of me first, and then you may play together."

Wow. His cock twitched. Never in all of his daydreams about being with Dani had he thought about the two of them sucking off a hot guy who would probably be comfortable wearing leather. He'd kind of envisioned her as the one who would save him from...*oh, shit.* He'd thought she'd be the one who could make him not want this. He'd thought she was the one who could make him fucking straightlaced.

Dani stared at him as though she could read his thoughts. Julian pulled her close again, his hands wandering, soothing. He wouldn't let her slide back to that place Finn had almost gotten her to, that place where his shame was more important than desire.

"Finn, it's okay, sweetie," Dani managed, her arms hugging Julian like she used to hug that big pink elephant Finn had won for her. "You don't have to do anything."

He didn't. He could put his clothes on and walk out, and then Dani would remain this perfect, pure dream. *Fuck that.* He didn't want that. He wanted Dani. He wanted her dirty and yet so, so sweet. He held his hand out, and she immediately took it. No hesitation from his girl. It suddenly struck him that maybe he hadn't been waiting for Dani to save him from the decadent road he wanted to go down. Maybe he'd been waiting for her to go down it with him.

He didn't bother to wince at the pain in his ass. It was a warm sensation that he hoped would last for a bit. Even the soreness was oddly pleasant. Yep, he was every bit the freak he'd thought he was.

"On your knees, my slaves."

That dark voice made Finn's cock stand up against his stomach. He wanted to stroke himself, but that was probably not a good idea. He settled for kneeling beside Dani. Her hand came out and stroked his thigh soothingly.

"You may kiss her, Finn. She has the softest lips." Julian gave them both a half smile as his hands went to the fly of his slacks.

He didn't wait. He cupped her face in his palms and pressed his lips to hers. He'd wanted to kiss her so many times, but this time felt right. This time he wasn't risking anything. They couldn't share this experience and walk away. Dani would be with him. He would accept nothing less. He molded his lips to hers. Julian was right. She was so soft. Gently, he requested entrance, running his tongue along the seam of her lips. At the first tentative touch of her tongue, he groaned, and his hands went right where they'd always wanted to go. He touched her breasts. Palms open, he cupped those luscious tits and marveled at how hard the nipples were against his skin. He rolled her nipples between his thumbs and forefingers, pinching a bit. She pressed against him as though requesting more.

God, he was kissing Dani. He was finally kissing Dani.

"Excuse me," Julian interrupted. "I believe you two were going to take care of me before you put on a show."

Dani broke off the kiss, leaning in and wiggling her nose against his in the sweetest way before turning to Julian. Her face was flushed, and she looked like a perfectly naughty schoolgirl. Dani was happy here. Her joy made everything seem right. He looked up at Julian, who towered over them both. He was naked, and Julian Lodge was a testament to masculine beauty. He was ripped everywhere. His long, dark hair hit his shoulders, framing his male model face. And then there was his cock. Damn, he'd never seen a cock so big. It was perfect, with a large, bulging head and a thick stalk that jutted from his pelvis. Big, heavy balls dangled between his muscular legs. Sheer perfection. Julian stared down as though waiting for something.

Top, he remembered. He topped Dani. "Lick him, Dani. Lick the Master's cock."

Dani leaned forward, and her pink tongue came out to swipe at the head of Julian's cock. Julian hissed lightly, and a small smile appeared on his face. He thrust his hand into Dani's hair and pulled her close.

"That's right. Run that tongue all over my cock. It feels so good. Finn, cup my balls."

Finn moved beside Dani, who bobbed up and down, sucking that big dick into her sultry mouth. He vowed he'd feel those lips around his own cock soon. He reached out and cupped the Master's sac, rolling it up, reveling in his groan. Julian's hips pumped. Finn leaned in close to Dani and lent his tongue to her campaign. Julian tasted good, masculine and clean. Dani sucked at the head of that monstrous cock while he licked up and down the stalk.

"Bad boy," Julian growled. "If that didn't feel so fucking good, I would tan your ass again. Switch places now. Finn, take me to the back of your throat. Make me come."

Dani started to lick up and down the sides of the cock they both played with, and he pulled the spongy head into his mouth. He nearly groaned at the salty taste on his tongue. The Master was close, and Finn was sure he could send him over the edge. He drew Julian into his mouth, sucking deeply.

"Danielle, allow Finn to finish." Julian's voice was ragged. "Come up here and kiss me, while I fill our partner's mouth."

Finn felt Dani move, but his whole concentration was spent on the throbbing dick filling his mouth. He softened his jaw and worked up and down on Julian's cock. His tongue rolled across the soft skin while his hand worked the base. He breathed only through his nose, finally managing to get that enormous organ to the back of his throat. When it pressed back and he was sure he couldn't take any more, he swallowed.

Julian groaned as he came. Woodsy, salty. The taste filled Finn's mouth, and he sucked, not wanting to miss a drop of that cream. Julian's hips pumped. His balls hit Finn's chin as he finally ceded every ounce he had.

Finn sat back on his heels, looking up. Julian kissed Dani one last time before stepping back. He slumped into the only chair in the room, a small recliner. He looked relaxed, and there was a happy light in his eyes. "That was exquisite, Finn. You may take your prize."

He was on Dani in a heartbeat. He stood and tossed her to the bed. She hit it with a little groan. Her legs splayed open, and he could see the dainty pink plug wedged high in her asshole. He shoved her legs even further apart. A savage need to get inside her rode roughshod over him, shoving the tenderness out of him.

She fucking belonged to him. Why the hell had he waited?

"Yes, Finn, take her. She can handle it. Take her rough. Take her hard. She'll like it."

Julian's voice was the devil on his shoulder. If there was an angel to balance him out, Finn didn't listen to him. He simply heard Julian's dark chocolate voice reaffirming what he already knew. Dani was his. Oh, they might yet belong to someone. To Julian. But she belonged to

Finn. Always.

"Finn, a condom, please. Danielle isn't on birth control. We'll remedy that after everyone has had a physical."

Condom. His brain wasn't quite working. She was so close all he could think about was getting inside her. He didn't want to wear a condom, but Dani was reaching for one. She passed it to him, and then her fist wrapped around his dick. Her hand stroked him, making his eyes roll to the back of his head.

"Fuck." He tore open the condom and rolled it on. He looked down at her. Dani was spread for his pleasure, her legs apart, her beautiful face wide open with desire. He'd waited for this moment since long before he'd known what sex was. It wasn't just sex. It was love and connection and finally being right with himself because he was a part of her.

"I love you, Dani," he managed to whisper. His throat felt too big.

Her hand came up, touching his cheek. Her lips trembled slightly as she replied. "I love you, too, Finn. Forever."

He took his dick in hand and pushed his way home.

Dani's eyes were wide as he slid into her tight pussy. Her mouth was open in a surprised *O*. "Oh, that feels so good, Finn."

It did. It felt good and right to be deep inside Dani. His friend. His champion. His love. Finn flexed inside that hot, tight pussy and prayed he lasted long enough to get her off. The plug Julian had shoved up her butt took up so much space that her pussy was cramped and snug. Finn thrust in and pulled back, the plug a hard drag on his dick.

Dani's legs came up and around his waist. She shoved her hips up, fucking him as surely as he fucked her. He began to pound inside. The heat, the pressure, everything about Dani sent him headlong into pleasure. He dragged his pelvis, grinding down on her clit. Her face flushed, and her blue eyes became dark orbs as she rushed to her own orgasm. When her pussy began to clench around his dick, Finn gave in. He thrust in over and over, letting the orgasm rush in. He felt broken in that moment. Broken and remade. New.

He fell forward, not bothering to withhold his weight. Dani's arms were around him, and he could smell the soap she'd used. He kissed whatever skin he could find and wrapped his arms around her.

"That was beautiful, pets." Julian's weight made the bed dip as he settled in beside them. Finn sighed as he felt the Master stroke his back. When he looked up, Julian's lips were pressed against Dani's. Finn kissed her breasts. He knew he should be jealous, but it was just another kink now. Besides, it was Julian. None of this would have happened without Julian. Somehow Julian completed them. Finn sighed and reveled in their connection.

* * * *

Dani felt like a completely different person as she walked down the steps and back into The Barn's main room. Of course, she looked like a different person, too. After another raucous bout of sex that had her screaming her orgasm into Julian's chest, he'd ordered her and Finn to shower. Finn had held her and washed every inch of her before drying her off and running a brush through her hair. She'd felt like a princess. Julian had laid out a pair of jeans and a perfectly respectable T-shirt. Apparently Abby kept some clothes here. She'd been informed that her denim miniskirt had managed to walk away all on its own and would likely never be seen again. She'd frowned at him but dressed in the clothes that actually covered her ass anyway.

Now she had one hand tucked into Julian's and the other in Finn's as they made their way down. She knew she should feel self-conscious. Everyone was going to know what she'd been doing, but she couldn't quite work up the will to care. Danielle Bay had two amazing men on her arms, and anyone who had a problem with that could suck it.

Loud country music pounded through the bar. It seemed that every eye did turn directly toward her when they made it to the dance floor. A quiver of excitement started in her chest, warring with a perfectly reasonable embarrassment. She'd done two guys in a room over a bar. It was a little slutty. Okay, it was a lot slutty, but there were all kinds of feelings involved, so that made it okay. There were feelings like deep affection when Julian licked at her clit and the overwhelming love she had for Finn when his cock hit that amazing place deep inside her pussy.

"What on earth is that look for?" Julian stared down at her, his lips pulled up in obvious amusement.

Finn leaned over so he could be heard over the loud music. "I think Dani is enjoying her role as town harlot."

Julian frowned. "Harlot? Why would she be a harlot?"

Dani and Finn laughed together. For the first time, they completely understood something Julian didn't.

"This is a small town, Sir," Finn explained. "All anyone is going to talk about tomorrow is the fact that Dani Bay snuck up the stairs at The Barn with two guys. Trust me, she is going to be called all kinds of names. Mostly to her back, though."

She shrugged. It was to be expected. At least no one would be feeling sorry for her.

Julian's face went dark, and his fingers tightened around hers. "They had better not say anything where I can hear it." He relaxed and nodded down at her. "I'm going to speak with Jackson, dear. You and Finn stay together. We'll be leaving shortly. We'll retrieve Finn's things and go back out to the ranch."

He turned and walked off, supremely confident that his orders would be met.

He turned back suddenly. "And stay out of trouble."

Dani grinned. He didn't look so confident that she would follow that edict. He walked away. She watched his gorgeous ass as it disappeared into the crowd. When she turned, she noticed that Finn was watching, too.

"I'm sorry." Finn pulled back slightly, his hand coming out of hers. That look was back in his eyes.

"Are you going to be an asshole?" she asked.

"What?"

"I thought we worked through this, but it looks like you're going to be an asshole." She wasn't putting up with it. Maybe she would have before but being with them had changed her.

Being with Julian and Finn together seemed to have altered something fundamental in Dani. It had been beautiful. She'd never felt as deeply as she did when they were kissing her, loving her. There had been that terrible moment when she was sure Julian was leaving, but he'd stayed. He had to care about her. He cared, and Finn cared.

She wasn't going to let anyone take that away from her or make her feel ashamed. That was hers.

Finn stared almost blankly and then shook his head. "I'm sorry. I spent so long trying to hide this from you."

"Hide what? That I knew you were gay? I was well aware of that. Why did you get upset because I caught you drooling over Julian's ass?"

His eyes slid down. "Damn it, Dani. This is why I stayed away. I knew it should be only the two of us, but I wasn't sure I could do it. I'm not sure I can stay away from men."

Julian was shaking his head at Jack, who seemed to be teasing him something fierce. Dani stared at him for a moment. She noticed she wasn't the only one. All around her, other women had their eyes on the hot new guy. They could look, but Julian was hers. He might not know it, but she planned on keeping him. And Finn. As soon as they ironed out a few things.

"And it never occurred to you to say, hey, Dani, here's the problem. Let's see if we can solve it? No, you decide to keep your mouth shut and almost let me marry someone I didn't love because you didn't want to admit you're bi."

"Damn it, I didn't want to lose you. I love you, Danielle. You're the only thing in my life that's permanent. I would rather keep you in my life than lose you because I can't be normal. It should be two people. A marriage should be two people."

Oh, yes, she had to fix his way of thinking. "Says who? The old biddies at church? Screw them. Why does everything have to be one way? What we did up there didn't hurt anyone. It isn't anyone's business but ours. I love you, Finn, but I think I'm falling for Julian, too. Can you handle that?"

"I can certainly try, baby. I was willing to love you from afar. I prefer loving you up close." He seemed tentative, but his hand went around her waist. "God, Dani, I loved fucking you."

She leaned into him. "I loved it, too."

His hand trailed down her ass right there in the middle of the bar. "How's the...you know? I know it seems rough, but Julian's right. It will, you know, prepare you and stuff."

She felt a slow smile slide across her face. Finn's voice had gone all husky and deep, as though he was thinking about what that plug in her ass was preparing her for. By the end of the week, Julian and Finn intended to take her together. Julian would fuck her ass while Finn took her pussy. It made her shiver.

"I'm looking forward to it, too," she whispered.

He kissed her cheek, and that momentary lapse of his seemed to be gone. Which was a good thing because she saw someone they needed to talk to. Now that she'd been fucked and loved into a more magnanimous state, she was ready to deal with the guy nursing a beer at the bar. "Come on, Finn. We have to talk to Jimbo."

Finn stopped, all arousal gone now. "I don't think that's a good idea. Julian told us to stay out of trouble."

She shrugged. "I don't intend to start trouble. I'm just going to talk to him."

"Oh, yeah. I bet that's what you said the last time, right before you started tossing hardware at his brain."

"Oh, no. I always intended to chuck something at his head the last time. Now I am calmer and more mature."

Finn snorted. "You've matured in the last hour?"

"Well, my ass is still sore. I'm going to try to avoid another spanking tonight. I've also seen some of the stuff they keep in the guesthouse out at the ranch. I would prefer to avoid that as well, for now." When she wasn't so sore, they could play around on the benches and other stuff. But for now, she had to get to the bottom of something. "Come on. We're going to talk to him. That's all."

Finn groaned but followed her. So much for him topping her. That was the only part of the evening that had rankled slightly. Oh, she didn't mind it in bed, but she would be damned if Finn told her what to do out of it. Julian was another story. The clothes she had on proved that. It wasn't that she would blindly follow him, but deep down Julian needed that control. It was essential to him, so she was willing to give it up. Finn had no such need.

"Dani, he's going to kill us."

She decided to be deliberately obtuse as she pushed her way through the crowd. "Nah, Jimbo isn't the killing kind. He's too lazy for that."

"I wasn't talking about Jimbo."

But now that she thought about it, it was true. Jimbo might be selfish and a little oafish, but he wasn't vindictive. She could see him putting her stuff out on the lawn, but could she honestly see him dousing it in gasoline and torching it?

"Hello, Jimbo." She held her ground as Finn sort of bumped into her.

Jimbo looked up and started. His hands came up. "Now, Dani, see here. I ain't gonna take another beating from you."

She held her hands out to prove she was perfectly unarmed. "I came to apologize."

Jimbo sat back, a wary look on his face. "You sure? Cause my head still hurts from the last time you came to apologize."

"Sorry. I was upset."

"I got that. You've been upset for a couple of days."

He hadn't been a horrible boyfriend. He simply hadn't been close to what she needed, and maybe the same could be said for her. "I know. I am genuinely sorry about the wedding. I couldn't go through with it."

He gave her a sad half smile. "I know. You don't love me. You always loved Finn. I'm glad he got his dick out of some guy's ass long enough to see what was standing in front of him."

"Hey, I'm right here." Finn stepped forward.

"Yes, you are, sweetie." She wrapped her arm around his waist.

Jimbo tipped his hat back and looked at them for a moment. His eyes held Finn's. "You get her out of this town. I don't give a shit where you put your dick as long you keep it in your pants around me."

"Like I would." Finn's eyes rolled.

Jimbo grinned. "Oh, I know all you gay boys want a piece of this. How can anyone resist my manly presence?" He got serious again. "But, you gotta get her out of here. The people of this town, they're gonna make her life hell. You two hitch your wagon to that rich boy and ride right on out of town."

She sighed because she'd been totally wrong. "You didn't burn my stuff, did you?"

He shook his head and took another swig of his beer. "Hell, no. I ain't about to hurt anyone like that. I know I can be a jerk, but I wouldn't do nothing like that. If I were you, I would look closer to home, if you know what I mean."

Oh, she knew what he meant. The betrayal hit her squarely in the chest.

"Val?" Dani asked, but she knew the answer.

"Val wouldn't." Finn didn't sound at all sure.

But she would. Her little sister had been nasty before, but the last couple of months she'd been sweet. Val had been the one to prod her into marrying Jimbo. She'd pushed for a date and helped with all the arrangements. She thought she and her sister had been making some progress. Now she could see Val had merely wanted her gone. And now that she thought about it, maybe Val hadn't been so sweet during her engagement. More than once, Val had hovered around Jimbo. A dozen tiny incidents added up to one huge betrayal. Maybe he *had* been a horrible boyfriend.

"How many times did you sleep with my sister?" She asked the question before she chickened out.

Even in the dim light of the bar, she could see the way Jimbo blanched. Finn tensed behind her, his hand coming to the nape of her neck, a soothing reminder that whatever Jimbo said, Finn was with her.

"A whole bunch of times," Jimbo admitted with a long sigh. "I'm sorry. I couldn't seem to give you what you needed, and she was real good at making me feel like a man."

She found she wasn't all that upset with Jimbo. The whole relationship had been a mistake on both their parts.

"Julian turned her down," Finn whispered in her ear.

He had. And Julian would never go behind her back. Despite his kinks and outward coolness, there was a warm honesty to Julian. If he decided he wanted to sleep with someone else, he would more than likely sit down and lay out the ground rules. He wouldn't lie about it.

"Where is my sister?" It was time to talk to her baby sis.

Jimbo pointed to the door. "She left with some skinny guy a while back. I ain't seen him before. I wouldn't expect her back until morning."

Then her talk with Val would have to wait.

"Danielle."

Wow, that voice got to her. She turned in tandem with Finn to see that Julian had come for them. "Are you ready to go?"

Julian looked between the two of them and Jimbo, as though assessing the situation. "Have you said what you need to say?"

"Yes, Sir."

"Then let's call it a night." He held out his hand, and Dani waved good-bye to Jimbo before taking it.

"I'm very proud of you. You managed a conversation with your ex-fiancé without any violence." He led the three of them through the crowded bar and out into the night.

"Yes, I'm saving my violence for my sister," she admitted as they walked through the parking lot.

Now Finn took the lead, his hands on his keys. He led them to his SUV. Julian had come with Jack, Sam, and Abby. Finn would have to drive them. "It's about time someone took her out. She's been terrorizing the world since she hit high school. She was Medusa in a cheerleader skirt."

"Yes, I do believe that the younger Miss Bay is more than likely due a bit of retribution. I'll consider it." Julian opened the back door and gestured for her to get inside.

She had no intention of allowing Julian to decide whether or not she had it out with her sister, but now probably wasn't the best time to fight about it. Her ass was still tender as she sat down. Finn opened his door and slid in, but Julian left the passenger door closed. He got in beside Danielle. He immediately pulled her into his lap.

"Is my poor little one's backside still sore?" He whispered the words directly into her ear, sending shivers down her spine.

"Yes, Sir."

His hand slid over her knee. "That's what happens when you disobey the big, bad Dom, Danielle. He does all sorts of nasty things to you. He might tie you down and force himself on you. You wouldn't want that, would you? You wouldn't want the big, bad Dom to take a whip to all that soft flesh before he fucks you senseless, would you?"

Did she? Hell, yeah she did. She was thinking about disobeying right now.

"That might have to wait, guys." Finn didn't sound aroused.

Finn's voice was quiet, thin, and reedy. Even from the backseat, she could see that Finn was tense. His eyes were focused on the seat beside him. "We have company."

That was when she heard it. It started low, but quickly made a sound every Texas girl knew meant trouble.

Rattlesnake.

Chapter Twelve

Finn tried to keep his entire body perfectly still. It was hard, since what he really wanted to do was run away screaming like a five-year-old girl. Instead, he froze as that fucking awful sound continued. That sound seemed like the only thing real in the whole world. Time seemed to slow, to grind to a halt. The very air felt frozen as he forced himself to breathe.

It sat perfectly coiled on the seat beside him. How had he missed that? How had he climbed in next to a fucking rattlesnake and not noticed? He'd been focused on Dani and Julian, wishing he didn't have to play chauffeur. He'd wanted to be back there with them. He hadn't noticed a thing until he looked down to turn on the radio, and then he'd heard that sound.

"Finn, I want you to stay completely still." Julian's voice was steady, a calm, quiet anchor reaching out to him.

"On it, Sir." He forced himself to reply, pushing the words out of his mouth and past his clenched jaw. It reminded him that he wasn't alone.

He stared at the snake, afraid to take his eyes off of it even for a second. God, he didn't want that thing to stick its fangs into him. He wished he hadn't parked under a damn light. It might have been easier if he couldn't see the thing. It sat there with dead, primeval eyes. He remembered everything his grandfather ever told him about snakes. They were supposedly more scared of him than he was of them. Bullshit. He was really fucking scared, and that snake looked perfectly happy. Maybe not happy, but certainly content. It also looked ready. Its diamond-shaped head was standing up, taking in its prey. It was waiting for him to make one wrong move. Just one.

Julian's voice broke through the tension. "Danielle, as carefully as you can, I want you to get out of the car. I want you to climb out, run back to the bar, and go find Jackson and Abigail Barnes."

The back door creaked slightly as Julian pushed it open. *Please. Please.* He prayed the motion didn't make the snake strike.

"I can't leave Finn." Dani sounded terrified.

He was willing to bet there were already tears running down her face. He had to stay calm for her. He had to keep it together for her sake, or she might do something foolish. It wouldn't be the first time she'd tried to save his ass.

He remembered vividly the day when he'd sprained his ankle. They'd been out at the swamp about a mile from Dani's house. They were ten, and he'd misjudged the sturdiness of the tree he'd been climbing. He fell at least twelve feet to the hard earth below. It was just before dark, and he'd been terrified of all the things that came out at night in the swamps of East Texas. Dani had carried him all the way home. She carried him through the mud and the dark. Her slender form had been strong enough, his weight no match for her will.

God, he loved her.

"Dani, you get out of here now. I mean it." He couldn't stand the thought of her being hurt. If he let her, she'd put herself between him and the snake. That was not happening.

The car shifted, but only slightly, as Dani turned to get out. Finn let his eyes shift to get a glimpse of her blonde hair as she got off Julian's lap and slid out of the car. When her feet touched the ground, she stumbled slightly and reached out to stabilize herself.

"Danielle." Julian's voice was a warning.

She caught herself, but the car moved slightly. It was enough.

The snake struck. Pain lashed like lightning on and up Finn's arm. It happened so fast. He only got a second's sight of the snake's fangs before the pain hit. The snake recoiled like a boxer going back to his corner. Finn had no intention of going another round. He cursed a blue streak and got the hell out of the car, tumbling to the ground. There was no delicate movement, just an insane need to get away. He hit the ground on his back, all the air rushing out of his chest.

"Go, now, Danielle," Julian shouted.

No need for quiet now. The world seemed very loud to Finn. Car doors slammed. People started to shout. There was a flash of bright light as he looked up at the street lamp, and then he felt his peripheral vision fading. Everything got foggy. All he could see were the twin holes on his forearm, and a mixture of blood and a weird, almost urine-like substance oozing out. It seemed so small for it to hurt that much. He tried to lift his arm, but movement failed him.

"Stay calm." Julian forced him to sit up. Julian pulled and prodded him until he was upright. "I've trapped the snake in the car. It won't bite you again. You have to stay calm. We need to keep your heart rate down, and I can't do that if you panic."

"Been snake bit much?" Somehow he couldn't see Julian as an outdoorsman. He groaned as his arm fell off his lap and hit the dirt of the parking lot. A strange almost metallic taste seemed to fill his mouth. Blood. He was biting his lip against the pain. He tried to force himself to relax.

"Not once, and I am grateful for that." Julian got in behind him, lending strength as he buoyed him.

Fuck, his arm hurt, but worse, a part of it was starting to go numb. His whole body started to shake.

Julian's arms came around him. "It's going to be okay. Danielle will be back in a moment. Abigail is a nurse. She'll know what to do, how to prep you for transport. We'll get you to a hospital."

Abby Barnes came running out of the bar. There was no mistaking her determination, even from Finn's distance. The pretty woman who seemed so soft and carefree had a ferociously competent look on her face. Her husbands were running right after her, but only Dani was managing to keep up. She ran next to Abby. Her mascara trailing down her face, making rivers of black where she'd been crying.

Abby fell to her knees beside him and immediately took his arm in her small hands. She briskly waved Julian's hands away, forcing

Finn's arm down. He winced at the pain as she examined him.

"Hey," Julian began.

Abby cut him off. "I need to get the bite below his heart, Julian. Let me do my job. This isn't my first rodeo. Sam, find something I can wrap Finn's arm in. I need something flexible. And get some short boards for a splint. I need to compress the lymph nodes around the bite. Then I need you to get the truck started. We can get him to the hospital faster than an ambulance at this point."

"What do you need from me, darlin'?" Jack asked, staring down, obviously willing to concede any and all control to his wife at this point.

"Jack, you get that damn snake. We need to know what kind it is." Abby Barnes was in charge. She looked down at his arm. "Unless you know the species. That would be helpful."

"Well," he began, gritting his teeth through the pain, "it was a snake with rattles, so I think it's safe to assume it was a rattlesnake."

Abby was not amused. She frowned down at him. "What kind of rattler? There are ten kinds in the state of Texas. This is important."

Dani was biting her lip as she looked down at him. "Please, Finn, they need to know what antivenin to give you."

"I don't know. It was whichever one had the biggest mouth and the evilest eyes. I didn't ask it for its contact information." Damn, Abby was poking and prodding. Every single touch hurt like hell, and now he was feeling nauseous. He didn't want to throw up, but he wasn't sure he could avoid it. Couldn't she let him die in peace?

"It's an eastern timber," Jack stated plainly.

Bile rose like acid in Finn's throat when he saw that the big cowboy had the damn thing in his hands. What the hell was he thinking? It twitched and rattled, and he held it like it was a kid's toy.

Jack held the head between his thumb and forefinger, locking down the jaw. "Good size, too. Bet that hurt like hell, Finn. Don't worry. We got an hour or two before it kills you. Last time I got bit, I managed to finish the fence I was working on before my hand went too numb. Baby, should I keep this one alive?"

Abby smiled up at him. "I think the hospital would appreciate it, Jack. They can always use antivenin."

Dani took his gone-numb hand in hers. "It's okay. I promise it's going to be okay."

He rested back against Julian's chest and let himself give in to the darkness that overtook him.

* * * *

Julian's footsteps echoed as he paced the empty halls of the ER, and the florescent light made everything slightly green. He wished the hospital was larger. It was almost a clinic. Would they give Finn the best care possible? He was surprised and a bit upset at the utter panic he'd felt at the thought of losing Finn. When he'd heard the snake rattle, he hadn't been afraid for himself. He'd seen Finn and Dani being hurt, and it sent a shock through his system. He'd truly only known Finn for a day, but what they'd shared had affected him. He understood Finn on a fundamental level. He'd felt very much the same way as Finn, always on the outside looking in. He'd been there. It was an honor to begin to lead the man on the path that would make him whole.

It had even been an easy decision to allow Finn access to Danielle. In the end, he hadn't been able to help himself. They wanted each other so much. Years of longing had been etched on their faces as they huddled together, waiting for his discipline. He'd been the one to give them that, to give them a way to finally be together. He'd watched the way Finn had taken her, desperately, as though he was starving and had been forever.

Julian had felt the same way as he watched them. He'd wanted to join them. The impulse had been almost overwhelming. He'd wanted to force Finn to turn Danielle over and offer that sweet ass up to him. He'd wanted to feel the slide of Finn's hard cock against his as they took Danielle together. He'd wanted to be a part of them.

"Hey, I thought you could use this." Jackson held out a Styrofoam cup of coffee.

He didn't need coffee. He needed a fifth of Scotch. Simply standing around in a hospital was making him antsy. He took the proffered coffee anyway. It gave him something to do with his hands. "What is Finn's status?"

It had already been an hour and he hadn't heard anything yet. It rankled. He wasn't in control. He'd started to argue, but Abigail had interceded and explained that the nurses wouldn't be intimidated. Nurses would simply call security, and before he would be able to buy the hospital and fire them all, Finn would either be well or dead, and Julian would have wasted his time. He believed her. For the first time in a long time, he'd been forced to back down. The doctors had been insistent on only one of them staying with Finn while he received treatment. Danielle's hand hadn't left Finn's free one all during the long night. He hadn't been able to force Danielle from his side. The fact that he was on the outside gnawed at his gut.

Jackson slapped him on the back. "Don't worry about it. Abby talked to the doctors. She says he's going to be fine. We got him here in plenty of time. He'll be sore tomorrow, and they'll more than likely keep him overnight, but he's not even going to need surgery."

His stomach turned. "Surgery?"

Jackson waved it off. "It's nothing to worry about. Sometimes the bite kills enough of the skin that the docs have to take it off, but Finn was lucky. He didn't get much of a dose of venom."

"Why the hell was there a snake in the car?" He hated the way his voice rose, but something was building inside him, something nasty and dark.

"Finn had a backpack on the floorboard of his car. He told the doc he'd had it with him out at Dani's earlier today. He set it down on the ground while he waited for her. I guess the damn thing crawled in. Sometime later, it slithered out and decided the front seat would make a nice place to nest. It's a bit unusual, but that's the only explanation I can come up with. He's going to be fine. There's nothing to worry about at this point. Why don't you sit down? Or I could have Sam drive you back to the ranch."

"I'm not going back to the fucking ranch. And I don't need to sit down," he said, a low growl in his throat.

A startled look flashed across Jackson's face before he nodded and took a step back. "All right, you need to be alone. I understand that. I'll take care of the paperwork. You relax. I'll come and get you if anything changes."

He checked himself as Jackson walked away. It wasn't Jackson's fault he felt so helpless. He sat down briefly, but stood again, the urge to pace overwhelming. Oh, how he hated hospitals.

Jackson could have no idea what being in a hospital did to him. He couldn't know that it made him feel like he was a child again. His hands clenched at the feeling. The smell of antiseptic and the chaos going on all around him brought him right back to the worst night of his life. Though he now wore ridiculously expensive loafers, he could still feel the cold linoleum under his bare feet as he went looking for his mother.

Memory tugged at his consciousness, pulling him along, though it wasn't a place he wanted to go to. He'd been so young. Only a child. He'd fallen asleep as his father drove them home. The insistent thud of the car rolling along had lulled him into peace. The wicked roar of the SUV tearing into the Benz had been the sound to awaken him. He didn't remember the accident, only the red and blue lights, and flashes of big hands pulling him out of the wreckage. It was mostly a jumble from there. He'd ridden in an ambulance, but not the one that had taken his parents. The fear of being alone and vulnerable was still stark in his mind, but the feel of that cold, slick floor under his feet was the physical sensation that haunted him. After the nurse had checked him out, he'd been left alone when another emergency called her attention away. He'd needed his mother. He'd walked through the loud ER, tears rolling down his cheeks, calling out for her. He'd just wanted to see his mother.

He'd wandered through the maze of identical rooms, with pained strangers in each, until he'd pulled back the right curtain, and he'd found her. She lay on a bed much like the one the nurse had put the six-year-old Julian on. Her dark hair lay on the pillow like it did on the mornings when he would bound into his parents' room and bounce on the bed until they laughed and tickled him senseless. He had sighed his relief and touched her hand.

Cold. Why was she so cold? He remembered rubbing her hands in between his, trying to get her warm.

They'd found him there, his arms wrapped around his mother's neck. It had been hours and hours before Child Protective Services took him away. Longer before his uncle had finally come to claim him.

"Julian?"

He was startled out of his memory by Danielle's soft voice. She looked tired, her face scrubbed clean and hair pulled back. There was a gaunt look in her eyes that was quickly replaced with compassion as she looked him over. She didn't say anything, merely walked into his arms and wrapped herself around him. The feel of her, the smell of her, overtook him, and Julian needed. He needed so badly. He twisted his hands in her hair and pulled her head back. He took her mouth with not an ounce of finesse. He shoved his tongue in, needing so badly to dominate her. More than his need to dominate, he needed her to submit. He needed her trust.

She softened against him. Her mouth opened, and her tongue slid in velvety softness against his own. Her nipples were suddenly hard nubs against his chest, and she wiggled against him as though attempting to lose herself, to merge with him.

He couldn't wait. He dragged his head from hers and glanced around. The hour was late, and even in a busy hospital, the halls were fairly empty at three in the morning. He needed someplace private. Bathroom. Julian saw the sign not ten feet away. He dragged Danielle with him, a savage need roiling in his cock, in his chest. He slammed the door open, shoved her in, and locked it. It was a single bathroom, luckily recently cleaned, but it wouldn't have mattered. He would have taken her anyway.

"Pants off, Danielle. Present yourself to me." The words came out harsh, harsher than he'd intended, but she simply obeyed.

Her face was flushed, as though she needed this every bit as badly as he did. She made quick work of her clothes, shoving the jeans off her hips, dragging the panties with them. Her pretty pussy came into view, and Julian's cock responded, engorging with blood, need. She tossed her shirt and the bra he'd made her wear off. She gave him the sweetest smile before turning and placing her hands on the sink, spreading her legs and flattening her back. His mouth watered at the sight of her curvy ass in the air, waiting for him. She was spread for him, trusting him. He wanted even more.

"Poor thing," he said, allowing his hand to trace the seam of her ass down to the plug he'd forgotten about. She'd worn it for hours without complaint. "You should have mentioned this. I would have taken it out."

"I'm used to it now, Sir. I pretended it was you. I pretended it was your cock. You were with me."

"Always, Danielle." The words were foreign but felt so right.

He shoved his pants down, freeing his cock. Without another thought, he lined his cock up to her soft pussy and shoved his way in. He loved looking at her in the mirror. The way her mouth came open and her eyes widened as she took his cock made him feel victorious. All the worry and stress faded away as he stroked into her. He let his hands wander up to find her swaying breasts. He stroked into her, forcing himself in an inch at a time as he toyed with her nipples, pinching and rubbing. She pushed back against him, taking him all the way to his balls. He twisted her nipples savagely. She moaned but held herself still.

"No, Danielle. I'm in charge. You keep your head up. Look at your Master in the mirror. Give me your orgasm."

Her head came up. Her brilliant blue eyes met his in the mirror. She was open, open to the sex, open to the experience, open to him.

He gripped her waist and slammed in all the way to his balls. Danielle groaned, and her slick muscles pulsed around him. She was so tight. The plug felt good and hard, bearing down on his cock. He imagined it was Finn there. Like Danielle had said, with them, always.

Julian gave up. He gave in. He pounded his cock into her, his finger trailing down to find her clit. He watched Danielle's beautiful face in the mirror as he slid over her engorged clitoris. He fucked in and out of her, the delicious feeling invading his bones. He felt the start of his orgasm as a tingle up and down his spine. His balls felt heavy and tight. He pinched down on her clit and felt Danielle clamp down as she came. Her face flushed furiously as she contorted in the sweetest agony imaginable. Julian couldn't wait. He joined her, spurting the orgasm in jets out of his body. He slammed in and held himself tight against her, gritting his teeth against the sensation of coming deep inside Danielle without anything between them.

Dear God, he'd taken her without a condom. The revelation sped through him, but all he could do was pull her up, sliding his hands to cup her breasts. He couldn't work up the will to see it as a bad thing. She was his. She was supposed to take everything he had to give her.

She was supposed to be filled with him.

She slumped back against him, obviously exhausted. He picked up his slave, because he couldn't think of her as anything less now.

"It's all right, little one," he whispered. All the bad thoughts seemed to have burned away. He was left with nothing but affection for the woman in his arms.

"He's going to be okay?"

"I'll make sure of it." Julian made the promise. Danielle rested her head against his chest.

They would all be okay. He would make very, very sure of it.

Chapter Thirteen

Val woke up to sound of her cell phone chirping. She groaned as she reached out and flipped the phone open.

"What?" She wasn't in a good mood. Sleep had been elusive. The minute she'd closed her eyes, all she'd been able to see was Jeremy carrying that bag. She'd dreamed about the sound the snake had made before he'd slammed the door to Finn's car closed.

"I'd like to know if you heard any news." Jeremy's voice was calm, as though requesting an update on the weather rather than whether or not his criminal activity had borne fruit.

Now she was fully awake and sitting straight up in bed. She had to swallow twice before she could answer. "It got Finn."

There was a silence on the line that Val could only construe as disapproval. As though she could control what a snake did.

"That is disappointing. I don't suppose he's dead."

She'd been on the phone half the night getting updates from Cece, who had a friend at the hospital. "No, they got him there in plenty of time. You know not a lot of people actually die from snake bites."

"I understand that, but sometimes it's important to make a point.

Julian Lodge should know that he's not the only predator here. He might have money and power, but even something as small as a snake can be deadly if handled improperly."

Val shivered. That snake hadn't seemed small. She'd thought about how Dani would feel when she realized there was a snake in the car. She'd wondered if Dani would be the one to open the passenger side door and slide in only to find it already occupied. Val's stomach turned. She'd done it anyway. She'd decided there was little risk that Dani would actually die, and maybe it would make her want to go with Finn back to Dallas.

Not that she would have had much of a choice. Jeremy had been insistent, and the truth was, he scared her. His bucket was pretty full of crazy, but if he could help her get rid of Dani, she would go along with just about anything.

"I was told that this Julian guy stayed at the hospital with Dani." She'd been a bit surprised at that. Why would a billionaire care enough to hang around?

"Yes, well, the Master always did take good care of his submissives. Until he was done with them, of course. Then they can rot for all he cares." Jeremy's voice took on that hint of gravel that Val now associated with his temper.

Even after only one night hanging around the man, she'd figured out his rage was directed at Julian Lodge. Jeremy was silky smooth when convincing her that he could help with her Dani problem, but his voice got slightly rough when he mentioned Julian Lodge's name. Jeremy was probably around her age, but there was a hardness about him that let Val know he wasn't to be messed with.

Still, if he could scare her sister out of town, she'd be grateful. And polite. She didn't want to give him a reason to sneak a black-market snake into the front seat of her sedan.

"So, what are you planning next?" Val would prefer to know so she didn't step on his toes.

"I have a project I'm working on in Dallas. I won't be back in town for a few days." He sighed. "Look, it's obvious to me that the Master is looking to take new slaves. He's auditioning your sister, and possibly this Finn person."

She wasn't sure about auditioning, but Dani sure seemed to be getting some from the man. Cece had gleefully spread the word that this Lodge guy and Dani had been seen sneaking out of the bathroom with their clothes mussed. What the hell did a guy that hot see in Dani? And what was Dani doing with such a total perv? If this Jeremy guy could be believed, Julian Lodge liked a lot of variety in sex partners. She couldn't see her uptight sister doing kinky things.

"From what I understand, they've gone back out to the Barnes-Fleetwood ranch. I don't think I would be welcome out there."

"Just make sure they don't leave Willow Fork." There was a click as the other end of the line went dead.

She let the phone drop as she slumped back against the bed. She thought about the offer she'd gotten on the place last week. Two hundred and fifty thousand dollars would buy her a whole new life. When she'd looked at that figure, she'd briefly thought about sharing it. A hundred and twenty-five thousand was a lot of money, but it didn't seem fair she had to share it. Dani wouldn't do anything interesting with it. Dani would probably give it away, and damn it, Val just flat deserved it.

She thought about the humiliation she'd felt every day since she'd gotten out of college and been forced to come home with her tail between her legs. She couldn't find a job. She hadn't been able to keep up, and she'd hated the city. No one listened to her there or gave a damn that she'd been the homecoming queen. She'd been a tiny fish in an enormous pond. The years she'd spent in college had been some of the most miserable of her life.

Of course, here in Willow Fork she was a big fish, but poor. Sure she could get married, but all the offers had come from working-class men. She needed cash or she would be stuck in this house or one like it for the rest of her life. She felt bad about Dani, but some things had to be done.

She sat in her bed for the longest time telling herself everything would be fine.

* * * *

"That's perfect. That is exactly what I want. Finn, on the other hand, needs to work on his form."

Dani kept her eyes down as she'd been instructed. She was kneeling with her hands on her thighs, palms up, and her legs were spread wide. With her back ramrod straight, there was no part of her that wasn't on display. Her pussy was right out there for anyone to see, and yet she felt more confident than she could have imagined. Naked in Julian and Finn's presence made her feel more powerful than she ever had before. Julian's hand touched her head, stroking her as he considered Finn.

"Finn, your spine should be straight, your shoulders squared off, and your head lowered submissively. I thought Abigail and Samuel talked to you about this."

Finn huffed. "They did. Sorry, it's not very comfortable. And Dani's had way more practice than me. You wouldn't let me get out of bed until yesterday."

They'd had words about it. Well, Finn had words about it. Julian had simply stared at him until he'd gotten back into bed. Dani had spent the last two days taking care of Finn and exploring the ranch with Julian when Finn rested. While Finn napped, Julian had taken her out to the barn and helped her saddle a horse. They'd ridden around with Jack and Sam, who showed them all over the seemingly endless ranch. Julian seemed to be perfectly comfortable with her. He'd openly held her hand and shown her great affection on their tour. At dinner, he'd pulled out her chair and made sure she had everything she could want. He'd treated her like a princess. It was far from how she had expected a submissive be treated.

"You were bitten by a venomous snake. I believe a few days in bed are called for. Besides, I didn't force you to sleep alone."

"I was grateful for that, Sir." There was a warmth in Finn's voice that let Dani know he was thinking of the night before.

While Julian had insisted Finn remain in bed, he hadn't left him unsatisfied. After dinner was done on the second night of Finn's bed rest, Julian had led her back to the guesthouse and up to the big bed. He undressed her and gently worked a larger plug into her ass. Finn had watched as Julian lubed her anus and fucked her with the plug before settling it deep in her rectum. There had been no mistaking Finn's interest. His cock had stood straight up.

Julian had chuckled, and he'd ordered her to take care of Finn.

She'd taken Finn in her mouth and sucked until he'd filled her. Then it had been Julian's turn. He'd settled her on his lap and told her to ride. Up and down. Up and down. She'd forced her pussy to take that enormous cock of his, every inch a pure pleasure. She'd shivered and cried when she came.

He'd still slept downstairs on the couch.

She'd been cozy in Finn's arms. It had felt normal and natural to snuggle down with her best friend, but she'd missed Julian.

He was an enigma, but one she felt compelled to solve. Since the night when Finn had been bitten, she had stopped questioning the relationship. He'd needed her that night. Though she had no idea why, her submission settled something inside him, so she gave it to him. The night before, she'd wanted to call out to him when he'd rolled her out of his arms, kissed her forehead, and quietly left the room. She'd remained silent. He wouldn't have answered her anyway. When she was sure he was asleep, she'd snuck down and made sure he had a blanket. She'd watched him restlessly shift, lost in some dream.

"Danielle, have we lost you?"

Julian's deep voice brought her out of her thoughts. "Sorry, Sir. I was thinking."

"I asked you to help Finn. I had to ask three times. There's no going into subspace without permission."

"Subspace?" Dani asked, lifting her chin.

"Yes, subspace. It's lingo for that nice floaty place you submissives find when doing a scene, though usually it takes some actual form of punishment to achieve. I was joking about the subspace. I believe you were simply finding the conversation between Finn and myself about proper positioning to be a bit dull. Let's see if we can liven things up for you. Please stand."

A little thrill went through her. He used that voice that promised something filthy was about to happen.

"Danielle, part of being my submissive is to obey me, but more than that it is to know what I want. I can't be with you every second of the day, nor do I suspect you would want that."

"Probably not, Sir," she answered honestly. Julian could be a lot to take.

He chuckled. "I can understand that. So when I am not with you, there have to be rules, as there are in any relationship. I expect you to behave in a manner that brings pride to yourself, Finn, and me. Part of pride in being a submissive is in your strict obedience. There are many times in play that a Master will loan his subs out to another Dom. This is considered polite in BDSM society."

The words dropped in the room like a bomb about to go off. Everything went silent and for a moment, she would have sworn she could hear her heart beating.

Danielle brought her head up. Tears pricked the back of her eyes. Loaned out? Like a library book?

"That is not happening," Finn said, getting to his feet in a hurry. His hand came down to haul her up. "Get your clothes on, Danielle. I'm not going to let him pimp you out."

Julian simply stood, his face a blank mask. He wore a pair of leather trousers and nothing else. His long, dark hair hung around his shoulders. She wanted so much for him to argue, to tell her she was different, but he stood there as though simply waiting for her to decide.

"Have you passed your subs around before?" Dani asked.

His answer was simple, nonemotional. "Yes."

"Fuck that." Finn began to pull her away, but she dug her heels in.

She studied Julian for a moment, much the same way he studied her. He wasn't a man to wear his emotions on his sleeves. Hell, he buried them so deep in the back of that closet of a brain that sometimes she wondered if he had them. Then, the night at the hospital happened. He'd been a hurricane of emotion that night, though he'd never said a word. She'd felt it rolling off him in waves. He'd needed her. Was this something else he needed? Should she dismiss it totally if he needed it?

"Stop." She tried to pull away from Finn.

He wasn't having it. "Dani, you can't let him tell you to fuck his friends."

She sighed. "He doesn't have friends. Haven't you figured him out yet?" She turned back to Julian. "Why would you want me to do that, Sir?"

"I didn't say I wanted you to do it," Julian corrected. "I said it's considered polite in some BDSM circles."

She fell back into her position, perfectly content with his answer. She lowered her head, but not before she saw Julian's face flush slightly. Happiness. She'd made him happy.

Finn sank down beside her. "Dani, you can't do this because it's polite. I get that you don't like to make waves, but can't you see this is wrong? I like the guy, too. Do you think I don't want to please him? I'm a lot like you, but I can't watch this. I can't watch him treat you like some toy he can pass around to whoever asks for it. And I can't let him do that to me, either."

Julian sniffed, the aristocratic gesture amusing to Dani. "I would never pass you around, Finn. You're far too obnoxious to foist off on someone else. Danielle isn't demonstrating her submissiveness. She's given me an enormous gift by giving me her trust."

She sent Finn a smile. He sometimes forgot to really listen to what people said. "He won't share me. He's too possessive. I suspect he passed around his other subs because they enjoyed it."

She also suspected that he'd chosen them for exactly that reason. From what she'd surmised, Julian wasn't one to get in too deep. He'd chosen his companions with great care and studied caution. Until her.

"Precisely," Julian replied, lifting her chin up so their eyes met. "It was written into their contracts that I had the right to give them away at any time. I had one particular submissive who wanted to be shared by many men. It made the sub feel wanted."

"Poor girl," Finn said.

"Oh, look, the morality police are here. He was a man, and, as it turned out, something of a criminal. I ended up turning him out when I discovered him conspiring with a guest against a friend of mine. I gave him what he required and he still turned on me, though I'm sure you see me as the villain of the piece. Perhaps you should look him up. His name is Jeremy. You can start a club."

"So you won't share us?" She heard the wealth of confusion in Finn's voice.

Julian's eyes narrowed. His lips curled back. "What I said, Finn, was that it is considered polite in some BDSM circles to share your submissives." He grabbed Finn by the neck and hoisted him up like he would an errant puppy. "I am not polite."

He began pulling Finn along across the playroom floor. She turned her head to see what was happening.

"Hey, I'm sorry if I misunderstood." Finn's feet tried to find purchase, but he ended up shuffling to keep up as Julian carted him to the bench he called a whipping chair.

"You continue to believe the worst of me. I think you're here because you want Danielle, not because you want to be part of our ménage. I would prefer not to make Danielle choose. She's had to make difficult decisions all of her life. Do you want to force her to choose between the two of us? Perhaps you would win. You have known her for longer, but what would it cost her?"

Everything. It would cost her everything. God, how would she choose? She knew deep down, if she was forced to, she would choose Finn. He was her best friend, but she wanted Julian so much. She needed time to show Finn that it could work. They could be like Abby, Jack, and Sam. They could be happy.

Finn stopped fighting and sagged down. "I don't want Dani unhappy. I love her. I am here for her, but, damn it, I'm here for me, too. I want to find out where this goes. I just…I couldn't stand the thought of you giving me away like I meant nothing. I can't mean nothing."

Julian stopped. His hold on Finn's neck loosened, and Finn slumped to the floor. "I won't ever share you. As long as we are together it will be you and me and Danielle. I will parade you around the club naked because your body and Danielle's body belong to me. I'll show you off because I'm proud to own such beautiful slaves, but I will kill the man or woman who touches you. I will show no mercy and give no quarter. For as long as you belong to me, you are precious to me and under my protection. I'll be honest with you, Finn. Even if you asked me to, I would not share you nor would I share Danielle. At times, my needs will be more important than yours, and this is one of them. Luckily, in this case, our needs dovetail nicely. Now make your choice. Get into the chair and accept your punishment or you may leave."

Finn didn't hesitate. She almost laughed at how quickly Finn assumed the position. He really liked to be spanked. Masochist. It defined Finn to a *T*.

"Danielle, please join your Master." Julian made the request as he opened one of the closet doors. An array of floggers, paddles, and whips came into view. She scrambled to join them.

"Thank you for your trust, love." Julian's arms wound their way around her waist. He dipped his head and pressed his lips to hers. "I would never share you."

"I know." She didn't need that. She needed him. She needed to be precious.

His lips curled up as he looked down at her. "What do you think we should use on poor Finn's backside today?"

It was deliciously decadent, like choosing a treat for a friend. It was, in a way. Finn would enjoy it. She let her hand rub along the array of tools laid out in precise order. *Paddles and floggers and whips, oh, my!* The leather tails of the flogger caught her eye. She picked it up, testing the weight in her palm before handing it to Julian.

"Is that the one?" Julian asked, taking it from her.

She nodded and stared down at Finn. He looked so perfect hunched over the whipping bench, his spine perfectly curved in submission. His muscled ass stuck out as though waiting, pleading, for attention.

"He's beautiful, isn't he?" Julian's whisper caressed her skin.

"Yes." This was what did it for Julian. This was the very reason he was a Dom. The trust Finn was showing him was a lovely thing.

"How many should we give him? He did misbehave."

"Thirty," Dani decided and was more than rewarded with the low groan that came from Finn.

"Thirty it is then," Julian replied. He reached down and placed a hand on Finn's back. "Danielle, I believe we'll need a bit more than just the flogger. It's thirty for disobeying, but I think a little torture is in order as well. We're going to need some lubricant."

She giggled as Finn swore. It looked like it would be an interesting afternoon.

* * * *

Finn relaxed as the flogger hit his ass. It was odd, but the pain seemed to fill some need in him long neglected. The flogger's tails screamed along his skin, lashing fire on his nerves and leaving him strangely sensitized. He gripped the handles of the chair so he didn't slip down. He counted as the flogger struck. *One, two, three.* The pain was king at first, but as it continued a lovely heat built, blocking the worst of the agony. *Four, five, six, seven, and eight.* Endurance was the key. It was a game. How much could he take? Finn was surprised that he put great pride in how much pain he could handle. *Nine, ten, eleven, twelve, and thirteen.* A sweet, floaty feeling invaded his veins. He forced himself to focus, to get the count out of his mouth. He'd rather float here in this nice cloud, but Julian would be disappointed.

The blows came quickly and without mercy. Finn counted all the way to thirty. When the flogger stopped, it took everything he had not to beg for more.

"Up, Finn. You're to place yourself on the ottoman and allow Danielle to bind your hands."

On shaky legs, he managed to get up and out of the whipping chair. Dani was already standing at the upholstered ottoman. He noticed now that it had handcuffs attached.

Where did these guys get their furniture?

He had a sudden desire to see Julian's club. Lucas had asked him to come several times, and he'd always turned him down. He'd been too afraid to go down a path that seemed so dark. Now he realized it was only dark if he made it that way. What might have happened if he'd gone with Lucas and Lexi? Would he have been introduced to Julian? Would he have begun a relationship that would have led them both to Dani?

As he knelt down and felt Dani's soft hands work the cuffs around his wrists, he let the thought go. It happened as it should have happened. If he had gone to the club with Lucas, he would have rejected it. He hadn't been ready to face himself. It'd taken Dani to get him to open up and accept himself for what he was.

A queer who couldn't be happy without one woman in his life.

A pervert who needed a Dom to spank him to feel complete.

A man who'd finally found what he needed. He let go of the labels and let himself be.

"You're smiling, Finn. What is that about?" Julian stood looking down at him, his dark hair a waterfall around his face. He was the epitome of alpha male. His cock hardened as he thought about the bottle of lube in Julian's hands. Fuck, he wanted that. Dani finished with his hands and went to stand beside Julian. They were so gorgeous.

"I just figured out I'm a freak, Sir."

A single dark eyebrow arched, and Finn could tell he'd confused the Master. "I don't know if I like that, Finn."

"I do, Sir. I think I finally get it. We're all freaks, aren't we? Maybe what we do is wrong for other people, but it's right for us. It's okay to be us."

Dani grinned up at Julian, her blue eyes bright with mischief. Finn wondered when he'd last seen her so confident and vibrant. Maybe never. "I told you he could learn."

"And I doubted you, little one," Julian practically purred back at her. "Perhaps we should see if Finn believes what he's saying."

Those silvery eyes turned back to him. From his position, he had to crane his neck up, but Finn could plainly see that the Master had other things on his mind. The pants he was wearing had tented, and Finn's ass clenched at the thought of taking that monster deep.

"Have you ever seen two men have sex, Danielle?" Julian asked as his hands found the fly of his pants.

Her face flushed. "Only on the Internet."

"Dani?" Finn was slightly shocked. "You searched for porn on the Internet?"

She shrugged, obviously not willing to expend shame on it. "It's the only way to get porn in Willow Fork."

Julian chuckled. He shoved his pants off his hips and handed them to Danielle. He leaned over and planted a kiss on her cheek. "I am going to have so much fun introducing you to the filthy civilized world. What do you say, Finn? Will Danielle like Dallas?"

Now it was his heart that clenched. Dani would come home with him. He just knew she would. The only question was, where would she stay? Would she stay at Julian's? Would he be the one left out? It didn't matter for now. He pushed the thought aside. What mattered was making Dani happy and pleasing Julian.

"I think we'll have a lot of fun showing her the X-rated world, Sir."

A low growl came out of Julian's throat, and Finn couldn't keep his eyes off the enormous cock that sprung from Julian's core. The man was a work of art. He was hard planes and perfect angles. Standing next to him was the softest, most heavenly bit of femininity Finn had ever seen. They were perfect together, and Finn had the sudden joyous suspicion he was going to be in the middle.

"Get me hard, little one. We need to punish Finn for a bit."

Dani fell to her knees in that graceful way of hers. Her blonde hair hung past her shoulders, and he only got the briefest glimpse of her lips and tongue caressing the Master's cock before Julian's hands tangled in her hair. His eyes closed as he guided Dani. Finn watched as Dani took that massive cock into her mouth.

"Yes, that's what I want. I want your mouth all over me before I ream Finn's ass."

Finn bit his lip to keep from groaning out loud. His cock was hard as a rock. He was going to die if Julian didn't fuck him and soon.

Julian pulled out of Dani's mouth. He raised her up and kissed her, treating her like fine china. Finn had noticed that about Julian. He treated Dani with perfect tenderness and care, as though he was trying to make up for years of neglect. Dani beamed under his affection. Then he turned his eyes to Finn. Finn shuddered at the savage lust he saw there. No tenderness for him, and he was past okay with it. He wanted Julian's primal lust. He craved it.

Julian broke off the kiss and strode out of sight. It was a mere second before Finn felt a hand on his back, smoothing down the line of his spine as Julian knelt behind him. It was a move Julian seemed to like. It made him feel like something fine and precious and worthy of praise. He shivered as he felt lube pouring down, sliding onto his anus.

Julian's fingers probed, massaging the lube into his ass. "Danielle, please kneel down beside our Finn. Coat your hand in the lubricant, and then you'll give him the hand job of a lifetime."

"I thought you were punishing me." He couldn't think of anything better. The two people he was crazy about would have their hands all over him. And he was crazy about Julian. Julian scared him, but he couldn't walk away. He had to know where this was going.

"I am punishing you. You're not allowed to come."

Now Finn didn't even try to hold back his groan. Dani got on the floor beside him, her small hand cupping his balls. Fuck. He was never going to last. "You're kidding. Please tell me you're kidding."

He felt something far bigger than Julian's fingers begin to breach his ass.

"I am not. Come and there will be hell to pay, Finn." Julian gripped his hips and started to penetrate Finn's hole.

He flattened his back and pushed out with the muscles of his sphincter. He gasped as Julian's cock slid in. So fucking full. He had never been so full. His asshole felt like it would burst, but Julian pressed in. He kept coming.

"Tell her. Tell her what it feels like because I'm going to fuck her ass very soon." Julian shoved in ruthlessly.

"He's so big. God, Dani, he's going to tear me apart. And I'll let him because it's going to feel so fucking good."

"I can't wait," she whispered in his ear. Her hand slid up and gripped his cock like a familiar friend. She grasped the base and sloped upward. "I can't wait to be between the two of you."

"I'm going to fuck that little ass of yours, Danielle. Finn is going to ram his cock into your pussy. You're going to be full of your men. Now, do as your Master requests. Rub him. Make him come."

It was unfair. He couldn't last. This really was torture. Finn tried to think of anything but the cock invading his ass and the hand running up and down his dick. Danielle was relentless. She stroked from the base of his cock to the tip where she brushed her thumb across his slit and then began the journey again. Every now and again she would cup his balls, running her finger along the perineum, making him shudder. She ran that dirty finger all the way to his anus, where she pressed in.

"Bad girl." Julian sounded throaty. "Fuck, love, do it again."

Finn felt tears in his eyes as she pressed her finger alongside Julian's cock. Damn. He wasn't going to make it. Then Julian finally seated himself fully. Every inch of Finn's ass was invaded and taken. Dani gripped his dick again and pulled as Julian dragged his cock back out.

Finn came, jets flowing out of his cock across Dani's hand.

She pressed a kiss on his jaw. "You lose, baby."

Julian sighed and pulled out. "Get the paddle this time. We'll start again. I can do this all night, Finn."

Finn slumped down, unable to stop the smile that widened his lips. He could do this all night, too, and maybe, if he was lucky, he could do it for the rest of his life.

Chapter Fourteen

Julian came awake with a startled shout. It took him a moment to remember where he was. Sunlight. It was morning, and he wasn't at home. He was in the guesthouse at Jackson's ranch. He breathed deeply and sat up on the couch. His mouth was dry and his head pounding. It was always that way after he had the dream.

God, when was it ever going to stop? He let his head fall to his hands as he attempted to let go of the images that played in his brain. It was his own personal horror movie.

Julian stood and stretched. It should be no big surprise that the dream was back. It came back with a vengeance any time he had to go to a hospital or felt like his life was veering out of control. When one of those things happened, images from the several years after his parents died played through his dreams. He saw the accident, though he didn't remember it in his conscious brain. In his dreams, there was a flash of light and the scream of metal attacking metal. In the dream, he saw his parents' blood flow, their bodies slumped over, never to rise again.

He'd wandered the hospital like a small zombie, feet shuffling, seeking only one thing. He'd sought his mother. He didn't call for her, simply walked the halls staring ahead, waiting for the sight of her, shivering in a hospital gown.

Then he was dressed in a suit. It chafed his young body. His uncle looked down on him like he was a piece of dirt on an otherwise pristine floor. His uncle explained he would pay for his schooling and appoint someone to run the business that would pass to Julian, but he wouldn't bring Julian into his home. He didn't have time for a nephew.

Julian hadn't seen the man again until he'd handed over the reins of the business when Julian turned eighteen.

It had been a series of nannies, some who tried, and some who beat the crap out of him when they realized no one cared.

He'd been twelve when he finally fought back, shoving his abuser down the stairs, breaking her arm. Only the fact that she could get in trouble for what she'd done to him had kept her mouth shut. The next day Candice had shown up, but Julian had understood. He wasn't lovable. People put up with him because he had money.

Damn. Leo would have a field day with the thoughts that ran through his head. Julian looked down, and his hands were shaking.

This was about the hospital. It had nothing to do with Danielle and Finn. They were simply good subs who would make perfect slaves. They needed him for now, and he would enjoy them, but even they were transitory.

Still, his feet moved up the stairs almost of their own volition. He was slightly overwhelmed by the need to see them. He would look in on them, and maybe join them. It was for sex, of course. The sex was good for burning off memories better left forgotten. Besides, he'd promised Danielle she could be in the middle. He'd only shared subs a couple of times before, and never his own. He would never have invited Jeremy to share Sally.

Why did Jeremy come to his mind? He was better off forgotten. He'd proven to be troublesome and a criminal, and yet Julian had thought of him a lot since he'd come to the ranch. Finn was far more problematic than Jeremy. Jeremy had never talked back or questioned him, and yet Julian had tossed him out without a thought after he'd caught him breaking club rules on tape. He'd watched as Jeremy slipped Lucas Cameron a roofie, and he'd calmly plotted to have him thrown out. He doubted he would have done the same with Finn.

No, if he'd caught Finn doing something like that, Finn would have paid. He would have been on his fucking knees. His backside would bleed, and he would have to spit out his safe word before Julian would stop. Then, and only then, would he allow Finn to beg for forgiveness. It would be a long time coming, but he knew he wouldn't allow Finn to leave. And as for Danielle, well, Danielle would never do anything that could hurt another person. He trusted her. If he saw her on tape doing what Jeremy had done, he would have known there was a damn good reason for it.

He stopped just before he made it to the bedroom door. He trusted Danielle. He trusted her deep in his bones, in a way he hadn't trusted anyone except Candice and Jackson and Samuel.

Was he in love with Danielle?

Julian turned away from the door. He couldn't look in on them. He strode down the stairs, found his clothes, and righted himself. When he looked smooth and calm, he walked to the main house. Coffee. He needed a bit of caffeine, and then he would be on the proper footing. Later, he would call Lucas and have him draw up a contract between himself, Danielle, and Finn.

Yes, that was what he needed. A contract would ensure all the proper boundaries were in place, and he would be back on an even keel.

He slipped into the house and immediately heard laughter. It was the throaty laughter of a man, and it was coming from the dining room.

"You seriously jumped into Julian Lodge's car and told him to drive?"

Another laugh, this one light and frothy and feminine. Danielle. "Well, he didn't exactly jump to do my bidding, Leo."

Julian's fists clenched at his side. She sounded flirty, his little sub. Yes. He needed a contract, one that allowed him to tear into her sweet ass when she flirted with other Doms.

"I don't doubt it for a moment, sweetheart. Julian prefers to give the orders, not take them. I should know. Now, if you had jumped into my Jeep, things would have gone differently."

Julian strode through the door. Leo was sitting altogether too close to his property. His Dom in residence poured coffee into her mug, while he beamed at her in that all-American hero way of his.

Jackson was right. Leo was an asshole.

"It would have gone exactly the same way, Leo," Julian said as he noted Finn was sitting at the end of the table staring a hole through Leo's head.

Finn sighed and seemed utterly relieved when Julian stepped into the room. He would have to train Finn to ward off potential poachers. He couldn't be allowed to mope while some Dom attempted to charm Danielle away.

Leo sat back in his chair. If he was intimidated, it didn't show. He simply smiled up and looked too young for Julian's comfort. "Good to see you, boss. I was getting to know Dani, here. Lovely girl."

"Yes, she is. Danielle," he commanded as he sat down.

She stared at him for a moment, seemingly confused. "Yes?"

"He wants you to sit in his lap," Leo explained. "It's his caveman-like way of telling me to keep my hands off you."

Danielle shook her head. "It isn't like that. He was just being nice."

Such an innocent. He turned to Leo. "Were you being nice, Leo?"

"Hell, no. I was trying to figure out how fast I could get her tied up and sink my cock in her ass. I bet she's a virgin there, Julian. She's one gorgeous sub."

Danielle's face went up in flames, and Finn stood.

"You keep your hands off her!"

Julian sighed. "Sit down, Finn. The time to beat the shit out of Leo has passed. We need to work on that. Don't concern yourself too much. Once she's properly collared, we need only worry about all the vanilla assholes who will hit on our woman. The Doms will back off."

Leo shrugged. "I thought I should give it a try before you collared her. She's lovely."

He was only slightly placated by Leo's appreciation for his sub. His lap was still empty. "Danielle?"

She was on her feet, the coffee in front of her forgotten. She hurried around the table, her clumsiness entirely endearing in Julian's mind. She almost stumbled into his lap. He'd had subs who never made a wrong move, so why was it Danielle who meant so much? Why was it Finn who drew him in?

"You can sit down now, Finn," Julian said, his arm circling Danielle's waist. Her arms went around his neck, her breath warm on his nape. "Actually, move your chair next to mine."

Finn moved, dragging the chair close to his. He sat down, and his hand came out, silently requesting contact, which Julian gave by covering it with his own.

"I still think he's a jerk."

"Who?" Samuel asked as he strode in. "Oh, Leo. Hey, Finn must be talking about you. Don't worry about him. He likes to play around with other men's wives. He doesn't mean anything by it. He's a pussy when it comes to commitment, so he falls for unavailable women."

Leo frowned. "That's actually quite astute of you, Sam."

Samuel grabbed a Danish from the buffet and sat down. "There's a brain behind all this masculine beauty. I don't use it often, but it's there. It's working overtime right now trying to figure out why the hell my partner and my wife had to take off for Dallas the minute you came in. I got a note, Leo. A fucking note. I was up all damn night with a calving, and now Jack and Abby are driving to Dallas with nothing more than a note telling me to watch out for Josh and Olivia. You tell me what's going on, and you tell me now."

Somewhere in his speech, Samuel had morphed from funny, goodtime guy to one pissed-off husband. He was all threat as he looked at Leo, and Julian was damn proud of the man he'd become. Finn could do that, too, if he was properly loved.

Loved. Could he do it? Could he love them and not lose himself? He felt his hand tighten over Finn's. Finn looked up, startled, but he threaded his fingers through Julian's and squeezed back. It was a sign. *I'll be there*, Finn said silently as he laced their hands together.

He turned back to Leo, who had gone very serious.

"Lexi is missing. Lucas called me last night, and she was supposed to come to his place for dinner, but she never showed up. He can't get her to answer her cell, and she wasn't in her apartment."

"Fuck me," Samuel said, standing up. His jaw clenched in anger. "I'm going after them."

"Sit down, Samuel," Julian said, using his darkest voice. "I have the feeling this gets worse."

Jackson would never have left him behind if there weren't

something more. As if conjured out of thin air, Samuel's cell trilled. He fumbled for it and sighed in relief.

"It's Jack." He strode off as he began to speak to his lover, his partner.

The back door came open and Julian's stomach took a deep dive. Leo hadn't come alone. Ian Taggart walked in, carrying a small tool kit. The big blond Viking of a man headed the company that provided Julian's security. If he was here, something had gone terribly wrong.

Taggart looked over at Leo. "The security system is working. I made a couple of tweaks, but the house itself is solid."

Julian turned to Leo. "Tell me what's going on. When did Lexi go missing and why is Taggart here and not out looking for her?"

Lexi Moore belonged to Julian's family. She might be a pain in his ass, but she was his pain to deal with. If someone had her, he would move heaven and earth to get her back.

"My brother and Liam are working on it back in Dallas. They'll meet Barnes up there. Sean is already with Lucas," Taggart explained. "Leo asked me to come down here with him. I wanted to check the security situation here on the ranch."

"Again, I don't understand why you're here when everyone on your team should be looking for Lexi."

Taggart glanced Leo's way. "You haven't told him?"

"I'm getting there. I don't know if Lexi has anything to do with this, Julian." Leo leaned forward, his bulky arms on the table. His face was hard as granite now, and Julian could see the Navy SEAL commando in his happy-go-lucky employee. "She's been a bit erratic since her wedding got called off."

"She would never worry Lucas by running off and not telling anyone." They had an odd relationship, Lucas and Lexi, but Julian knew she would never hurt him in such a fashion. She clung to Lucas. He was her life raft.

Leo nodded. "Then we should worry. I've seen a disturbing pattern over the last few months. It started with your car being trashed."

Danielle sat up in Julian's lap. "Someone vandalized your car?"

He stroked her back. "It happens in the city. Even in protected places, it can happen."

"I don't think that was a random crime," Taggart said, setting his tool kit down.

Leo shook his head. "I did, at first, but Taggart brought his concerns to me and now I agree with him. I don't like the fact that someone took out the security camera. Those cameras are small. You have to know where they are. And the only vehicle they damaged was yours. Then there was the fire on the street level of the building that houses The Club."

Julian felt a chill. "I thought the insurance adjuster decided that was an accident."

Taggart huffed, a superior sound. "That adjuster would have done anything to close the case."

Leo frowned up at him. "Well, whose fault is that? You stood over the man the whole time. He practically crapped his pants every time you walked in a room."

Taggart shrugged. "I don't get paid to make people comfortable."

Danielle cuddled closer to him. "Someone tried to set your club on fire?"

Taggart seemed to soften a bit as he looked down at Danielle. Unlike Leo, there was zero flirtation in his demeanor. It was another reason he'd backed Taggart's business. The man was an excellent Dom. "I believe it was an attempt to get Mr. Lodge's attention. Maybe on the outside these acts look random, but when you put them all together, I don't think so. Did you know that Sally's house was recently burglarized?"

"No." No one had told him.

"Yes, about two weeks ago," Taggart continued. "Whoever broke in didn't take anything, but they trashed the place, paying special attention to the pictures she had of you. Those were torn up. Luckily, she and Stephen were out at the time."

Leo leaned in. "When I talked to Lucas this morning, he mentioned a couple of days ago he'd had his tires slashed. That's when I finally talked to that damn reporter."

Julian felt his indignation rise. People he cared about were being targeted, and Leo was talking to a reporter who wanted to do a tabloid piece. "I told you to ignore the reporter. Damn it, Leo. We do not need publicity. Where did you get the number? I told Candice to lose it."

"Don't blame Candice," Leo replied nonchalantly. "She was perfectly threatening when I asked for the thing. She should be in leathers, you know. She would make an excellent Domme."

"Could we stop talking about my secretary's potential kinks? It disturbs me. If Candice didn't give you the number, how did you contact the reporter?"

Leo sat back, crossing his arms over his chest. "I know Candice. She's a good assistant. If she thought you would ever need that number again, she would keep it. All I had to do was search her desk while she was at lunch."

"You're fired." He meant it this time. Leo had gone too far.

Leo sighed, and his eyes rolled. "Yeah, yeah, I'm fired. Well, you're going to want to do more than fire me when you find out what I did next. Tricia, you can come out now."

The door that led to the kitchen opened, and a tall, slender woman with large brown eyes walked out. Though Julian could tell she was nervous, she was also resolute.

"Mr. Lodge, my name is Tricia Walker. I need to talk to you."

Leo's face had gone stony, as though he expected Julian to punch him. Julian had no intention of doing anything so uncivilized as starting a fight. He had other plans for his now former employee.

"Up," he commanded, and Danielle hopped off his lap. She sat back down in the chair after Julian rose and stalked to Leo. The reporter he ignored. Leo was the one who had his attention. "You brought a reporter to my friend's home?"

Taggart's hands came up. "Not my idea. I don't like any of this."

"I'm not—" Tricia began but stopped the minute Julian turned on her.

"I do not require your input. You may leave and be glad that I only intend to see that you never write another word in Dallas again. If you don't quit your job, I'll buy the paper and fire you. Choose another city, Miss Walker. You are no longer welcome in mine." He turned back to Leo. "I have other plans for you, Mr. Meyer. I intend to ruin you on every level. You might want to leave the country."

Leo stood, his stare heavy with irritation. "Fine, I'll leave the country, but not until you've heard her out. Damn it, Julian. I'm sick of this. You've been more than a mentor to me, but you have no concept of what it means to really be a friend. Maybe because very few people have ever fought for you. Well, guess what. I'm willing to do it. So sit down and shut up. Ruin me later; listen to her now."

"I want to hear what she has to say," Danielle said.

Julian turned to her, frowning. "I did not ask your opinion, Danielle." He glared at Finn. "Nor did I request yours, Finn. This is not a democracy."

Danielle stood up. "Julian, you're being stubborn and not looking at the big picture."

All of his buttons were being firmly pushed. Between the dream he had the night before, and the chaos of this morning, he was in no mood to deal with a bratty sub. He looked to her for stability, not more uncertainty.

"Am I not, Danielle?" He heard the sarcasm flow. He tried to quell it, but anger had taken over, and a cold tone was all he seemed capable of. This was precisely why he should never have taken a sub without a contract. Danielle should know to never behave as she was behaving now.

"Leo wouldn't do something to hurt you."

Julian felt his heart rate tick up, the pressure slowly building. Leo was charming. Leo was younger. Leo probably had a variety of things in common with Danielle and Finn. Though Leo didn't swing both ways, it didn't seem to bother Danielle. Danielle seemed to be taken with the Dom. "You'll forgive me if I don't take your advice. You're not exactly worldly. This is between me and my employee."

"Julian, can't you listen to the woman?" Finn asked, exasperation plain in his voice.

"You are both dismissed. Wait for me in our rooms." He would deal with them later, when he had his anger under control. He would set a proper punishment and decide how to proceed. He wouldn't touch either of them again sexually until he had a contract in place. A hot anger was starting to build. He needed to get it under control.

"I'm not going anywhere," Danielle said. Her blue eyes were almost sad as she looked up at him. "Leo's right. No one has cared enough to fight with you or for you. I do."

"Which simply proves how little you know about me. I do not

fight. Finn, take Danielle back to our rooms and pack your things." His gut turned at the thought of sending them away, but he had standards to keep up. He couldn't, wouldn't, allow them to push him into a corner. If he lost his temper, he could hurt her. He could hurt Finn. He could still remember pushing that woman down the stairs. He'd taken pleasure in doing it. He'd been twelve. What kind of damage could he do to them now?

"Can't give an inch, can you, Julian?" Leo asked, his voice heavy with disappointment.

Samuel Fleetwood strode back into the room and stared at the reporter. "I don't give a damn what Julian wants or doesn't want. Do you know anything about my stepdaughter's disappearance?"

The reporter's eyes grew watery. "I hope not, but I wouldn't put it past him. Since he got out of jail, he's been unhinged."

"Who?" Julian asked. He wanted to get this over with so he could leave. The quicker he put distance between Danielle, Finn, and himself the better. He knew he was being a bit of an ass, but he couldn't help it. The simple act of her talking to Leo had set him on edge. He had never been so righteously possessive before. Part of him was pushing to leave before they got under his skin. He should walk away now, when it wouldn't hurt so much. He would walk away before he had a chance to hurt them. The other half knew he was never going to allow them to leave.

"My brother. My brother's name is Jeremy Walker, and I believe he used to be your lover, Mr. Lodge. I think he's trying to kill you."

* * * *

Finn stared at Julian from across the table. His face was smooth, placid, showing none of the hostility from before, but he could sense that his Master was not pleased.

Dani wasn't happy either, for that matter. She'd kept her head down for the most part as Tricia got to her story. When she bothered to look up, there was a red cast to her eyes that told him she was fighting hard not to cry. Finn had to force himself not to put a fist through Julian's face until he really watched him. He was beginning to understand his lover, and there was no doubt that Julian was his lover. He could still feel the slide of that big cock ramming deep inside him. It had been more than sex, and that was what scared the shit out of Julian. That was what had Julian saying things he shouldn't.

Unfortunately, he'd said the one thing guaranteed to make Dani feel as low as she possibly could. He'd tossed her aside for a single mistake. He doubted Julian would actually have let them go. He'd watched the way Julian sighed as he came in contact with Dani. He was in deep, and it scared Julian. But that wouldn't matter to Dani. He knew her too well. She'd heard absolutely nothing past Julian telling her to get packed. He knew the only thing that kept her sitting at the table was the fact that she was Lexi Moore's friend. Otherwise, she would have done exactly what he said. She would have packed and asked Finn to take her home. Now she sat, her hands twisting on the table in front of her, and listened to Tricia Walker.

"What did he go to prison for?" Julian asked. There was a blandness to his voice. He could have been asking about the weather. He glanced down at the report Taggart had given him. Apparently the blond dude who looked like he ate nails for breakfast was some sort of security expert.

Tricia swallowed. It was obvious she was intimidated. "Drugs. He got caught with cocaine at a club. It was his third strike. He went a little crazy after you kicked him out."

Leo spoke up. His fists hit the table. "I explained this to you. Jeremy broke the rules of The Club. He attempted to drug an associate member and give him over to a man who meant him harm. You do understand what your brother did?"

Tears welled. "Yes. He was troubled for a long time. It isn't the first assault he attempted, though my stepfather kept it quiet. He gave it up after he got caught with cocaine. I'm afraid my brother blamed you for his trouble."

"I'm sure he did," Julian said quietly. "Jeremy was good at blaming others. Unfortunately, he was also good at acting like a sane human being."

"I made it worse, I'm afraid," Tricia said. "I hadn't seen him in the last couple of years, and when he came by and told me about you, I listened. I fed into his fantasy about ruining you. You have to understand what a great story you are. Billionaire businessman runs underground sex club. It's the kind of story that could make my career."

"It will be the end of your career if you don't drop it," Julian said, glancing up at her.

She nodded, and Finn sensed some backbone in her now. "Yeah, I get that now. You're a very scary man. I'll drop it, but I went to his place a couple of days back. He wasn't in, but I have a key. I went in to check his computer to see if I could find another number for you. I couldn't get past that Nazi secretary of yours."

A faint smile crossed Julian's face as he looked back at the arrest and police records Taggart had compiled. "Yes, I believe she's earned her bonus this year."

"What did you find?" Finn asked. All of his investigative instincts had been on high alert ever since Tricia walked in. He knew a witness with a story when he saw one.

"Pictures of Mr. Lodge. He's been following Mr. Lodge around for the better part of a year, from what I can tell. Ever since he got out of jail."

"He's the one who vandalized my vehicle," Julian mused. His fingers drummed along the tabletop. His eyes found Leo's. "And The Club?"

Leo frowned. "Oh, yeah. I think he started the fire. Little things add up. When Sally's place got trashed, I couldn't let it go. That's when I called Taggart in. I've had him working on this for the last couple of weeks."

Julian sighed. "Fine. You're rehired."

"Maybe I don't want to be rehired," Leo returned.

"At a ten percent raise."

Now Leo was all smiles. "Nice working for you again, boss. I swear your stubbornness is going to make me a millionaire."

Sam was back on the phone. He started talking as he left the room, relaying the new information to Jack.

Finn still didn't understand. "What does Lexi Moore have to do with any of this? Does she know your brother?"

Tricia shook her head. "I don't think so, but from what I can tell the only person my brother hates as much as Mr. Lodge here is Lucas

191

Cameron. I assume this Lexi is his girlfriend."

Finn felt his blood run cold. "Not exactly, but he would be devastated if anything happened to her."

Julian was on his feet in an instant, and Finn could see Julian was following the logical path. "Danielle, you will not step foot out of this house until this man is caught."

Her mouth set in a stubborn line. "Really? I thought I was packing my bags."

Julian rounded on her. "Do not test me right now. I am willing to admit I acted in a bit of haste, but I won't discuss it now. Now you will obey me and stay in this house."

"You dismissed me, Julian," Dani pointed out. "You told me to leave, so I think I'll make up my own mind about this. Besides, this Jeremy guy won't come after me. He's going after people you care about, not your vacation flings. I think Finn and I are safe. Now, where would he have taken Lexi?"

Julian got down on one knee. Finn could see his face was flushed. He was shocked to see that Julian's hands had a fine tremble to them as he gripped Dani's arms. "You will obey me, Danielle. You will stay here, and you will do exactly as I say. You will lock yourself in the guesthouse, and you will not answer the door for anyone. Mr. Taggart will call back to Dallas and have bodyguards brought here immediately. They'll guard you and the children. Do you understand me?"

Dani frowned at him. "Fine. I'll sit and wait with the children. Now let go of me. You're hurting me."

Finn didn't move to help her. He'd known Dani far too long. She wasn't hurt. She was pissed, but Julian didn't seem to know it. His hands came off her arms right away, and he stared at her skin as though waiting for the bruises to show up. His skin was pasty white now, and he stood quickly, moving away from her. He stared at her for a moment, and when he spoke again, his voice was hoarse.

"Leave all you like after Jeremy is caught, but I won't have you in danger. Whether you choose to believe it or not, Jeremy will come after you. If he's been watching me, he's seen us together, and he'll know that harming you would be far worse than killing me. Stay put, Danielle. Finn, take care of her." Julian turned and walked out of the room without a backward glance.

Tricia Walker stood. "I think Mr. Lodge is right. I do think my brother's been down here for the last few days. I tried to call, and he didn't answer. He wasn't at his place, but he sent himself some e-mails on his computer with pictures of Julian and Danielle in a bar."

"Yeah, that would be The Barn. We were there the other night," he said, his skin prickling. There was really a psycho out there, and he wanted to hurt Dani and Julian. Finn turned to the door Julian had exited through. Every instinct he had told him to go after him, but Dani was firmly in her seat. She wasn't moving.

Taggart pulled out his cell and started talking, while Leo stepped out of the room. Finn turned his attention to Dani. Her eyes faced forward and were glazed with a solid pain he wondered if he could ease.

"Dani," he began. "Baby, you gotta listen to me. He didn't mean any of that."

He understood Julian in this instance. Julian had pushed her away for the same reason Finn had held her apart. They were both scared to death. He would bet his life on it. He'd been scared Dani would reject him and Julian...well, Julian was scared of a lot of things as far as Finn could tell. Julian might be incredibly comfortable with his outward sexuality but his heart—not so much. He probably wasn't even aware he had one.

Finn was. He'd seen the way Julian worshipped Dani. Julian was more loving than he thought he was. It was up to them to prove it.

Dani simply sat at the table, staring at the buffet that was left largely untouched. She pushed out of her chair and started to stack the plates.

"You have to know he's scared," Finn said.

"I don't know anything at all," she replied, her voice bland.

Taggart slid his cell into his pocket. He looked at them, first at Finn and then Dani. "You two going to give me trouble?"

"Why would we give you trouble?" Dani asked.

Taggart crossed his arms over his massive chest. "Well, several reasons. First of all you're involved in some crazy three way and I think Lodge just fucked that up. He's emotional and that man never gets emotional. It's weird and I don't like it, but then I don't get the weird threesome thing. Can you wait because in about an hour this douchebag named Adam is going to be here and he totally gets the threesome thing and he loves to Oprah all the emotional shit. Can you wait that long to do whatever stunt you're going to pull? Because I would rather you talked all this out with Adam than I had to deal with it."

Dani crossed her arms over her chest and went toe to toe with the man. It took everything Finn had not to reach over and pull her out of the way of the man's potential wrath. Instead he stood back and let her make her stand.

"I don't have to talk about it at all," she said, looking him in the eyes. Unfortunately that meant her head was bent back. Way back. "And my crazy three way is none of your business."

"It becomes my business if you do something stupid like try to run." Taggart stared down at her.

"I'm not going to put myself in danger because Julian Lodge is too stupid to see how good I am for him," she replied. "You tell him he doesn't have a thing to worry about because I don't stay where I'm not wanted."

Taggart's lips curved up slightly. "Just so you know you're wanted right here."

She finally stepped back. "I'll stay until it's safe to go, Mr. Taggart."

"Good. And if you're serious about not giving Lodge another chance and you don't mind mouthy metros, maybe I'll set you up with Jake and Adam. They're always looking for a gorgeous, open-minded woman."

Now it was Finn's turn. "I'm always looking for target practice."

A brilliant smile crossed Taggart's face. "Awesome. I win either way. Now stay put. I've got a couple of calls to make. I'll be in the living room. Scream if someone attacks you."

Dani picked up the plate of Danishes. "Do you want one before I put them up?"

For the first time the man looked slightly happy. "I can always eat. What flavor do you have?"

She glanced down. "I think all I've got left is lemon."

Taggart's whole face shut down, the light leaving his eyes.

"Thanks, but I don't eat lemon. Ever. It's far too sour for me."

He turned and walked out.

Dani was silent, her eyes on the door.

If he didn't do something, she would turn in on herself and he would be left out. "Come on, Dani. Let's go out to the guesthouse. We can watch some movies while we wait."

He'd work on her. He'd talk to her and get her to see that the Master would take a little teaching himself. No one was perfect. They had to work to get what they wanted. He'd take Leo's lead. Leo seemed to do what he thought was best, despite Julian's anger, and he came out on top anyway.

Dani nodded, though her expression was vacant. "Sure. I just need to use the restroom and then we can pick a movie."

Finn kissed her before she moved out of the dining room.

Chapter Fifteen

Dani felt her heart pounding as she pushed out of the dining room doors. She could hear the men behind her. Even Finn had gotten in on the conversation. They were talking about strategies and how best to protect her. Julian had Ian Taggart bringing in some professional bodyguards. He was flying them down despite the fact that it was only a couple of hours to drive. She was going to be watched after by someone named Alex and another guy named Liam. Julian had just about had a hissy fit when Taggart told him Adam and Jake were coming. That had been a long conversation where Julian had threatened to fire more people.

Why the hell would Julian care?

It took everything she had not to sob. The tears were right there, stuck in her chest. She'd promised herself she wouldn't fall for Julian Lodge, but she had. She'd been so stupid. She should have known he didn't give a real damn about her. She'd been obedient. That flipped Julian's switch. The minute she stepped out of line, he'd dumped her.

And then ordered her to protect herself. She could still feel his hands tightening around her upper arms. He'd held on so tight as he'd ordered her to the guesthouse. His face had been a mask of cold rage, but his eyes had told a different story.

Damn him. She could see in his eyes that he was far more

engaged than he let on. Why couldn't he admit it? Why did he have to pull all this bullshit? Even if he did care, if he never admitted it, what did it mean?

It made sense to Dani. It was the way her whole life had gone. Nothing had been easy. It was only fitting that the two men she'd loved were hard cases. Finn was only now accepting who he was, and Julian—oh, shit. She loved Julian Lodge.

Why? Why did she have to love Julian Lodge?

"Dani?"

Dani whirled around. Leo Meyer stood in the doorway. He was dressed simply in a T-shirt and jeans. He was a delicious-looking man, but he couldn't hold a candle to Julian's sophistication or Finn's easy western charm. And right now she found him annoying. "What the hell do you want?"

A hard glimmer came into those eyes, and Dani remembered what he was. He was the number two Dom in Julian's private world, and right now, he looked the part. An indefinable air of authority came over the man, and he seemed to grow an inch as he stared at her.

"I would greatly prefer to be friends, Danielle."

She wouldn't want him as an enemy. And she had been rude. "I'm sorry, Sir. Do I call you Sir?"

Just like that, the easygoing man was back. A smile crossed his face. "Yes. You would call any dominant either Sir or Ma'am, as applicable. It's polite. Julian, you would call Master, after everything is settled between the three of you."

Like that was going to happen now. He would be Sir forever if he had his way.

"Hey," Leo said, walking up to her. Concern was written on his face. "Don't look so sad. We already called the police. Julian and I are going to meet with the sheriff in a few minutes. Ian's going to stay here until he goes to pick up Alex and Liam. Sean is driving back with Jack and Abby and they have Lucas. We'll call in the feds if we have to. Julian has long arms. He won't let anything happen to you."

"I'm not afraid," she stated dully. She wasn't. She seriously doubted anyone would come after her. She wasn't important enough. That was the trouble. She would follow orders because it was stupid to fight him on this. Everyone was worried about Lexi and rightly so.

She wasn't going to add to the trouble in order to prove some stubborn point.

"Then why do you look so sad? Is it about that fit Julian threw? Sweetheart, that was actually progress. It gives me great hope for the future that he got that upset."

Somehow she couldn't see it as good. He'd told her to get out. If he did that every time she made a mistake or had a different opinion, her life would be miserable anyway. She couldn't live like that, always afraid she would make a misstep. God, she'd lived like that most of her life. It had been easier when she was a kid, but even then judgment had been the air the people of Willow Fork breathed. She'd always been that trashy Bay girl. Her mother had worked as a waitress at a truck stop. She hadn't had the best taste in men, but she'd been a good mom. It hadn't been her fault that first her dad and then Val's had run out, neither one willing to get married.

It had gotten so much worse after her mother died. She had been eighteen years old raising an eleven-year-old girl. The lectures had come hard and fast from the church ladies. Hillary Glass and her cronies had shown up after the funeral with Jell-O molds and tuna casserole. They'd explained that she had to be a role model for her little sister. She had to watch her step or someone might call social services.

She'd known from that day on that she had to be perfect or she could lose everything. Tears clouded her vision. She couldn't do it anymore. She could handle the spankings. Hell, she kind of craved that. For Julian, it was a weird way of saying he cared. It was the complete and utter dismissal she couldn't take. She couldn't worry about making a wrong move and losing what she loved. It was too much.

"Don't, sweetheart." Leo's arms came around her as she began to cry.

"Leo, is there a reason you're pawing my slave?"

Dani looked up, and Julian was staring at her from the doorway. Finn was at his side. He started toward her, but a single hand stopped him. Julian moved in front of Finn, taking a dominant position.

"She's upset. You can't tell me not to help her when she's upset," Leo said, but his arms were quick to release her.

"I certainly can. She's mine. If she requires comfort, she'll come to me."

Danielle frowned. "You're the reason I need comfort in the first place. I don't want comfort from you."

Julian's broad shoulders inched up in a negligent shrug. "Then you may go without. Leo, if you're through molesting my property, we need to go to the sheriff's office. We're taking Ms. Walker with us to give her story to the local police. Ian is going to meet the private jet. He won't be gone for more than half an hour. Samuel and Finn will remain here. Samuel, I assume you know what to do."

"I'll shoot anything that even vaguely looks like that weasel. Don't worry. As long as Dani and Finn stay here, we won't have a problem." Sam already had a shotgun in his hand. He looked like a man who knew how to use it.

A small woman with dark hair walked out of the kitchen. Benita was the Barnes-Fleetwood family's housekeeper. She also had a shotgun in her hands. "The children are playing quietly. Two of the ranch hands are watching them. Ricky is enjoying playing princesses with Olivia. Truly, I never expected he would look so nice in a tiara."

"Is everyone armed now?" Dani asked.

Seeing the housekeeper with a firearm brought home the danger they were in. Maybe Julian was wrong about this Jeremy guy coming for her, but he was out there, and he meant Julian harm. Despite the fact that he was a jerk, Dani couldn't stand the thought of something happening to him.

"Yes," Julian replied gravely. "Everyone is armed, and they will protect you. Once the McKay-Taggart employees are here, they'll transport you, Finn, and the children to a safe house. Abigail will be joining you."

Sam's eyes got wide. "Damn. Does she know that yet?"

"I don't believe Jackson has informed her. I believe he intends to have her taken into custody whether she likes it or not. You should mind him, Samuel, or you'll go to a safe house as well."

"Okay, I get it, but can we tell her that I didn't have anything to do with it?" Sam asked. "I would just like it to be on record that I didn't have anything to do with locking her up."

"This is why you're not the Dom, Samuel," Julian said. He turned back to Dani, and she felt the weight of his stare. "I see your mind working, Danielle. I know what you're thinking. You're thinking it isn't fair that Jackson would lock up his wife."

It had been exactly what she'd been thinking. "It's her daughter. She has the right to look for her."

"And she's Jackson's daughter, too. She became his responsibility the day he fell in love with her mother. He cannot properly track her if he's worried about Abigail. Abigail will be his chief concern, and that is not what she needs. She needs her husband to be an animal with one thought and one thought only—find Lexi, bring her home."

Sam shook his head. "Damn it. I have to agree. I'll be in the doghouse, too, now. I hate logic. I'll pack a bag for her. It's the least I can do."

Sam walked out, and Benita followed, the shotgun on her petite shoulder. Dani looked at Julian. She was with Sam. Logic sucked.

"I'll stay put. I'll go with the guards. I won't make trouble." She would go quietly and then figure out what the hell she would do with her life from there.

Julian stood staring as though judging her truthfulness. He finally nodded. "See that you do. I'll contact you as soon as it's safe. Finn, make sure you're both ready to go when Mr. Taggart comes for you."

He turned and left without another word.

"Give him time," Leo said with a sad smile before he turned and followed Julian.

Finn's hair fell over his eyes, and he pushed it back, much as he had when they were kids. The gesture made her heart soften and then clench a bit. Would he be mad that she'd gotten them tossed out? Would he want to go with Julian or stay with her?

"Baby, don't look like that." He reached out, tentatively at first, and then more forcefully, as though he'd made the decision to take the lead. He grasped her arms and brought her close. "It's going to be all right. You'll see."

She let him hold her for a moment but then pulled away. Emotional wasn't something she could do right now. She needed to keep it together. Later, when everything was over, she could fall apart. "Can you go grab my bag?"

Finn kissed her forehead and headed out to the guesthouse to retrieve her bag. It was the only thing she owned anymore besides that ramshackle house she shared with her sister.

Dani's cell trilled. She pulled it out of her pocket and glanced at the display. Val. Speak of the devil. She hit the *answer* button, perfectly ready to spew some venom at her sister. Finn's near-death experience had taken precedence over her sister's much-needed ass kicking, but now seemed like a good time to at least tell Val that hell was coming her way.

"Val, you have a lot of nerve calling me, little sister." She kept her voice low. There were a whole bunch of things she meant to say to her baby sis that she didn't want anyone else to hear.

"Dani? Is that you, Dani?"

Val sounded strange, as though she'd been crying. The words were muffled and almost hard to understand.

"Val, where are you? I can barely hear you."

"I'm so sorry. I didn't mean for it to go this far. Please, please—" Val's voice was abruptly cut off.

"If you would like to see your sister alive again, you'll do exactly what I tell you," a low voice said.

Dani went cold. She turned and looked for someone, anyone, but she was alone. Oh, god, she'd been wrong, and Julian had been right. Jeremy was coming for her. He was already here.

"Don't even think about going after your boyfriend. I have a gun to your sister's head, and I broke into the security system feed. I can see everything that's covered by his security cameras. I know Julian and Leo left with my traitor bitch sister. The big blond asshole is gone, too. I know your boy is in the guesthouse, and I know Sam Fleetwood is pacing on the porch. You're going to do exactly what I tell you, or I kill your sister. I would kill the other one, but I really want old Lucas to watch her die, so Valerie it is. Are you going to do as I ask, or should I pull the trigger?"

"Please!"

Dani could hear Val crying. She wailed, and then something thudded, and Val went quiet. Dani didn't have a choice. She couldn't sit here while her sister was killed and Lexi waited to die. She had to act, even if it meant she was the one to go. It was better than living with the consequences of inaction. "What do you want me to do?"

A low chuckle vibrated over the phone. "Well, Danielle, I want you to walk outside and take the Master's car. He keeps a spare key in a magnetic box over the driver's side wheel. I know my Master well. You will take his car and drive to your family homestead, which I have also rigged with cameras. You will get the instructions I placed in your mailbox and follow them to the letter. Oh, and before you leave, I expect you to look at the camera outside the back door and drop your cell phone. You'll find another in the mailbox with your letter. You have ten seconds to comply."

There was a click, and Dani took off. She didn't think, didn't debate, simply ran for the back door. When she opened it, she turned and found the small black camera that looked out over the back porch. She held up her cell phone and dropped it to the ground before running toward Julian's Audi.

The key was right were Jeremy had said it would be. She slipped inside the car and thanked the day Finn had taught her to drive a stick shift. Tears clouded her vision. She might never see him again. Or Julian. How angry would he be? Would he even understand?

It didn't matter. She had to go. Her soul demanded it. Dani put the car in drive and took off.

Chapter Sixteen

Finn zipped the bag closed and glanced around the small bedroom looking for anything he might have lost there.

Despite all the anxiety of the past hour, he felt a wide grin split his face. He'd actually lost a lot in this little house. He'd lost his shame. He'd lost his fear. He'd lost his freaking heart.

Love for Dani pounded through his system. It was so different now that she was his. He felt more than he'd ever thought he could. Making love with her had changed something fundamental inside him. Watching her embrace her sexuality had helped him to accept his own.

And then there was Julian. Julian thrilled him in a way he never could have imagined. Even when Julian scared the crap out of him, and he did when Julian turned that icy stare his way, Finn had never been more attracted to a man. Julian pushed his boundaries like no one had before. Julian didn't try to coax him along. Others had tried, and it hadn't worked. In his mind, Finn had come up with one excuse after another to hold on to his shame. Julian left no room for anything as useless as shame.

Despite Julian's poor handling of Dani earlier, Finn felt an optimism he hadn't felt before, maybe ever. He was in a good place.

As soon as Julian took care of this Jeremy person, he had the feeling he'd have no real trouble getting Dani to move to Dallas with him. Julian would insist on it. They could see him, date him, whatever they wanted to call it. The three of them would work it all out.

He would have a family. He would have Dani. He would have Julian. He would have it all.

After they survived this apparently crazy dude.

He jogged down the stairs carrying his suitcase. He had all the things Julian had bought for Dani over the last few days. It was only the essentials, toothbrush, a couple of pairs of jeans, T-shirts, moisturizer, anal plug, and lube. When they got wherever they were going, Finn would see that he expanded her wardrobe. Julian would more than likely expand the toy selection.

He couldn't wait to see The Club. Now he was certain he'd made the right decision in not accepting Lucas's offer to visit the underground BDSM club. It was better to experience it for the first time with Julian and Dani.

Lucas. God, what must he be going through? Finn felt for his friend. He would do anything he could to help him find Lexi. Lucas would do the same for him if Dani was missing.

He wasn't even going to think about that. His stomach rolled at the idea. He needed to focus on something else or panic would take over.

Finn paused by the sofa. He sighed before folding the blanket he found there. He had no idea why Julian refused to sleep with them, nor would he ask. When Julian was ready to explain, he would. Until then it would be like beating his head against a brick wall. He would have to be happy with having Dani all to himself during those hours. He got to cuddle her and wake her up. Somehow in the morning, when they were both groggy with sleep, it seemed easy and sensible to be the aggressive one. This morning he'd rolled her over and been deep inside her before either of them were fully awake. He'd rocked into her over and over until he'd come, and then he'd fallen back to sleep beside her.

The door flew open, pulling him out of his memory. Sam stood in the doorway, his face set in hard lines he didn't normally associate with the fun-loving cowboy.

"You better go after your girl, and you better go now. She's gone insane. Do you have any idea what Julian's going to do to her?" Sam asked, his voice getting louder and more insistent with every word.

He dropped the bag. A sick feeling nestled in his gut. "What do you mean go after her?"

Sam pointed out the guesthouse's doorway toward the long, paved drive. "I mean Dani just took off for God knows where in Julian's Audi. What the hell is she thinking? I can't go after her. My kids are holed up in a bedroom. I'm not leaving them, so you have to go after her."

Finn felt his stomach turn. "Dani wouldn't leave."

"Well, she damn sure did. I guess she was more pissed off at Julian than we suspected."

"No," Finn replied. If there was one thing in the world he was certain of, it was that he knew Danielle Bay. He knew her inside and out. "She wouldn't leave. She wouldn't cause trouble when so many lives are at stake. There's no way she stole Julian's car because she was mad. Something happened. Something, or someone, made her take off."

He pushed his way past Sam and started to jog toward the house.

"Why? If Julian had called, wouldn't he have called you, too?" Sam asked, following behind.

"Or Dani would have told me she was leaving. Besides, Julian would never allow her to go alone. He wouldn't have called her. He would have called me." Finn stopped when he saw the small, black box on the back porch. Now he was panicking. He could feel the blood rushing through his veins. He rushed to pick up the phone he recognized as Dani's.

Sam stared at the phone. "Damn, there's no way she dropped it. She had that phone in her jeans. It wouldn't have fallen out."

"And she left her purse behind. How many women do you know who leave their purse behind unless it's an emergency? And she doesn't have Julian's keys. How the hell did she hot-wire a car?" Nothing added up. He picked up the phone, hoping to see who might have called. When the screen came on, he saw the last thing she'd done. It was an unsent message. Three characters in stark relief.

<3 U

Love you. He felt his heart drop to his feet because that felt like good-bye.

* * * *

"But this girl was taken from Dallas. I don't see what that has to do with us here in Willow Fork. Girls don't go missing in Willow Fork."

The sheriff was grating on Julian's every nerve. His laconic speech and lazy manners made Julian want to punch the man who was supposed to protect and serve his people. Apparently women from the big city weren't his concern. Julian shifted from one foot to the other, unable to stay still. The mid-morning light filtered through the sheriff's department's windows. Casting a glance outside, he could see that the rest of Willow Fork moved along as though nothing untoward was happening under their noses.

Perhaps he should have brought Taggart with him. Leo was too reasonable. He thought talking to the sheriff was the way to handle this. Taggart would have stormed the building and taken over all their resources. Oh, they would likely all end up in jail, but at least they wouldn't be talking endlessly.

"We have every reason to believe that this woman was brought here," Leo was saying. The sheriff simply nodded as Leo continued to talk, as though actually following the conversation.

These people wouldn't help him. They didn't have the resources even if they had the will, and Julian doubted they wanted to help him. This town seemed to think anyone who wasn't born here was an outsider and unworthy of support. Even the ones who had been born here were up for rejection. Danielle and Finn had been miserable in this small town. They had been outsiders looking in.

How long could he keep them? The question flitted through his mind as Leo argued with the sheriff. He could get them under contract. He could move them to his penthouse. He could control much of their lives, and they would still leave him. Everyone left.

Not everyone. Some he'd pushed away. Some he'd shoved away, and now it was coming back to haunt him. He thought about that night almost three years ago when he tossed Jeremy into the streets. It was the night he'd set everything in motion.

Julian had stared up at the stage. Samuel was lovely in his submission. He had finished his count of twenty, his body sagging forward. He was being punished for causing trouble at The Club, but it wasn't truly punishment for someone like Samuel. For someone like Samuel, finally being on a St. Andrew's Cross was something akin to redemption. Jackson tenderly helped his partner off the cross. Julian had handed a robe up to them, though covering Samuel's magnificence was the last thing he'd wanted to do.

His heart ached a bit, but it was a good thing. Samuel belonged with Jackson. They both belonged with Abigail. Something sad lodged itself in Julian's chest. They were happy. He would content himself with that.

"Boss." Leo's voice had pulled him away. "Have you forgotten about the other situation we have to deal with?"

Julian had sighed. Yes, Jeremy. He had almost forgotten about Jeremy. He should never have taken the young man on, but he'd seemed so eager to please. He'd been a lovely young man with a lanky body and large eyes that seemed to plead for someone to take care of him. He was a sucker for that.

Jeremy had conspired against a guest of The Club. He'd drugged Lucas Cameron's drink. He'd done it at the behest of someone looking to harm Lucas, but the simple act of bringing the drug into the building was a punishable offense. It was far past time to cut the fucker loose.

In the end, it had been easy. He'd simply had him carted out. Julian hadn't listened to offered explanations. He hadn't listened to pleas. He told the man who had shared his home and bed for almost a year that he was done. Julian struggled to remember the words, and then the night came back in vivid color.

"I am no longer your Master," he'd said.

No longer. He'd watched as Jeremy struggled with the bouncer at first, and then when he realized it was never going to work, something had died in his eyes. Jeremy had slumped down, and the bouncer had to carry him. Julian had turned back to the drama at hand, his former slave completely forgotten.

There had been weepy voice mails. Each time, Jeremy promised to be good. He'd promised to be a better slave, to give Julian free access to anything and everything he had. Jeremy had offered to take any kind of punishment the Master saw fit. He'd begged and pleaded.

Julian had changed his phone number.

When Jeremy had sat outside the building for two days in the pouring rain, Julian had the police escort him away. He'd delivered the young man a restraining order the following morning.

He had been quiet after that, and Julian had forgotten.

Jeremy had not.

Would Danielle and Finn pay for his mistake?

The sheriff's voice pulled him from his memory. "Now why would this boy kidnap this particular woman? Is she real good-looking?"

Julian hissed through his teeth, and he saw Leo tense. Leo knew him well. Leo seemed to sense that he was about to explode. "Alexis Moore is Jackson Barnes's stepdaughter. I expect you to speak of her with some respect."

The sheriff's eyes got wide, and he sat up straight in his chair. "Damn, man, why didn't you say that in the first place?" His hand flew toward the phone on his desk. He dialed a number with more vigor than he'd seemed capable of moments before. "Maudene, I need you to get the Dallas police liaison on the phone for me." He looked up. "This won't take but a minute."

Leo sat back in his chair. "Damn, we're far from home, boss. I never thought I'd see the day when someone was more afraid of Jack Barnes than you."

"It's only because he doesn't know me," Julian murmured. He toyed with his phone. Dani and Finn. They were running through his brain. The urge to call one of them was almost overwhelming. The thought that he wouldn't be able to see them or touch them again until this was sorted out gnawed at him.

The door to the main office opened and closed. That man Danielle had almost married walked in wearing some form of polyester work uniform. His name was stitched on the right side.

Jimbo. How atrocious. He could never have appreciated Danielle's loveliness.

"Hey, Maudene, is Andy around? I got a problem out at Momma's house. She said someone's been prowling around Daddy's old hunting shack. I looked last night and I didn't see anything, but she's on my ass about it. There were tracks, but it's just kids, I know it. You know how they go out there and hang out. If Andy could talk to her about it, she might let me alone."

Julian shook his head. He didn't need to hear about the man's problems. He had real problems.

Leo stood and stared out the window behind the sheriff's desk. "Is that Finn?"

Julian stood immediately. The SUV that pulled up was Finn's. Finn slammed out of the car and started running for the building. His heart raced.

Leo was frowning. "You'll have to punish him. He had clear orders."

"Shut up, Leo. He wouldn't have disobeyed without good reason." *What had happened? Was it Danielle?* He raced out of the cramped office and met Finn in the hall.

"Sir!" Finn's boots nearly slid on the floor. His hair was wild and his hands shaking.

"What is it, Finn? What's happened? Where is Danielle?" The questions raced through his mind. A thousand scenarios, each worse than the next, played out in a manner of seconds.

"She's gone. She took off in your car."

Leo was right behind him. "She did what?"

Finn placed a hand on Julian's arm, the warmth of his body a comfort to him. He felt icy cold everywhere else. "Julian, please, you have to hear me out."

"About what? We don't have time to talk. Somehow that fucker got to her. Was she alone for any amount of time? Is it possible she got a phone call you didn't hear?"

A sigh that could only be relief swept out of Finn's mouth. "Yes. I'm sure that's what happened. Sam checked the tapes. He called me on my way here. He said Dani looked up at the rear camera and dropped her phone, like she was trying to show someone she was doing it. Then she took off in your car."

"Damn it. He told her about the spare key I keep." Jeremy had known his habits.

Leo was on the phone already. "Yes, ma'am, my boss has just had his vehicle stolen. Could you please turn on the tracking? Thank you. I have the passwords."

Finn was staring up at him. "I checked the last number on her phone. It was Val's. He used Val to get to her. I know it. Val's phone is old. There's no way we can track it unless he calls again. How are we going to find her?"

Julian cupped Finn's face. "I promise I'll find her. I won't let anything happen to her. I will find her, and I will bring her back. Now why didn't you call me? We could have turned on the GPS on the Audi immediately." He tried to keep his voice calm. The last thing he wanted to do was chastise Finn. Finn had dealt with things the best way he knew how.

"I tried, Sir. It kept going to voice mail."

Julian rammed his hand in his pocket and came out with his phone. *Damn it.* He'd put it on silent the night before. He didn't want to be interrupted with mundane things like business when he was playing with his subs. Though he'd almost never turned off his phone before, his time with Danielle and Finn seemed different, almost sacred. Nothing should interrupt that. He'd forgotten to turn it back on.

Julian flipped the switch and immediately saw that he had more calls than he should have. A fission of fear crept across his skin. There was a text as well. It popped up when he pushed the button.

I suggest you answer me, Julian. You'll note I don't call you Master anymore. A true Master never neglects his slaves. Well, your slave has the power now.

Pure terror flooded his system. Before he could process any of the facts, his phone was ringing. The number was unfamiliar, but Julian knew who it was.

"What is it?"

There was a purr of pure pleasure that saturated the line. "Worried, are you? Don't be. I have Danielle. Might I say she's a step down from Sally? What are you thinking, Master...I mean Julian. At least Sally was slender and lovely. This girl looks like she fell off a trailer."

Leo was asking Finn some questions. It gave Julian a moment to step away. He pushed the door open and walked outside. He didn't want the others to overhear what might be a private conversation. There was only one reason to take Danielle. Jeremy wanted to lure him into a trap. If it saved her, if it spared her a moment's pain, he would go willingly. He wouldn't risk Finn. He needed to know that one of them was safe.

"What do you want, Jeremy?" He wouldn't waste time with bluster. He could tell Jeremy that he would kill him if he so much as harmed a hair on Danielle's head, but Jeremy would almost surely know that to be a lie. Julian would kill him no matter what he did at this point. Today or somewhere down the line, if he survived the day, he would make certain that Jeremy Walker died.

"Oh, so many things, but I'll start with you meeting me at a time and place of my specification. This is going to be different for you. You don't call the shots now. You aren't in control. I am."

It rankled. That alpha part of him growled and clawed to be let out. But Danielle needed him. "I'm walking to the car now. I want to speak with Danielle."

"No can do. She's a bit indisposed."

Julian stopped. "I won't come to you unless I have some proof that she's alive."

There was a long-suffering sigh and then a feminine voice. "Julian?"

"Lexi? Lexi, are you all right?"

"No, I am not. Some freaky asshole shoved a needle in my neck and when I woke up, I was chained to the set of *Deliverance*. So, no, I am not all right. I am as far from all right as a person can be." There was a jostling sound as though Lexi was moving. "Stop it. Fine. I'll tell him. Dani's here. She's alive, but I don't know for how long. You have to tell Lucas to stay away. He'll kill you bo—"

Lexi's scream was abruptly cut off. "See, she's alive. How long she stays that way is up to you. I've left a map in a black Jeep. It's at a café on Main Street. The keys are under the driver's seat. Come alone or I'll kill Danielle. There's a map in the car leading you to

211

where I will meet you. Don't try anything, Julian. The Jeep doesn't have GPS. You can't be traced, and I'll know if you try. I have planned this very carefully. There's no way out. You have twenty minutes. If you're a second late, I'll slit her throat."

Julian knew the café. He'd had lunch with Jackson there the day before. It was less than a block away. He could make it in under a minute if he ran. He would have to in order to get away from Finn and Leo. The time limit was there to ensure he didn't make any side trips. Of course, he could always call.

"Now drop the phone. My sister is watching. She'll tell me if you make a wrong move. Poor thing. She's always been a bit sad. Don't blame her, though. I kidnapped her cat. It's the only thing she's had to love since her husband died. Whatever you do, don't tell her I already killed the fucking thing. Your twenty minutes starts now."

Julian dropped the phone and ran for the café.

He heard Finn behind him but couldn't—wouldn't—stop for anything. He had the car in gear and was off before Finn could catch up. His eyes caught Finn's as he drove by, and the terror in Finn's eyes haunted him. He was sure it mirrored his own.

Julian picked up the map and followed directions.

Chapter Seventeen

Dani came awake slowly, her head pounding and the sound of a woman crying leaking into her brain. She tugged at her hands. The feel of tight, hard plastic on her wrists was jarring, forcing her out of that fuzzy place.

She opened her eyes. The world came into focus in fits and starts. Brown walls. Wood. The scent of gun oil. Where was she? Oh, yes. She started to piece it together. She was in Jimbo's family hunting cabin. Set back on the Smart family land, the small cabin had been his father's retreat, and then Jimbo's. She'd come out to this place on several occasions, mostly to pick him up when he was done "shooting deer and drinking beer," as he put it.

It came back in flashes like pictures in her mind. She'd done everything Jeremy had told her to do, though this time obedience had been a vile thing. She'd driven Julian's car to her house and traded it for an old sedan. The sedan had a map, but she'd known immediately where she was going. She'd stood outside her house and wondered if she dared to run inside and call someone, but a cell phone had rung in the sedan and she'd been told she had ten minutes to get to the cabin before he put a bullet in Val's head. Unsure if she could make it in time, she'd flown down the highway and up the back road. When she was on the dirt road that led through the woods, she'd never felt so alone. She'd gotten out of the sedan with tears in her eyes, certain she would never see Finn again, never feel Julian moving against her again.

It had all happened quickly. One minute she was stepping onto the rickety stairs that led to the door, and the next she felt something sink into her shoulder. A sting and the world had turned odd and soft. She'd had the barest moment to register a face looming above her before she hit the ground.

Her vision wasn't one hundred percent as she pulled at the zip tie that held her wrists together. She seemed to be tied to a hook that was anchored into the ceiling. It must be new, because it wasn't something she'd noticed before. There were only two rooms in the cabin. There was a living space and a small bedroom. There wasn't even a bathroom. She always remembered to go before she came out here because she was never going to use that outhouse. The small cabin, well, it was more like a shack, barely had electricity. What electricity it had was run from a generator. There was very little in the way of furniture. There was only a sofa bed, an easy chair, and a scuffed table with two chairs. She managed to turn her face.

"Val?" The words felt heavy in her mouth. At least she could remember why she was here. That monster had her sister.

She saw Val, tied similarly on another hook from the ceiling, just four or five feet away from her. Her head came up at Dani's words, and a manic look came over her face, her eyes bulged, her mouth opened, and she shook.

"Dani. Oh, Dani. You have to get us out of this. You have to."

There was a whine to Val's voice that cut through her brain like a hacksaw. Still, she had sort of been the one to get Val into this. This Jeremy person must have taken her sister in order to get her to comply.

"I will. You have to give me a minute. Is he here?" Dani forced herself to try to focus. Everything was still a little fuzzy, and her mouth felt as dry as a desert.

Val kicked out at her. "He walked outside. I think he's waiting on someone. Maybe he's brought someone in to kill us all. You give him whatever he wants."

"Shut up," a husky voice said. "You're getting exactly what you deserve, you deceitful bitch. You think I didn't overhear your conversation with our giant ass of a kidnapper?"

"Lexi!" Dani strained to twist around. Lexi huddled in a corner, her legs bound with rope, and her hands seemed to be tied behind her. "Oh, Lexi, are you okay? Everyone's looking for you."

"She's fine," Val whined. "She would be better if she kept that big mouth of hers closed. She's been spitting bile ever since she got here."

Lexi's deep blue eyes rolled. "Sorry, I guess I didn't get the pamphlet that went over the rules of how to behave when an asswipe takes you off the streets. Next time he should hold a seminar or something. Or I could take a few lessons from you. After all, you've spent so much time with him, you should know his habits by now."

Dani turned to Val, the quickness of the motion churning her stomach and making her queasy. Her shoulders ached from the weight being held on them. She forced herself to stand, though her legs felt wobbly.

"Lexi, please, give her a break. She's never handled stress well." Some of Lexi's words were starting to penetrate. "What do you mean she spent time with him? Val knows Jeremy?"

"No...I mean I met him in a bar. He lied to me. I thought he liked me." Val sputtered, and her hands went still.

Lexi snorted. "Sure you did. I don't know a female over the age of ten with a gaydar so fucked up she can't tell Jeremy plays for the other team. Don't try that line of bull with me. Like I said, I heard the two of you talking, though mostly it was Jeremy talking and Val crying. Seems like her conspirator turned on her. Tell me something, Val, how much did he offer you to turn over your sister?"

She wanted to look at her sister and ask her if it was true. It would be useless. Dani knew deep down that it was true. Something was wrong with Val. Anger and rage warred with guilt in Dani's heart. Had she failed Val? She couldn't see how. She'd done her best. She'd sacrificed and worked hard to make Val's life the best it could be under the circumstances. She'd told her sister she loved her, and she had, though it had become harder and harder as the years went by.

"Damn it, I never meant for it to go like this," Val tried, obviously giving up the innocent routine. "I only wanted to scare you.

I wanted you to see that leaving town was what's best for you. I was giving you the shove you needed to be with Finn. Can't you see I was trying to do this for you?"

Or not. Dani felt tired in a way that had nothing to do with the drugs that had been in her system.

"Bravo, Valerie," a new voice said. It was soft but menacing. Dani got her first look at Jeremy Walker. He was thin and handsome, in a pretty boy way. "I admire you, dear. You're a liar right to the end."

"Please don't hurt me," Val sobbed. "I helped you, damn it."

Jeremy sighed as he looked Dani over. "God, I hope you're better than these two. This one can't stop crying, and Lucas's whore over there can't stop raging. It's giving me a headache."

"I'm glad, motherfucker," Lexi spat. "If I can do anything else to screw up your day, please let me know."

Jeremy shook his head. "I have no idea what Lucas sees in you." His head turned Dani's way. "Of course, I have no idea at all what Julian is doing with you, dear. Slumming, I suspect, though he jumped fast enough when I told him I was going to slit your throat. He should be here any minute. I have plans for the two of you."

"He doesn't care about me. I'm just extremely submissive. He likes that." Dani kept her voice low and her words calm. She'd dealt with more than one anxious patient at the clinic she worked at. The key was to remain even and calm. It would also be best to get him away from talking about Julian. "Now tell me what my sister's done."

Jeremy crossed to the table. There was a small duffel bag sitting there, and he opened it. His hands disappeared inside as he replied. "Well, your sister has been an excellent accomplice. She's everything I could want in a partner. Stupid and greedy and easily cowed, with the right amount of pressure."

"Don't listen to him." Val shifted from foot to foot as she pled.

Dani ignored her. She focused on Jeremy, who pulled out a small vial of clear fluid. Her stomach rolled. *Who was that for?* "What did she want from you? Money?"

A hypodermic needle came out next. Jeremy plunged it in and gauged the dose.

Lexi answered when Jeremy seemed too interested in his

medication. "She wants you to sign over your house. Something about her making a bunch of money off of it. When Jeremy turned on her, she offered to split it with him."

"I am not interested in money." Jeremy turned. Dani stared at the needle like it was a snake coiled and ready to strike. "What I have in mind is so much more important. You see, Julian thinks of himself as a teacher. I was his student. He is going to find out today exactly how much I learned from him. Julian is merciless, you see. Do you know what his first act as CEO of the company his mother left him was?"

He turned, and Dani tensed, waiting to feel that needle plunge in, maybe for the last time. Was that his plan? Would Julian get here and be confronted with her dead body?

"Please don't." Val squirmed as though she could shrink back.

Jeremy paid no attention to her. He stared at Dani. "No? Don't follow the business world here in Willow Fuck? Pity. Julian's first act was to begin a hostile takeover of a company his uncle owned. It was his uncle's baby. He'd spent thirty years of his life building that company. Julian took it apart in a matter of days. I think his uncle is in a nursing home. The best of care, of course. Everything money could buy, except companionship and his dreams."

"Why would he do that?" There had to be a reason. Julian was ruthless. She knew that beyond a shadow of a doubt. But she hadn't seen any true cruelty in him. He was concerned about the people around him. He'd taken such good care of her.

"I'm sure he'd tell you it was all a good investment, but I know the truth. You see, you have to study the things you love in life. I've made a comprehensive study of Julian Lodge. His uncle became young Julian's guardian after his parents died. He didn't have any time to spend on a child. He was too busy building his own company, software of some kind. He hired nannies, but he hired them off the street, without references of any kind. He paid them little, and he looked the other way when they abused their charge. When they left, he would simply bring in another one. Once, one walked away and Julian was left alone for weeks. I believe he was ten at the time. It was only when the gardener came that Julian was found. It wasn't that there wasn't the money for good help. His uncle had tens of thousands per month for Julian's care. He simply preferred to use it on himself."

How chaotic must his life have been? Her heart bled for him. Even though her own childhood had been money poor, at least she'd had her mom. She'd worked most of the time, but she'd been there at night to tuck her in. Julian's life had been a series of transient abusers.

"Don't believe him. He's making shit up," Lexi said, shaking her head. "He doesn't know anything. Julian would never have told him anything so personal."

He struck and quickly. The needle was in Lexi's arm before she could scream.

"Bastard." Lexi's eyes were glazing even as she said the words.

"Probably, though Mother claims not." Jeremy sighed. "I really can't have her yelling. You never know when the yokels will be listening in. I would have gagged her, but I'm afraid she bites. She's just as much trouble as her mother. I'll never understand the Dom who wants a willful slave."

Dani couldn't help it. "Because you were so well behaved? I heard what you did."

His eyes lit up. "The Master…I mean, Julian spoke of me? Of course, he did. I was the best slave he ever had. The truth is he didn't deserve me. I was far too good for him. And I'm right about his childhood. I lived with him, you know. I also worked in the building he owned. His secretary was given a cushy suite after her husband died. She was his final nanny, the one who stayed. He worships the ground she walks on. She keeps a diary. I read it. Mostly boring crap about her kids, but I found the volumes about Julian's childhood to be illuminating."

Dani didn't doubt it. Nor did she doubt Julian would be horrified if he knew someone had read such intimate details of his life. "Why are we here? Why don't you go and find another Master? I'm sure there are many who want an obedient slave. Of course, they might not after you murder your former Dom." Dani decided to try logic one last time. "Come on, Jeremy, you still have a chance to make this right. Julian isn't here yet. You haven't actually hurt anyone."

"Speak for yourself. He slapped me." Now Val sounded sullen.

Jeremy's face hardened. "If you speak again, I'll seriously consider setting my friend on you. You remember the other night. I bought more than one snake, Valerie. Would you like to meet the second one? I'm certain he's antsy by now."

"You tried to kill Finn." The truth rushed into Dani's consciousness.

Jeremy shrugged. "If it makes you feel better, I was trying to kill Julian. I saw him talking to this Finn person. I had Val point out his vehicle. I knew Julian would go home with him. I know that look in his eyes. However, I thought Julian would drive. He always has to be in control. How was I to know he would change his habits?"

It seemed to Dani that maybe Julian was changing a lot of his habits lately. She fell silent, using all of her concentration to stay on her toes.

"I feel sorry for you, really I do." Jeremy continued on, obviously enjoying the sound of his own voice. Dani briefly wondered if Lexi wasn't the lucky one. "Julian will make you fall in love with him. He'll give you everything you need for a time, and then when you think it's all going to work out, that you'll be the one who can truly change him, that's when he finds a new slave and cuts you loose. He might be kinder about it with you than he was with me. Perhaps he'll find you a new Master as he did for many of his former slaves, but in the end, you're just another in a long line of interchangeable bodies. You don't matter. Not really."

It wasn't anything she hadn't thought before. Only hours before, Julian had dismissed her for the simple act of having a different opinion. Was she fooling herself into thinking she was different? Would she end up like Jeremy if she stayed with Julian?

He stared down at Lexi's unconscious form. "As for her, it's truly better she ends here, too. I've been watching her for months. She's filled with rage, so much rage and pain. She seems fine when she's in public, but she's not. Not even Lucas seems to reach her. I've often wondered what happened to her. They don't have sex, you know."

That was news to Dani, but she kept her mouth closed. Jeremy put the needle back in the bag and came out with another two sets of zip ties. Dani wondered if he'd gotten a special deal since he seemed to buy them in bulk. He carried them to the far side of the room along with one of the chairs. He placed it far from anything else and then attached a set to each arm of the chair, leaving the open end dangling, waiting for someone.

Julian. He intended for Julian to sit in that chair. Was Julian coming here? Was he coming for her?

Jeremy turned back to her. "I managed to get myself into Lucas's house through his cleaning service. You can't trust the help these days. I set up cameras. Poor Lucas. He won't fuck her no matter how much she begs. He'll whip her, spank her, tie her up and use a vibe on her, but he withholds his cock, and would you like to know why?" Jeremy laughed and shook his head. "She won't tell him she loves him. Who would have guessed that Lucas Cameron would hold out for a declaration of love? Pity. He should have fucked her while he had the chance. Carpe diem and all that."

Jeremy's head swung around. He cocked an ear as though he could hear something Dani could not. A wicked smiled creased his youthful face. "Looks like he wants you to live." He strode to the table and pulled an odd-looking gun out of the bag. As he made it to the door, he turned. "Scream if you like, Danielle. I think Julian will appreciate it. He always did like the sound of a woman in pain."

She kept her terror firmly lodged in her chest as Jeremy walked out the door. Julian wouldn't like it. It would horrify him. Julian liked to play. He played out his own fantasies even as he indulged her own. He enjoyed her cries as long as he knew they would lead her to something pleasurable. Julian would be horrified if he caused her pain that wasn't erotic or didn't seem to be something she needed. It was why he was harder on Finn. He would raise welts on Finn's ass, and Finn would come all the harder for it. On her he used a light hand. He barely made her bottom pink.

"See, if you hadn't decided to sleep with that sicko, we wouldn't be in this predicament." Val's sullen pout was back.

"Shut up, Val, or I swear I'll kill you myself." She strained to see out the window. The ties bit into her wrists and her neck hurt at the unnatural angle. In the distance, she glimpsed a black Jeep coming up the back way. It rolled up the dirt road that ran from the highway, if you knew where to look for it. It didn't go by the Smart house, so there wasn't anyone to warn.

"I really wasn't trying to kill you, Dani." Val sounded small now.

She looked down at her sister. "You wanted the house? I was going to sell you my half."

"I don't have the money for your half, and then—"

"And then what?"

There was a small pause and then a deep, heaving sigh. "And then the mayor told me there's going to be a big development right on our land. They're going to build an outlet mall. It's going to be huge. My piece of the land is worth two hundred and fifty thousand."

"Well, it's good to know my life was at least worth six figures to you." Desperation edged out anger at her sister. She could deal with her later, after she'd figured a way out.

"I told you I wasn't trying to kill you. Just scare you into leaving with Finn."

"I don't care. Take the land. I don't care. All I care about right now is the fact that that whackdoodle is going to come back in here any minute and use me as a sacrificial lamb to punish Julian." She slipped as she tried to get a better look outside. She groaned as her wrists took the full weight of her body.

"Be careful. You're going to break the damn roof if you keep swinging like that."

Dani got her footing back and stared up at the ceiling where the hook was bolted. Sure enough, Val was right. There was a crack right there, snaking out from where the hook met the ceiling. A bit of hope soared through her. Jimbo's father had built this place himself over twenty years before. The elder Smart hadn't been known for his perfectionism. He'd been just as lazy and apt to cut corners as his son. She looked at the hook above Val's head. It was taking her weight with ease. Never before had Dani been so happy to have twenty pounds on her sister.

"What are you doing?" Val's attention was focused now as Dani took a deep breath. "I don't think you should do it, whatever it is."

"I'm done listening to you. If I decide to save you when all this is over, I don't think I want to be your sister anymore." Dani braced herself because this was going to hurt.

She grabbed the ties with her hands and pulled. The crack opened a bit more, but not enough. It would take more than a simple pull. Dani brought her feet up and dangled. She swiveled her hips and started to sway.

Val tried to turn to her. "You're going to bring the roof down on top of us. This is your plan? You're going to kill us before he can?"

Dani pulled and pulled. She gained ground, but not enough. It would take time to work the screw out of the beam. She let her full weight hang. The beam groaned but held.

The door opened, and Dani's time was up.

* * * *

Finn sat back in one of the old vinyl chairs that dotted the sheriff's department's waiting room. All around him people were buzzing like flies in a flurry of activity, but he felt completely still, held in place. His brain screamed for everything to stop. He wanted it all to stop so he had a minute to process the fact that they were both gone.

They were gone, and he didn't know where they were. He didn't know what was happening. He stared down at the phone in his hand almost waiting for it to ring. Julian had dropped his phone just like Dani had dropped hers. Leo had picked it up and had confirmed it was the same number that had called Dani, Val's old-model cell. He'd called and called the number, but it simply went to voice mail. The phone company was trying to trace it, but it would take time, and there was no way to know if Jeremy had dumped it somewhere. His own phone had been completely silent.

Leo had been on the phone with Taggart, who was on his way, but how would they find Julian? Dani was out there and Finn couldn't protect her. Julian was walking into a trap and Finn was…alone.

He wanted to be with them.

Why wouldn't it ring? Damn it, but he wanted to be where they were. Fuck the consequences. He didn't want to be left behind. He'd run after the Jeep Julian had been driving until he couldn't anymore.

"Finn, I got the location on the Audi. The sheriff and I are going out to take a look. Would you like to come?" Leo stared down at him. He seemed perfectly cool and collected. Finn bet there wasn't a screaming idiot inside of Leo waiting to get out.

"No. I'll wait here." What was the point? Dani obviously had ditched the car, and Julian had driven off in a Jeep. They were following someone's plan. Finn was certain Leo would find the car without a driver, and there was no way to trace the Jeep. Julian was gone the same way Dani was gone.

"All right, Finn." Leo's eyes were sympathetic. "It's probably for the best. I'll be back as soon as I can. Jack Barnes should be here in about twenty minutes. Taggart is on his way, too. Let them know what's going on."

Leo walked away. It wasn't a moment before there was a hand on Finn's shoulder. He looked up into the face of his nemesis. Jimbo Smart. *Damn it.* This was not what he needed.

"Finn, what the hell is going on? Someone said Dani went missing."

Finn softened slightly. The big man honestly seemed concerned. "Someone's after Julian, and he thinks he can get to him through Dani."

"Is Julian the rich guy?"

Finn nodded, though his attention was taken by Tricia Walker, who sat by the big window staring at her cell phone, too. Finn studied her carefully. Her head was down, and she didn't seem to notice anyone around her. She was so quiet for a reporter. Finn had met many reporters in his time, and the one thing they all had was an innate confidence. They had to. Tricia lacked that confidence.

Wasn't that odd?

"I knew he was trouble," Jimbo was saying. "What's a guy like that doing here anyway?"

"Taking a vacation," Finn said as he stood and crossed to Tricia.

Her eyes came up, and before she could settle a mask on to her face, she was open. Finn read her like a book.

"Is he really your brother?" He asked the question gently. One thing Finn had learned to do in his years as a lawyer was to properly gauge the witness. Some required a firm hand, but many needed sympathy to get them to properly tell their stories.

Tears welled in her eyes. "Half-brother, but yes, we're related."

"He scares you."

"Well, hell, Finn, of course he scares her if he runs around kidnapping people." Jimbo stood right behind them. Finn thought briefly about shoving him back, but he had other fish to fry.

"I think he's perfectly capable of doing everything he says." She leaned in a little. "But then I'm scared of that Julian person, too."

Finn bet she was. "And what paper did you say you worked for?"

A pause. "*The Dallas Morning News.*"

Her eyes had flared briefly. Finn knew he had her. It was time to make her afraid of him. A small lie was called for, but then a good lawyer always knew when to lie and when to tell the truth. "Really? Because that's not what you said this morning."

He watched as she tried hard to think. She finally bit her lip and clutched at her phone. "No. I said it. I know I did."

"Because he told you to say it?"

Again, a brief flaring of her wide eyes. He bet she couldn't play poker to save her life. If he'd been watching her closely this morning, he would have seen this, but he'd been distracted.

"I don't know what you're talking about."

Finn turned to Jimbo. "Jim, I need you to contact *The Dallas Morning News* and ask if they employ one Patricia Walker."

Jimbo's eyes widened, but he gamely started to pull out his cell phone.

Now her hands shook. "No, don't. I don't work there. I work for a suburban newspaper. I write a pet care column, but I do have press credentials because sometimes I cover dog shows. Jeremy made me call. He said it would cause chaos, and this Julian guy hates chaos. Jeremy made me say it. He took someone precious to me. I have to get her back."

He didn't care. Nothing in the world was more precious than Dani and Julian. "Where is he?"

"I don't know. He's been in the area for days. He doesn't tell me anything. He just calls me on this phone, and I do what he says. I don't even know how to contact him."

And Finn believed her. He took the phone from her trembling hands. He turned to Jimbo, who was watching avidly. "If you were going to take someone someplace secluded, where would you go? It has to be someplace fairly close."

One big shoulder went up and down. "Damn, there's a ton of places outside of town. This is East Texas. We have woods and swamps. You could hide for a long time in places like that."

Tricia sniffled. "He wouldn't like that. He's not an outdoorsman." Her tears were flowing freely now.

"Yeah, but there are plenty of hunting shacks…oh, fuck, Finn, I think I know where they are." Jimbo's breathing became ragged. "I think he might be holed up on my land."

"Do you know how to get there without alerting them that we're coming?" Finn glanced around the station house. There was only the deputy left and the secretary. All in all, he would rather go in alone. He didn't trust Andy.

"Hell, yeah," Jimbo replied. "I know those woods like the back of my hand. But I'm telling you, if you get Andy or the sheriff involved, they'll go in with guns blazing. I can be a hell of a lot quieter than either of those two."

"I agree. I would call Leo, but I don't have his number. I think we're it." Finn couldn't wait. He knew he'd been told to stay here until Taggart came for him, but he couldn't. He had to get to them. Every second he waited something terrible could happen. "But, Jim, I'm going to need a gun."

A wide smile split Jimbo's face. "I think I can help you out there."

Finn ran behind Jimbo. He held the only way for Tricia to talk to her brother firmly in his hand. Her cell phone. She wouldn't be able to warn him even if she wanted to.

As Jimbo pulled out of the parking lot, Finn sent out a silent prayer. *Keep them safe.*

Whether they liked it or not, he was the only cavalry they had coming.

Chapter Eighteen

Julian saw him the minute he put the sedan in park. His greatest mistake in human form. Jeremy stood in the doorway to a small structure, his thin frame seemingly too gaunt to cause any real damage.

How wrong he had been.

Jeremy smiled as he jogged down the steps. He looked excited, as though Julian were a welcome guest, not a victim. Everything seemed normal except for the oddly shaped gun in Jeremy's hand. God, was Danielle already dead? He wouldn't accept that possibility.

"Welcome, Julian." Jeremy stopped feet from him. Far enough that Julian would have to jump to get him. Far enough that Jeremy would have time to shoot him.

"You wanted to get me here. Well, I'm here. Now, you will let Danielle leave here unharmed or we will have trouble." He used his darkest voice, the one assured to get every sub in a five-mile radius on his or her knees.

And he could see the impulse written on his former slave's face. Jeremy wanted to do exactly that. Unfortunately, it looked like he'd tamed his impulses. Jeremy pulled the gun out, and now Julian could see it was no ordinary gun. He braced himself because he had the feeling this was going to hurt. He cursed himself for not keeping a gun in his car. If he survived this he was applying for a concealed license, and the next time someone freaked out on him, he would just shoot the bastard. He was certain Taggart could teach him how to use all the weapons.

Jeremy held the gun level to Julian's torso. "I don't think that works for me, Sir. I think I would rather give you a dose of your own medicine and see how you like it."

A spark flared from the end of the Taser. The probes shot out of the end of the Taser and lodged into Julian's chest. He lost all control in an instant. He hit the ground, knees first, his chest falling after, and he shook. Pain filled his every sense. He would have sworn he could smell that pain, hear it in the creaking of his bones. There was no control at all, merely the random spasm of every muscle in his body. He tasted dirt as his muscles shook violently for what seemed like forever. Julian tried everything. He commanded his body to do his bidding, but in the end he had no control. Pain screamed along his nerves until finally, blissfully, the pain ceased, and he was left quivering, all his strength sucked away.

It took everything he had to merely get air into his lungs.

"You're so big, Julian. I didn't want to get too close. These suckers can get you from fifteen feet away. I had to modify the output. I upped the ampage." Jeremy reached down, and Julian felt the pull on his dress shirt. His body flipped over at Jeremy's command. The probes from the Taser were still in his skin. Jeremy began to pull him by the back of his shirt. "You'll forgive me, but I didn't think you would actually cooperate with me."

Julian tried a snappy comeback. Tried to tell the fucker he'd never cooperate, but he couldn't seem to make his limp noodle jaw move. He was pulled along the ground like a sack of shit, and his only vision was of the sky above him. It was blue and pure, so unlike his situation it was perverse. He should be lying out by the pool at the ranch, Danielle and Finn at his side. Again and again he tried to make his arms move. His frustration boiled. What good was he to Danielle? He'd intended to trade himself for her or at least throw his body in front of hers and take whatever came their way. He was useless like this. His eyes burned with the knowledge that he'd gotten her into this.

"Don't bother," Jeremy said, a malicious glee in his voice. "With the electricity you took, it should be a while before you get function back. By then I'll have you nice and secure. You like bondage, Julian. I couldn't use metal cuffs, but I think you'll like the ones I bought for you."

"Ffffuuuckkk offff," Julian managed to stutter.

He was finally able to clench his fists. He rotated his feet in a deliberate manner. Yes, he was getting control back. In a moment, he would pull the Taser probes out of his flesh. He would reach out and grab the little fucker's legs. He would pull his ass down and beat him until he was dead, and then he would get Danielle, and he was never going to let her go. He would wrap her up in the tightest contract he'd ever written. He would never, never tell her how much of his heart she and Finn held. He would be their Master, their lover. He would never, ever let them go, but he couldn't love them. He couldn't afford to love them. To love them was to ache the way he was aching now. Why couldn't he let them go? He wished he could, but they were essential now. Somehow, they had wormed their way in. How could he handle it? People died. People left. They all left in the end. But if he wrapped them up, he could keep them. He could hoard them, like gold. They were precious. He'd gotten them into this position.

He looked up and saw the beginnings of the roof. He felt his head bump against something hard. Stairs. He moved his knee, flexing. Almost time. Just another minute and he would kill Jeremy. He would enjoy it. He would let the beast that lived inside him out and have his way with the prick. He would be covered in blood by the time he was done.

There was that horrible crackling sound as Jeremy struck again. His body convulsed as lightning flared through his system. Hated tears leaked out of his eyes and down his cheeks. Every muscle convulsed from the pulse sent through the probes, and he heard his own animal groan. He'd never felt so helpless, so vulnerable. It was like acid in his gut as he struggled to regain control.

Make it stop. Please. Please. Please.

The begging in his head felt toxic. He held it in. He wouldn't give anyone the satisfaction of hearing him beg. Not ever again. He'd begged his uncle. He'd gotten on his knees and begged to be allowed into his home with his aunt and cousins. He'd so wanted to be a part of a family. He'd cried that day.

His uncle had sent him away.

He would never beg again.

His body sagged in exhaustion as the shock finally stopped flowing through his system.

"I can do this all day, Julian." Jeremy knelt beside him, Taser in hand.

He wanted to shrink back, to crawl away like a wounded animal, but he couldn't move again. Control was so far away. Jeremy's hand came out and caressed his face.

"Isn't that what you used to say while you fucked me? 'I can do this all day, slave.' I dream about those words at night. I longed to hear them for so long. So I want you to know that I intend to make our last day together memorable."

Jeremy's eyes were big and soft, as though he was talking to a beloved lover rather than a victim. He hated the word, but *victim* was the only way to describe him. God, what had this psycho already put Danielle through? Was she even fucking alive? Please, please let her be alive and whole.

Jeremy got up and resumed his previous occupation of dragging Julian's dead weight into the shack that would probably be the location of his death. He heard the door open and the soft sound of a woman crying.

Danielle? Was Danielle crying?

"Oh, god, Julian. Julian. What have you done to him? You asshole."

Yes, that was his Danielle. He'd never heard her curse. It sounded savage. His sweet Danielle sounded like a warrior. His head turned as Jeremy pulled him, and he was able to see her. She was bound and still in her clothes from this morning. At least it appeared Jeremy hadn't raped her. God, he hoped not. He tried to reach a hand out to her. He'd promised to protect her. There was no contract between them, but she'd taken him into her body, into her heart. It was contract enough, he suddenly realized. He was the one who had broken the promises their bodies had made. First he'd said words meant to hurt her, meant to make her feel small and inconsequential.

Then he'd gotten her into this mess. He'd be the reason she died.

Tears streaked down her face. "Please leave him alone."

Jeremy pulled him along. "I can't, dear. He's the reason we're here."

Julian felt his torso being dragged up against something solid. He could see Danielle, and now he could see Lexi huddled in a corner. She was so still. Her black hair fell over her face, and she didn't move at all. Lucas was going to be devastated. Lucas might not survive losing her no matter what their current relationship status was. Lucas loved her.

Like he loved Danielle. Like he was coming to love Finn.

Time, he needed more time. If he had a little more, maybe he could have made it work. His hands were brought up one by one, and he felt the hard plastic wrap around his wrists.

"I love you, Julian." Danielle's voice eased over him, the only soft thing in a world that seemed so full of pain.

He wanted to give those words back to her. He'd never said them aloud since that day his uncle had sent him away. He'd used them that day. He'd told his uncle he loved him in hopes of getting what he wanted. Now he wanted to say them, to shout them, but his voice was mute. His mouth was a useless thing.

"Please don't hurt him again," Danielle begged. Her hands were over her head, attached to a hook in the ceiling. He could see where the ties were too tight. Her wrists were chaffing. She would be bruised.

If not for him, she would be safe somewhere.

A third woman cried next to Dani. Julian stared at her briefly. She had the same features as Danielle, but there was something weak about the slim woman. Her sister. She looked different without the mask of cosmetics. She didn't matter. Danielle mattered, and Lexi mattered. He knew he was a bastard, but he would let this woman die in order to save the other two.

Jeremy sighed as he walked up to Danielle. "Poor girl. She thinks you care about her. She doesn't understand that you would have come here for any of your slaves." He gave Danielle a pitying glance. "You see the Master is serious about his contracts. Those contracts mean more to him than the actual slave. He doesn't have a heart, but he does have an enormous sense of responsibility and guilt. Which is precisely why I know this is going to hurt him."

Jeremy slapped her across the face with brutal force. Julian managed to kick his feet weakly in a show of protest. Danielle gasped, her head snapping back. There was an angry palm print across her delicate skin when she looked back. Rage churned in his gut, and the vile taste of bile was in the back of his throat.

A thin trickle of blood was on the edge of Danielle's mouth. She spit it out and turned back to Jeremy. "Is that the best you have?"

Don't. Don't tempt him, little one. Cry and plead with him.

Jeremy stared at her for a moment. "Interesting. I chose her because I thought the man was a pain slut. He had that look about him. She looks so soft. I thought it would bother her. But if you like it…"

Jeremy crossed the room. There was a bag on the table, and he reached into it. Julian watched in horror as he pulled out a baton.

"Don't." Julian managed to push the words through his lips.

"Don't what?" Jeremy asked with a smile on his face.

"Don't hurt her."

He shrugged. "It's not what you think it is. I'm not going to beat her with it."

Danielle was shivering. "I know what it is. It's a cattle prod."

Shit.

Jeremy knelt down to get at eye level. "I'm going to use it on your cow, Julian. I'll warm her up a bit, and then I'm going to shove it up her ass. We'll see how much she can take."

He had lied to himself. He'd promised to never beg, but now he knew he'd do anything to spare her. "Please."

Jeremy's face lit up.

"Julian, don't. I can handle it."

Danielle, so sweet, so brave.

The words were bitter, but necessary. "I'll do anything. Please."

"Begging like the dog you are. I'm surprised. You really will do anything to keep up your end of a contract. It's your Achilles' heel." Jeremy set the prod down and came back with a dog collar. Julian lay passive as it was clicked around his neck. It chafed and bit into his skin. "You're my dog now. Good puppy. And I'm still going to hurt her."

"Fucker."

Just like before, it didn't matter. Begging didn't work. Pleading didn't work. And still he tried.

"Please leave her alone. I'll come with you. I'll do what you want. I'll be your fucking dog." He'd never felt so small, but watching Danielle die would be worse.

"Oh, yes, you'll do everything I say, Julian. I'm the Master now." Jeremy flicked on the cattle prod. The sound sizzled through the air menacingly.

It was nothing compared to the scream that came out of Danielle's mouth.

* * * *

Finn heard the scream. It seemed to echo through the forest.

"Holy shit," Jimbo said beside him. "That sounds like Dani."

He started forward, but Finn stopped him. He understood the impulse. He wanted to run through the fucking forest like a barbarian and kill everything in his path, but he had to control it. He had to stop and think it through. The worst thing he could do was rush in without any knowledge of what was going on. The old Finn would have blustered his way in and probably gotten himself caught in the same web. The new Finn held his breath for a second. Julian was out of commission for all he knew. He could only count on himself. He was their best shot.

"How many windows are there on the cabin?"

Jimbo checked himself. "Two. There's a big window on the side facing us and a smaller one in the back. If you're thinking about sneaking in through the small one, don't. We're both too damn big. Though we oughta be able to shoot through it if the target is visible. But what if she's already gone?"

He refused to believe it. "I don't think so. Julian couldn't have been there long. I think this Jeremy person wants to torture him before he kills him. The way to torture Julian is to hurt Dani. He'll play with her for a while."

"Fuck."

Fuck was right. It tore him up that Dani was being hurt. She would have to take it while he set up her rescue. After, he'd love her so much she'd heal. Dani was strong. She'd had to be.

The hunting cabin came into view as he and Jimbo quietly slunk through the trees. Every sound made Finn wince. He had a rifle in his hands. He could see the big window, and what he saw made his heart clench. Dani was clearly visible. Her back was to them.

"Is that Val, too?" Jimbo's soft whisper held a note of desperation.

"It looks like it."

A long, tortured sigh came from Jimbo's throat. "Damn it. When the time comes, I'll take care of Val. She's a bitch, but damn it, she's kind of my bitch. I don't know why, but I got a thing for her. If we make it out, I'm going to make sure she understands."

Poor guy. He didn't envy anyone who had the hots for Val.

A slender male figure came into view. Jeremy. He could see him through the glass. His hands stroked Dani's hair almost lovingly. *Bastard.* He'd pay for touching her. Finn strained, but he couldn't see Julian. Was he even here yet?

"Hand me the binoculars." He held out his hand for the slim binoculars. Jimbo's truck had proven to be a treasure chest of hunting aids. He kept rifles and ammo, knives, vests, and binoculars. Finn looked through the binoculars. He could see Dani's lovely form hanging limply. Jeremy had some sort of baton in his hand. He stared for a minute before his gut churned and he passed the binoculars to Jimbo. "Is that what I think it is?"

Jimbo's face went white. "Cattle prod." He brought the binoculars down and put his hand on Finn's shoulder. "It's actually good news. Unless he modified it, it won't kill her. It hurts like hell, but she'll be fine."

"How the hell do you know?" The thought of someone treating his Dani like a cow had him clawing at the rifle. Jeremy was too close. He'd never make the shot without hurting Danielle.

"Hell, Finn, I'm a redneck. You think I've never been hit with a cattle prod? That's a regular Saturday night around here. My point is we have some time."

Finn nodded, now happy he'd spent his childhood on the outside if cattle prods were regular weekend toys around here. His mind raced. "We need a distraction. I need to get Jeremy to a place where he's not so close to Dani. If he moves to the left, I can get him."

"Yes, can you use that rifle?"

"Of course." On that Finn was completely confident. The only occasions his father had spent real time with him was on the shooting range. He'd never liked hunting, but he'd always had a fondness for target practice. "Three years as the 4-H sharpshooter."

"That's what I like to hear. Now I'm going to give you a distraction. When that bastard heads for the door, be ready."

"What kind of a distraction?"

Jimbo shrugged. "I thought setting off some firecrackers right outside the door oughta scare the shit out of him."

"Why the hell do you have fireworks? They're illegal here."

Jimbo looked at him like he was a complete moron. "That never stopped a redneck from celebrating."

Jimbo set off, silently making his way toward a shed on the back of the property. Finn got into position and prepared to wait.

He promised himself he wouldn't miss.

Chapter Nineteen

Dani shook. Every inch of her body felt bruised and battered from the inside out. It felt like someone had twisted her insides around over and over until nothing seemed to be in the right place anymore.

"He's in agony you know." Jeremy had taken to talking to her like they were girlfriends gossiping. "Not over you. He hates the fact that he hasn't protected someone he's contracted to protect. You're like property to him."

"We don't have a contract." Dani heard the words coming out of her mouth, but they sounded foreign. Her eyes were on Julian's form. She couldn't stand to see him like that. The last ten minutes had been hell. Jeremy had shifted his attention between the two of them. He would work Dani over with the prod and then zap Julian. Watching her big, strong man shake and writhe was worse than feeling the pain herself. She could take the pain, but not the agony of watching Julian's pride fall away.

Jeremy stopped. "What do you mean?"

Dani tried to focus on him. "No contract."

"I thought you were sleeping with him."

"I didn't write a contract on her, asshole." Julian's words sounded weary. He leaned back. "I never meant to keep her. She's a vacation fling, nothing more."

The words stung, but she knew what he was doing. He was trying to protect her.

But Jeremy didn't seem to know what to do with that. "You don't have flings."

Julian laughed, but it was a shallow, bitter sound. "Shows what you know. I only came after her because you pissed me off."

"Really?" Jeremy moved toward Julian. "I think you're lying. I think you actually might give a shit about her. Why fucking her? Sally was more beautiful, and I hated Sally. Why women at all? Why do you need a fucking hole? I never understood that. I never understood why I had to share you with a fucking cow. Do you know how that made me feel?"

Even his eyes were wild now. He was building. She could feel it. Val cowered as much as she could. Dani tried to catch her eyes, but she was lost to terror. Lexi was unconscious in the corner. Julian was firmly bound, and even if he managed to get out, Dani doubted he would be able to move. He'd been hit several times with the Taser.

She managed to shift her feet. Her arms felt numb above her. The pain had gone away a long time before, but if she concentrated she could still move. She turned her head up to the ceiling. The crack was there, perfectly visible, simply too small to give her what she needed.

"I don't care how you felt, you little prick. I never cared." As tired as Julian sounded, the bile kept spewing out. Since that moment when he'd begged Jeremy to spare her, she'd watched as he retreated further and further into himself. There seemed to be nothing left but an indefatigable rage. And then she saw it. He moved his foot with purpose when Jeremy turned his back. He flexed and pointed it straight her way. The hardness was still in his eyes, but he wasn't giving up.

"I knew that, too. And you call yourself a Master." Jeremy reared his foot back and kicked Julian straight in the gut, the sound a dull, resounding thud that filled the room.

Beside her, Val cried out. She begged to no one in particular.

"Shut up!" Jeremy screamed the words. He dropped the cattle prod and shoved his hands in his hair, pulling and pulling.

"He's crazy," Val said, tears streaking down her face.

"You think?" Dani couldn't help the sarcasm. If she gave in to the terror, she would be utterly useless. Sarcasm seemed safer. "What gave it away?"

Jeremy stopped and turned to her. The resolute look on his face nearly stopped her heart. He was done playing.

God, she wasn't done. She wasn't done with anything. She wasn't done with life or love or any of it. She couldn't die when she'd just started to figure out who she was. But her body didn't agree. She couldn't find the strength to pull anymore.

"Let's see how much of a fling you are." Jeremy spun her around until she was facing the window. At least she could see the sunlight.

"Fucking leave her alone!" Julian's shout was hoarse. She could hear him pounding at something, most likely the floor. He was giving away too much. He was panicking.

"Not a chance," Jeremy returned.

Dani shivered as she felt hands on the waist of her pants. She remembered his promise from before. He was going to do it. He was going to shove that damn prod where it shouldn't go and turn it on. Her previously numb hands shook. How could she take this?

"Please." There was a shaking cry to Julian's words, and her heart broke. He was begging for her. It would kill a piece of him.

Jeremy's voice shook with rage. "I begged you once, Julian. I cried and begged. It didn't do me any good. It won't do you any good, either. You don't deserve forgiveness. You never have. There's a reason you're alone. There's a reason terrible things happen to the people around you. I'm merely helping the universe along, Master."

Jeremy pulled at her jeans, and Dani struggled. Tears filled her eyes. Nothing was working. She stared at the woods in front of her. She'd played in them as a child. She'd run through the woods pretending she was somewhere else. She'd never go anywhere, never be anything now. She'd seen a future, and now it was all about to end. He was going to kill her.

And then she saw him. He stood alone in the woods, his back to a pine, his face peering out.

Finn.

Finn had come for her. Numb or not, Dani felt a thrill of hope run through her body. She couldn't see him plainly, but she knew it was him. A brief thought played in her brain. It could be a trick. Her mind could have made up the sight of Finn, like a mirage of an oasis in the desert, but something made her discount the idea. Even if it wasn't true, she had to fight. She had to fight until she took her last breath. If Finn was out there, he was waiting for his chance.

She saw the rifle in his hands. He couldn't shoot Jeremy because she was in the way.

Why was he alone? Where were Leo and Taggart and the police?

Suddenly there was a loud popping sound, and Dani thought she might know where they were. It sounded as though they were right outside the door.

"What the hell?" Jeremy jumped back.

Dani twisted her head to look at her kidnapper. He was staring at the door but made no move toward it. When she looked back at Finn, she could see the frustration in his stance. The rifle was up. He was waiting, but he couldn't get a shot because she was in the way.

With a burst of energy she was sure she didn't have left, Dani pulled her legs up. She brought her knees to her waist. Every ounce of her weight hung by that small hook. Her wrists ached, and she thought she could see a thin line of blood beginning to trickle from where the zip tie bit into her hands. She groaned.

"What do you think you're doing?" Jeremy asked.

"Danielle," Julian started to call out to her, but he was interrupted by a long groan that came from the ceiling and finally, blissfully, a loud crack.

One minute Dani was suspended, and the next, her knees hit the hard floor. She jerked forward. She looked up, and Jeremy stood over her, a scowl on his face. The cattle prod was in his hand.

"You think that will stop me, bitch? Nothing is going to stop me."

"Don't you fucking touch her again," Julian shouted. Dani could see he was pulling at his own bonds. His face was chalky white, but he fought, trying to get to her.

Jeremy practically glowed as he pulled the prod up. "No one's going to stop me. Even if that was the cops, they're too late to save her. Live with that, Master."

She gasped as the sound of glass breaking cut through the air.

Jeremy stopped and looked down at his shirt. A slight stain broke through the fabric, blooming like a rose opening to the sun. He staggered back as he was hit again. Two to the chest. He fell to his knees with a low groan.

"Was that the cops?" Val asked breathlessly. "The cops are here?"

"No, it was Finn," Dani replied, struggling to get to her knees. Her legs felt wobbly, but she started to crawl toward Julian. He stared at Jeremy's body, his gray eyes colder than she could ever remember.

The front door flew open with a crack. Jimbo strode in, rifle at the ready.

"He dead?" Jimbo looked down at Jeremy's body. One side of his mouth quirked up. "Damn, he took out both lungs. Remind me not to get on Finn's bad side."

"Dani!" Finn burst in and completely ignored the body on the floor. He was at her side in a second, pulling her up and taking her in his arms. "Baby, I was so worried."

"Get Julian out." Dani couldn't take her eyes off of him.

There was something about how still he was, how cold his eyes were that made her wonder if the worst wasn't yet to come. He should be relieved, but there was nothing in the way Julian held himself that told her he was happy this was over. The rest of them were relaxed. Even Val was sagging into Jimbo's arms as he pulled her off the hook. Julian was stiff, his gaze on Jeremy's body as though he expected him to get up.

Finn kissed her cheek and helped her sit up. "Jim, you got a knife?"

Jimbo snorted as he reached into his pocket.

"Yeah, I know. Dumb question."

Finn quickly sawed through the bindings on her hands and moved toward Julian. She got to her wobbly feet, rubbing her wrists. She bit back a groan as the blood started flowing again. The pain meant she was alive, so she would take it gratefully.

The minute Finn pulled Julian's hands free, Dani tried to get into his arms. If anyone needed a hug, it was Julian. She remembered all the terrible things Jeremy had said to him. At least her torture had been purely physical. Jeremy had been ruthless in his mental torture of Julian.

"Are you okay?" Dani asked, trying to get close.

"I'm fine." Julian turned to her, his face a blank mask. "You call the police now, unless Finn brought them with him."

Dani shrank back. He might need a hug, but every signal he gave off told her he didn't want one from her.

"Here, let me help you up, Sir." Finn held out a hand.

Julian stared at it. "I'll manage on my own."

There was the sound of sirens and cars squealing up the road.

Jimbo held Val in his arms as he looked out the window. "Looks like the cops finally figured it out. Damn, I think that's Jack Barnes's truck. That kid there should be glad Finn killed him. I don't think he would have liked what Barnes would have done with him."

Finn knelt next to Julian, who struggled to get the Taser probes out of his chest. Finn reached down to help him, but Julian pushed his hands away.

"I didn't tell you to touch me, sub. Back off." Now Julian's eyes had some life in them. Unfortunately, it was rage that Dani could see. He was so angry. He pulled the probes out and tugged the collar off. He tossed it away as though it was diseased.

"Come out with your hands up." Someone was yelling through a bullhorn. Then Dani could hear someone shouting. "Damn it, Barnes. There's a protocol involved in this."

All she could see at first was a massive gun and then a huge man who looked an awful lot like Ian Taggart was sweeping his way through the room, that big gun in his hand.

"Clear," the slightly smaller version of Taggart yelled.

Jack Barnes's enormous form suddenly filled the doorway. He held a shotgun in his hands. His green eyes quickly surveyed the space. He looked down at Jeremy and then around the room.

The blond Viking of a man shouted out to the cops. "We're going to need a bus! Two if you have them."

"Lexi?" Barnes shouted the question through the small cabin. When he finally saw Lexi's form, his face fell, and the shotgun was on the ground at his side.

Lucas Cameron shoved his way past his brother. He looked like a younger version of Jack, but his eyes were wild with worry. He was completely unkempt. He stopped when he saw Lexi's still form.

"Oh, god, no, no." He looked like he might fall over.

"She's fine." Dani prayed that she was telling them the truth. "She's just unconscious."

Lucas had tears rolling down his face as he knelt down next to Lexi and pulled her into his lap. He moved her dark hair out of the way and stared down at her.

"Is there anyone else, or was this bastard working alone?" There was an odd tremble to Jack's voice, as though he was containing his emotion, afraid to let it out.

"He was alone. You can bring Abigail in." Julian's voice was perfectly steady. It scared the hell out of Dani.

Jack waved a hand and Abby rushed through the door, followed quickly by Leo and two police officers. Abby was at her daughter's side in a heartbeat. Lucas had already gotten her bindings undone.

"Thank god, she has a pulse," Abby said. Her hands moved up and down her daughter's body, checking her.

Lucas wouldn't let her go. He stood up. "We're taking her to the hospital."

Jack nodded. "I think we should take Julian and Dani, too."

"Please, take Danielle. I need to stay and clear up all the legalities. Mr. Taggart, if you don't mind." Julian held a hand out to the other Mr. Taggart. With help from the new guy, Julian managed to get to his feet. Every movement was careful and seemed to take something out of him, but his face remained perfectly placid. "Sean, I would like a report, please. I take it you were with Jackson in Dallas when the call came in? Did you break land speed records?"

Sean Taggart inclined his head. "We were already on our way back and I know a few shortcuts. My Scout moves faster than you think it would. When we realized Lexi was likely being held here in Willow Fork, we made excellent time. Ian is on his way."

"Excellent," Julian said, completely ignoring everything around him, including her. "Go and make sure the ambulance is on the way and then call your brother and have him meet Jackson at the hospital. I want someone watching over them."

"No, I'm not going to the hospital until you do," Dani said.

Julian didn't look at her, but his spine straightened. "You will do exactly what I tell you to. You will go with Jackson and get yourself checked out." He looked to the man he'd called Sean Taggart. "Please inform the EMTs that she was hit several times, and he used a cattle prod on her, not to mention the fact that he drugged her. They need to check her for nerve damage. She was hung like a side of beef for far too long. She needs blood tests and a thorough physical."

"I don't need anything but you." Dani felt herself choking up. Julian's coldness felt worse somehow than the damn cattle prod. He'd come for her. He'd put himself in danger for her. Why wasn't he holding her?

Finn's arms came around her. "The ambulance isn't going to be able to get through. It'll be faster to drive out."

"Sean, if you don't mind," Julian said.

"I can get them out of here quickly. I'll make sure they're safe," Sean promised.

They were leaving Julian?

Finn nodded Sean's way. "Come on, Dani. We'll get in the truck. You and Lexi need to get checked out. Jim, can you bring Val?"

"Yes," Jimbo said, nodding. "I think the drive will do her some good. I have a few things to say to her."

Val's eyes got wide. "I don't know what it could be."

"Nothing you're going to like hearing, babe. And I think I'm going to start taking after this crowd. You give me trouble, and I'm going to spank that ass of yours."

"You jerk. You touch me and I'll call the cops."

Jimbo shrugged. "The cops? You mean my uncle and my best friend? Good luck with that, babe."

Jimbo strode out of the cabin, Val bitching in his arms.

"Come on, Dani." Finn hauled her up as Lucas walked out of the cabin with Lexi. He turned back to Julian. "You feel free to take care of the legalities, Julian. I'll take care of my girl." He looked at the cops in the room who were staring down at the dead body. It was probably the first gunshot homicide they had ever seen. "If you want a statement, I'll give you one. I killed that fucker because he messed with my girl. That's my statement, and I'm sticking to it. If you need more, I'll be at the hospital."

Dani watched Julian's face as Finn carried her out. He stood there, stoic and proud, though Dani knew he'd been utterly broken.

She might never be able to put him back together.

* * * *

"This is how you deal with tragedy?"

Julian gritted his teeth. Of all the people he didn't want to deal with at this moment, Leo was the third. Danielle and Finn would be worse, but Leo was definitely not someone he wanted to talk to. He'd hoped Leo would stay in the main house. It was just his luck Leo had followed him to the guesthouse where Julian had spent twenty minutes packing his clothes and trying not to look at the bed where he'd taken Danielle and Finn.

Julian closed his suitcase and glanced at the clock. It had been hours, and there was still no word on when Danielle would be released. He'd spoken to the Taggarts earlier. After he'd finished with the police, he'd sent the entire security team to the hospital. Lexi was still unconscious and, though the doctors believed she would be fine, being kept overnight. Sam had already gone to the hospital by the time Julian had finished with the cops. Danielle was fine, Ian had informed him. They were waiting for her blood work and she would be released.

Julian intended to be gone long before then.

He turned to his troublesome employee. "I don't consider Jeremy's death a tragedy. I wish we'd killed him when we caught him trying to dose Lucas. As for my exit, I believe it will be easier for everyone to get on with their lives if I head home."

Where he would never again try this whole huggy, love crap. The next time Jackson called, he would be busy. Jackson didn't need him. Samuel didn't need him. He would treat Leo as the employee he was from now on, and he would never again take a slave. He would fuck the subs in his club, but they wouldn't belong to him.

He'd begged. He'd pleaded. God, he'd known that if Jeremy hurt Danielle the way he'd threatened to, he would have rather died than live knowing what he'd cost her. He couldn't handle it. He couldn't be in that position again. It wasn't worth it.

"You're running. Can't you see that?" Leo asked the question on an exasperated sigh.

Of course he was running. He was running as fast as his not fully functional legs would take him. If he didn't, Danielle would be here and he would have to deal with her. Finn would be here, with his hard eyes. He'd felt every inch of Finn's wrath when he'd carried Danielle out of the cabin that had served as their torture chamber. He certainly hadn't missed Finn's pointed use of the word "my" when he talked about Danielle being his girl. Not "our" girl.

It was far better that way.

"I prefer to think of it as knowing when I've overstayed my welcome." The next time he needed a vacation, he'd rent an island and go alone.

"I don't think Dani and Finn are going to feel the same way." Leo's muscular arms were crossed over his chest. "I think they're going to feel used, Julian."

Acid burned in his gut. He knew how Danielle would feel. She would feel small. She would feel confused since he'd given every indication that he wanted her to come with him when he left. If he were in Danielle's position, he would be very angry. But he wasn't Danielle. Danielle wouldn't be angry. Her heart would break.

"That isn't my problem. I didn't sign a contract. I owe them nothing." The words tasted bitter on his tongue, but it was best to break the tie now. If he didn't, he worried he would never break the tie. He would never be able to give them up. They would be the ones to leave. He couldn't handle that.

"You and your contracts." Leo's eyes were rolling in a fashion that got Julian's back up. "You think those contracts will protect you, but they can't. If you had Dani and Finn sign a contract, they could still leave you. They could still die or fall in love with someone else or just decide they made a mistake. Believe me, I know. I signed a pretty fucking permanent contract, and years later I was signing divorce papers. Nothing is for certain."

And that was precisely why Julian wouldn't do anything like this again. "Thank you for making my point. As it happens, I've changed my mind about contracts. I don't think I'll sign another. I think I'll keep everything casual from now on. Better for everyone."

"It sure isn't better for you. You're not going to understand a word I say, but I'm going to say it anyway. Nothing is certain, but you got to try, man. You think I'm going to let the fact that my ex cheated deter me from finding someone else, someone to spend my life with? I'm looking. When I find her, I'm sure not going to let past heartaches keep me from future happiness."

Julian felt his fists clench. Sanctimonious prick. Leo had no idea what he was talking about. Julian hadn't had his wife walk out on him. He'd had his world destroyed. First by an accident, and then by his uncle's neglect.

Jeremy had merely pointed out to him that it could all happen again. He'd almost taken Danielle from him. The hole in his life would have been huge, and he'd only spent a few days with her. What if he brought Danielle and Finn to live with him? How much would he ache when they left? The only way to protect himself was to not give a shit. Apathy protected him. It protected Danielle and Finn, too. He'd been the one to put them in danger. With the enemies he had, it could happen again. "Stay out of this, Leo."

"I've stayed out of it for years. What are you so fucking afraid of?"

A low anger churned in his gut. Leo thought he could psychoanalyze him? Well, he knew a thing or two about his Dom in residence. Leo wasn't as brave as he made himself out to be. "That is none of your business. And you're quite the hypocrite to call me out. You have a doctorate, and yet you spend your time in a BDSM club spanking submissives. What a crock. Why don't we talk about what happened in Afghanistan, Leo? You talk about that, and maybe I'll think about listening to you. You've used my club to hide for years."

Leo's jaw firmed and a low snarl came from the back of his throat. "I might be hiding, but I'm not hurting anyone. I'm not letting people fall in love with me and then dumping them the minute the going gets tough. You know what? You're a coward."

Julian practically teared up in joy. This was what he needed. He reared back and let his fist fly, connecting firmly with Leo's jaw. The younger man's head snapped back, but Julian wasn't through with him. Not by a long shot. He struck again, sending him stumbling back out of the doorway and into the playroom.

"Stop it, Julian!" Leo growled, holding his bleeding nose. "You hit me one more time, and I'll hit back."

There was nothing he wanted more. He punched Leo straight in his gut and was satisfied when he fell back over the spanking bench.

"Feel free," Julian said.

Leo was on his feet in a second. "Maybe I'll see if Dani wants to come to Dallas with me. You don't give a fuck, right? I'd love to get into her panties. So soft. She looks so fucking sweet. Tell me something, Julian. How's she in the sack?"

That hurt far worse than a fist to the gut. Julian was determined not to let the asshole see how much that hurt. The thought of his Danielle in Leo's arms knocked the breath out of him, yet he was a consummate actor. "She'll be quite suitable after she's properly trained."

There was a soft cry behind him, and Julian caught Leo's grimace before he turned and saw Danielle, Finn, Jackson, and Taggart standing on the stairs. Danielle's face was stark white and already tears were leaking. Finn's hand curled into hers. Finn would always be there, his hand open to her, offering comfort and support.

Julian's hands felt so cold.

"I didn't think I was that bad." Danielle's eyes bore through him.

"He's being an ass. He's scared shitless, and he's running," Leo said. "It's not a reflection on you." Leo pushed past him. "And yeah, I know, I'm fired. Hell, I quit. If this job is years more of watching you shut everyone out, then I don't want it. It's gone past pathetic."

Leo strode out of the room.

Jackson moved to allow the former SEAL to leave, then turned back to Julian. "I take it you're leaving? Would you even have said good-bye? Forget about the fact that you're walking out on the people you've been sleeping with. You were going to walk out without even finding out whether or not my stepdaughter is alive."

"I talked to Taggart earlier." It sounded like a pitiful excuse even to his ears.

Jackson was having none of it. "You know, I have always given you the benefit of the doubt. I know a bit about your past, so I let you act like a cold, unfeeling bastard because I knew it was only armor to protect yourself. I know, man. I've been there. But there comes a time to take off the armor and take a fucking risk. You can't live like this the rest of your life."

He could. He was going to. He stared at Danielle and Finn. Danielle, for all her curves, looked delicate and fragile. Finn's eyes had changed during the course of Jackson's speech. They had gone from angry to something softer, something that looked much more like pity. Julian hated that look. He would have greatly preferred Finn smacked him. He would have taken it.

"Leo was right, baby," Finn said quietly. "Don't take it wrong. He's in love, and he's scared out of his mind. He's not being a Dom right now. He's just a man in the end."

"No one asked your opinion, Finn." Why wasn't he walking away? He should simply walk out. His feet wouldn't move. He felt planted to the floor.

Finn stepped away from Danielle. "I know, Sir. Look, I'm going to lay it on the line. I think I'm falling in love with you. I know Dani is. I think we could be something amazing. I think we could make it. I want you, and I want Dani. I want to live together, and if it works, I want to have a family. I think this is forever, but if it's not for you, then we'll move on. We'll be like a person who loses a limb. We'll always miss you, but we'll learn to walk again. It won't be the same, but we won't let losing you ruin us. Do you understand what I'm saying?"

He forced himself not to reach out and pull Finn in. The impulse was almost overwhelming, which was exactly the reason he should ignore it. He understood exactly what Finn was saying. Finn was saying that he, Julian, would be the only one to lose if he walked out. "It doesn't matter. Believe what you want. This was a vacation fling for me. Nothing more."

"You came for me. You put your life on the line to save me." Danielle stepped up. Her blonde hair had escaped the ponytail she wore, and it wisped around her face. She looked tired. She needed to be in bed, being coddled and loved back to life.

He couldn't do it. He couldn't love her. "I would have come for anyone. I'm quite the humanitarian."

She shook her head. "No, you aren't. You're a bastard, but I love you anyway. Does that count for anything?"

He couldn't let it count. "No, Danielle. I'm going to leave, and I won't see you again."

Now she would plead. She would cry, and it would hurt his heart, but he had to let her go.

"All right, then." There were tears in her eyes and a sadness that kicked him in the balls. "It wouldn't have worked out anyway. I really, really hope you find someone. You just know that I'm out here, and I love you. If you need me, I'll come."

She backed away, though he felt her need. She wanted to put her arms around him. God, what was she thinking? She should be raging at him. She should shout and scream the place down. He'd used her, and now he was throwing her away. How could she say that she loved him?

"Why?"

She turned, startled by the question. "Why what?"

Julian knew he was being cruel, but he had to try to understand. "You keep offering. Everyone has refused, Danielle. You've told me your story. I've heard it from Finn and Jackson, too. Everyone in this town has rejected you in one way or another, yet you offer yourself again. Are you stupid? Is there something wrong with that brain of yours that you love the ache that comes with rejection?"

Finn started to respond, anger clearly taking the forefront again, but Danielle held her hand out.

She brushed her hair back. "Maybe I am dumb, Julian, but I won't stop. I won't stop trying to love people. I won't cut my heart out and store it somewhere because life's been crappy. If I do that, then all the people who stomped on me get to win. You taught me so much. You taught me that the world is a way bigger place than I ever thought it was. I want to know it, and I don't just mean places and other people. I need to know me. If I spend the rest of my life closing myself off, I'll never do that. As for loving you, well, it's way more important to love than to be loved. Loving people makes us better, even when it's not returned. So I'll love you till the day I die, but I won't stop living for you."

He felt numb. Danielle was younger than him, with so little life experience, and yet she understood things he hadn't begun to comprehend. Things he didn't want to comprehend. They deserved better. He wouldn't change. He would simply put them under a contract, and after a while they would just be slaves. He would never change.

Jackson shook his head as though disappointed. He put his hands on Danielle's shoulders and looked down at her. He was in full-on Dom mode, and it raised Julian's hackles.

"Dani, don't worry about a thing. I'll take care of you and Finn. I'll make sure you get everything you need," Jackson said.

Finn stepped up. "No, Sir. I appreciate that, truly I do, and I would love to be able to call you if we need something, but I'm responsible for her now, and she's responsible for me. We'll be fine. I've been reading up, and I think I can be what she needs. I can be a…what do they call it? A switch."

Jackson stood back. "You're wrong. A switch is merely someone who likes to both top and bottom. What you're talking about is something different. You're talking about doing whatever it takes to love a woman. We call that a husband, Finn."

Finn took Danielle into his arms, and she buried her head in his neck. Her chest heaved up and down.

Julian brushed past Jackson on his way down the stairs. He'd been frozen in place before, but now he couldn't move fast enough. He ran down the stairs. He couldn't breathe. The sight of Danielle and Finn clinging to each other made him ache in a way he'd never thought possible.

The door slammed behind him, and he dragged long breaths into his lungs, but it didn't help.

Distance. He needed distance. Once he was back in his condo, he would find his balance again. He needed normalcy. He needed control.

He needed his car.

"Take my truck." Jackson stood in the doorway. He tossed the keys to his big black truck at Julian's chest. They hit him and then the dirt at his feet. "It'll take hours to get your car back. When the police are done with it, I'll have someone drive it to you, or hell, you're not attached to anything. You can buy a new one."

There was a derisiveness to the younger man's tone that normally would have set Julian off. Now all he could think was that he deserved it. He reached down to pick up the keys as Jackson walked into the house.

Julian stared after him. Jackson would walk in and soon he would be surrounded by his family. He would be enveloped in their warmth. Abigail and Samuel would open their arms to him. Jackson had once told him that Doms all too often forgot their subs owed them comfort, too.

How long had it been since arms had wound around him seeking nothing more than to comfort him? He'd treated his subs as something to show off, something to prove his status. He'd never once lost himself in one's arms.

Until Danielle.

God, some of the sex he'd had with her had been so vanilla. It hadn't been sex at all. He'd made love to her. He'd taken her with no protection. He might have made a baby with her. It was unlikely, but he'd taken the chance.

If he let her go, she would move on. Her heart was strong, stronger than any he'd known. She would build a life with Finn, and Julian would be on the outside, forever staring in. They would have a family, raise children. Perhaps they would even find another Dom.

And Julian? He could see his life, too. He would go on as he always had. He would play the generous benefactor. He would give of his money, sometimes his body. He would let his heart rot because it was a useless, dangerous thing. He would let those moments when he'd been abused and neglected rob him of everything that could have healed the hurt.

"It gets easier."

Julian started and realized he wasn't alone. Ian Taggart was standing across from him, his face a stony mask. "I'm sorry. You can go, Mr. Taggart."

"Go where? Back to work? That's what I have, you know. Work and sleep, and sometimes if I get desperate enough I'll find a sub to fuck. I've learned a lot from you, Mr. Lodge. I always put them under a contract. I won't touch anyone without a contract," Taggart said.

Rules. He had so many of them. Jackson always told him that his rules would keep him from something good someday. Julian's rules stated plainly that it was time to walk away. He stared at the guesthouse where he was sure Finn was holding Danielle while she cried. Rules and contracts. That was what his life came down to.

Those rules were his safe word. He'd been screaming his fucking safe word for twenty years.

"And it works? The contracts protect you?" He knew the answer, hated the fact that someone like Taggart would think to learn from him.

"It reminds me that I didn't have one with her. Not one that stopped her from dying. Not one that stopped her from taking me with her when she went," he replied.

"Her?"

"My wife, and if you ever mention her, I'll kill you. No one knows about her. She's dead and buried, and the best piece of me went with her, so I'm going to tell you how this goes because you taught me so much. It'll hurt in the beginning. You'll feel hollow, and nothing, no amount of liquor or drugs or fucking, will ever fill that place, so you let it be empty. You let it be hollow. And one day you realize you're cold and that's so much better than being warm. Because you'll never be warm again, so welcome it, brother."

Welcome the cold? A cold bed. A cold life. A life where he never spoke of them. Never talked about them. Never let anyone even know they had existed. "Your brother doesn't know?"

"About my Charlie? No. I try to forget about her but she's always there. Sometimes I can get through the night without dreaming of her, but not often. Maybe it'll be different for you because you made this decision. You didn't love them."

"I did. I do."

"No, you didn't because if you loved them, you wouldn't have walked away. I would sell my soul for one more minute with her. I would give away the rest of my fucking life to hold her in my arms one more time, and I hate that bitch as much as I ever loved her. She lied and used me, and I would give anything to be with her one last time so no, Mr. Lodge, if you can walk, it's not love." Taggart glanced over at his truck. "So why don't you let me drive you back to Dallas and we can both get on with our pathetic lives."

Could he stop? He thought he couldn't change, but hadn't he changed already?

There was something wet on his cheek, sliding down toward his mouth. He brushed it off and then gazed at his own hand. Tears. He was fucking crying. More and more rolled down his skin. Another broken rule.

He'd begged. He'd pleaded. He was crying. All broken rules. He had two choices. He could get into that truck and drive home and pull all those rules around him like a protective sheath.

"Or you can walk back into that house and thank god they're alive and they love you," Taggart said. "You fill that fucking hollow place inside with them and be whole. I'll never be whole again. I'll never be the me I was when I was with her. You could be better."

He could be as brave as his Danielle, as steadfast as his Finn. He could sink into them and let them be a balm to his wounds.

If something happened down the line, at least he would know he'd loved them. At least he would know that he'd lived.

He dropped the keys in the dirt and, tears blurring the world around him, walked back into the house.

Chapter Twenty

Finn's lips were soft against her cheek. His arms hadn't left her since the minute Julian had walked out. Dani took a deep breath and relaxed against him, his strength and the warmth of his body a comfort to her. He sat on the bed, cradling her gently. She closed her eyes, but she could still see the horrors of the day.

Finn's arms tightened as she shivered. "You still scared, baby? It's okay. Nobody's going to blame you. You need to know that I won't let anything happen to you. I swear, I'm going to watch you like a hawk from now on."

She nodded because she was going to watch him, too. She would worry about Julian because he wouldn't let her watch him. She wondered how far down the road Julian had gotten. How many miles separated them?

"You'll see. It's going to be better when we get home. My condo is nice, but if you don't like it, we'll move. We'll find someplace that suits us." He seemed willing to talk about anything but the fact that Julian was currently driving away from them. "And if you need to talk to someone, I can find a good shrink. I'll go with you."

She shook her head. She didn't need a shrink. She needed Julian, but that wasn't going to happen. The whole time she'd been in the hospital all she could think about was the blank expression on his face. It didn't fool her at all. He hadn't been unaffected. He'd been a ball of emotion, but he would never show it.

"I don't want to see someone," she said, measuring her words. The last thing she wanted was for Finn to feel slighted. "I promise I'll talk about it if I get scared or have bad dreams. But there is something I want to do once we get settled down."

"Anything. We can do anything." Finn's voice was breathless, as though he was excited she was asking for something.

"I want to go to The Club."

Finn stiffened. "I don't think that's a good idea."

She sat up. She was sure she looked a mess, but it didn't matter with Finn. He wouldn't care that she had a red nose or that her makeup was long gone. She pushed her hair out of her eyes. "Tell me you don't want to experiment. Tell me you don't want to play anymore."

His handsome face fell. "I told you, I'll top you. I can do it."

He would try, and she didn't doubt he would do it. But it wouldn't fulfill him. Julian had taught them so much. For so long they had been cut off from whole sides of themselves. She doubted Finn could be happy without D/s playing some role in their lives. "I don't think either of us is going to be content until we explore this part of ourselves. I'm okay with playing around at home, but I think we should try The Club or, if Julian refuses to let us in, maybe some other club. I heard the bodyguards talking. They have one called Sanctum. We could try going there."

Finn's voice was low, defeated. "I don't think he'll care either way, Dani. I think once he makes up his mind he's done. Hell, if you want to play, I bet Lucas can get us in. Julian probably won't even notice we're there."

Dani sniffled. She couldn't seem to help it. Maybe one day the ache of losing him would lessen, but it was still a raw, gaping wound in her chest. "Probably not. He'll probably have other subs by the time we're ready. He'll have some pretty, thin thing under one of those contracts."

"No, I won't."

Dani spun around, gasping at that deep, dark voice she had been sure she wouldn't hear again. "Julian."

He stood in the doorway. His tall, muscled frame took up most of the space, making everything seem small in comparison. His hair was loose, making him look younger than his forty-plus years. His silvery eyes were hesitant, though. Still, he held her with his gaze. "I'll never sign another contract. Not another BDSM contract."

Finn's hand was suddenly in hers. He squeezed her fingers. "I thought that was important to you. I thought you never took a lover without one."

"I didn't. Until I met the two of you."

Dani felt a surge of hope. He was here. He hadn't left. But she had to know. She couldn't go through this ping-pong of emotion. "Why? Because we were a fling and those don't count? Because I'm not up to your standards?"

His face went a scarlet red, and his fists clenched. "Damn it. I won't listen to anyone talk that way about you." He took a deep breath. He visibly got himself under control. "Please, little one, don't test me. I'm at the end of my control. I won't allow anyone to put you down, least of all yourself. You and Finn mean more to me than I can say."

"Try." Finn scooted beside her. His voice had a slightly hard edge, but his arm curled around her reassuringly. He wouldn't simply let Julian back in. Finn would make him work for it. She'd known Finn all her life. He could hold a grudge. She would have to make sure he didn't in this case.

She watched as Julian swallowed. She waited for him to tell Finn to fuck himself and walk off. A thousand scenarios played through her mind. Julian could simply leave, deciding they were too much trouble. He could start his Dom routine and bark orders at them. He could have come back simply because he wanted to explain why he had to leave. He wasn't a monster. Maybe he wanted to soothe them. He might promise to find them a new Dom. That scenario hurt most of all.

"I think I love you."

His hoarse words sent her reeling. Of everything he could have said or done, she hadn't expected it would be that.

"Okay," Finn said.

She turned her face up. Finn had a smile that caused Dani's heart to clench. Finn understood that there was no place for grudges now.

She looked back at Julian. "Okay."

He stared for a moment, seemingly dumbstruck. "Okay? That's all you have to say?"

It wasn't. Not for Dani. "I love you, too, Julian, but I have a few conditions."

Every muscle in his body tightened. His jaw clenched. "All right. I'll listen to conditions."

She contained the smile that threatened to burst over her. Moments before she'd been dead tired, but now a new energy rolled through her system. "I don't want to be your slave, though I do want the sex part. I know I'm submissive, and I'm willing to be sexually submissive, but I want to take charge of my life. I want you to help me do that."

His red-rimmed eyes suddenly held a wealth of warmth. "Yes, Danielle. I will help you do that."

One hurdle gone. The worst was yet to come, though. She took a long gulp of air. "I won't sign a contract with you. I know that's important to you, but I need you to trust me. That contract won't hold me to you. My love will hold me."

"I told you no contract, Danielle. But I want you and Finn to live with me. I want you with me always. I want to try. I want to give you the things you need."

Finn got to his feet. "You can't run again."

"I won't." Julian met his eyes. Something passed between the men. "I promise you. Whatever problems we have, we'll talk it over or fight it out. I won't ever leave again. But you should know something. I don't think I'm good at the love thing. I haven't really tried it before, never wanted to. You might have to be patient with me."

Patience was Dani's middle name. She got to her feet. She could be more than patient with him on an emotional level, but on the physical plane she wanted more, and she wanted it now. She walked straight up to him and planted her body close to his. He was stiff for a moment, as if he wasn't sure what to do, but then he sighed, and his arms curled around her body. She sank into his heat, nuzzling his neck, listening to the firm beat of his heart. She felt his left arm open, and Finn snuggled in. Finn's arm wrapped around her waist, and she was complete.

"Forgive me." The words from Julian's mouth were hoarse and unnecessary.

She'd forgiven him even as he'd walked out on her.

"I love you." She and Finn whispered it at the same time, a benediction for their soul mate, for the man who made them whole.

"I love you. I love you so much. I'll never stop." Julian leaned down and kissed her. His lips grazed against hers softly before his tongue came out, requesting entry. She opened beneath him and was rewarded with the strong surge of his tongue rubbing against hers, dancing in a slow grind she felt in her pussy.

He released her mouth and pressed his lips against Finn's. Dani watched as they kissed for the first time. It was tender. Emotion and promise played along their lips. They were so beautiful together. Dani wanted to step back and watch them, but they held her close.

"I want to make love," Julian whispered against Finn's mouth. "I want us to share Danielle, to make her understand that she can rely on both of us."

Their heads turned together, both gorgeous men watching her with undisguised lust in their eyes. One pair of gray eyes and one pair of green caught her. Their skin touched, and their hair mingled. It seemed to Danielle they had a single purpose. Her.

Her heart rate sped up. The air in the room suddenly seemed too heavy to breathe.

Julian suddenly pulled away as though something had just occurred to him. His hands were on her clothes, pulling her shirt up. "What did the doctors say, Finn? Perhaps she should be in bed."

Hell, no. She was not getting put to bed and treated like an invalid. She didn't need to be coddled. She needed them. She wanted everything their eyes had promised her. She allowed Julian to tug the T-shirt over her head. "I'm fine. Surprisingly the doctors say they see the cattle prod thing more than you would think. No permanent damage and no need to rest."

Finn slid around to her back, his chest a solid warmth on her skin. "I don't know about that. I think some rest is definitely in order. I think you should lay back and let your men take care of you."

Julian stared at her skin. His fingers came out to trace the bruises left on her flesh. "He hurt you."

His voice was haunted. Dani reached down and tugged his shirt from his pants. She quickly undid the buttons, and his magnificent chest was revealed. She wasn't the only one with bruises, but Julian's went deep. She leaned over and brushed her lips against the angry red marks where the Taser probes had bitten viscously into his chest.

"I'm not the only one he hurt." She kissed the skin on and around his wounds. She let her hands skim his tapered waist.

Julian's fingers came up to frame her face while Finn's cupped her hips. She sighed as Julian's forehead touched hers. She could feel Finn's erection pressing into the seam of her ass.

"I deserved it. You did not," Julian said gravely. She started to argue, but his finger came up to cover her lips. "Don't deny it, little one. Karma finds us all, and Jeremy was my karma. Of course, karma works in mysterious ways. Had he not done what he did, this would not end this way."

"How would it have gone?" She thought she knew, but it would be good to hear it from him. It would make the agony seem worthwhile. Finn's hands moved from her hips to her breasts, molding the nipples and tugging them, shooting fire down into her belly.

A smile played on Julian's lips as he watched Finn play with her breasts. He brought a fingertip down to touch the nipple. "I would have taken you both home with me. I would have made you my sweet slaves. I would have bound you in a contract that dictated every aspect of your lives. For Finn, I would have taken charge of his career, telling him when and where he could work. Most likely, I would have become his only client. For you, I would have selected your clothes and given you a schedule each day."

She smiled back at him. "I know I'm submissive, but you should know that I would have shoved that schedule right up your ass."

He threw back his head and laughed. "Which is why karma is our friend." He got serious again, his face lined with concern. "I might take a while to adjust, you know. I've lived my life this way for a long time."

He needed a certain amount of control, and he always would.

"We can be patient." One of Finn's hands reached out to grasp

Julian's shoulder. "And I don't think either one of us wants you to change completely. Just bend a bit from time to time."

"I promise to try. I believe I would like to bend a bit now." He bent his head over and pulled her nipple into his mouth.

Heat raced through her system. She let her head fall back against Finn's neck.

"I love you." Finn's tongue licked along the shell of her ear. "I want to spend the rest of my life with you, beside you, inside you."

She wanted that, too. God, she had never wanted anything more.

"Take off her pants, Finn." That hard edge was back in Julian's voice, and she felt Finn's cock twitch behind her. Her own pussy already felt moist and ready.

Finn's fingers did a sensuous slide down her hips, slipping under the band of her pants and lowering them down along with her panties.

Julian got to his knees. His mouth pressed a line of kisses down her stomach all the way to her pussy. Her legs were caught in her jeans. Finn pressed his erection against her ass, forcing her pelvis to bow out toward Julian. He growled before burying his nose in her labia.

"Oh, god!" Her whole body shook, but Finn held her upright.

"Does he feel good, baby? Do you like him feasting on your pussy?"

And he was. She groaned as Julian's tongue laved her tender flesh. His tongue slid over every inch of her pussy. She looked down at his dark hair. It was silky and smooth and all the more perfect for being mussed. He sucked at her, kissing, nibbling until she thought she was going to scream. He was torturing her with soft passes and long strokes.

"Oh, please, please." She couldn't stop the cry that came out of her mouth. It was maddening. He was leisurely eating at her pussy as though he could stay there all day, teasing and tantalizing.

His face turned up. She could see her cream on his lips. "Please, what? Tell your Dom what you need."

"I need to come."

His lips turned up. "Is that all you need?"

Not even close. "I need you and Finn inside me."

Julian stood. There was no mistaking the erection in his slacks.

He quickly moved to unsheathe himself. He tossed his slacks aside and shrugged off his shirt. His glorious body was uncovered, and Dani grinned as she felt Finn sigh behind her. She knew exactly what he was thinking. That gorgeous hunk of man was all smooth skin and muscle, and he was all theirs.

Her breath caught. He was hers and Finn's, and she belonged to them. She belonged. It had been so long, maybe never, since she truly belonged somewhere, but she belonged between these two men. Tears caught in her eyes. For so long home had been a place. It had been walls and floors, ceilings and furniture. But now home was two men and their hearts. Home was their arms around her, their voices whispering to her.

"Danielle." Julian reached out for her.

She threw herself into his arms. When she'd been alone in that terrible place Jeremy had taken her, they had come. They hadn't left her. She mattered to them. "I love you so much. You came for me." She put an arm out to draw in Finn. "You both came for me."

"Always. I will always come for you." Julian held her so tightly, as though he would never let her go.

"You're my world," Finn said, his lips in her hair. "You always have been. You always will be. We'll never leave you alone."

Warmth coated her heart. They would stand beside her, a bulwark to the world when it was cruel, partners to enjoy it when life was wondrous. She wouldn't be alone. Not ever again.

"On the bed, little one. We need you." Julian's rasp filled her with desire.

She shimmied out of her jeans and practically threw herself on the bed. Her muscles ached, but it was nothing compared to how much she needed them. She scooted back to give them plenty of room, but when she looked up, Julian had his hands on Finn. She watched, completely transfixed, as Julian pulled Finn's clothes off. His hands ran down Finn's muscular chest toward his straining cock.

"Let me kiss you, Sir." Finn was still under his hands. "I want to taste her on your lips."

"She's on more than my lips, Finn." Julian's mouth hovered above Finn's. "I can still taste her on my tongue."

He devoured Finn. Their heads slanted as they kissed, and she caught a glimpse of their tongues playing, exchanging the juice of her arousal between them. Their hard cocks rubbed against each other. Julian held Finn's head still as he plundered his mouth. Though dominant, the hold was gentle. She felt the growing love and trust between the two men. After a moment's sweet play, they broke away and turned to her. Two hard, enormous cocks pointed her way. Dani felt a pulse deep in her pussy. If they didn't fuck her soon, she was going to die. Her muscles ached. Her skin was bruised, and none of that mattered because she wanted them inside her. She needed the reassurance that came with making love. She would know she was alive and wanted and loved.

"Finn, you take her pussy," Julian said.

Finn leapt onto the bed. He covered her with his body, spreading her legs. His fingers parted her, playing in her juices. "You're so wet for us, baby. Do you know how crazy that makes me?"

If the size of his erection was any indication, she could guess that it made him really crazy. Dani sighed as he pushed his fingers into her cunt. It felt so good, so right, to have him inside, and it would feel even better when Julian joined him.

Julian chuckled at the end of the bed. He held a tube of lubricant in his hands as he watched them play. "Finn, I think you'll find I need you in a different position. Let Danielle be the sweet cowgirl she is. Let her ride you."

Finn growled as he flipped her around. He reached to the nightstand and picked up a condom. "Put it on me."

A thrill went through her at Finn's dark command. He sounded rough and demanding. It did all kinds of things to her pussy. She took the packet out of his hands but wanted him in her mouth before she did anything else. She leaned over and licked at the head of Finn's weeping cock. She sucked, drawing the salty pre-cum into her mouth, and was rewarded with Finn's deep groan.

"Lift your ass in the air," Julian commanded. "I'll prepare you while you prepare our Finn."

She felt Finn's fingers tangle in her hair as she moved her ass up, wiggling it invitingly. Finn grunted as he spread his legs and thrust up into her mouth. He didn't seem to need the same things from her that he needed from Julian. From her, Finn seemed to need softness and submission. Perhaps he was closer to being a switch than he thought he was.

"God, Dani, suck me. Take my cock all the way in. I want to feel the back of your throat." Finn gently guided her head down, helping her swallow his cock inch by inch.

Dani whirled her tongue around his dick, enjoying the salty taste of him. She sucked him in deep, long passes, taking him in until her chin bumped his balls.

"You two are beautiful, you know," Julian said. She felt him get on the bed with them. His big hands cupped the curves of her rear. "I enjoy watching you. I never liked that before, but I believe one of the things I'll have you do regularly is put on a show for me."

She shivered at the thought, and her mind took it one or two steps further. She could see herself at The Club, making love with Finn for their Master's pleasure while everyone watched. It was inconceivable, but she felt beautiful enough to do it. Julian chuckled as he slipped two fingers into her pussy.

"You like that thought. There's an exhibitionist in there."

Dani felt his hands worshipping her curves. Julian's lips kissed the skin at the small of her back. She could feel the soft sweep of his hair on her hips as she licked and nibbled on Finn's cock.

She groaned when Julian parted the cheeks of her ass.

"No one's taken you here before?"

"No, Sir." Oh, he was going to do it. She shuddered in anticipation. He was going to shove that huge cock up her ass while she rode Finn.

She felt a dribble of lube just before his finger rimmed her.

"Not Sir. Never again. If you want to play, you may call me Master, but I am Julian. I think I see what Jackson means now. There are many Masters, but only one Julian for you and Finn."

Dani groaned around Finn's dick. Julian's finger felt huge in her anus. How was she ever going to take his monster cock? It would ache, but she looked forward to it. It meant he was with her.

"Put the condom on me, Dani. Damn it, if you suck me any more, I'm going to come," Finn said.

An amazingly happy sense of power surged through her. She put a kiss on the head of his cock. "Don't do it, Finn. Julian might spank you."

That sent a shiver through Finn's body. His cock surged, and arousal glistened on the head as she slid the condom on. Yup, that just did it for Finn. And it worked for her, too. She loved to watch Julian work Finn over. She loved the fact that both her men got what they needed.

"Do not come, Finn," Julian commanded. "You don't go until we're both deep inside her. Danielle, take our lover inside that pussy of yours."

She swung a leg over Finn's hips. His hands came up to her waist. She slid onto his cock, pleasure spiking through her. He felt so good inside her.

"God, I love you, Dani. I love you so much."

"I love you, too." She sighed as she felt Julian gently pressing down on her back. She twisted her head around to look at her other lover. His hair was around his broad shoulders, and his face was a mask of desire. "And you, Julian."

He leaned over and pressed his lips against hers. "I love you, too. And Finn. Now hold on to him and let me in. Press against me. Don't fight my cock."

Dani gasped as she felt the pressure of Julian's big dick beginning to breach her asshole.

"It's all right, baby," Finn whispered in her ear. "I know. He's so fucking big, but you can take him. You can take him all the way."

Julian was advancing in increments. It burned, and the pressure was immense. She whimpered and felt Julian's breath hitch. It gave her comfort. He had changed, but not too much. He was still her gloriously, slightly sadistic Master. She wouldn't have him any other way. Now that he'd introduced her to play, she couldn't imagine her life without it. She didn't try to hide her discomfort. It would add to Julian's pleasure. She trusted him to never hurt her. All she had to do was say her safe word, but she wanted this. She wanted to take him deep.

"A little more. Can you take more, Danielle?"

"Yes." She curled her hands around Finn's shoulders. The burning increased. Tears leaked from her eyes as she bit her lip. Julian pushed in as he pulled back on her hips. With a low groan, she felt him slide all the way in. His pelvis was flush against her backside.

"You feel so amazing."

She could feel them stretching and filling her. It seemed like there wasn't an inch of her they weren't touching. It was the most intimate moment of her life.

Finn stared up at her, his green eyes hooded. "I can feel him, Dani. I can feel both of you. Julian, please, I need to fuck."

He chuckled behind her. His hands tightened on her hips. "Yes, Finn. I need her, too." He began to draw out gently. "I need you both."

She prepared for pain, but was shocked at the jangled, jittery pleasure that came with the long slow drag of Julian's dick. It was a brutal pleasure, but it lit her every nerve and caused her to gasp. She moved with him, trying to keep that big cock inside her, wanting more of the sensation. Finn pulled down, shoving his cock and grinding his pelvis against her clit. Now she wanted more of that, but Julian was the aggressor again. He tunneled into her ass with ruthless precision as Finn pulled back. She was a precious toy between them, pulled this way and that for their pleasure. She gave up control. She rode them, allowing her men to take over, trusting them to give her everything she desired. She felt the pleasure build until it detonated like a bomb in her womb. Dani shook from the powerful orgasm that flooded her system. She felt Julian lose control behind her. His cock plunged inside her, and she felt the warmth of his release fill her ass. Finn bucked up and held himself tightly against her. He reached in between their bodies and circled her clit with his finger, sending her over the edge again.

She fell forward onto Finn. His arms came up around her. Julian slipped out of her ass. He pulled her down with him, spooning her. He tangled their legs together, and his hands wound around her and found their way to Finn's skin. They were bound together.

"Dani," Finn whispered, pushing hair from her eyes. There was a smile playing on his face, and his lips were inches from hers. "He's asleep."

Tears filled her eyes as she felt Julian's steady, deep breaths. He was asleep, pressed against her. Dani settled down, warm and happy between them.

Chapter Twenty-One

3 months later

Julian Lodge knew they talked about him. They had talked about him before his marriage, and they certainly talked about him now. As he walked through the dungeon, he heard the whispers.

"I never would have believed that the Master could go so soft."

"He married her without a prenup. He's gone insane."

Julian didn't bother to glance back at the women talking about him. They could talk all they liked. He had better things to do. Besides, all of it was true. He'd gone back on his promise about the contracts. He'd needed one more to legally protect his loves. He had married Danielle in a small, lovely ceremony attended only by a few friends and Danielle's amazingly obnoxious sister. It was the only real fight the three of them had engaged in since he had moved Danielle and Finn into his penthouse. He'd found it surprisingly easy to be indulgent when it came to his lovers, but he'd been angry with Danielle's utter refusal to allow him all-out vengeance on her sister. She'd told him he wasn't allowed to have her murdered. Taggart had offered. He'd even promised to do it in a humane fashion, but Danielle had been insistent. He wasn't allowed to send her to prison. He hadn't even been allowed to bar her from their wedding. Danielle had been perfectly willing to accept punishment for arguing with her Master, but she wasn't willing to budge. She believed her sister could change. After all, she would say, Julian had changed.

Of course, he hadn't changed as much as Danielle suspected. And Finn, it turned out, had just as much of a vicious streak when it came to protecting their woman.

Speaking of his little devil…Julian felt a wide smile spread across his face as Finn walked into the dungeon, followed by Lucas Cameron. Finn looked ridiculously out of place in his three-piece suit and slightly messy hair. He carried his briefcase, and the look of elation on his face told Julian that he and Lucas had more than likely concluded their latest venture.

"You should whip him, you know." Leo stepped out from behind him. "He's not wearing his collar."

It was a point of some contention between his Dom in residence and his partner. Finn didn't see the need to go all the way up to the penthouse and come all the way back down when he got off work and wanted to see Julian and Danielle. Danielle was far more obedient. She wore the small diamond necklace Julian and Finn had placed around her neck every day without fail. It matched the ring he'd placed on her finger. Finn wore a ring as well. It was a duplicate of the one Julian wore.

"I'll see to Finn, Leo," Julian said evenly. Since he'd rehired Leo, after a heartfelt apology and a fifteen percent raise, the Dom had taken charge of The Club while Julian concentrated on Danielle and Finn. Julian had never noticed how devoted to protocol his second-in-command was until Julian himself had begun breaking the rules. "Perhaps we'll play out a heavy scene this evening."

"Like the one you two played out with Danielle after-hours last night? The cleaning crew nearly called the cops." Leo groused, but there was warmth in his eyes. "Tell me something, Julian, did you really chase her down while wearing a Viking helmet?"

Julian laughed. He noted that it caused almost everyone in the dungeon to turn and stare. "My wife has some rather involved fantasies. It is up to her husbands to make them come true. Let me tell you something, Leo. Those horns are heavy, and I greatly prefer my leathers to the loincloth she insisted on. Danielle looked extremely sweet in her nun's outfit though. Well, she looked better once Finn and I ripped it off her."

Leo shook his head. "One of these days I'm going to find my own sweet little perv. Speaking of sweet pervs, Abby Barnes just checked in upstairs. I take it she's in town to spend time with Lexi."

Julian nodded, and his eyes strayed back to Finn and Lucas. How was he going to tell Lucas about the man who had come to visit him earlier in the day? Aidan O'Malley was back in Dallas. Lexi's ex-fiancé had explained a lot to Julian that he was sure not even Lucas knew. And he'd asked Julian to train him. He was determined to win Lexi back…and to bring Lucas in.

Julian would have to think on it. He already had Taggart working on a dossier on exactly what O'Malley had been doing since he'd left. He wanted Lucas happy, but wasn't sure he had the right to interfere. He would have to talk it out with Danielle and Finn. They would help him decide what to do.

As though he'd conjured her, Danielle raced up to Finn. She threw her arms around him and kissed him soundly. Lucas nodded at them and then noticed Julian. While Danielle and Finn were in their own world, Lucas walked down the hall and greeted Julian. There were lines on his face that made him look older than his twenty-six years.

"I left the final paperwork with Candice. You and Finn are now the proud owners of a development group specializing in shopping centers. I'll be happy to inform the Willow Fork City Council that we'll take our outlet store elsewhere." Lucas pulled at the tie around his neck.

A nice warm sensation settled in his heart. Danielle hadn't forbidden him from buying the business that was going to make Val wealthy and ensuring that the deal didn't go through. She also hadn't made him promise he wouldn't send inspectors out to condemn her home. He didn't feel bad about it. It would send her straight into Jimbo's arms. Julian had no idea why the mechanic would want her, but he intended to send him a very nice set of canes. Jimbo would need them.

"I'm heading out." Lucas glanced around the dungeon. "I think I'll stay away from The Club for a couple of days. Abby's in town with my brother and Sam. It's awkward to run into them when I'm escorting Lexi around and she's wearing nothing but some PVC and a collar. And since I've started thinking of Abby as a potential mother-in-law, I find it disturbing that she looks so freaking hot when she gets her ass whipped." He shook his head as he walked away.

Leo slapped him on the back. "And I need to go make sure Jack Barnes's scene is properly prepared. It's the least I can do. He's upset because apparently the younger Taggart was very flirty with Abby earlier today. Who would have guessed Little Tag would like older redheads? He's going to have to get in line. Will you be around later, boss?"

"Not tonight," Julian replied. Danielle turned and caught sight of him. Her whole face lit up. Finn followed her line of sight, and they both began rushing his way. "We're staying in tonight."

"Have fun, boss." Leo left, making his way toward the center of the dungeon, greeting people all along the way.

"Hello, Mr. Lodge," Danielle said with a smile that lit up his world. She walked into his arms.

He gave her the words she wanted. She loved her new name. He'd pulled strings to facilitate her name change. "Hello to you, Mrs. Lodge-Taylor."

Finn laughed. "She thinks it makes her sound elegant."

Her nose crinkled up. "It does make me sound elegant. And it's true. It's my name. I got my new driver's license in today. Now I can go down to the campus and get my student ID. Before he knows it, I'll be running Julian's company."

Julian shuddered to think about it. She would try. The wife he shared with Finn was a sweet thing, but her ruthless side came out when she talked about having a career. Of course, she also talked about starting a family. Danielle was determined to have it all, and Julian was determined to give it to her.

"I don't think that's a good idea. That would mean I was sleeping with the boss," Finn said.

Danielle snorted and began to walk toward the door. "Like you don't do that already."

Finn followed after her. "It's different with Julian. He's like the boss of everything."

Julian watched them for a moment, his heart fuller than he could have imagined. Danielle had told him that she'd learned the world was a bigger place than she could have imagined. He'd learned the opposite. He'd learned how amazingly small the world could be. His whole world was encompassed in two people. Four arms that could surround him. Two hearts that loved him. Two souls to share his own with.

The world was small, and he would have it no other way.

"Are you coming with us, Julian?" Finn asked. He held open the door as Danielle walked through into the bar.

"Always," Julian said as he caught up to them and took Danielle's hand.

* * * *

Lexi Moore, Lucas Cameron, Aidan O'Malley, and the whole Texas Sirens gang will return in *Siren Beloved*, now available.

Author's Note

I'm often asked by generous readers how they can help get the word out about a book they enjoyed. There are so many ways to help an author you like. Leave a review. If your e-reader allows you to lend a book to a friend, please share it. Go to Goodreads and connect with others. Recommend the books you love because stories are meant to be shared. Thank you so much for reading this book and for supporting all the authors you love!

Sign up for Lexi Blake's newsletter
and be entered to win a $25 gift certificate
to the bookseller of your choice.

Join us for news, fun, and exclusive content
including free short stories.

There's a new contest every month!

Go to www.LexiBlake.net to subscribe.

Siren Beloved
Texas Sirens Book 4
By Lexi Blake writing as Sophie Oak

Aidan O'Malley left his fiancée, Lexi Moore, and their best friend, Lucas Cameron, after a night of passion left him shaken to his core. Years later, Aidan is back and he knows what he wants. He wants Lucas and Lexi forever.

Lucas has always been in love with Lexi, but he knows they need something more. They need the perfect Dom to complete their family. He never expected Aidan would be the Dom of their dreams.

Lexi is hiding a secret. She knows she's drowning and the time has come to heal, but her anger at Aidan holds her back from moving on with Lucas.

When Lexi's life is in danger, Aidan knows he'll do anything to win them back—and keep them alive.

* * * *

"What are they doing?" Lexi's voice had the slightest shake to it. She hated the sawhorse. He would never put her over one.

"I'll find out." He gave her hand a squeeze.

Lexi preferred the comfort of the whipping chair or the St. Andrew's Cross. When he'd started playing the role of Lexi's Dom, he'd introduced her to all of the equipment in the dungeon. Some of it hadn't appealed to her at all, and he'd never pushed her on it. He had the handcuffs he'd had made for her. They were lined with faux fur so her wrists never chaffed. He pulled them out as he approached Master A.

The enormous mountain of a man picked up a strap and tested it against his own hand. He had a table full of torture implements. None of them were the ones Lucas had brought.

"There seems to have been a miscommunication, Sir." He was exceedingly polite. He was suddenly intensely aware that he'd agreed to sub for this man. At the time, it had seemed like an afterthought, something incidental. BDSM scenes required a chain of command. When he'd signed his name to the bottom line of the contract, he'd been thinking more of Lexi than himself. Now, as Master A turned and his dark chocolate eyes pinned him, it seemed pretty damn serious.

"What's wrong, Lucas?" His voice was like gravel, as though something had damaged it, but a lyrical quality still held. Up close, his scars were like rivers crossing his powerful chest. Some were thick and wove across his skin, others a mere whisper, but together they made a map of the man. "Why aren't you waiting with Lexi?"

Lucas felt that voice deep inside him. It was much more than mere sexual attraction. He could be sexually attracted to any number of people. He'd learned to ignore it entirely. His cock didn't have the best of taste, but it had stopped ruling his life long ago. This was more. This was the instant, soul-deep recognition of someone he knew could top him. Master A was one hell of a Dom.

But he wasn't Lexi's Dom. He might be for the evening, but that was Lucas's full-time role. Though he'd signed over control of the punishment to Master A, surely the man would take advice from the sub's permanent Dom. "We need to move that sawhorse out of here. Lexi prefers a whipping chair. Actually, it would be better if we used a whip. She's comfortable with a St. Andrew's Cross."

There was a long pause as Master A stared a hole through him. There was no hot dimple in his cheek now. There was only a simple stony silence emanating from the man. Lucas fought not to fidget under his stare. This was how he'd felt when he'd done something stupid at the ranch and Jack wanted him to know he was a dumbass.

"So, should I set up the whipping chair?" he asked. Master A was obviously not amenable to the cross for some reason. He silently cursed himself. He should have tightened that contract, but he hadn't been the one negotiating. He placed a lot of trust in Julian, especially when it came to contracts.

"You should take your place beside Lexi. I'll let you know when I need your help. We'll be using a sawhorse. If Lexi has a problem with it, she can use her safe word. Leo is waiting in case she requires assistance off the grounds."

Lucas felt his face flush. Bastard wanted to play rough? "So, it's your way or the highway?"

Master A took a slow step forward, his boots thudding across the hard floor of the stage. "Yes, it is, sub. Welcome to D/s.

About Lexi Blake

Lexi Blake is the author of contemporary and urban fantasy romance. She started publishing in 2011 and has gone on to sell over two million copies of her books. Her books have appeared twenty-six times on the *USA Today*, *New York Times*, and *Wall Street Journal* bestseller lists. She lives in North Texas with her husband, kids, and two rescue dogs.

Connect with Lexi online:

Facebook: Lexi Blake
Twitter: authorlexiblake
Website: www.LexiBlake.net

www.ingramcontent.com/pod-product-compliance
Lightning Source LLC
Chambersburg PA
CBHW020310200626
46814CB00006BA/2183